I0571759

A Sweeping Ocean

By Zvi S. Lazar

Translated from the Hebrew by Anna Mowszowski

The characters portrayed in this book are works of the author's imagination and any resemblance to actual persons, living or dead, is purely coincidental. However, the book does reference specific real-life dates, events, and incidences, which did indeed occur.

KIP – Kotarim International Publishing, Ltd.

Translated and Edited by: Anna Mowszowski
Proofread by: Shalom Bar-Eretz
Graphic Design by: Bat-Chen Nachmani
Cover Painting by: Zvi S. Lazar
Illustrations by: Tsofit Shalom

Publisher: Moshe Alon

ISBN: 978-965-7238-31-8
Printed in Israel 2016

This book is dedicated to the memory of my sister,
my dear Ada Rotter,
who helped and supported me during my writing.

Thank you to Doron Yaacov,
the Jerusalem Academy of the Hebrew Language.

A special thanks goes out to Dan Chamizer.

Glossary of nautical terms

Ballast tank - A compartment that retains or releases water in order to maintain the ship's stability.

Beaufort scale - The scale by which wind force is measured.

Bilge - A compartment at the bottom of the hull of the vessel where water collects so that it may be pumped out later.

Bitts - Pairs of posts mounted along a ship's bow for fastening ropes or cables, using a figure eight knot. Made of iron, with the round top resembling a *pita*.

Bollard - Pillar on which lines are fastened at a dock.

Bulk carrier - A merchant ship designed to transport unpackaged bulk cargo, particularly grain.

Cargo hold - Place for stowing cargo.

Chief - Nickname of the ship's first mate.

Davit - A small crane used to raise and lower the lifeboat.

Davit span - A fixed cable along the edge of the davit.

Derrick - A lifting device on a vessel used to load and unload cargo.

Economic speed - The optimal speed for financial savings, considering fuel costs and freight weight.

Gross tonnage - The total volume of a ship's internal spaces.

Hatch - The opening to the ship's hold, or cargo stowage.

Hatch cover - The doors to the hatch.

Knot - A unit of speed, equaling one nautical mile per hour.

Lifeline - Ropes dangling from the davit span from which people can be raised or lowered.

Motorman - Rank below chief engineer; in charge of daily operation and maintenance of machinery.

Nautical mile - A unit of length equaling 1.852 km.

Porthole - A round window in the ship's cabins that looks out onto the water.

Ranks - Crewmembers of varying ranks.

Rigging - Ropes and cables used to keep moving parts of the ship in place.

Rubbing strake - A protective strip, usually made of rubber, running along a boat's side below the gunwale.

Shackle - A metal closure that secures ropes and cables.

Ship breaking - The dismantling of a ship to use its parts or raw materials for future use.

Tween deck - An additional storage space between the hold and the main deck, opened by either a hydraulic engine or crane cable.

Winch - A mechanical device used for hoisting lines or cables.

Prologue

He parked his car in front of the black iron gate that had a Star of David painted on it, at the entrance of the cemetery on the southern outskirts of the city of Haifa in the Carmel region of Israel. When he arrived, it had already begun to get dark.

In the month of November, autumn had made place for winter. The skies had opened, the rains began to fall, and a cold westerly wind blew in from the sea. He zipped up his jacket, and as he made his way down the path, he took the note from out of his pocket – for the millionth time – and reread the directions. He was alone in the oppressive silence. A few leaves fell with each gust of wind and from a far off treetop a raven called, breathing life into the land of the dead. The sound of his footsteps on the gravel path quieted his thoughts of what was to come.

The simple granite headstone caught his eye. Wild plants – moss and ferns, the results of the seasonal rains – had sprouted out of the earth and climbed up the stone, painting it in shades of green and yellow. He read the engraving again.

Priel Porat
1942-1969
Lost at sea
R.I.P.

Five years had passed since that terrible day. This was his first time in this place. Until now, he had pushed away all thoughts about Perry from his mind. Tears began to trickle down his face. The thoughts came flooding back – all those crazy, extraordinary days they had together onboard the *Cormoran*, all those shared experiences.

The darkness began to overcome the last remnants of faint evening light. He turned away and started back on the gravel path toward the black iron gate where his car was parked. When he reached the gate, he washed his hands – as is customary – in the cold water of the faucet in the wall. The engine roared back to life and he began driving toward the coastal road, going south to his house in north Tel Aviv, to his wife Nellie and his two sons Perry and Tom.

Priel Porat

She burst through without warning.

Within a few minutes, the sea began to rage. The bow of the *Cormoran* climbed high and plunged down with the crashing waves. The howls of wind were heard throughout the ship. The shift mechanics scrambled to run the hydraulics that close the skylights to keep the engine room dry from the spray. The grey-black sky began to show scatters of white, but the tireless, enveloping waves swept away the snow. Tons of water were hurled onto the *Cormoran*, and each wave was a reminder to the ship and its crew that it was still too early to dismiss the powers of the netherworld forces that were swirling furiously around them, ready to take them below. Neptune kept his fierce eyes on the *Cormoran*, his wrath and fury pummeling her, wave after wave. A commotion was heard coming from the direction of the bow. I looked out of my porthole and suddenly, with a flash of lightning allowing a moment of clear view through the mist, I saw two barrels of oil – whose lines had snapped loose from near the hatch of cargo hold one – roll their way along the deck, crashing into all sorts of cargo. The primary danger was a group of twenty barrels, each containing 25 liters of flammable, explosive materials. I immediately ran to the bridge. There, Captain Bar-Noy stood, wide-legged, red beard covering his face, his ever-present pipe hanging from the corner of his mouth, his eyes fixed on the raging storm.

Second mate Mordechai (Moti) Lev was seen in the chartroom hunched over a map of the North Atlantic, tracing the probable current position of the *Cormoran*. The shift sailor Carlos Antonio – "the Spaniard" – was at the automatic wheel, which had been switched to manual due to the storm, his eyes staring at the shining compass readings, his strong and steady hands trying desperately to keep on course as the needle spun wildly. I approached the captain and as I was about to speak, Bar-Noy stopped me with a wave of his hand, saying:

"Go, get two crewmen and go guard the loose cargo. On your way, knock on the door of the first officer's cabin and send him to me at once! Meanwhile, I'll give orders to the engine room to lower the rotations so we can steer the ship against the wind and waves and stabilize ourselves as much as possible, so you can catch and secure the barrels. Remember to go out on deck from the portside, and if you hear a long siren, drop everything and get back inside immediately. The officer on duty and I will maintain visuals as much as possible. Did you understand?"

I nodded. I replayed his words briefly in my head and started on my mission. Two decks below the bridge was First Mate Itzik Shahak's quarters. I found him curled up in a ball of wool blankets. It took some precious seconds to rouse him from hibernation. When he was conscious enough to absorb what I was saying at that hour of the night, I gave him a rundown of the captain's orders.

Two decks below, in the crew's quarters, I stopped at the cabin of Eli Ben-Tzur and Shaul Shauli, two professional and knowledgeable seamen. I spoke to them clearly and concisely: They had to put on their storm uniforms as quickly as possible and wait by the portside exit facing the main deck. I lay topside one deck to my cabin and put on my own yellow storm uniform, grabbed the flashlight that always hung on the hook near the cabin door, and strapped it to my shoulder. I turned to leave, but remembered one thing I was leaving behind in my haste. I went to the liquor cabinet, took the bottle by its neck, and took a deep swig. I put the bottle back in its place and went to meet Ben-Tzur and Shauli. Ben-Tzur was already there and Shauli could be seen making his way down the passageway. Together we opened the exit door and, struggling against the ferocious wind, we looked for a post on which to steady ourselves.

"Shit!" I cursed to myself and started toward the main deck, trying hard to keep balanced. From out of the corner of my eye I saw Ben-Tzur and Shauli advancing along, using each surge of sea to propel them forward. I estimated the wind speed to be about 60 knots. The whole sea was covered in white, sloshing foam.

"Goddamn it! This is one hell of a storm! Someone must've forgotten to pay that nice girl at the port, and now she's cursed us!" I muttered to myself.

I spotted the first of the wayward barrels stuck between the bulkheads of the cargo hold, all bashed up and dented. The three of us were drenched from the flood of waves slamming the iron vessel. Together, we swiftly stood up the barrel and pushed it between the bulkhead of cargo hold one and the foremast, so that both the barrel and we had a moment of respite from the rage of the waves. Nimble-fingered, we fastened the barrel to its new place. We then set out to search for the second barrel. The biting cold penetrated into our bones and our teeth chattered like castanets. We had to find and secure the second barrel before we could return to our warm quarters. The *Cormoran* rose and fell like a yo-yo with each wave. An image flashed before my eyes of the painted prostitute Sandy, with a Mona Lisa smile on her face, lying naked on white silk sheets, wagging her finger at me. I pushed her out of my thoughts and focused on finding the barrel and then:

A colossal wave lifted high the bow of the ship. As the wave reached the stern, the bow began to plummet, but as it fell, another, larger wave began to roll toward us at lightning speed. "My God!" managed to escape my lips as the gargantuan wave hit me, tore my hands away from whatever I was clinging to, and flung me somewhere. The water enveloped me and did with me as it wished. My body was being beaten and thrashed through the whole ordeal. An unbearable, excruciating pain crawled all over me. I tried aimlessly to grab hold of something, but my hands grasped only water. Images from my distant and recent past played before me like a film. For a moment, I had the thought that this was the way of all flesh. The shrieking of the wind became a pleasant melody. Peace and quiet washed over me. I wanted to sleep... to sleep... to sleep in that sweet heaven. But no! From the last bit of consciousness and with inhuman strength, I lifted my eyes to see the hull of the *Cormoran* rushing away from me, followed by the receding navigation lights. I began to scream, but no sound came out. I tried again and again, but nothing but silence escaped my throat. It felt as if my voice was muted by some higher power. I tried to at least wave my arms, but they were heavy as lead. The water covered me, and my body began to sink, slowly, slowly, toward the abyss. The final glimmer of hope had disappeared. In despair and acceptance, I felt my remaining willpower retreating far away from me. My lungs began to fill with water, my mouth gaped open despite my resistance, and in it rushed volumes of murky seawater. A few last tremors fluttered through my body, and just before expiring, I woke up.

I reached up and switched on my lamp, and was flooded in yellow light. A glance at the clock showed it was 4:32 a.m. My bladder nagged. Still fogged by the nightmare, I shuffled over to the head to drain the pressure. I washed my face in the sink and lit myself a cigarette. I considered going below to Ben-Tzur and Shauli's cabin, but rejected the notion. Sleep was lost. I stretched out on my bed, with my hands under the pillow supporting my head, and my eyes narrowing in on some spot on the overhead. This time of watch was silent, but you could still make out all sorts of background noises, like the creaking of the wood surrounding the compartment, the rattling of the doors in their frames, the clinking of glasses in the liquor cabinet, the shaking of the mirror on the cupboard over the sink, the flow of air through the vents, and whistling from mysterious places that you couldn't pinpoint. You could also hear, of course, the ever-present sound coming from the engine room and the constant vibrations that were the result of the enormous pressure the shafts put on the ship's propeller. There's no question, all that racket sometimes gave you the feeling that you're living on an old jalopy. But the more you spend time with her, the more you get to know her and love her. It seems that even before she left the shipyard on her maiden voyage, when the plans were drawn up and the build began to take shape, when they decided on her dimensions, her height, width, and breadth, the first trace of life was molded into her, her specific characteristics that set her apart from others. Sometimes she's compared to a wife; and your relationship is indeed a lot like a marriage. You give and take, love and hate, bless and curse, indulge and cherish her just as you would a wife. And both the wife and the ship treat you the same way in return, it just happens to be that one is made of flesh and bones, the other of iron.

The grey matter of my brain continued to wander from subject to subject, like fingers walking along piano keys with no specific melody in mind. That's how I came to see the first light of dawn, when it slowly began to overcome the artificial light of my lamp and revealed the cabin in its true form. I pulled myself out of bed and took the three steps there were between me and the porthole that looked out toward the front of the ship. The Jalopy's bow was crossing the water in an idyllic calm, and aside from a few ripples, the blue ocean looked remarkably smooth and quiet. Sunset is famous for being breathtaking, but sunrise is just as beautiful. As you watch, as you see the ball of fire slowly peek over the sea's horizon, painting the world crimson, your heart skips a beat and you feel as if you are a trespasser in a forbidden place, witnessing a glimpse of the secrets of creation.

A light knock on my door broke my string of thoughts and brought me back to reality. After getting my brusque "Yes," Carlos Antonio, the shift sailor, opened the door halfway, leaving most of his size hidden, which in turn highlighted his face, whose most distinguishing feature was the expertly groomed moustache in the style of Clark Gable.

"Boss, it's 06:15. The weather conditions are warm and pleasant, the water is smooth and calm. The first mate asked to wake the deck crew, and when you're ready, for you to go see him on the bridge." As he finished his speech, he gave a big smile, showing two rows of straight teeth, gleaming bright and white.

"Gracias, Carlos," I replied. Carlos disappeared behind the door, closing it softly.

As I was still getting ready for the beginning of the day, a second knock was heard on my door. This time it opened without waiting for my response. "This is for you, boss. I also woke up the crew to switch out the night shift." I thanked Carlos for the coffee and he left humming a Spanish tune under his breath, whose melody kept ringing in my ears. *Carlos is a special breed*, I thought to myself as I sipped the steaming hot coffee. Over the past nine moons that we'd served together on the Jalopy, he'd never once let me down. He was always in the right place; a professional seaman of the highest order, there weren't many like him. I remember one day on the Jalopy at the Port of Balboa, when we'd crossed the Pacific the long way around – from Tokyo to New York, and we'd stopped at the beginning of the canal in order to refuel and stock up on fresh fruits, vegetables, and dairy products. He didn't make a good impression on me at first, as he boarded the gangway onto the ship and asked for "the Big Boss." When they pointed to me, he immediately came over, ignoring everyone else, bulky and large, with a wide smile on his face, and put out a large, rough hand.

"Carlos Antonio Delgado, Andalucía, España," he introduced himself to me. With his smile still on his lips, he brought his other hand toward himself and gave a theatrical bow, as if her were an actor in a one-man, off-Broadway show. Yup, that's Carlos, a real seaman in his early fifties, with thirty years sailing the seven seas under his belt.

"Morning, Chief," I said as I reached the bridge. I photographed him with my eyes only centimeters from the captain's chair.

"Oh, good morning Perry," he said, with wide innocent eyes, as if he didn't know that most of his crewmen had tested their butts on the raised Captain's chair. But it was my little secret; of course I ignored his actions. Itzik was really quite pleasant. It was good to work with him. He was steady and sensible, and it seemed that as much as you tried, you could never get him riled up. He knew how to appreciate the crew's hard work, a trait that translated in him giving longer shore leaves as a special bonus for meeting his expectations.

"Well, Perry," he started. "We've got a really busy day ahead of us. We need to prepare the ship for arrival at port. We're expected to rendezvous with the pilot boat close to midnight, so the first order of business for you is to get the lines ready at the bow and the stern, raise the derricks at cargo holds one and three, release the hatch covers and prepare them to be opened immediately. Likewise, prepare the pilot ladder, lifesaver, heaving line, and the lights. After finishing all the preparations for docking, we need to swab and scrub the old lady, to clean her and pump some adrenaline through her veins. Before arrival, and in coordination with me, walk out the anchors and ready them for letting go." When my hand was already on the handle of the chartroom door, which led to the passageway toward the ladder, Itzik stopped me.

"Perry, don't forget to ready the rigging on the gangway and prepare it for lowering, including the safety line and lighting."

"Okay, Chief. It'll be fine, I won't forget a thing and the ship will be swabbed and ready for arrival."

The crew was already waiting for me, ready to get to work. There was no doubt about it, we all could smell the scent of the approaching harbor. The day of arrival at port was usually a festive time, which wasn't surprising considering the long days and weeks of sea and sky, when we're completely disconnected from the rest of the world. Ben-Tzur and Shauli stuck out in the crowd, after my long night, and I kept my eyes locked on them.

"Good morning, everyone," I said loudly. "We'll start by loosening the rigging on the bow, and we'll try to get this done by breakfast. Don't forget to grease the shackles." I sent Jeremy the deck boy to the bridge to order the engine room to power the winch. And once they were on deck, I returned to my quarters.

Everything is familiar there, in my compartment. It's not more than four-and-a-half meters long to the porthole, and it's only three-and-a-half meters wide. There's a beech wood bed built along the length of the compartment, under which there's storage. The closet is also made of varnished beech wood. The rest of the furniture is also a shade of brown, like the couch under the porthole upholstered in a brown plastic. The table and two chairs are next to the couch, bolted to the floor to prevent shifting during a storm. The liquor cabinet – built with my own two hands and the pride of my compartment – is on the right bulkhead. The lighting is decent; there are two main lights and additional lamps above the table and the bed. I sometimes like to play with the lighting, brightening to resemble daylight, sometimes giving an atmosphere of a dark alley bar in late afternoon. On the bulkhead hang two seascape paintings, reproductions of anonymous painters, and a map of the world on which I've marked routes and places where the ship has sailed. On a bookshelf next to the writing desk are two nautical books and about a half a dozen reading books. Also, scattered throughout the compartment are various souvenirs and mementos that I've purchased from ports around the world. The head is connected to the compartment, separated by a door, and has all my hygiene necessities. Here I've lived for about ten straight months, and this place, it's a part of me.

Thousands of nautical miles from Puerto Cortes in Honduras were reduced to a few dozen, and you could smell the odor of soot, carried over the sea from the numerous factories along the northern coast of the Netherlands. The final destination for the Jalopy – which was carrying in its cargo hold eight thousand tons of Chiquita bananas, bound for markets all over Holland – was getting closer, almost as if one could reach out and touch it. Now it seemed that I couldn't help but think of Gertie.

Five long months had passed since my last visit to the lively port city of Rotterdam, where I first met Gertie. And as it happened, so it began. Gertie worked as a head hostess at the city's swanky nightclub, Oasis, which was a bit far in the city's entertainment district of Katendrecht. The club's windows looked out onto the

Old Port. And from these windows you could watch the ships and other vessels flowing in and out, the thousands of lights flickering across the water, the shadows of the giraffe-like long-necked cranes, and the white moonbeams. In a moment of nostalgia, you could leave the bouncing club and sail away on your thoughts and memories, to cling to your chest the girl you left somewhere, far away and long ago.

The exotic, flashing neon sign above the club – in the blue/white/red of the Dutch flag – could be seen from far away, beckoning all to come, and it was what caught Shauli's eye.

"Listen, Perry, last night a few of us wound up in some night club, called Oasis, in Katendrecht. We had an unforgettable night. It isn't like our regular holes-in-the-wall. There's a floor with a bar, a restaurant floor, a casino, and the main hall has decent live music and a dance floor. The dance floor is surrounded by tables, each candlelit, with a red tablecloth and a tulip in a vase. There are lots of shows throughout the night, like jugglers and magicians. But most importantly: there are plenty of ladies looking for a good time. The place's main attraction is this spectacular girl named Gertie. All our attempts to get close to her failed. The chances of getting her are impossible, she just smiles and evades you smoothly and elegantly. But seriously, Perry, she's a rare thing, this Gertie. She's a queen, uncontested. She's over 1.7 meters tall, with long auburn hair that tumbles in waves over her fantastic breasts, deep blue eyes as clear as the sea on a summer's day, luscious, inviting lips, amazing curves, and a pair of perfect legs that seem to go on forever. She's overflowing with sex, and all eyes are on her. This girl knows what she's got and knows how to use it."

And that's how I found myself that evening making my way to Oasis in a cab, with Shauli at my side. And he was right – the place wowed me right away. We rang the doorbell and the heavy wooden door, covered in unique carvings, creaked open, and out came a large, bearded bouncer who sized us up, like a horse dealer looking over prospective purchases. When he found no fault in us – and after a few bills were exchanged – he waved us through. We entered a magnificent foyer with thick amber-colored carpets, decorated in different varieties of tulips, covering hardwood floors and silencing our footsteps. The architecture was a visual feast. It was resplendent with lines and curves in bright colors in the Baroque style. The walls were made of wood painted the color of French cognac. A scantily dressed, smiling hostess led us to the entrance of the main hall, at our request. There, we signaled an accommodating waiter in a blue tuxedo. Once again bills were exchanged, and we were seated at a central table in front of the dance floor and bandstand. I glanced around the room – the place was packed. A few couples were dancing to the band's pleasantly soft music. Some girls sat together in groups looking around hungrily for some object of entertainment to justify their night out. The dance floor was made out of a thick, translucent green glass, which was lit up from underneath by psychedelic, rainbow-colored lights, changing to the beat of the music.

Shauli was checking out some blonde who had given him some not-so-subtle signals. He mumbled something incoherent to me, got up, and smiling like a professional, asked her to dance. My eyes followed him, and the tart didn't say no to his invitation. Together they went onto the dance floor and disappeared among the rest of the gyrating couples.

"How 'bout a drink?" said a voice from behind me. I turned and saw a pair gorgeous, long legs, wrapped in a long evening gown with a slit up the side, expertly done to excite the senses. I slowly raised my head, my eyes taking in a perfect body, until they reached her own. A sly smile, barely noticeable, could be seen in them. A few seconds passed before I could reply, jokily:

"Of course. When encountering a cute thing like you, it's no wonder that a person would need a double shot of Dimple, with a single ice cube, and a bottle of sparkling water on the side." The nymph looked at me curiously and without saying a word, gracefully turned and walked to the bar to fill out my order. Her walk hypnotized me and I could feel my manhood harden. *I have to pick her up,* I thought to myself. *This must be the Gertie that Shauli was telling me about, there's no way she's anyone else.* I glanced over at the dance floor. Shauli was still dancing closely with the girl, and it seemed like there was a mutual understanding between them. Gertie returned with the drink, bent over, and placed it on the table. An exotic perfume wafted up from between her breasts. My pants began to stretch again.

"Hello, Queen of Sheba," I said. "How would you like to sit down for a drink with a lonely man who's just lost his whole world and is in need of some comforting?" She considered my thoughtfully with her eyes, hesitated a minute or two and said:

"You know, I'm inclined to accept your offer. I like your peculiar audacity." As she spoke, she sat down in the seat next to me, smiled angelically, and held out her hand.

"My name's Gertie. And you?"

"Priel, Priel Porat," I said. "You can call me Perry," I added. A waiter walked by and I waved him over. "What will you have, sweet Gertie?"

"I'll take a gin and tonic," she said. I ordered another Dimple on ice. The waiter gave a nod and went on his way. Shauli continued dancing with his lady. It didn't look as if he was returning any time soon. I looked at Gertie, but I wasn't the only one – several sets of eyes were on the two of us.

After the drinks arrived and we toasted to the health of a lonely man whose world had returned, Gertie turned to me and asked:

"What are you doing in Rotterdam and how long are you here for?"

"Well, I got to you directly from Puerto Cortes, Honduras, in Central America, on the deck of a reefer ship named the *Cormoran.* She's a sweet old jalopy who's trekked the world's oceans, so that our travels are always shrouded in a bit of mystery. You don't always know what port you may dock at next, what side of the world you'll be on, other than this time, after unloading the cargo we're expected to stay here awhile because of a problem in the main engine." I thought I saw her eyes flicker slightly.

"What happened to your engine?" she asked.

"Well, it's a bit complicated. Three days ago, we stopped the engines in open waters in order to identify a malfunction in the engine room. We found that one out of the three cylinders had ceased to work because of some buildup. This caused the rotor to go off balance, which caused more damage, which forced us to cut the cylinders and allow the ship to dock at the port at a moderate speed. It was decided to unload all the cargo – even the ones going on to other destinations – and keep the ship docked until all the necessary repairs are completed. The work itself shouldn't take long, but we have to wait for the parts to arrive, which can only be ordered from the original shipyard. That's more or less the current situation. I can't really get into the mechanical details of it all, since it's not my area of expertise. The important thing is the time we have, I mean the crew, and that's good for all of us." Gertie gave me the impression that this unexpected meeting was welcomed. I couldn't take my eyes off her porcelain skin, or her bewildering curves.

The hours passed by quickly, as did the refills. It was as if we had our own personal waiter at our beck and call, alert to every hand gesture or head nod. His eagerness on other fronts bothered me a bit: I would only put out a cigarette in the ashtray and immediately it was replaced by another clean one, sparkling in the lights of the dance floor. Gertie stuck by me, and I felt the drinks influencing her, too. For a minute I thought she might just be bored. But then, she wouldn't stay so long in my company. Then we were holding hands. Most of the other patrons began filing out, and with them Shauli with his new friend, while he gave me a wave of good luck. For a few seconds we sat silently, feigning to watch those leaving. Meanwhile, my mind raced. *What's going on with you Perry?* I thought to myself. *Are you waiting for her to make the first move? Where's your spine?* I cleared my throat and said:

"What do you think, Gertie my dear, about getting a coffee and a sandwich someplace?" Her answer surprised me, even though somewhere in my subconscious I had waited for it.

"Why don't we go to my apartment? It's only a few blocks away and I'm sure you'll be more comfortable there, if I'm not mistaken by the look on your face. So come on, let's leave this joint." I read a challenge in her clear eyes and I doubled up. The bill was facedown on the table. I turned it over and without a second glance, I placed the necessary amout of guilders down along with a generous tip. Our "personal" waiter picked up the cash while muttering some words of gratitude and flattery.

A set of wooden stairs led up to the second floor. Potted plants and flowers of all colors lined the stairwell. "Typically Dutch," I thought to myself as I admired them. Her apartment was surprisingly modest and tastefully decorated. It was obvious that Gertie's own personality was woven into the place, and I was taken in by its simple beauty. Gertie called to me:

"The bar is over in the left corner. I'll take, as usual, a gin and tonic. I'll be right back, darling."

I heard her getting into the shower. I made the drinks and found the radio and turned the dial. A quiet, familiar tune began to play. My damn pants began to stretch again, this time forming a noticeable bulge. The bathroom door opened and Gertie entered the room wrapped in a sheer robe that left nothing to the imagination. Her intoxicating scent wafted through space and tickled my nose. She gracefully walked over to her glass of gin and tonic, brought it to her lips, and stood in front of me like a runway model. Her flawless figure drove me to distraction as her beauty shot through my chest like an arrow. Her long legs ended in an enchanting triangle. My eyes continued to climb upward and paused at the hills of her breasts. They were perked and inviting, reminiscent of a young maiden. I began to peel off my clothes, tossing them aside. I took a deep swig of my drink and lay down on the carpet near the table, grabbing a cushion. Gertie knelt down and began to crawl toward me. Her eyes looked me over. Her magical fingers traveled up my body, lingering, touching and not touching, surveying and probing my torso and below. I slowly brought her beneath me, my own hands caressing and exploring her physique. Sighs and gasps came silently at first, but increasingly turned into moans. Her movements became more and more intense. Hands, legs, lips, bodies, and sweat blended together. "Yes," she said. "Like that. More. Now. Fuck me." And then all at once the whirlwind of senses broke, and a tranquility washed over us, like the calm following a storm.

I lit a cigarette. A pleasant melody quietly sounded from the radio. A morning zephyr played with the curtains. Gertie fell asleep, her head resting on my shoulder. One of her legs wrapped me entirely, and her breasts pressed against my chest. I carefully untwined myself from her. Gertie sighed faintly and turned over onto her stomach, with one leg akimbo. Her auburn hair flowed over the pillow. Her posterior was raised slightly. I took a blanket from off the bed and covered her. A grabbed the bottle by the neck and drew a drink, and while still clutching it, headed over to the bathroom. I splashed myself with water, but it didn't help. My head pounded. "Perry, you old man," I said to myself. "You drank past your limit tonight." So I left the bottle there, on top of the toilet seat.

I found the kitchen, and as I started the water for a cup of black coffee, I devoured a few slices of dry salami. I felt a bit better, so I returned to the room. Gertie was still how I'd left her. Her naked body, which lay between the blanket and our little encounter made me feel something. Through the swaying curtains came the first glimpses of dawn. Slowly and delicately, I ran my fingers across Gertie's body. With sleep still lingering in her eyes, she began to respond and join in. I flicked my tongue along her curves and reached her divine rose. This time we reached new heights of passion culminating in a simultaneous explosion. Afterward, we enjoyed some time together in the shower, under the droplets of water and soapsuds, lathering each other. Still dripping, we padded over to the kitchen, leaving wet footprints along the floor. Gertie began fixing breakfast. The enticing smell of eggs teased my stomach. As I lounged on the couch in the living room, sipping on another sup of coffee and listening to the banging of the pots and pans in kitchen, I thought how only the night before we'd been strangers to each other, and here, in this moment, it felt as if we had been together since always. Everything seemed to be so natural between us, like the familiar routine of a long-time couple.

The noises of the morning began trickling in. The Jalopy was waiting for me, and because of this, without wanting to, I started getting dressed. Gertie watched me with a look of astonishment and said:

"Where are you off to, Perry?"

I explained it to her.

"Will I see you tonight?" she asked.

"Of course, Queen of Sheba. I'll be at the Oasis."

"No," she said. "I'll be waiting for you here, at the apartment."

Outside, I whistled at a passing cab and it came shrieking to a halt right at my feet. The port was teeming with life. My watch showed 7:45. *I'll still be able to make it in time to give out the orders for the day to the crew.* But before I even reached to the Jalopy I saw four long cranes working at a break-neck speed to unload the crates of bananas. An alarm went off in my head and my mood immediately sank. *What's going on?* I thought. *Did they really start unloading the cargo overnight? And if so, why?* These questions went unanswered, but kept racing through my mind, so I picked up my pace. As soon as I started up the gangway I caught sight of Ben-Tzur, standing above me. He understood from the look on my face that I had questions. I knew that he had been busy with the deck's night shift.

"Change of plans. We push off tomorrow at dawn, for Hamburg. No repairs will be made in Rotterdam," he shouted down to me. Itzik Shahak, the first mate, repeated Ben-Tzur's report, confirming my worry.

"Yes, it's true, shore leave ends tonight at midnight. Part of the cargo will be unloaded in Hamburg and some of the necessary repairs will be done there at the Deutsche Werft shipyard. The decision was delivered by telex directly from corporate."

The crew was already waiting for me, so I sent them to the bow, where the supply hold was located. While I assigned the work, I noticed that Carlos Antonio was missing. I would have to check in on him when I was free. I distributed the paints and tools that were needed to make repairs to the outer hull of the ship, where the cables had damaged the wood. Shauli seemed tired and heavy. Dark circles outlined his eyes. I knew that in his present state he wouldn't be able to work effectively. I asked him to come with me to the bow's cargo hold, and when we were alone I told him that he could go hibernate in his cabin for a bit. He thanked me and went off to his quarters. Once the crew all turned to work, I also made my way to the living quarters. I knocked on Carlos Antonio's door a two or three times until it cracked open slightly and smiling face could be seen. Behind him I saw a slight movement from underneath the sheet on his bed, and before he could say anything I said, "It's OK, go back to what you were doing. I'll need you later." I then turned and walked to my own cabin.

In one swift movement I opened the liquor cabinet and pulled out a bottle. I got a glass and threw in an imperfect ice cube. *My freezer seems to work less often than I do on shore leave*, I thought to myself as I poured half a glass. The first gulp did something to me, and the events of the night suddenly came flooding in. Her image came back to me as from the depths of the past, so far away, yet so recent. As I was lost in thought, Jeremy, the redheaded deck boy, called for me from the other side of my door to say that the first mate was looking for me and wanted to see me in his office. I finished off the last drops from the glass and instinctively wiped my lips with the back of my hand and lay topside to Itzik Shahak's office. Itzik was busy calculating the cargo that was being unloaded. He gestured to a chair and said:

"Take a seat Perry, I'll be with you in a minute. Have something from the cooler." I took out a beer, opened it with my cabin key, and sipped quietly. "Well, there's another change of plan," I heard him say through the fog. "Shore leave has been brought back to 17:00 this afternoon. The pilot will come immediately after the unloading has completed. Get everything ready to leave port by 19:00. We'll sail slowly to Hamburg to unload the remaining cargo and then the port's tugboat will steer us to the shipyard. After the repairs have been finished, we'll set the engines for the Port of New York." His eyes went back to the complicated papers on his desk.

"Great, perfect," I said, mostly to myself. He lifted his eyes and said:

"What's going on with you, Perry? You look tense. What's wrong?"

"Truthfully," I said. "There's a problem, and I need to go into the city for a few hours to settle something. Ben-Tzur can replace me until I get back. Is that OK, chief?" Itzik raised his head from the paperwork and looked at me closely. "The way you look, you definitely have something urgent to take care of over there." A slight smile crept in and he continued, "I won't keep you. Just don't forget yourself out there. I need you here on the ship. We've got a hell of a lot of work ahead of us and I need everything to go smoothly. You work it out with Ben-Tzur." And with that, he went back to his pile of paperwork.

I walked quickly between the line of ships at the dock and the cranes and cargo containers toward the exit. Outside, I stopped a passing cab.

"Number 68 William Street," I said, and the taxi took off. I climbed the familiar wooden stairs. I reached the door and rang the bell. I heard a muffled voice.

"Who's there?" she said.

"It's Perry," I answered. The door swung open. She stood there naked, with a look of wonder on her face. I gave her a brief of the news. She put on a flowered robe, took out a cigarette, and sat down on the couch looking pensive. Tears began to well up in her eyes and she was dangerously serious.

"Gertie," I said. "Let's go to bed." We went, but it didn't start

out well, so we stopped. Silence weighed heavy on the room
and the minutes flew by incessantly. We were both so stressed
that I offered that we get dressed and go out and get some fresh
air. We walked for a good hour, hand in hand. We paused by a
canal where ducks and herons floated on the water, every once
in a while dunking their heads down for a fish. Some kids were
throwing stones into the water, creating circles of ripples across
its surface.

We found a busy café just nearby. We had to wait a bit until they
found us a table for two near a window overlooking a green and
winding promenade. A waiter in a white jacket took our order: A
latte for Gertie and a Heineken for me.

"You know, Perry," she said. "You've done something to me
in here," and she touched a finger to her heart. "I feel like a young
girl about to lose her virginity. For some reason, I'm going to
really miss you. And I still can't fully realize that I won't see
you again." As she looked at me, tears welled up in her blue eyes
again. She reached into her grey bag and took out a handkerchief
to wipe her eyes. She then put her hand in mine. I gave her a weak
smile and said:

"It's not the end of the world, my darling. I'll be back to see
you. The *Cormoran* will be returning soon and everything will be
alright." Again, a heavy silence fell upon us.

"Can I at least write to you?" she asked. As she said this, I
wrote down the ship agent's address on a napkin. The sounding
of the clock reminded me of the Jalopy. When it was my time to
leave, Gertie stood to accompany me to the port. We held each
other silently in the cab, until it stopped at the somber iron gates
of the dock. The driver was impatient, as it seemed he was in a
hurry to get somewhere. I leaned over, kissed Gertie on the cheek,
and opened the door. I turned and walked to the entrance without
looking back. I heard the taxi's engine roar back to life.

The wind picked up and dark, depressing cumulonimbus clouds
began to gather, rapidly covering the sky. The rain would come

soon. I zipped up my jacket and quickened my pace. A group of longshoremen passed me on their way out of the dock. I felt like joining them. The Jalopy was eerily silent. The same cranes that had been working furiously when I left were now motionless. A small spark of hope lit up. *The departure must have been postponed. How else could you explain the cranes? The ship's derricks aren't set for sailing yet, either.* I went up the gangway and raced to Itzik Shahak. He sat busy with stability calculations.

"What, we're not leaving port tonight?" I asked. Itzik glared at me as if I'd gone nuts.

"We've been waiting for you, Perry. You wasted a serious chunk of our time. Unloading finished an hour ago. The crew's waiting in the mess. Gather them up and get the ship ready to set sail. The pilot will arrive in two hours from now."

Yes, five months had passed since then, and here I was again at the mouth of the port of Rotterdam. *Will I see her? She may have moved out of her apartment or changed jobs. Or she may have forgotten about me.* She did write some letters of love and longing at the beginning. I also sent her a couple of postcards. But for some reason, time and distance did their share, and the letters began to dwindle, until they stopped completely.

By early evening the Jalopy was swabbed and clean, ready for port. The derricks were all raised uniformly, like two rows of soldiers standing at attention. The gangway was rigged and ready. The pilot ladder, lifesaver, heaving line, and lights were also all set on the hatch of cargo hold number three, close to both the port and starboard side of the main deck, waiting for the pilot's orders depending on which side he wanted to board. That decision was of course subject to the weather conditions – the winds and the directions of the waves. Dinner was quiet. The crew's messman almost had no work, as most of the men opted out of eating. The day of arrival at port typically excited all crew members, meaning that after all the preparations are completed, many chose to pass the remaining time with a friend in his quarters, over a beer or some liquor. Someone might bring out some delicacy he purchased at the previous port, like gourmet cheeses, cured meats, canned oysters, etc. Someone else will bring vegetables from the crew refrigerator, bread, plates, and cutlery. Unlike on the rest of the days at sea, on this day the cook's menu suddenly seemed lacking. Gradually, more men gather in the quarters, a radio is turned on, cigarette smoke begins to waft, and until they are called for duty, they pass the time telling stories from their times at the previous ports and, of course, imagine what's to come.

I showered and put on clean clothes. I took out a beer from the fridge and lay topside to the stern of the ship to get some fresh air. I leaned on the railing. I filled my lungs with clean sea air. The sky was strewn with stars and the full moon's light made the ship's propeller glisten. The clamor from below had a calming effect, like a beloved melody. My thoughts – how could they not? – returned to Gertie. My brain replayed the night and day we had spent together, and my longing for her intensified. The image of her beauty stood before my eyes as if it were real.

The Jalopy arrived early to the rendezvous point, and the port authorities agreed to send out the pilot boat without delay. The crew was called to the connection point. The pilot ladder was rigged on the port side, as requested, one meter above the water. The helmsman was already on the bridge, ready for manual steering, following the vocal commands of the captain without hesitation or delay. The officer on duty, the third mate, gave a visual confirmation by binoculars of the red lights of the approaching pilot boat and reported to the captain. Speed was reduced to minimum and visual contact was kept until the officer's authorization was heard – and he was sent to oversee the pilot board and confirm that he did indeed arrive and was making his way to the bridge. After some brief greetings, the pilot began to direct the ship toward the designated pier. He gave instructions to dock the ship on its port side. The first mate was at the bow while the second mate was at the stern. Two tugboats waited for us at port. One was secured at the bow's starboard side and the second was toward the stern, also starboard. Right around 22:30, the sweet old Jalopy, restful and calm, was docked. The vibrations ceased, the noisy main engine quieted, and the emerging sounds of the port's water lapping against the ship signaled the end of our journey at sea and the arrival at solid ground to all of the eager crew.

And here I was walking between the piers toward the exit, with Shauli at my side. A beautiful, starry June night. Wonder, adventure, and expectation were all nested deep within my heart and mind.

The cab stopped outside of the Oasis club. We rang the doorbell and the bouncer let us in after carefully looking us over. We passed through the familiar foyer into the club. It looked exactly the same as our last visit. My "personal" waiter from before recognized me immediately. He must have remembered the generous tip and that I had left with the queen of the place. With a smile and a slight bow, the waiter led us to the same table where I first met Gertie. We ordered drinks. While ordering, someone came up behind us and covered Shauli's eyes with her hands. He didn't have to think hard to know it was the same blonde "old friend." Shauli beamed with satisfaction. He knew that the night was already "in order." The waiter brought the drinks and Shauli immediately ordered another, for the blonde. I glanced around the club in hopes of seeing Gertie, but she wasn't there. Daringly, I asked the blonde:

"Does Gertie still work here, miss?"

"You can call me Nellie. As for Gertie, we haven't seen her for two days."

Maxim Shaulov

Maxim Shaulov was born to parents Igor and Katia on a horse farm, at midnight in the middle of a snowy January in 1917, in the village of Vasilevka. It was a particularly turbulent year in history. In March, Tsar Nicholas II was forced to abdicate during the Russian Revolution. World War I, which had started in 1914, was still raging across Europe and did not skip the Ukraine. In the same year, Ukraine took advantage of Russia's weakness following the Bolshevik Revolution and declared its independence, but it would not last long.

As Katia went into labor, and her contractions intensified, Igor hitched his mare to his cart, wrapped himself in a heavy wool coat, and put on a Cossack hat. Igor made his way to the home of the village midwife, cursing the raging winter. At that time of night, the village was asleep and no one would be out in such weather. Everyone was boarded up warm in their houses, their fireplaces keeping the bitter cold at bay. Most were already fast asleep, in preparation for the hard day of work ahead. The smoke coming from the chimneys looked grey against the white of the falling snow.

The midwife's house was nine kilometers from his farm, and his horse dragged the cart slowly. The snowflakes continued to fall, and his thick moustache turned white. Finally, Igor arrived at the home of Svetlana the midwife. The house was dark and he knocked loudly on the door. An eternity passed until the midwife opened the door. Svetlana, big and round, took one look at Igor and – knowing Katia was heavily pregnant – realized what this late night visit meant.

"Give me a few minutes and I'll get everything I need ready for the birth. And congratulations."

They began the journey back to Igor's farm. Still the snow fell. It was even heavier than before, and the horse, as if in spite, drudged on at a terribly slow pace. The extreme weather was taking its toll on her.

Katia lay in bed, moaning as the contractions grew stronger and more frequent. Svetlana prepared a clean cloth, filled a bowl with water, took tools from out of her bag, and with Igor's help, moved the dining table as close as possible to the mother. On it she placed the cloths, the bowl of water, and the birthing tools. Svetlana bent Katia's legs and began the birthing process. Igor couldn't watch Katia suffer, so he left the room, went into their modest living room, pulled out a half-full bottle of vodka, and took several gulps. As he sat and thought, drinking occasionally, he heard the cries of a baby. He still didn't know if it was a boy or a girl. He wanted to go into the room, but he decided to wait. After some time, Svetlana came into the living room, pale and distraught. Blood stained her apron. She looked at Igor and said:

"You've got a beautiful baby boy, weighing 2870 grams. But a tragedy has happened. Katia died while giving birth. She suffered internal complications. I did everything I could, but it was no use. Perhaps it was God's way of bringing a good soul under the wings of his angels. Katia was a wonderful woman. I join in your pain." Igor's voice broke in his throat, and he stormed into the room. Katia looked so beautiful, and so happy. Tears flooded down his cheeks. The next day, in the early evening, Katia was laid to rest. There wasn't even a *minyan*. There were the two undertakers, the rabbi who was called in from the nearby Zaporojye province, and a couple from the neighboring farm. After the funeral service, Igor was left alone with his cavernous pain. Finally, he turned back home.

A nanny from the neighboring farm was brought to watch over little Maxim. The child grew. Nastasia the nanny raised him with love, as if he was her own. To Maxim, Nastasia was a real mother. He continued to grow and thrive. One day when he was six years old, as Maxim approached one of his beloved horses – perhaps he didn't stand in right spot, or perhaps the horse was spooked by an insect or something – suddenly, she stood on her hind legs, whinnied loudly, and kicked her left leg and struck Maxim's right knee. Little Maxim fell and could not get back up. His leg was broken. He lay for a long time in the stable before Igor found him half conscious. Some more time passed before the village doctor arrived. The doctor treated the leg and set it in plaster. He then delivered the news:

"Igor," he said. "Your son was injured severely in his knee. The damage is irreparable. He will be crippled for the rest of his life and will have to walk with a cane."

As the days, weeks, and months passed, the wounds closed, but Maxim's leg would twitch and he strained as he limped. Igor carved a walking stick for Maxim. Maxim grew and developed well over the years. Nastasia cared for him devotedly, and even taught him to read and write. But Maxim was lonely and had no friends. He no longer went near the stables, but he did enjoy walking around the farm, between the fields and the woods, all the way to the distant hills. He loved when the flowers blossomed, especially during the spring and autumn, and he would listen to the birds calling and the noises of the wildlife. He would watch the sunset and would often return home has night was falling. Though it was difficult to walk, he limped on. As the years passed, Maxim grew into a fine young man, tall and sturdy. His limp improved, and during summer days he would even go without his walking stick. He kept busy with different jobs around the farm; mended the surrounded fences, cut down trees for firewood and stored them for winter, made repairs on farmhouse, and planted various seasonal vegetables. Sometimes Nastasia would bring him a book and he immersed himself in it. His favorites were Fyodor Mikhailovich Dostoyevsky's *Crime and Punishment*, Lev Nikolayevich Tolstoy's *Anna Karenina*, and Gustave Flaubert's *Madame Bovary*.

All those same years, Igor delved deeper and deeper into his devastation over losing Katia, and for his grief he found comfort in vodka. He rarely left the living room. Nothing interested him, not the farm, not Maxim, nothing at all. Nastasia did all she could to ease his suffering, but it was impossible to get through to him. He was never himself again. One fateful day, when Maxim was 14 years old, Igor hung himself. Nastasia found him in the stables. She hitched the mare to the cart and rode to the neighboring farmhouse. When the farmer and his son heard what happened, they immediately went with Nastasia, while the farmer's other son rode to the village council in order to get help. The neighbor and his son brought down Igor's body and brought him into the small living room. There, they cleared the table, laid him down, and covered him with a blanket. Nastasia lit several memorial candles. After mourning with them a while, the neighbor and his son returned to their farm and left Nastasia and Maxim to grieve. Maxim stared at the blanket covering his dead father's body. Many minutes went by in painful, mournful silence. The candles flickered, looking to Maxim as if the passing soul was breathing on them.

This time, too, there was no *minyan*. Besides Maxim and Nastasia, there was only the rabbi who came from Zaporojye, the two undertakers, the neighboring farmer, his wife, and two sons. Igor was buried next to his wife Katia, whom he so loved. One day, a month after the tragedy, a man from the village council arrived with two others. One of the men held a paper folder. Nastasia opened the door after she heard them knocking. The councilman told them that he had some important information for them, and so she let them in and offered them something to drink. Maxim came forward, limping slightly. They sat at the table and the man with the folder took out several documents.

"We regret to tell you that the farm is in heavy debt. We have a document signed by Igor, may he rest in peace, stating that if he is unable to pay his debt, the farm and all of its contents will go to his creditors." Nastasia read the document over and over, unable to move.

"What will come of us?" she asked.

"You are to leave the farm. We will give you thirty days to

prepare your things; please see this as a gesture of goodwill. We are very sorry, but it is out of our hands." Maxim suddenly burst out angrily:

"Leeches! Miserable bloodsuckers! Extortionists! Thieves! Get out of my face before I hit you!"

The three quietly got up and left. Nastasia went to Maxim crying and brought him to her chest.

"Don't worry," she said. "As long as I live, I will make sure that you grow into a proud and independent man."

Nastasia had a married sister who lived in Zaporojye. The sister, her husband, and their three children lived in a neighborhood in the southern part of the city. It wasn't a wealthy neighborhood, but they had a small house with a green garden, and nearby they managed a notions store. Nastasia's sister was herself a skillful seamstress and she had several regular customers. They didn't make much profit, but they had enough to run their household and raise their children, though they owned no other luxuries. In despair, Nastasia decided to write to her sister Irina, telling her about recent events and asking for help. As soon as Irina read the letter, she knew she would do everything in her power to help her sister. She discussed it with her husband, Gregory, and together they came to a decision: They would clear out the attic of all the clutter and turn it into a living space for Nastasia. Regarding Maxim, as they had no place for him in their house, they had no choice but to register him at the city's boarding school for orphans. He would always be welcome to stay with them on holidays. In this spirit, Irina wrote back to Nastasia.

On the morning following the thirty-day grace period, the councilman and his companions returned to the farm. Once again, they knocked on the heavy wooden door. Nastasia opened it. Wasting no time, the man with the folder took out several documents for Nastasia to sign. After she signed everything, the three men seemed relieved and even happy. Finally, the man from the council said:

"You have to clear out of here by the end of the day. I know this is difficult, but it is out of my power to stop this legal procedure. The only thing I can do is to give you a day or two to organize your things and to allow you to keep the mare and the cart." The three then went on their way.

Nastasia and Maxim immediately began to gather up the few things they felt they needed with them and loaded it all on the cart. Nastasia filled a basket with some food and a few bottles of water, which she anticipated would last them the long journey. On the night before they were to leave, their only thoughts were on the future and what lay ahead. Early the next morning, they hitched the cart to the horse and gave one last glance back to the farm and its surroundings. It was a sad day. For Maxim, a period of his life was ending, and yet he did not know what new stage was about to begin. They started out on the long road that lay before them. They passed by the village's main streets, up toward Zaporojye. The village of Vasilevka was similar to dozens of other villages scattered along the Dnieper River, whose populations were sparse. Through its center ran a main road that began in the Crimean Peninsula and went to the capital of Moscow. Vasilevka sat on the bank of the Dnieper River, and over time the government established there an artificial lake and hydraulic power station. In addition to the main road, the village was also crossed by railway tracks. The villagers earned their livelihood by growing crops such as corn, beans, melons, and more. They also raised horses, cows, sheep, and there were even vineyards. Now, as Nastasia and Maxim were getting further away from the village, they passed by field after field of green. The hills and the woods that surrounded the carefully plotted fields echoed their pain in leaving this place. Vasilevka became smaller and smaller as the distance between them grew, until it disappeared altogether, never to be seen again.

It was a warm day. The sun peaked through between the clouds and the pastoral landscape soothed their sorrow somewhat. In the afternoon, they stopped on the side of the road. Nastasia took the basket and placed a tablecloth on the ground under the shade of a tree. She brought out some food and the two began to eat, enjoying the quiet and the calm that they both so needed. After some time, they continued on their way. By evening, they could begin to see on the horizon some of the houses of Zaporojye. The horse seemed to understand that the journey was nearing its end, and began to hasten her steps.

The lights of the city were already lit when they arrived at Irina and Gregory's house. Nastasia knew that Maxim would have to go to the boarding school, so before they entered her sister's house, she explained to him the decision and what he might expect.

Priel Porat

My eyes darted between the tables, the bar, the dance floor, and especially in the direction of the entrance of the club, but there was no sign of Gertie. Nellie and Shauli sat holding hands, exchanging loving looks. He answered her questions about his recent journeys around the world since we left five months ago. They looked every bit like a couple in love, but who knew if Nellie was the real deal; Shauli had managed to have many "true loves" along his travels. I ordered another round of drinks from my personal waiter and then I decided to walk around the place a bit. There was no sign of her at any section of the club, not the gambling hall nor the restaurant. I returned disappointed to our table. Now, in the seat next to mine sat a nice looking girl with light-brown hair cut short, who followed my gaze as I approached. As I sat down, Nellie said:

"Perry, meet Brigitte, a good friend of mine. She'll know how to take care of you." Shauli ordered another round. He and Nellie got up and went to the dance floor. I was left sitting with Brigitte, but my thoughts were elsewhere. The cigarettes were finished, so I pulled out a new pack from my jacket pocket. Brigitte stared at me for a few minutes and then tried to break me from my reverie.

"Perry," she said at last. "You're giving the impression of a closed off, withdrawn man. I don't think that's your true nature. Why don't you loosen up a bit and let yourself enjoy the club and the company?" I looked at her, and suddenly noticed that she was a stunning temptress.

"You're right," I said. "I haven't been in the best mood. I'm very sorry." Nellie and Shauli came back. He requested permission to return to the ship in the afternoon, and it was granted.

As I left the club, I stopped a cab and gave him directions: Port entrance number seven, as close as possible to the pier where the *Cormoran* was docked. It was already 3:00 in the morning when I got to my cabin. I didn't see another soul, though I knew that there at least two people on the night watch, most likely on deck near where the cargo was being unloaded, and of course, the officer on duty. I took out the key to my cabin, but the door wouldn't open. I tried a few more times, but it was stuck. I checked the number on the door – maybe I was too drunk and was trying the wrong door? But no, it was mine. Perhaps I hadn't locked it when I'd left? I tried the handle, but had no luck. Something must have happened to the key, I thought, and warped it. I knew that every door had a spare key and that first mate Itzik Shahak had a master key that opened all of the doors on the ship. I didn't want to wake Itzik, so I decided to look for the duty officer and get the spare key, which was usually kept in a closet in the office. The officer on duty was Zeev "Zevik" Tichon. I couldn't find him on deck, in the mess, or on the bridge. I went to look for him in the control room for the main engine. *Bingo*, I said to myself when I saw him next to the panel that controlled the pumps of the ballast tank, which kept the ship stable when the uneven loading and unloading of cargo shifted the ship's weight. Zevik had completed the duty officer training course only a few months prior. The *Cormoran* was the first ship in his command. Before he went ashore to train, he'd sailed for a year and a half as a cadet for the company in preparation for the course. When I told Zevik why I'd come to find him, he said that he would be finished within ten minutes and would be with me right after. Together, we went to the deck office. He found the spare key and we went to my cabin. He tried the lock, but once again the door refused to open. We looked at each other dumbfounded, neither of us knowing what was going on. Zevik rapped loudly on the door and tried jiggling the handle a few times, and then suddenly, the door swung open, and there stood Gertie.

The surprise that Gertie had made for me was perfect. I was astonished to see her in my cabin. I couldn't have imagined it in my wildest dreams. Gertie, half asleep, jumped onto me and hugged me tightly. We stood embracing each other for several minutes, stroking each other's hair and kissing without either of us saying anything. After we calmed down, we went to sit at the table. I saw that Gertie had found the liquor cabinet, as a bottle of Chivas Regal was out, and next to it a nearly empty glass. I took out another glass and poured for both of us. I waited for an explanation. She told me that she'd been in contact with the ship agent and had learned that we were to dock in the nighttime. She'd decided to come and surprise me, but when she arrived, she was told that I'd already gone ashore about a half an hour beforehand. The first mate was the one who had opened the door for her. We sat talking at the table for an hour. Her extraordinary beauty captivated me.

"Gertie," I said finally. "Perhaps we should freshen up in the shower together?"

A stream of water flowed over both of us. We lathered each other. Her perfect body, slippery with soap, could awaken even the dead. I couldn't hide what was happening between my legs. Gertie did not ignore it. I turned off the tap and we quickly toweled ourselves off and raced to bed. The memories of our lovemaking five months before flooded back with full strength, until we both fell asleep, entwined in each other's embrace.

My sleep was roused by loud knocking and Ben-Tzur's voice calling from the other side of the door:

"Good morning, Perry! It's 07:00. Welcome to a new day!"

"OK, thanks," I muttered. I grudgingly got out of bed – cold shower, shave, toothbrush, comb, and straight to the mess. Breakfast is served at 07:30. On the table was spread a green salad, cans of sardines, cream cheese, sliced cheese, a tub of yoghurt, jam, and a basket of fresh rolls – baked in the early morning by the cook. I requested from the messman to prepare me a cup of coffee and an omelet. After I finished eating, I made up a tray of the same for Gertie. She was still sleeping when I came into the cabin. Reluctantly, I woke her up to eat the breakfast I'd brought for her. I told her I had to go on deck to give the crew their jobs for the day and that I would come back afterward. Her body drugged me, I felt like stopping to have a quick screw, but the first mate and the crew were waiting for me.

Itzik the first mate and I coordinated our work schedule. He explained that the second mate had reported some erosion to the ropes at the stern that may cause them to tear, so we'd need to worm, parcel, and serve the damaged section. On the bow, we needed to scrape off the rust and scrub the hull, and then paint it over. At 10:30, there would be a lifeboat drill.

"We'll lower the starboard lifeboat into the water. Send the carpenter to grease the davit pulleys, the winch, and all other moving parts."

Ben-Tzur and Jeremy, who had been on the night watch, were released to rest in their quarters until the drill. I sent Carlos Antonio, the midshipman, and Doron, to mend the ropes at the stern, and I sent Shauli and Yossi to the bow. Gershon the carpenter was sent to the starboard side. After coordinating with Itzik, I released the two other sailors, Ehud and Yonatan, on a day's shore leave, so that they could do some shopping and return for the night's watch.

Gertie was still sleeping when I returned to my cabin, having barely touched her breakfast tray. I didn't want to wake her, so I left quietly, closing the door carefully behind me. I went to the stern to watch over and help with the repairs, but there was no need. Carlos, the perfect seaman, had worked on the ropes extraordinarily well. Doron had helped him with the worming of the lines, parceling them, and serving them securely. I left them and went to the bow deck. The work was being handled to my satisfaction there, as well. Shauli looked up from what he was doing, looked at me and with a deliberate wink said:

"A little birdie told me that Gertie's on the ship. Well done!" I appreciated that Shauli had come back early, even though he had been given permission to stay with Nellie until the late afternoon.

After the coffee break between 10:00-10:20, the entire deck crew, including Ben-Tzur and Jeremy, lay topside to relieve the crewman on duty. Captain Bar-Noy stood with the walkie-talkie on the portside bridge wing, watching what was happening on the lifeboat. First mate Itzik also stood with a walkie-talkie monitoring the drill. He ordered them to release the line and lower the lifeboat to the embarkation deck. The team began lowering the two hooks fastened forward and aft. The drainage plug was checked and in place. The bow line was also released and hitched to the bit on the main deck. The lifelines connected to the davit span were released and lowered into the boat, ready to be used. After a final check, Itzik gave me the signal to lower it to the embarkation deck. I carefully raised the winch's brake and the boat began to lower. Its weight transferred to two tricing pendants and it stopped on the embarkation deck. I returned the winch brake to its place. The launching crew began to board. Third mate Zevik stood at the rudder and Avraham, the second engineer, stood near the engine, checking to make sure everything was in order and that there was enough fuel, water, and oil. After his OK, he shifted to neutral. The tricing pendants were let go carefully and the weight of the lifeboat shifted to the davits' pulleys. Itzik reported to the captain that the boat was ready and requested permission to lower it. Permission was granted. Following Zevik's directions, the boat crew held fast to the lifelines then I was given the signal to begin lowering the boat into the water. I raised the winch lever and the boat began to lower until it slowed as it touched the surface of the water and the pulley cables slackened then quickly unhooked. Aided by a rod, the boat pushed off from the ship, the bow line was unhitched, and with the third mate's orders, the engineer put it into gear. Zevik began to steer the boat away from the ship's hull and kept a reasonable distance from the rest of the ships at the dock. The crew was told to move to the stern of the lifeboat so that the bow could be raised and to facilitate cruising speed. Avraham kicked it into high gear, and the boat slid along the surface of the water at the speed of 7 knots. After a half an hour, the first mate radioed Zevik to return to the ship and begin lifting the boat back onto the ship. He turned the boat and began sailing it back toward the pulley cables. He approached at a moderate speed and then directed the lines to them. The hooks were attached forward and aft and I pulled the cable taut to prevent it from unhooking at the rocking of the boat in the water. The bow line was hitched. The lifelines were brought into the boat. Avraham the engineer turned off the engine. After all of the preparation was confirmed, Zevik relayed it to the first mate. The air compressor motor was already connected. After it was confirmed that all crew members had taken hold of the lifelines, Itzik ordered me to began lifting the boat. I turned on the air compressor motor and the boat began to rise slowly from off the water's surface.

But as the boat was halfway up to the embarkation deck, disaster struck. Due to pressure applied to the pulley whose cable was attached forward, the line tore suddenly. This is an extremely rare occurrence and was completely unexpected. The bow plunged downward, and with a huge crash the boat hung by the stern. Everyone fell into the water. The only one still clinging to the lifeline was Carlos Antonio. When the line broke, Gershon, the carpenter, hit his head hard and fell with the rest of the boat crew into the water. He lay there motionless, floating with the help of his life vest. The water surrounding him turned red. The rest of the crew, still in shock and some moderately injured, swam in all directions, not comprehending what had just happened. Carlos let go of the lifeline and swam to Gershon. Captain Bar-Noy immediately alerted the port officials and requested urgent medical assistance. A rescue boat with a doctor, nurse, and a team of paramedics set out directly to the scene of the disaster. An ambulance and an additional medical team, equipped with a stretcher, were also called to the ship. The rescue workers pulled out the crewmen scattered in the water and brought them into the boat. The port doctor pronounced Gershon's death.

Gertie Van der Giessen

Gertie was born in the spring of 1944 to Hans and Joanna in Amsterdam. They managed a small hotel on Dam Street, which Joanna had inherited from her parents. It was called the Will Hotel, named after Joanna's late mother Wilhelmina. It was three stories tall. A restaurant and bar were on the first floor, and the restaurant could seat 36 diners comfortably. There were an additional eight seats at the bar. The second floor had eight rooms that were rented out on monthly basis to patrons who worked in various jobs near the hotel. Some came from out of town and would go back to their families on the weekends. The third, smaller, floor housed a two-bedroom apartment with a living room, kitchen, bathroom and all of the necessary amenities. The apartment was airy and bright, with several windows and a small balcony overlooking the streets and canals. Joanna managed the hotel's employees: there was a cook, two waiters, a bartender, and two maids. She especially watched over the activities in the kitchen. Hans managed the administrative side; he worked with their suppliers, managed the accounts, and took care of the maintenance of the hotel. Gertie was their only child and they raised her with love and dedication.

Holland, like the surrounding countries, suffered under the Nazi occupation, and only after the end of WWII did life begin to return back to normal. Hans could not forget, however, the May 15, 1940, the day that Holland surrendered to the Nazi invaders, nor August 4, 1944, when Anne Frank and her family and the rest of the Dutch Jews were hauled off by the Gestapo to the death camps. Hans had had several Jewish friends who had disappeared, never to be seen again, their property given over to the government. But life conquered all. Hans and Joanna survived the tough times by running the hotel. A few times they needed to sell some of their personal belongings in order to buy food, as customers were few and far between. Some only came to sit at the bar and drink away their troubles. Following the difficult Operation Market Garden, fought in the Netherlands by the Allied forces against the Nazis in September 1944, and after Dutch liberation in May 1945, Joanna and Hans began rebuilding the hotel, hoping for better days.

Gertie grew up loved and pampered. Her parents gave her everything they could. Her room was full of toys, and she especially loved to play with her Dolly. She had blue eyes, just like Gertie, which could close and open when she played with her. As she crawled into bed, Gertie would hug and kiss Dolly, and would drift off to sleep with her tight in her arms. When Gertie was three years old, her parents put her in a day care next to the hotel. There, she blossomed, as she loved playing with other children her same age. She quickly became the queen of the nursery. Her greatest pride was her watercolor paintings, which her parents kept safe in a special pink binder. She enjoyed taking walks with her mother or father – never together, as one always had to watch over the hotel. She especially loved playing at the park; to sit on seesaw and fly into the air, to walk barefoot on the green grass, to watch the ducks swimming in the canal from the benches. She liked walking through the streets of the city and wonder at the mannequins in shop windows. She also loved going to the zoo and throwing bananas to the monkeys, sharing her sandwich with the pelicans, and listen to different sounds all of the animals would make. Once a year, her father would take her to the amusement park, where her joy and laughter would overflow. She was amazed by the Ferris wheel, and even felt a little scared, but with her father by her side she knew she was safe and that nothing bad could happen to her.

When she turned six, Gertie started school. Her mother accompanied her on her first day of school. Two days before, Joanna had bought her a beautiful school bag and stationary for her new adventure. Already at this age, it was impossible to ignore Gertie's unique beauty. She was tall for her age and her eyes were bright blue, sprinkled with splashes of turquoise. Her hair was a shiny auburn that fell in waves to her shoulders. It was no wonder that she captured the attention of all of her classmates from the very first day.

In fourth grade, when Gertie was ten, she began excelling in school and quickly passed all of her classmates in grades. She made studying suddenly very popular and was loved by her friends. She worked hard on homework, was always punctual, and if she was ever unsure about something, she wasn't afraid to raise her hand and ask for an explanation from the teacher. Her best friend was named Margareta and they would always sit together at the same desk. When the school bell would ring at the end of the day, they would both gather up their books and pencils and walk together to the school gate. They would usually go to the hotel afterward, chatting and gossiping the whole way there. When they arrived, Joanna would serve them lunch at the restaurant's corner table. Then, they would go up to Gertie's room and start on their homework. After they finished, they would often go out onto the balcony and watch the people passing by below them. Joanna would bring them tea and cake and they would sit and share secrets together on the balcony, promising that they would stay best friends forever. It was nice to sit there, especially toward the evening when the smells of the flower blossoms would waft up to them as they drank their tea and were wrapped in warmth and tranquility. Sometimes they would play together in Gertie's room or sometimes Hans or Joanna would take them to the park. At the end of the day, they'd say goodbye to each other and each one would return home, knowing they'd see each other the next day.

Toward the end of her last year at middle school, Joanna suddenly fell ill and had to stay in the nearby hospital. Gertie would visit her after school and sometimes Margareta would even join her. Hans learned from the doctor that Joanna's illness was incurable and that her days were numbered, but he did not have the heart to tell their daughter. He was forced to take on a hotel manager in order to cover Joanna's duties. At night, when he was alone in his room, the tears would stream down his face, like a river on its way to the ocean. He loved Joanna with all his soul and knew that when she left, he would have a hole in his heart for the rest of his life. One day, as Gertie sat next to her mother's bed, Joanna reached out her hand and asked her daughter to help her sit up. She then looked at her and said:

"Gertie, you're a big girl now, almost 14 years old. Soon you will be an independent woman. Time ticks on like a clock. You must always be careful and sensible. Life is not always pretty. Your father and I lived through the war and saw terrible things; the suffering of many at the hands of a few. There were days that we went hungry. You should always save now, because you do not know what is to come. Do all that you can to stay out of trouble. One can never know what fate has in store for us, and there are always surprises along the way. Take care of Papa and be good to him, because he loves you so much, as I love you. My hope is that I can leave this hospital and return to you soon, but if God has other plans, I'm asking you to both stay strong, as that is just the way of the world. Now, please, help me to lie back down because I'm tired and want to rest." Joanna passed away that same night, in her sleep. When Hans heard the news, even though he'd been prepared for it, he let out a scream of pain that tore through his entire body. The hotel's employees, the regular customers, and a few friends attended the funeral. Joanna's coffin stood on the platform, surrounded by flowers and candles. Her face was one of peace and serenity. One after one, all of the mourners paid their respects and the priest delivered a beautiful eulogy.

On her last day of school, Gertie came to the decision that she would not continue on to high school, but would help her father run the hotel. Patrons loved visiting the bar and enjoyed the atmosphere of the place, as well as the food and the staff. Margareta went on to high school and she and Gertie never saw each other again.

Maxim Shaulov

Nastasia rang the doorbell and Irina answered. The two sisters embraced each other warmly. It had been nearly six years since they'd last seen each other. Nastasia introduced Maxim to her sister and Irina kindly touched his head and said:

"Maxim, don't worry, we will all do what we can to help you grow into a happy and good man."

They entered the house, where Gregory and the three kids were already waiting for them. Irina introduced Nastasia and Maxim to everyone and then went into the kitchen to bring out dinner. After dinner was finished, Irina told the kids to go get ready for bed. The eldest, Sonia, who was nine years old, bid everyone a good night, kissed her parents, and went up to her room. Maria, who was six, did the same. As she had no room elsewhere, Irina offered Maxim a mattress on the floor in the room of the youngest, Nikolai, who was four. After the children had all fallen asleep, Nastasia, Irina, and Gregory sat around the living room table. Gregory poured himself a vodka and lit a cigarette. They discussed the idea that Gregory and Irina had come up with even before their arrival: Nastasia would help at the notions store until she could find something more suitable. In this spirit, they each went to bed.

Maxim began his studies at the boarding school, named after Symon Petliura, who had been a Ukrainian nationalist leader. Nastasia and Gregory accompanied him on his first day and after he was registered and had settled in, they said goodbye. Maxim was placed in a spacious room that had four beds. After he introduced himself to his three new roommates, they told him all about the boarding school. The rules were strict, and the teachers made sure they were followed, but in general the students enjoyed various sports and activities. The grounds were well maintained and were lush and green, full of colorful seasonal flowers. Benches were scattered among the grass and the trees. The sports equipment in the gym was old, but met the needs of the students. The cafeteria food was plentiful and filling, though repetitive not particularly exciting in terms of flavors and range. Lights out was at 10 p.m. sharp.

Maxim got along particularly well with his roommate Alex Dimitry, or Dima for short. They often would tell each other about their lives before their arrival at the boarding school. They became fast friends when they found out that they both had Jewish roots. Maxim recalled how his father had told him, after he had had his accident, that he had Jewish ancestry and that he should always be proud of his origins. Even though they didn't practice religion in their home, Maxim still remembered the menorah that sat on shelf in the living room, the Star of David on the wall next to the pictures of his grandparents, and the pair of candles lit on Friday nights, whose lights would cast a warm orange glow over the house. Dima shared his secret about what he heard about Palestine, or Eretz Yisrael, and about its capitol, the holy city of Jerusalem, which was mentioned in a sentence that his parents had repeated: "If I forget thee, O Jerusalem, let my right hand forget her cunning." Another phrase that he had heard was said at the end of Yom Kippur prayers at the synagogue: "Next year in Jerusalem." Dima told Maxim that one day he would "make *aliyah*" (immigrate) to Eretz Yisrael.

Maxim would spend his few vacations at Irina and Gregory's house. Everyone pampered him and made sure he enjoyed his short time off, most of all Nastasia, whose eyes would fill with tears when she saw him. She truly thought of him as her own son.

In 1932, Maxim's second year at the boarding school, Stalin implemented the *Holodomor*, or the Famine Genocide, in the Ukraine. For more than two years, the collectivization of agriculture and other policies led to the starvation of an estimated seven million Ukrainians.

Priel Porat

Work on the dock stopped following the tragedy. Longshoremen, port authorities, crewmen, and curious onlookers gathered in groups watched the rescue boat approach the dock slowly. The paramedics who arrived with the ambulance began helping the injured onto the pier and tended their wounds. Second mate Moti Lev, whose duties included overseeing the ship's sickbay, took down the names of the injured and got instructions from the paramedics for their ongoing treatments. Captain Bar-Noy spoke with the ship agent over the phone and reported the incident. The agent straight away phoned the shipping company in Israel and reported the name of the deceased, as well as those of the injured. The Israeli embassy in Holland was also notified, which worked with the Dutch authorities in order to get Gershon's body transferred to Israel. Under the captain's instructions, and with Moti's guidance, the necessary paperwork concerning Gershon's death was completed. One copy was sent to the shipping company and another one was sent to the Ministry of Transport, Administration of Shipping and Ports. A third copy was filed onboard. The captain also filled out a complete report of the accident and the incident was recorded in the ship's log. Work started up again and everything went back to usual as if nothing had happened.

A floating crane and some crew from the nearby shipyard were brought to put the lifeboat back in place. Carlos Antonio remained on the embarkation deck, at my request, to provide support if needed. It was a sweltering summer day, which added to the weight felt by all of us. The air was stale and motionless, giving no respite to the heat that enveloped us. The injured were sent to rest following a crew-wide talk with the captain, who briefed everyone about the details of the unexpected incident and listened to the lifeboat crew's own feelings about the matter. At the end of

the meeting, we all stood for a moment of silence for our friend
Gershon. The Israeli Merchant Marine flag at the stern was flown
at half-mast.

Midday arrived. In the mess, crewmen bent over their plates,
looking forlorn. They had little appetite. I decided against eating,
but I asked Yaacov the messman to make up a plate for Gertie. I
took the overflowing tray up to my cabin. I knocked lightly on
the door and without waiting for an answer, I opened it. Gertie sat
next to the table, flipping through a booklet she found, listening
to some upbeat music on the radio. She was barefoot, in black
underwear and an oversized T-shirt that she'd found in my drawer.
She seemed bored. I glanced over the room; the bed was made
and the cabin was clean. I put the tray down on the table, hugged
her gently, and went straight to the liquor cabinet. I took out a
bottle of Vat 69 whiskey and poured myself a tall glass. I sat next
to her at the table and watched her busy with her lunch. Gertie
noticed my mood.

"Did something happen?" she asked. I told her about the
accident, about Gershon's death and the other's injuries. Gertie
said that she'd woken up to the sound of a loud bang on the ship,
but she would never have guessed that it would be such a disaster.
The glass emptied and was refilled. I felt the need for a cold
shower to rinse away the events of the day.

"Gertie," I said. "Let's jump in the shower quickly and then
go out and find some fun." We threw our clothes onto the bed and
went into the shower. Her body once again had its effects on me,
and we ended up losing ourselves under the water. As we were
getting dressed, Jeremy the deck boy knocked on the door, and
hearing my answer, entered the cabin. He reported that the first
mate was waiting for me in the office.

"Gertie, my Queen of Sheba, I'll be right back," I said. As I
walked into the office, Itzik said without hesitating:

"Perry, we sail tomorrow evening to Hamburg, Germany.
We'll stay there a single day and then from Hamburg we sail to
Kingston, Jamaica without cargo. Those were last instructions we

received from the ship agent." My eyes fell and Itzik understood; he'd met Gertie.

"What a bleak day," I murmured, and turned back to my quarters.

Gertie's face also dropped after I'd told her about the Jalopy's plans. I poured both of us a glass. As we sat drinking, Shauli came in through the open door. I poured him a glass of Vat 69 as well. He broke the silence and offered that we go out that evening.

"I made plans to meet Nellie at the Oasis, you two should come, too."

"Good idea," Gertie said. "What do you think, Perry?"

"Sounds perfect," I replied.

Daylight had already begun to fade when we disembarked and made our way out of the port. At the request of the guards, we showed them our passes, including Gertie's, which we'd arranged in advance with Itzik Shahak and the ship agent, with Captain Bar-Noy's knowledge. We stopped a cab and asked that he drive us to the Oasis club in the Katendrecht district. The taxi zipped through the streets of Rotterdam, lit up in the bright summer night, up to the entrance of the club. *God. This place is so familiar to me, as if it were already a part of me. It's such a pity that we're leaving tomorrow again, for such a long trip over the ocean. I'm going to miss Gertie terribly, and who knows when we might meet again?*

Our familiar "personal" waiter led us to our same table near the dance floor and immediately took our orders, probably remembering again the nice tip he received the last time. Nellie joined us at the table and sat next to Shauli, giving him a loving kiss. Gertie told her about the tragedy that happened on the ship and Nellie gave some words of comfort. Our personal waiter, as usual with his white towel hanging form the crook of his elbow, tended to all our needs. Gertie looked at me with her big eyes, trying to read my thoughts. I gave a small, unconvincing smile and held her hand in mine.

"Perry," she said. "It doesn't matter the distance or the time passed, you are stuck inside here," and she pointed to her heart. "You and your unique personality have changed my world. I will wait for your return, for all my life."

Nellie and Shauli got up and went to the crowded dance floor. I felt some pressure from my bladder, so I begged her pardon and found the men's room. After I finished, I washed my hands and face with the tap water and dried myself with a paper towel. On my way back to the table, I saw from afar Gertie arguing with two men I hadn't seen before. As I neared, I heard her say:

"It's none of your business who I go out with. I don't owe you any explanation and I'm asking you once and for all: Leave me alone." The man closest to her suddenly smacked her across the face loudly, twice, and grabbing her collar, pulled her up from the seat. I didn't hesitate much and bounded toward them while grabbing something off a nearby table. Adrenaline pumped through my body; I was young, tall, and strong from my work on the Jalopy. The difficult events on the ship just added fuel to my fire. I smashed into them without warning and they fell to the floor. I continued to punch them, even as they lay there helpless, until two pairs of strong arms pulled at me. Two bouncers, accompanied by our personal waiter, took me away from the men. Gertie, whom everyone recognized as the head hostess, got up from the table and came toward us, a red mark still on her face from the slaps. He told her side of the story and our waiter confirmed the details. The two bouncers told Gertie that there wouldn't be any more trouble and that they'd deal with the offenders. Nellie and Shauli were already at our side. We decided to leave the club, so we paid the bill and, of course, left a nice tip. This time it was my turn to thank our waiter. We found a nice, cozy café nearby and ordered espressos and cold water for the table. Later, Shauli and Nellie took their leave.

Gertie said that she would like to join me on the ship and stay there until we sailed. Of course, I agreed and was happy of the fact. I still hadn't asked her about the two men as we made our way back to the port. I preferred to wait until we were alone in my cabin. As we made our way down the passageway, I glanced at the shore leave notice board, upon which was written in white chalk:

Port of Rotterdam
Date – 07/07/1969
Time – 17:00

The Vat 69 was still on the table. I washed the glasses, took out some ice from the freezer – as usual, imperfect – and poured out the contents of the bottle.

"Gertie," I said. "I'm going to the crew refrigerator to get some snacks." I toasted a few slices of bread, and piled up some cheese, sausage, vegetables, and green olives. I salted the veggies a bit and took out a pair of forks and knives and when it was all ready, I placed my handiwork on a tray and returned to my quarters. A single light above the bed cast a romantic yellow glow over the cabin and music played from the radio. Gertie was still sitting at the table playing with her glass, but now she was topless. I put down the tray and joined her. I lit a cigarette and finished the remains of my glass. I went to the liquor cabinet and took out another Vat 69. I wanted to know about the two men, so I finally asked her. She looked straight at me and began to explain:

"The man who slapped me is named Willem. He was my boyfriend for about a year. Before I started working at the Oasis, I worked at a bar that he and the other guy you saw owned. From our first meeting, Willem was so nice to me. He spoiled me, showered me with compliments, and would buy me presents and leave generous tips. His generosity and kindness is what 'sold' him to me, up until the day I found myself packing my bags to move in with him in his large house. At the beginning, everything was great, but gradually, cracks in his personality began to appear. He would fly into jealous rages, which increased on a daily basis. He would accuse me of cheating, and his anger soon changed from verbal abuse to physical. He controlled every part of my life and monitored my movements. I prayed for the day that I would get enough courage to leave him. One day the opportunity came: Willem went out to take care of some business having to do with the bar and I knew he'd be gone for a few hours. I took advantage of his absence and packed my clothes and belongings, and when everything was ready, I sat and wrote him a note telling him that I was leaving him forever, that I didn't love him, and that he better not try to contact me. I found an apartment to rent – the same one that you've seen – and I soon found work at the Oasis. Tonight was first time since I left him that they found me."

Fatigue began to set in. All of the long day's events – the morning's disaster and the evening's run in at the bar – were taking their toll. Gertie herself looked wiped. There was little time left to sleep, so we went into bed, made love sleepily, and fell asleep until my wake up time in the early morning.

Departure day from port is usually a busy one. Many different jobs need to be finished, which takes the efforts of the whole crew. Most of the work involves the ship's hull, like scraping off rust, repainting a base coat, and finally painting a top layer. Then there's the painting of the draft numbers on the hull, the name of the ship at the bow and both sides of the stern, and the name of the home port. The crew also needs to ensure all of the cargo is tied down, to secure the equipment in the holds, to secure the hatches, and an endless number of additional tasks that have to be done before the ship leaves port. Between all of these jobs, I stole a few minutes here and there to look in on Gertie in my cabin. The impending separation did not sit well with us.

"Perry my love, when you get back, I'm prepared to go with you back to Israel, if you wish," she said to me.

The last of the longshoremen left the Jalopy and the deck crew finished up the final jobs before the imminent departure. We waited for the harbor pilot and the tugboats to release the ship. And that was it. It was time to say goodbye to Gertie. I went to my cabin. She was ready. I helped her with her bag and together we went to the gangway. We stood there embracing silently for five minutes until we heard:

"Deck, bow, stern crews to their stations. Helmsman – to the bridge." The port authority crew arrived in the harbor vehicle. On the side of the car was a blue logo showing interlocking anchors and the words "Port of Rotterdam, Docking Crew." They split into two groups, taking up spots at the bow and the stern, next to the bitts, ready to unhitch. The pilot went to the bridge and the tugboats began their approach. One last wordless embrace and Gertie disembarked. She remained there on the dock, watching me at the bow. She took out a flowery handkerchief from her bag and waved it until the ship was out of sight. *She didn't know it would be the last time she'd see Perry.*

The short trip to Hamburg passed quickly, and I mostly thought of Gertie. *I really will miss her*, I thought. I always loved being in Hamburg, especially the famous St. Pauli quarter, with its wild nightlife. But this time I chose to stay onboard. My body's batteries were nearly empty. The ship was docked at the designated pier and the preparations for the final unloading of cargo finished. Since they were free and weren't on night duty, Shauli, Ben-Tzur, and Carlos Antonio decided to go check out St. Pauli. They tried to sway me to join them, but I stuck to my original plan and stayed on the ship.

The next day, ahead of the long voyage to Jamaica, a new carpenter named Yoav Artzi arrived from Israel to take the late Gershon's place. We once sailed together on another of the company's ships. I remembered him as a good seaman, with a good sense of humor and well-liked by the guys. After Yoav settled into his cabin, he lay topside to First Mate Itzik Shahak's office and gave him a package of newspapers and letters for the captain and the crewmen. From Itzik's office he lay below to the chief steward's office and gave him his embarkation papers and his mariner's card. He got recorded into and signed the ship's crew list. After all the formalities were taken care of, he returned to his cabin, changed into work clothes and went straight to me on the main deck. We shook hands and after a brief "Welcome to the ship" and a bit of gossip, I told him about Gershon. He said that there were reports about the accident on the radio and in all the papers. There were also reports published in the newspapers that were sent from Israel to the crewmen (as usual).

Late that night, at around midnight, we were on our way. On the captain's instructions, Moti Lev drew out on the map our course, a great circle passing northwest over the Azores islands, starting at the Isles of Scilly on the southwestern border of England near the mouth of the English Channel – or La Manche, as the French call it – not in a straight line, which lengthened the voyage slightly. Since it was still summer, and the North Atlantic was relatively calm, it was the preferred route.

Daily life at sea does me good. The fatigue from port disappears. The workday goes from 08:00-17:00, leaving ample free time. Sometimes we put in an extra hour or two to finish a job. In the evening, after dinner, the crew usually gathers in the day room to watch a video, play cards, play board games like backgammon or checkers, while others read books or newspapers. Some sit in their quarters drinking and eating, telling stories and jokes they've all heard before, usually surrounding the topic most close to them: the sea. As the evening progresses, and the drinks begin to have their impact, loud singing commences. One crewman might even empty a garbage can and use it as a drum. My favorite day is Friday, when we finish our work at 14:00, and everyone – besides the crew on duty – are free.

That's how it was on our first Friday out on route. Dinner was celebratory and different from the rest of the week. A white tablecloth was used instead of the usual colorful plastic one, and on it were bottles of wine and various salads, including carrot, beet, cabbage, a green salad, hummus, tahini, eggplant, and pickles. In the middle of the table lay a fresh baked challah bread, made by the cook and his assistant. On Fridays, starters were usually a mushroom pastry or Saint Peter's fish baked in a Moroccan style with red pepper, tomato, hot green pepper, coriander and other spices. For the main course, a juicy beef steak made to order – rare, medium, or well done – with fries. Dessert was canned pineapple or fruit cocktail. Sometimes we got ice cream and seasonal fruits. We enjoyed a relaxed atmosphere and full stomachs. After dinner I liked to go out to the stern, light a cigarette, and be by myself, looking out on the wide-open ocean, watching the colors of the sunset, and listening to water in the wake. This time, of course, my thoughts returned to Gertie. I passed about twenty minutes thinking about her there by myself. I tossed my cigarette butt into the blue and white foam and went back to my cabin. I took out a bottle and poured myself a decent sized glass. My radio doesn't work out on open water, so I sat in silence, sipping every few seconds, until Shauli knocked on my door and asked to join me. He preferred beer, so I got him a can. Since it was Friday, we weren't pressed for time and could stay up late, as there wasn't work to get up for in the morning. Shauli told me that his plans for him and Nellie were serious. He loved her, and she him. When his contract was up – which was in about five months – he planned to bring her to Israel, stop sailing, rent an apartment, and try to live together on land. She had agreed fully to this proposal. I was happy to hear it and I even encouraged his ideas, but I did warn him that they might encounter all sorts of bureaucratic and social problems. It would be really tough at the beginning, but it was clear that it was worth trying. As we sat, drinking and talking, a few more guys began showing up. First came Ben-Tzur, then Carlos Antonio, and it didn't take long for Doron and Yossi and finally Yoav Artzi, the replacement carpenter, to join. The mood was warming, as was the temperature of the cabin, which was full of cigarette smoke and alcohol vapors. Everyone started telling stories about their travels, and no one interrupted each other. Ben-Tzur quickly went to his quarters and brought back a recorder and out came the sounds of Greek bouzouki music. I revealed to them that I was guilty of writing songs and Shauli was graced with the art of composing, so I suggested that we all took a crack at singing something. I took out a song I'd written from a drawer and began reading it to them.

At the Tavern

In a dark corner, at a dark table,
Two sailors and a girl are willing and able
To throw back the drinks, driving full throttle,
One by one grabbing the neck of the bottle.

The dear bottle, their own joy and pride
Glasses sitting half-empty at its side,
While a small red candle flickers and burns,
Shining a spotlight on each face, in turns.

Chorus:
So lets drink to these three,
The two sailors and she,
As the white seagull guides us
To safe shore and lighthouse.

A girl and two sailors sit, and they drink,
One smiles brightly, the other bright pink.
And that sly lady, with her sly eyes,
Gets both of them caught in her love and her lies.

Eyes dart, lips part, the girl plays with her hair,
And all round the table hints fly through the air.
Full glasses are swallowed, again and again,
Toasting the health of the woman and men.

Chorus

And so it began, in quiet and silence,
Two loving sailors contemplating violence.

Jealous glances flicker to and fro,
A tense calm before the storm, before the first throw.

Without a word, the war is declared.
While begging the pardon of the woman they shared.
They take to the floor of that dark tavern
To fight for the hand of the bewitching siren.

Chorus

In a dark corner, at a dark table,
A girl sits alone, crestfallen, unable,
While a small red candle shines a spotlight
On the face of the girl, with no sailors, that night.

Chorus

Shauli liked the song so much that he asked Yossi to go and empty
the aluminum trash can. He then took a shot of whiskey, turned the
trashcan over and placed it between his legs, and began drumming
a beat and a singing the song. We all joined in, really feeling
the muse's presence. The mood took over and even influenced
other crewmen who heard the music from down the passageway.
Eventually, the night began to wind down as it got later. The first
to "fall" was Carlos Antonio, who gave a muttered "goodnight"
and hobbled back to his quarters. One by one everyone left and
I was finally by myself again when it was well past midnight. I
reordered the cabin a bit and then went to the crew preparation
room to make myself a cheese and tomato sandwich. When I got
back to my quarters, the fatigue really hit me and I was soon in
bed, my thoughts sailing back to Gertie.

On the evening of the seventh day at sea, a flashing lighthouse
beam could be seen on the horizon. I knew that it meant that
the Jalopy was going to soon pass the Azores islands. These
are a group of islands in the heart of the North Atlantic Ocean

that belong to Portugal. Even though we only passed them by, the event still gave us a good feeling after days of sea and sky. When you only see the dome of the sky touching the circle of water surrounding the ship, it can feel as if you were alone in the center of the world. Gradually, we began to see slivers of coastline appear, scattered lights from the villages twinkled like stars, and soon even the rooftops could be spotted. Even the rhythmic lights of the lighthouse became brighter.

I went to the crew refrigerator and got myself some slices of bread and then went to the stern. I listened to the call of the seagulls fishing for their dinner, their sharp eyes watching the silvery wake from the ship hoping for a fish to spring up. I threw over the bread slices and the seagulls dove expertly and caught them. Satisfied, I returned to my cabin, turned on the radio, and turned the dial until I fell upon a local station playing lovely Portuguese music. I poured myself a glass and looked through the porthole, watching the villages passing by the portside of the *Cormoran*. The little avocado plant that I'd placed on the sill of the porthole needed water, so I added a bit. I thought of that wintery day when I first set aside the avocado pit to dry out for a month, after which I speared it with four wooden skewers I'd retrieved from the ship's galley. I rinsed out a plastic jam jar, filled it with water, and placed the pit into it. Three months later, it sprouted a root, which had only grown stronger since. Soon after, its first two leaves sprouted. It now had two stems with sixteen leaves and the bottom of the jar was filled with a tangle of roots. Every morning I peeked in and for every new leaf I felt a new feeling of accomplishment. A small plant gives you the sense that you're not alone in your cabin, and helps with the loneliness that comes with being out on the ocean.

Later in the evening the lights of the islands disappeared, and with them the lighthouse, until only its reflection still showed on the surface of the water, and soon that, too, vanished. The radio began to crackle with static, signaling our entrance into the dark ocean.

I turned off the radio. But sleep eluded me. I poured myself a glass and took it topside to the stern. A cool breeze caressed my face. The moon made the wake of the ship glisten silver. The roar of the waves played me a beautiful melody. I leaned on the railing, enjoying the calm of the universe. The mice on land could never understand life out in the heart of the ocean with its endless expanse. To watch the sunrise and sunset painting the heavens in the colors of the rainbow, or that night in the light of the moon, alone with myself on the stern in soothing tranquility. I loved the Jalopy. I knew each of part of her – her masts, decks, holds, and engine room. It's a love that is hard to explain to anyone besides another seaman who had also spent a long time on a ship. I'd heard of and also seen ships that were on their last voyage. There were those that sunk and those that were broken up, erased from the registry. I always felt a deep sorrow for those sad endings.

Sleep remained evasive. I decided to go to the bridge. In the map room, I met Second Mate Moti Lev, who was on the night shift. Moti was bent over a map of our present location, marking the ship's current position. He smiled when he saw me.

"What's up, Perry? Can't sleep?" I didn't reply. "Well, make yourself a cup of tea or coffee and we can chat on the bridge. There's hot water in the kettle."

I made myself some tea with a slice of lemon. Moti watched the radar to make sure there were no ships in the vicinity that could present danger.

"I'm going to the starboard bridge wing to get some fresh ocean air," I told him.

"I'll join you soon, just after I finish up here," he answered.

The moment that Moti joined me, we both noticed suddenly that there was what seemed to be a refinery ship with a red distress signal on the bow's starboard side. Moti ran to the radar and reset the range to six nautical miles. He could barely make out the little flashing dot. It was about five nautical miles away. It looked as if it was adrift in the water. He went to the telephone and called Captain Bar-Noy to the bridge. Then, using the international frequency on the radio, he tried to make contact with the unidentified ship, to no avail. Bar-Noy arrived immediately and the second mate briefed him on the situation. The captain called the chief engineer to ready the engine room for an emergency. He asked me to get Carlos Antonio, the helmsman, and to wake up the deck crew and get the starboard side lifeboat ready to launch. The captain contacted the station on Faial Island, part of the Azores Islands, informing them about the refinery ship in distress and that he was deviating his course to offer assistance. He added that they should keep in contact until the state of emergency was lifted. As the ship approached the vessel, it turned out that it was a small yacht. The ship stopped half a mile from the yacht. I boarded the lifeboat along with the other crewmen, together with blankets, water, and food. Moti took with him a first aid kit and a radio. Onboard the yacht were a young English couple, who looked to be about thirty years old. Apparently, their radio had stopped working and then their engine had also given out on them. Avraham the second engineer checked the engine and quickly fixed the issue. The ship's electrician also repaired their radio. They thanked us for the unexpected help. We left them some food and water and went on our way. The coastal station received a report and the event was recorded in the ship's log.

Maxim Shaulov

Five years had passed since he'd arrived at the boarding school. Eighteen-year-olds Maxim and Dima, like the rest of their classmates, completed their studies and thus their time at the Symon Petliura Boarding School came to an end. They were to clear their rooms, to make space for other orphaned and abandoned children now flocking to the school's doors. That summer of 1935, they still had no idea what would become of themselves, where they would sleep at night, what they would do, or how they would earn a living. It was clear that they would have to find jobs as soon as possible. Maxim suggested to Dima to go see Irina and Gregory and ask for their advice in the matter. When they both agreed to the plan, they gathered what little belongings they had and were on their way.

When Nastasia opened the door and saw Maxim, she wrapped her arms around him in a tight embrace and kissed him on the forehead. He had grown tall and sturdy and was quite handsome. His limp was almost unnoticeable. They sat down at the dining table and Irina served dinner. After they'd finished, Gregory offered them a glass of vodka. When Gregory, Maxim, and Dima were alone in the living room and Gregory had filled and lit his pipe, Maxim laid out his problems. Gregory listened intently and then sat thoughtfully for a while. After some time, he said:

"Tonight you will sleep in the living room, as it's our only option. Tomorrow morning we'll begin all the necessary arrangements for you each to stand on your own two feet. I have a good friend who has a small shoe factory. I hope that I can convince him to find some work for you there. As for where you'll live – I know that sometimes he rents out the house adjacent to the factory to his workers." Maxim and Dima thanked him for his help and hoped that his plan would come to fruition. They bid him good night and went to sleep.

The next morning, the three of them set out for the shoe factory, which was not too far from Gregory's house. They met Gregory's friend Mikhailovich in his office. At first glance, he seemed very strange: He was short, stocky, and bald, with mousey eyes that darted back and forth and stubby hands that couldn't stop fiddling with the papers on his desk. His voice was hoarse and high pitched and he spoke so fast that it was hard to understand what he was saying. After listening to Gregory's request, Mikhailovich looked at Maxim and Dima and said finally:

"Until Romulus and Remus over here can prove their worth, I'll hire them to do deliveries. They can stay in the next door housing, but they'll have to pay for their own meals." They shook hands and the deal was done.

The room they were given was terrible. It had a small window facing the factory's courtyard, two cots that were meant to be beds, a small wooden table, and two chairs. A bathroom and shower was at the end of the hall, for use by all the employee residents. Once a week there was hot water, but if they wanted to shower during the rest of the week, they had to do so with cold water. They began their work in deliveries, as they had agreed. Maxim and Dima each got a bicycle with a large trunk attached to the back. They signed an official agreement stating that if a bicycle went missing or stolen, they would have to pay for it out of their salaries. And thus passed the days, the weeks, and the months.

Eight months later, the two were still working as delivery men, but were happy, since most customers usually gave them a tip for delivering their package quickly and without damage. They opened bank accounts and saved their money carefully; they would deposit their salaries every month and kept a log of income – including salary and tips – and expenses – including food, clothing, and entertainment. Dima still dreamed of one day departing for Eretz Yisrael, and this dream captured Maxim's heart as well. They made a decision to never tell anyone about this plan.

Once a week, on Saturday, Maxim would go to Irina and Gregory's house to enjoy a hearty home-cooked meal. Afterward, he'd return back to his apartment. Since they both had Sundays off, the two would then usually go out to a club or the local bar, where they'd sit in the corner and order a vodka.

One evening, as they sat drinking, two girls sat next to them, also enjoying some vodka, smoking cigarettes, and chatting. Maxim and Dima kept looking over to the young ladies and noticed out of the corner of their eyes that they, too, were looking at them. Finally, Dima had the courage to approach them, turning to the girl who sat nearest to him and introduced himself and Maxim and offered to buy them a drink. She looked at her friend to see what she thought, and she gave her a slight nod. The girl introduced herself as Marina and her friend as Natasha, and that they'd be happy to have a drink. Dima asked the bartender for four vodkas, and after they clinked glasses, Dima and Natasha switched places so that she was sitting next to Maxim. She asked them what they did, and they told her about their job at the shoe factory. She told them that they work as saleswomen at a clothing store and live together in a two-bedroom apartment near their work. Maxim watched her face and eyes. She was nice-looking. *Definitely pretty enough*, he thought. Their conversation had some false starts, but then began to flow. The vodka certainly helped his confidence. Maxim had never been with a woman. Sure, he'd had wet dreams and pleasured himself sometimes, but he was still a virgin. At the end of the night, they said goodbye, but not before setting a date for the following Saturday evening at the same bar. On their way back to their building, Maxim and Dima exchanged stories and expressed their hope that the next time they saw the girls would be even better.

Saturday arrived and Maxim went, as usual, to eat at Irina and Gregory's house. When dinner was finished, Nastasia gave him a big hug and kissed him on his forehead, and they said goodbye. He then met Dima back at their building and together the two returned to the bar, hoping to see Marina and Natasha again.

The two young ladies were sitting in the same spots as the week before. They were smoking cigarettes and on the bar in front of them sat two glasses of vodka. Blue-grey smoke swirled around and up toward the ceiling. After greeting them, Maxim and Dima sat down next to the girls. Everyone seemed happy about seeing other again; they were already able to talk freely and naturally. As the evening went on, three musicians brought out instruments – a balalaika, violin, and accordion – and began playing some bouncy folk music for the patrons. One of the customers, who had probably had one vodka too many, got up and started a lively Russian dance, stomping hard on the wooden floor. The evening was pleasant and enjoyable. Dima stroked Marina's hand, and she caressed his in return. They sometimes whispered to each other, already exchanging shared secrets. Maxim still could not gather the courage to touch Natasha, even though she seemed interested. He was not yet ready to show his inexperience with women, which he was ashamed to admit even out loud. At the end of the night, as they were leaving the bar, Maxim shook Natasha's hand. Dima and Marina held each other and kissed. A love between them already seemed to be blooming. They once again set a date for the following week at the same place and then went their separate ways. On the walk home, Dima told Maxim that on their next date Marina intended to invite him over to her place. He added:

"Maxim, you need to move things along with Natasha, Marina told me that she's interested in you. If you make your move, then we could both go to their apartment and have a little fun." Maxim said that he was interested, but he had reservations because of his lack of experience. Dima tried to calm his nerves:

"Be confident, Maxim, and the moment you get into bed, everything will just flow naturally. I remember my first time with a girl. I also had doubts, but everything worked out for the absolute best."

Sometimes, at the end of a long workday, after eating dinner and washing the dishes, Maxim and Dima would each light a cigarette, pour themselves a vodka, and play checkers. They'd chat and always return to the same subject: making *aliyah* to Eretz Yisrael. As a year and half had passed since they began working, their savings had grown and they decided that within six months – at the age of twenty – they would fulfill their dream. The winter of 1936 arrived. They had no heating in their room, and even when they sat in their thick wool coats, the cold still crept into their bones. Icicles covered their single window, blocking their view of the factory courtyard. Snow fell, piling up on the tree branches and the roofs. The wind whistled through the door, sounding as if at any second it would come in a join them.

Saturday arrived quickly. Wrapped up in their coats, they walked to the bar, to Natasha and Marina. Snow was falling, covering them in white. They quickened their pace in order to warm up and also to escape the snow. Natasha and Marina were sitting in their same spot, with two glasses of vodka, as usual. The fireplace warmed the air. Maxim and Dima took off their coats and hung them on the coat rack near the door. The girls noticed them coming in, and they looked happy to see them. Dima hugged Marina, gave her a kiss, and sat down. Maxim held out his hand, and Natasha took it warmly and pointed to the seat next to her. The three musicians from the week before were playing again and everyone enjoyed themselves. After a little while, Natasha and Marina suggested they join them at their apartment for a cup of coffee. They boys agreed.

The apartment was simple and nice – a small living room, two small bedrooms, a bathroom, and a kitchenette. They went to the living room and Natasha turned on the radio. Marina went a got a bottle of vodka and glasses, and some snacks, like sliced smoked beef, salmon, cut vegetables, and dark bread, and put it all on the table. They ate the food to the radio music, and drank and smoked together. Then the inevitable moment came, as the sexual tension between Dima and Marina hung thick in the air and they left for the bedroom. Natasha then took the initiative and made the first move: She reached out to him and drew his face to hers. Lustily, she told him:

"Come on, let's go to my room." Her look was determined – even aggressive – and there was no way out. They stood up and went to her bedroom. As soon as they entered, Natasha didn't hesitate and began to take off her clothes. She lay down on her bed and beckoned to him. Maxim was slightly embarrassed, but her naked body did something to him, and he felt a great urge to go to her, which he did, while taking off his own clothes. Natasha was free and open. She knew what she wanted and directed him naturally on what to do and how she liked it. She pulled him toward her through her thighs, took his fingers to her breasts, held his member and guided him into her. He came to quickly and Natasha frowned.

"Maxim, smoke a cigarette and then come play with me, and don't hurry to finish, hold back." He obeyed her. He lit a cigarette and when he finished smoking, he went back to her and played with her as she told him to. This time Natasha climaxed, scratching her fingernails down his back and moaning deeply. They both came, but it wasn't enough for her. She wanted more. Maxim complied, happily. It was his first time in bed with a woman, and he wanted more and more. He reached supreme and incomprehensible satisfaction and beamed with happiness. He now knew what a woman was.

In the morning, the girls prepared a breakfast of eggs, salad, toast and butter, and coffee. After eating, they said goodbye to each other. Natasha looked happy. She hugged him and kissed him and it looked like it was hard for her to leave him. On their way back to their building, Maxim and Dima exchanged stories. To the question of how it was, Maxim told Dima how free Natasha was and how the sex had flowed. They then began their deliveries for the day.

In the middle of the week, Mikhailovich called the two to his office. When the got there, he lifted his mousey eyes from his paperwork and said in a hoarse voice:

"Look, Romulus and Remus, you've been here for more than a year and a half. Customers are happy with your work, and of course, I am too. I thought that the time has come to move you to another department where you can earn more. You'd get a raise, but it's your decision. You do good work and shopkeepers are happy with you. If you decide to continue with deliveries, I can give you a small raise. You don't have to answer now, think about it for a couple days and come back to my office." When they left the office, they discussed it and decided that they would tell Mikhailovich that they'd like to stay in deliveries.

On Thursday morning, as Maxim was going to the bathroom, he felt a burning in his penis. At first he didn't pay much attention, but throughout the day, each time he went to pee, it burned. He then noticed a small green-yellow rash on the end of his penis. He didn't understand it, so he told Dima about it. Dima asked to take a look and as soon as he saw it, he burst out laughing.

"Maxim, my dear friend, Natasha gave you VD. You've got gonorrhea, and you have to go to the doctor as soon as possible." Maxim grabbed his head in disbelief. That nymphomaniac had given him an unwanted prize. What a slut. That's just what he needed, to get VD on his first time. That same day, after they finished their work, Dima went with Maxim to a doctor. The doctor gave him a prescription for sulphur tablets and told him not to drink any alcohol for at least a week after finishing the medication. Over the next few days, Maxim took his medicine meticulously, focused on his work, and went to bed early, and even woke up uncharacteristically early in the morning.

On Saturday, as he was about to leave for Irina and Gregory's house, Maxim told Dima that he didn't want to meet Natasha again, but asked him to tell her what had happened so that she could get treatment. Dima promised that he would do so. As Irina was preparing dinner in the kitchen, Gregory invited Maxim to have some vodka in the living room.

"I think I'll have some juice instead, but I'll keep you company anyway," Maxim said. He wondered if Gregory would guess the real reason he declined. After a wonderful meal, he said goodbye.

He returned home and Dima wasn't there, so he figured he'd gone out to meet Marina and Natasha.

Dima had indeed gone to the bar and saw Marina and Natasha there. He asked to speak with Natasha outside and then told her about Maxim. He said that it wasn't right that she hadn't gotten checked by a doctor and that she needed to confront Maxim because he didn't want to see her again. Natasha gave a wry smile and said,

"If that's what he wants, that's fine. There's a lot of guys out there who would love to keep me company." Dima decided that he didn't want anything to do with these two easy girls, and left without even saying goodbye.

Summer, 1937, arrived. Two years had passed since Maxim and Dima had first come to the shoe factory. They now had enough money to follow their dream. It was decided, as they had agreed to earlier, that they would travel to the Crimean Peninsula and buy cruise tickets for Constanta, Romania. In Crimea, they'd go to a travel agency that arranged guided group tours. In Constanta, they'd disembark with the permission of the tour guide and contact the local Jewish community. At first, when they told him that they were quitting, Mikhailovich was reluctant to part with the boys, but when he understood that they were serious and that he most likely wouldn't see them again, he gave them their remaining salary with a nice bonus and wished them the best of luck. They didn't tell him the truth about their final destination. They had to keep that detail a secret, because if it ever got out to the wrong person, their whole plan – which they'd worked toward for so long – would crumble. Despite his appearances, Mikhailovich was a good man with a good heart and they would look fondly on the time that they'd spent at his factory. It was a shame that they had to leave him behind.

Leaving Nastasia, Irina, and Gregory was extremely difficult. Nastasia dissolved into tears, refusing to accept that she wouldn't see Maxim again. He promised to write to her as soon as he was settled into his new place. He still hadn't told her where he was going. He so wanted to share with her all the details of his plans, as she was like his very own mother in every respect, but he could not. Nastasia held on to him, refusing to say goodbye, but the moment had to arrive, and he finally turned and went. Dima was also forlorn. He didn't have anyone to say goodbye to or to share his secrets with. Finally, the day came. Maxim and Dima packed their bags, making sure they hadn't forgotten anything essential for the trip. They went to the train station and bought tickets to Sevastopol in Crimea. The train pulled out of the station noisily, wheels screeching and whistle blowing, and smoke billowing, toward a still unknown future.

Gertie Van der Giessen

On the one hand, Hans was happy to have his daughter help him with the management of the hotel, but on the other hand, it pained him that she gave up on studying, especially considering her good grades. He was consoled when Gertie told him that it would never be too late to go back to school, and that maybe one day she would continue her studies. He gave her the responsibility of managing the staff as well as watching over the activities in the kitchen, just as her mother Joanna had done. Over time, she became a wonderful manager and even improved the overall functioning of the staff and kitchen. Her work was reflected in increased profits. Her age was not a hindrance; quite the contrary. The workers appreciated her drive and her talents. Her astonishing beauty, quiet composure, fierce dedication, and her kind treatment of the employees melted hearts and made everyone love her.

In the Spring of 1961, on Gertie's 17th birthday, Hans invited the whole staff and the regular clients to the restaurant to celebrate. It was a successful evening, and at the end of the meal, the cook and his assistants brought in a three-tiered cake, designed to look like the hotel, and decorated with frosting the colors of the Dutch flag with a floral border. On the cake read: "Happy Birthday, wishing you success and happiness Gertie!" The bartender poured everyone coffee or tea. A string quartet, which Hans booked early for the event, played beautiful Dutch melodies. Toward the end of the evening, the staff presented its present to Gertie. It was in a big box wrapped in colorful paper. She untied the ribbons and ripped the paper to discover its contents: A burgundy colored gown, fit for special occasions, brown shoes – which were very "of the moment" – and a matching purse and makeup. She was so ecstatic about the gift, which must have cost a lot of money, and thanked each person with all her heart. Later, when she was alone in her room, she tried on the dress and shoes. They both fit her perfectly, and her wavy auburn hair went well with the new outfit. She looked at the makeup and tried some on her face and lips. Tired, but happy, after a long day, she then climbed into bed.

Over the winter of 1962, Gertie noticed that her father was spending more and more time with one particular woman who visited the hotel. She was quite nice looking, though on the plumper side. She was of average height and had flaxen hair. One day, while they were in their apartment above the hotel, Hans said:
"Gertie, please meet Tineke. We are going to marry and ask for your blessing." Gertie was completely taken aback, and was even a bit embarrassed, but she held out her hand and wished them both good luck. In that moment, she realized that she would no longer hold the top place in her father's heart.

Following the wedding, Tineke began to be involved in the work at the hotel. Slowly and carefully, she got in Gertie's way and eventually took over. It turned out that Hans was as weak as a little puppy and wouldn't stand up for Gertie. His daughter resolved to leave. She was almost eighteen and decided to start out on her own. She hadn't yet spoken about it, because she thought it would be best if she found another job beforehand, since she'd need to find an apartment in addition to some work that met her experience. When she was "given" some time off by Tineke, she started to look around and try her luck. This was how, one afternoon, she found herself in front of a popular restaurant with a large sign reading "Free Dutch Restaurant, popular prices." She went in and sat at the bar. She ordered herself a steak, a baked potato, a salad, and a glass of wine. Next to her sat a nice-looking young man, who looked to be in his mid-twenties, wearing a grey business suit with a blue tie. He was drinking a green cocktail and had a plate of shrimp in front of him. They exchanged glances a few times and then he turned to her and said:
"Hello, my name is Henrik. You look a bit lonely. What's your name? If you don't mind, I'd be happy to get to know you."
"I'm Gertie," she said. "I live not far from here. My father

owns a hotel, but I'm looking for work now where I can use my talents. What do you do?" Henrik looked into her eyes and said:

"I'm here on business. I arrived this morning from Rotterdam and I'm returning tomorrow. I own a nightclub there. My father managed it all his life, but when he retired, he gave it over to me. I came here to check out some equipment I'm interested in buying for the club." They sat and talked some more about various subjects, telling each other a bit about their pasts. Finally, Henrik said:

"Gertie, if you'd like, and if you're not busy tonight, I'd love to take you out to a nice club here. I know the owners and maybe you could get a job there after I talk to them." They set a time to meet that evening and said goodbye to each other.

The club was full to capacity. It was considered to be one of the best in the city. It was right on the canal, where the boats sailed. It shared the street with cafés, restaurants, and several bars, lit up with blinking neon signs. There was a long row of trees, under which were benches to sit and admire the view. Gertie and Henrik found a small corner table next to a stained-glass bay window overlooking the trees and canal. A sweet looking waitress came to take their order: A glass of Riesling for Henrik, a gin and tonic for Gertie, and a plate of fries. When the waitress came back with their order, Henrik asked her if the owner, Rudy, was there. She said that Rudy usually could be found in his office, and he thanked her. After clinking glasses and taking some sips, Henrik excused himself and said he would go see Rudy about a possible position for her.

"It shouldn't take long," he said. "I'll try to be quick and come back to you."

When she was alone, Gertie looked around the club. It really was lovely. It was large and well-decorated and very full. Several couples were dancing in the middle of the dance floor to the band's lively music. Waitresses darted between people and tables, trays full of drinks and food. She suddenly found herself thinking about Henrik. He was quite handsome and seemed so nice, even though she'd only met him that day. Too bad he was going back to Rotterdam the following day, before they could get to know each other better.

More than a half an hour passed before Henrik returned to the table. She could immediately tell on his face that Rudy didn't have a job for her. All of the positions at the club were already taken. Additionally, Rudy had a long waiting list of waiters that had passed the initial interview and were in line for a position to open up, so it just wasn't feasible at the moment. Henrik ordered another round, lit a cigarette, and looked around the club. He thought about Gertie's divine beauty, her unique personality, and her quiet but straightforward character. You could tell that she came from a good home, he thought. The band began to play a slower tune. He turned to her and asked her for a dance. Gertie agreed happily and they set out to the dance floor. Henrik held her gently. A scent of his shampoo and cologne wafted up to her and she began feeling herself attracted to him. The feeling was mutual. When they returned to the table, Henrik ordered two cups of coffee. As they began sipping the aromatic coffee, he said suddenly:

"Listen, Gertie, I just got an idea. I could take you on to work in my club in Rotterdam. You'd start out as a waitress, but I promise you that in no time, after you get a little experience, you'll be put in charge of the whole staff. With my help, of course. The only problem is that you'd need to move to Rotterdam. I can help you there, too, because I've got three apartments, and one just opened up. I'm going to leave you the address and my phone number. Think about it. When you come to a decision, call me, and we'll take care of everything."

The offer was enticing. Finally, she could be independent and make a living on her own. Nevertheless, she felt a strong hesitation deep in her stomach. She didn't know where it came from. Until she was sure of herself, she decided to try it out and not tell her father about it. Gertie didn't want to look overeager, so she said she'd think about it. She'd get in touch with him either way. Henrik said that he hoped she'd say yes and added that she had nothing to worry about. He'd stay by her side to help her along the way.

Henrik walked her back to the hotel and before saying goodbye, he moved close to her and kissed her on her lips. It was the first intimate kiss she'd had.

Priel Porat

Long days had passed since we were near the Azores, until one warm, bright morning we saw the beaches of the Bahamas. Carlos Antonio, as usual, brought a coffee to me in my cabin and briefed me on the weather conditions. A day earlier, we could feel the end of the journey in the air. Sea gulls had appeared out of nowhere, following the *Cormoran* in hopes of getting some scraps. We saw fishing boats on their way out to sea and others on their way back to port with their catch. We could see other ships with the same route sailing toward the Caribbean Islands. It was always exciting for me to pass between the exotic Caribbean Islands, if for no other reason than the unbelievable experience I'd had that had lasted nearly a year. It went like this:

Three years before, I sailed on a big bulk carrier. The ship carried unpackaged grain from ports in the United States' Gulf of Mexico, for the Dagon silo in Haifa. The journey took 24 days in each direction. Sometimes, when the ship owners ordered an economic speed, to save on fuel costs, the trip could last 30 days in each direction. The whole way from the origin port to the destination port, the deck crew would be busy swabbing and scrubbing the giant cargo holds and scraping rust off the bulkheads and decks. The work was dangerous and required skill and professionalism. Cargo hold floors would be fully repainted and, finally, disinfection to get rid of pests, so that the ship would pass USDA inspection and get the required permits. One day, on a Summer evening following the long journey from the Mediterranean, across the Atlantic, through Providence Channel in the Bahamas, as we approached the southern tip of Great Abaco Island to the place strangely named "Hole in the Wall", hundreds of birds of all different colors and sizes suddenly landed on deck, picking at leftover grains. Since I loved birds – and probably also because of the loneliness from sea – I decided to try and catch some of the docile ones. The ship's cook, who was a friend of mine, helped out. We were able to catch forty birds, consisting of three different types. The small ones – which were the majority – resembled sparrows, but unlike in our country, they had multicolored feathers. The medium sized ones looked like white parrots and the large ones looked like young hens.

Birds in the Caribbean

I brought all the birds respectfully into my shower. I filled a bowl with water, brought some grains like wheat and sorghum, and also sprinkled some breadcrumbs. Then I closed the door. In the morning, I carefully opened the door, and to my dismay, all of the sparrow-like birds lay dead on the floor. I gave them a burial at sea. The ones left were two parrot-like birds and eight hen-like birds. I decided to build a proper birdcage, so I went to the deck equipment warehouse at the fore of the ship and began building a wooden cage whose frame was 120 cm long, 75 cm wide, and 90 cm tall. At the top and bottom of the frame I build a plywood floor and roof. I placed little outposts for the birds inside the cage, made out of a broom handle. I then wrapped the cage in chain-link fencing, with a door. Finally, I sprinkled sawdust on the bottom, and I was happy with the result. I worked and sweated hard for hours building the "Villa". The finished birdcage was very heavy, and I needed four crewmen to help carry it to my cabin. I placed it in a nice space between my bed and the table. The cage went right up against the bulkhead, and since it was so heavy and large, I wasn't worried about the rocking of the waves. Gabi the ship's cook gave me two plastic jam jars, and I used one for water and the other for food. Then, all that remained was to move the birds into their new home. I was very happy with the result, and also because I knew that in just two days, we'd be docking in New Orleans after 30 days at sea. Later in the evening, Gabi came to my cabin. I took out a bottle of whiskey and poured two glasses. We looked at the cage and the birds inside. Gabi took out a bag from his pocket and rolled a joint. When it was ready, he offered me some, but I declined. I preferred Marlboro. We sat, drank our whiskey, and talked about the upcoming shore leave and what we planned to do there. A little while later, Gabi got up and said he'd be right back. He came back with some snacks for his munchies. We sat together until midnight and then bid each other goodnight.

At the port of New Orleans, I gathered a lot of grain for my beloved roommates. During their first days in captivity, you could see that they were in shock – they huddled together, almost motionless. They barely ate and never sang. This made me very sad, but I believed that they would soon get used to their new lives. One morning, about three weeks after I'd caught them, I awoke to find one of the parrot birds dead on the floor of the cage. I was heartbroken, but I carefully picked him up and gave him a sailor's burial. Three days later, the other parrot bird died. Only the eight hen birds were left. They lived to see the Haifa port. The smells of the grains and the harbor seemed to lift their spirits. But only two days after we set sail again, one hen bird lay, fluttering, at the bottom of the cage. She stopped breathing before my eyes. She, too, got a proper sea burial. Now I had seven hen birds. Days, weeks, and months passed, and it seemed that they had finally gotten used to their new home. They began being more active: They walked around the cage, climbed on the poles, stretched their wings, ate their food hungrily, and even tweeted. After a long day's work, I liked to watch them. I sensed that they had overcome the trauma of captivity. I felt it most when I would change fill up their food bowl and changed their water. They no longer feared me or tried to escape. And so the months passed. The ship continued on its regular route between the Haifa and Gulf of Mexico ports. I noticed the birds get happy when I would return to my cabin after a day's work. One evening, I decided to release them into my cabin. I opened the cage door and helped them out one by one. As soon as they were out of the cage, they stretched their wings and began walking around the cabin. Some climbed high up, while others seemed happy to walk along the linoleum floor and even approached me. In the days following, they let me pet them and pick them up. That time we had together was perfect. I loved them like a man loves his dogs, and I would spend hours in their company, just watching them.

Almost a year had passed since I first got the birds. Once again we left the Haifa silo toward the Gulf of Mexico port. The Mediterranean was stormy and fierce, but it was nothing compared to what was awaiting us in the Atlantic. In the afternoon, as we passed the Strait of Gibraltar, the radio officer brought the captain a weather forecast of a storm with a force of 10-11 on the Beaufort Scale, raging in the Northern Atlantic. We were sent to check and reinforce the lifeboats, the davits, the deck equipment, and the rest. The engineers and maintenance crew made sure everything was in order and all rigging was secure. I wasn't worried about the fate of the birdcage, since it was so large and stable. I believed with my whole heart that it could withstand any turbulence. The storm hit the ship in the early evening. As the hours passed, it only grew stronger, the wind shrieking and ringing in our ears. The ship rocked violently. I slept – or rather, poorly dozed – spread eagle in order to maintain balance. After each particularly bad wave, I would check on the cage to make sure it was still OK. I still wasn't very worried that anything would happen, though. But something did happen, at around three in the morning. Suddenly there was a really powerful wave, and it seemed as if the ship was about to flip over. The ship went soaring up, held suspended in the air for several seconds that felt like an eternity, and then, all at once, it crashed down at an impossible angle. I could hardly hold on in my bed, when I heard a terrible bang. The unbelievable happened, and the cage lay on its side in the middle of the cabin. I struggled to lift it up, and then stuck a chair between the bed and the table, as a replacement to the nonexistent rigging. It hurt me to see four of the birds lying motionless on their sides. The three others looked shocked and miserable. Pity overwhelmed me and I decided in that moment to set them free, once we reached the Hole in the Wall again.

Two days later, the storm subsided and it was as if it never happened. The ocean was calm and quiet. The sun emerged from behind the clouds. Another week passed and once again we caught a glimpse of the beauty of the Bahamas. Toward the evening, we approached Great Abaco Island. The Hole in the Wall could be seen on the horizon. The time had come to free the three hen birds. Unhappily, I gathered them up in my arms and took them to the main deck, where I put them down carefully, pet them each one last time, and it was done. They hopped along the deck, but showed no signs of leaving. I looked at them one last time, turned away, and started walking toward to the door to the living quarters. Right as I was about to enter, I turned my head once more, and they were scrambling, single-file, toward in me, not wanting to let me go. I closed the door and left them to their fate. I'm known to be tough, but at this point, tears welled up in my eyes. The end to the long year I had shared with them in my cabin was very difficult. When I returned to my cabin, it looked empty. The cage was barren, and joy had vanished. All that was left was to bring out the bottle to drown my sorrows. A little while later, Gabi joined me in my loss while rolling a joint. Early the next morning, I ran topside hoping to see them, but they had gone.

Now, as we once again passed by those Islands, it was obvious that I would be thinking about them, but I also thought about our next stop at the port in Kingston, Jamaica, which was fast approaching. As we neared Morant Point, Jamaica's easternmost spot, we began the preparations for arrival at port. Itzik came to report to me that there was yet another change in plans: We weren't returning to northern Europe, but rather were going to load up on bananas, pass through the Panama Canal, and continue on a south-easterly route to Sydney, Australia. Once again, my heart sank when I heard what to me was bad news. I consoled myself with the fact that my contract would be up in five months, along with Shauli. Perhaps during the break, I could fly to Rotterdam to meet Gertie. Shauli would most likely join me, seeing how he had serious plans with Nellie.

There were four letters from Gertie waiting for me in Kingston. Shauli received letters from Nellie, too. After all my work duties were completed, I went to my cabin, placed the letters on the table, poured myself some whiskey, lit a cigarette, and with trembling, excited fingers, I opened the first letter, and then the second, and the third, and the fourth. I read their contents a few times through, while refilling my glass now and then. Love and longing poured through the lines on the paper. My radio picked up some Reggae music, easing my emotions a bit. In the evening, Shauli joined me for a glass and told me about his letters from Nellie, about her love for him and her intentions toward him. Later, we decided to go out on the town.

At the entrance to the port, we hired a car. These guys wait for hours in front of the entrance and hope for customers like us. After making all the arrangements, we were on our way. The car was really old, so much so that in Israel it would have been considered a collectible, but most of the cars we saw were similar. In the center of Kingston, we stopped at a five-star restaurant and the driver waited for us outside. The restaurant was next to a swimming pool, and in the middle was an elliptical shaped bar. A chocolate-skinned songstress led the evening with her collection of English-language songs for the crowd, who were mostly Western tourists. The menu was diverse and was served buffet style. I went and filled my plate with a juicy steak, oven-baked potatoes, cabbage salad, carrot salad, lettuce salad, and a little bowl of sauce for the steak, whose name I didn't recognize but was delicious. After finishing the amazing food, and having a short rest, we went back to the buffet. This time I chose a tropical fruit bowl, a cup of coffee, and a slice of cheesecake. After the plentiful meal, we went to the bar and ordered a whiskey. The bill was very reasonable. Satisfied and happy, we went out to meet our driver. He was waiting next to his car, and when I asked about a good place to go to, he recommended a Reggae club that a lot of women liked. We agreed, and he started the car. The club was built like a large bungalow. Loud Reggae music blasted from the speakers. Blacks, whites, and mixed-race people were squeezed in like sardines. Dozens of dark-skinned, beautiful girls walked through the crowd, hoping to make a little cash. One of them came up to me and asked my name. I told her. She said her name was Marie and went on to her second question: Would I like to buy her a drink? She hinted that it 'would all work out.' I ordered a round and then another, and Shauli didn't lag behind. She started to put her hands on me and asked:

"How about a quickie? You won't be disappointed, I'm something special." After a short argument, we agreed on a price for her services. I asked Shauli to wait for me.

"It won't take long," I said. She put her hand in mine and we went outside the club. There, behind the bungalow, she asked me to pull out my member, rubbed it quickly, then expertly put a condom on it, hiked up her dress and pulled down her underwear and said:

"Come here, sailor, enjoy the fruits of my garden. But no hands and no kissing. Do it quickly, I don't have much time."

When I went back into the club, I asked Shauli why he wasn't letting loose. His answer was abrupt. Black girls weren't his type, he preferred blondes. Well, we got what we could – or rather, I did – out of the Reggae club, so our driver took us back to the port.

Marie the prostitute, Kingston Jamaica

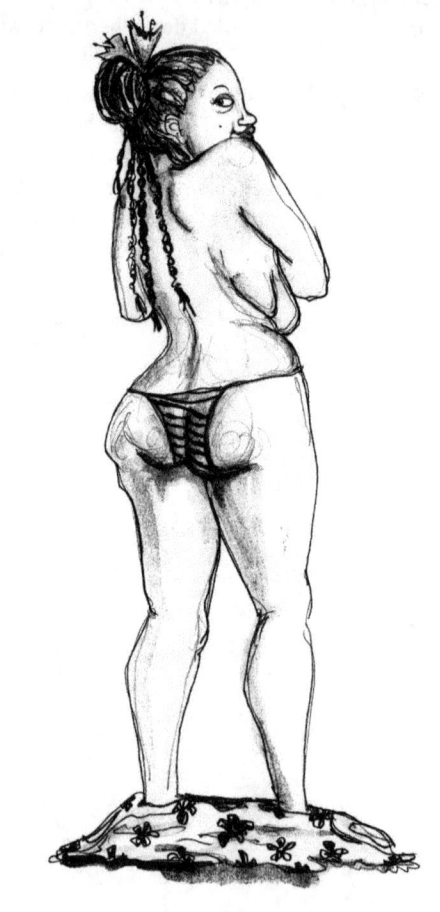

We set sail a week later. Kingston and Marie the prostitute receded into the background behind the Jalopy. It took two days before the *Cormoran* anchored in the breakwaters of Cristóbal in Limon Bay, the northwestern entrance to the Panama Canal. The ship waited her turn for the convoy that would pass the fifty nautical miles of the canal to the southwestern entrance ending in the Pacific Ocean. At 03:00 in the morning, it was our turn to join the convoy. Two pilots and marine personnel boarded the ship. The pilots went to the control bridge and the personnel went took positions at the bow and stern. Transitioning the Panama Canal takes about nine hours, but because of the wait times at the artificial lakes and locks that are in place to allow for safe passage of the opposing traffic, a number of hours are added to the total crossing time.

Entering the locks is a special experience. The ship is guided into the lock with steel cables, and when the gates close, a valve is opened and water flows into the pool, raising the ship to the level of the next lock. In this way, the ship passes through one lock to the other, until, in the final series of locks, the water level goes down to the level of the Pacific. The passing scenery is breathtaking and quite a few crewmen bring out their cameras and take photos. Jungle lines both sides of the canal, and if you're lucky, you can see monkeys, birds, crocodiles, and other animals. The lakes themselves are full of tropical vegetation, such as mangrove trees and shrubs, whose roots go deep into the swampy earth, creating miniature islands. Several waterfalls lead into the canal and here and there you can make out wooden cabins belonging to the locals. *It's 1969*, I thought. *I wonder how many ships have passed through this canal since it opened in August 1914, after ten years of construction.* At 16:00, we passed the city of Balboa and were swallowed into the waters of the Pacific Ocean, on our way to Sydney, Australia.

We once again returned to the routine of life at sea. Each day like the one before. Up at 07:00, jump to the bridge to figure out the day's work with First Mate Itzik, breakfast at 07:30, begin the assigned jobs on deck at 8:00, a 10:00 coffee break, back to work at 10:20, lunch break between 12:00-13:00, another coffee break at 15:00-15:20, and finally 17:00 is the end of the workday and dinner. After dinner, a shower and a drink. At 18:00, I would go to the day room where there'd be a movie showing. Usually after the movie, Shauli would join me in my cabin where we'd drink and talk about anything and everything. A little later, we'd hit up the crew refrigerator for a light snack and then it was off to bed in preparation for another day. Only on Friday did the routine change, since in addition to Shauli, Ben-Tzur, Carlos Antonio, and others would come to my cabin and we'd drink, eat various foods, tell stories, and always end in song. Carlos Antonio – strong, sturdy, and solid – told us once about one of his adventures at sea: On one of his ships there was a particularly violent man, the ship's donkeyman, in charge of the engine room. Every day, he'd pick a crewman and bully and tease him for no apparent reason. Everyone was afraid of him and tried to stay out of his way if they could.

"Even I tried not to confront him," Carlos continued his story. "Truthfully, I was a little intimidated by him, even though I've never been considered a wimp. One day, when we arrived at the San Pedro Port of LA in California, I was going to go out on the town that evening. He came to my quarters and asked to join me. I didn't like it at all. I just really couldn't stand him, but I agreed anyway.

"We arrived at a Puerto Rican pub and sat at the bar. I ordered two beers for us. A girl sat at one of the tables, and he went up to her. The table was behind me, so I didn't see what happened. I continued drinking my beer, ignoring him completely. Suddenly I heard him scream in panic: 'Carlos! Help me! They're going to kill me!' I turned around and saw him – face white as a sheet – running out of the bathroom toward the exit. Chasing him were three Puerto Ricans holding knives. I didn't hesitate, I grabbed the beer bottle by its neck, smashed it, and ran after them while shouting at him to stop. But even though he was a big guy, he was really quick, and disappeared into one of the alleyways. So then they turned to me, wielding their knives. Believe me, since I was so angry at the donkeyman, I didn't flinch. I wasn't afraid of them. The first one that got close received the full weight of my anger. In one swift kick, I knocked the knife out of his hand, and at a speed that even surprised myself, I stabbed the broken bottle into his face, between his eyes, nose, and mouth, and rotated it, ripping him up mercilessly. He roared in pain and dropped like a sack of potatoes. I then turned to the two others, but they immediately dropped their knives and surrendered. Blood streamed from their friend's mangled face. I told them to take him and get out of there. I knew there was still a running tab that I had to close that night. Back onboard, I silently opened the door of the donkeyman's cabin – unfortunately for him, it was unlocked. He was sleeping like a baby. I grabbed him by his bull neck and surprised him with my punches. Blood streamed down his face and only after he begged me to stop did I relent. I spat in his bruised face and told him what I thought of him: Just a bloated pussycat, a piece of garbage that was all talk. I warned him that he better not even think about teasing another crewman. He wet a towel and wiped his face and said that it was a mistake and that he was sorry about everything. He'd change his behavior immediately, but he begged that I wouldn't tell anyone about what had happened that night. From that day on, there was never another incident, and the crew had no idea what had come over him. To them, it was a complete mystery."

Ben-Tzur cracked a half smile and said, "That's one fucked up story, Carlos. I wonder what ever happened to the Puerto Rican."

In order to lift everyone's spirits, Shauli asked me to bring out another song from my notebook, so I began reading one in a clear voice.

Alone

Out of my porthole
As I watch the waves kiss the irons of my ship
I think of all I wish to say to you.

Out of my porthole
I see the light of the moon and the stars
Faraway from my home and my love.

Out of my porthole
The ships are moored in the quiet bay
And a seagull flies in the night.

Out of my porthole
A red line over the horizon
Tells the world to wake again.

Out of my porthole
I think of all I wish to say
If only tomorrow.

As usual, Shauli emptied out a trashcan and began putting the words to music. We all joined in, even though some of us couldn't hold a tune.

In the second week since crossing the Panama Canal, tragedy visited to the *Cormoran* once more, but this time it was shrouded in mystery. Carlos Antonio did his rounds waking up the crew, but he couldn't find Yossi in his cabin. The bed was made and it didn't look like it had been slept in. He looked at the mess and the day room, throughout the passageways, and even lay topside to the main deck, but Yossi couldn't be found anywhere. Carlos went to the bridge and reported on Yossi's absence. The first mate radioed Captain Bar-Noy and told Carlos to call me quickly to the bridge. When I got to the bridge, the captain was already there.

"Perry," he said. "Divide the crew into three groups and search every corner of this ship. Report back to me on anything. I'll wait here on the bridge. Get to work."

There wasn't an inch on that ship that we didn't turn over, to no avail. But near the railings of the stern, I found four cigarette butts and a few used matches. The last person to have seen him turned out to be the ship's cook Arieh, a little before midnight. In his opinion, Yossi had shown no signs of distress. They had even exchanged a few words and said goodnight. When the captain received my report from the search, he immediately told the first mate to change course and turn the ship around to retrace our route. Additionally, men were put on lookout at both sides of the bridge, at the stern, and at the bow, equipped with lifesavers. The radio officer was told to put out a distress signal warning of a man overboard to all of the ships in the region. Another message was sent to the company headquarters in Israel. We were stuck in the middle of the ocean, far from any settled land. We had to retrace our steps seven hours back, the amount of time since Yossi had last been seen. The ocean was higher than before, and a white foam covered most of it, which made our search even more difficult. Our eyes burned from our efforts, but it was all in vain. Yossi was never seen again. The water had taken him, and his secrets.

The Jalopy returned to its original route. Toward the evening, we gathered in the day room. The first mate announced the loss of Yossi. We stood for two minutes of silence in his honor. Additional announcements detailing the case were sent to the company headquarters and to the ship agent in Sydney, to inform the local authorities that Yossi was lost at sea, and his name was removed from the ship's crew list. Again, numerous forms were filled, to be sent to Sydney. A detailed report was recorded in the ship's log, with the estimated location of the ship, including the wind speed and wave height, the weather, and other necessary information. The crew was hurting from losing Yossi. For the rest of the journey, we didn't sit together and 'make merry', because our hearts weren't in it. He was a great guy, a diligent sailor, who had been up for a promotion in rank.

At the Sydney Harbor, there were port authorities, government representatives, the ship agent, a company representative, and an investigator with the rank of captain sent by the Ministry of Transport, Administration of Shipping and Ports waiting on the dock to look into the incident. With them was a sailor named Yaacov ("Jackie"), who was sent from Israel to replace Yossi, resting in Heaven.

Maxim Shaulov

On the day that they disembarked from the cruise ship at the port in Constanta, and after they had gone through border control and had their passports stamped as tourists, Maxim and Dima rented a room at a modest and inexpensive hotel in the center of town. Their goal was to find the Great Synagogue first thing the next morning and to seek urgent help from the Jewish community. They knew that the cruise ship was scheduled to depart within 48 hours, and if their absence was noticed, they would be declared deserters and illegal aliens. A cab brought them to their destination. The synagogue was remarkable. It was surrounded by a wall and in the middle was an iron gate, from which a paved path led to the synagogue steps. A guard was standing at the gate and asked what their purpose there was. They told him of their situation, and despite the difficulty breaking through the language barrier, he understood the young men's desperation and resolve. Finally, the guard said:

"Ask for Mr. Schwartzman. He can probably help you. But entry into the synagogue is forbidden without a head covering." The guard lifted the lid of a small wooden box that lay next to him and took out two black yarmulkes.

The congregation was in the middle of morning prayers when they found a spot to sit. When the prayers were finished and people began filing out, they asked someone about Mr. Schwartzman. He pointed out a tall, stocky, silver-haired man in a grey suit. He was speaking with one of the other worshippers. Maxim and Dima waited on the side until he finished his conversation. When he turned to leave, they went and introduced themselves. From their accents and stammering, Mr. Schwartzman picked up right away that the two weren't locals, and replied to them in their own tongue. It turned out that his Russian was excellent. When he asked them where they were from and what they wanted, they told him their whole story and their life goal. Mr. Schwartzman saw the fire in their eyes and decided to help them.

"Listen, my young friends," he began. "This is not an easy matter. First, we have to find you a hiding place within the community. I don't know if you know this, but *aliyah* to Eretz Yisrael is illegal, according to the official policies of the British Mandate. It's true that there is a yearly quota for legal immigrants, but acquiring a visa is nearly impossible. You should also know that the Jewish community there is harassed by Arabs. Also, life there is extremely difficult and full of hardships. Additionally, it could take months to organize a ship with other immigrants and to get it to set sail when the conditions are right. All of this, of course, would be coordinated with representatives from Israel who come to Europe in order to get as many immigrants and pioneers to Eretz Yisrael as possible. Now, if you will, please show me your passports." He looked at their passports and seemed satisfied.

"You still have time to decide," he said. "Before your cruise ship returns to Crimea, because afterward, you won't be able to change your minds." The two stood their ground. They wanted to reach Eretz Yisrael, despite all of the challenges that he'd listed.

Another congregant gave the young men a ride back to their hotel, after speaking with Mr. Schwartzman. They paid their bill and packed the few belongings that they had brought with them, and went back to the man's car, who'd waited for them outside. He drove them to a suburb quite far from the city center and finally parked the car outside of a charming two-story house. An elderly couple greeted them at the door. They had been expecting them, as they'd received a message beforehand. The man with the car bid them farewell, but before leaving, he warned them not to wander around or show their faces to anyone, in order to protect themselves and their gracious hosts. Once night fell, they could stretch their legs in the garden, but should not go further than that. Then, he turned and left.

Their hosts, the Berkoviches, were kind and courteous. They were of few words, but made sure all their needs were met. Maxim and Dima's room was on the second floor, and for meals, they were invited to the couple's table. They had no children, and Maxim inwardly felt sorry for them. During the day, Maxim and Dima helped out around the house and tried to do everything they could to ease their load. In addition to housework, they also worked in the garden, and it flourished in their hands. Months passed, but there seemed to be no end in sight. Each day they'd say to themselves, *Perhaps today we'll get the good news.* The wait and uncertainty weighed heavily upon them, but they believed with all their hearts that in the end they would find themselves on the deck of a ship headed to Eretz Yisrael. Their ears rang with the echoes of March's invasion of Austria by Nazi soldiers, a fact that pushed them forward in their resolve to pursue their goal.

In the wintery August of 1938, after spending many months with the wonderful Berkovich family, the news they'd been waiting for so long finally arrived. One evening, there was a knock at the door. Mr. Schwartzman and another man stood at the entrance. After the initial greetings, he said:

"Please meet Moshe. He's a Betar man from the Revisionist movement, who was sent here from Eretz Yisrael in order to encourage and organize immigration, and from now on he's responsible for you. He will help you and do everything that's needed to ensure your safe passage." Moshe turned to them and said:

"You're going to board a ship that has been currently moored at port for a few days. There are still a few details to work out, such as bureaucratic problems and issues with the money and food donated by the Jewish community in the city and from other cities. Authorization by the Romanian government to set sail is still pending and we are still waiting on other immigrants, who are making their way as we speak to the Black Sea. You will most likely board in Sulina. As you've already been told, this is illegal, according to the British Mandate in Eretz Yisrael. British destroyers patrol the coast and the whole eastern Mediterranean. If they identify a ship to be illegal, they stop it and usually deport its passengers to camps in Cyprus, an island that neighbors Eretz Yisrael.

Ten more days passed until Moshe returned to the Berkovich home.

"Be ready," he said. "Tomorrow at midnight, you'll be taken to the ship. Good luck." He shook their hands and left.

On the day of the journey, Mr. Schwartzman came to say goodbye. Maxim and Dima thanked him for all his help. He exchanged a few words with the Berkoviches, wished the boys luck, and disappeared. At around midnight, just as Moshe had said, a car came to collect them. Maxim and Dima hugged the couple and thanked them, as well, for all their kindness and help. Mr. Berkovich said that if they were younger and stronger, they would do the same – move to Eretz Yisrael.

"We wish for you, from the bottom of our hearts, that you have a safe journey to your new country." Their escort pressed them to hurry, and so they said one more goodbye and got into the car.

The vessel was a small merchant ship, steam powered and flying a Panamanian flag. She had a gross tonnage of 643 tons, had been built in England in 1918, and had been used as a patrol ship. She looked shaky and it didn't seem possible that she'd be able to make the journey through the harsh sea. Her top speed was about nine knots. The living quarters and engine room were in the middle of the ship. There were two cargo holds, covered with tarpaulin, one in front of the main structure and one behind. At three in the morning, the ropes were released from the bollards at the dock and pulled onto the deck by the sailors. The ship was on its way, giving a whistle for peace and blessings. About an hour after setting sail, all of the immigrants were asked to gather at the back cargo hold. The ship's captain and two other men stood before them. The captain gave the general rules of the ship, announced meal times and the locations of the toilets, and explained the importance of establishing a cleaning rotation. He then introduced the two other men as Betar representatives from the Revisionist Zionist "Af Al Pi" project, who were to explain the security rules. He then wished them all a safe, quiet, and successful voyage. After him spoke one of the Betar men:

"During daylight hours," he began. "Everyone must stay in the cargo holds, which will be covered by tarpaulin, in order to keep you hidden from patrolling British planes. When night falls, you will be allowed to go on deck and take in some fresh air, but not before. The plan is to anchor near one of the shores more populated by Jews. Netanya has been chosen as a preferred location. There will be skilled personnel waiting for you on the beach to help bring you ashore with rowboats. From there you'll head to absorption centers. Any questions?" No one said anything.

The ship was named *Draga B*. Most of the passengers had originally boarded the *Melek*, a cruise ship that was moored near the Danube customhouse in Vienna. Gestapo forces checked the passengers, told to bring with them only personal items. Finally, the ship was authorized to leave. It had been a ship built to carry 80 passengers on short river tours, but it was now taking 500 souls to join the dozens of others already waiting at the Sulina port. When they were on their way to Sulina, they heard rumors about Kristallnacht – the night when, all over Germany, Jewish businesses and synagogues were destroyed, about 90 Jews were murdered, and tens of thousands were sent to concentration camps.

For three weeks, the *Draga B* sailed on. The rules were strictly kept. One day, a British plane passed overhead, but luckily it paid no mind to the innocent merchant ship. Once, a British destroyer could be seen on the horizon, but again, to their great fortune, it didn't approach them. Eventually, after much rocking and swaying one night, when they were about a day's journey away from the shores of Eretz Yisrael, a smaller ship named the *Artemisia* approached them. It took on 200 of the immigrants, among them Maxim and Dima. The *Artemisia* sailed toward Netanya, which had replaced Tantura as the main gate to Eretz Yisrael. The radio officer, who was a local, used a flashlight to signal the coast. The answer was quick to come: Rowboats came to bring the immigrants to the secure shore, with the aid of

Etzel members. On the beach, everyone was given blankets and hot drinks. Dima bent down to the ground and kissed his new homeland. Then, all of the immigrants gathered in the hall of the "Esther" movie theater. There, they passed their first night in Eretz Yisrael. In the morning, they were put on buses and brought to absorption centers around the region, which had been chosen ahead of time. The National Workers Federation would handle the work arrangements for those who hadn't been recruited by Betar. Before receiving their jobs, the immigrants would stay at the National Immigrants House in Tel Aviv, where they receive their first stipends.

The *Draga B* and the *Artemisia* completed their missions without a hitch. After bringing the immigrants to shore successfully, the *Artemisia* sailed back to sea until it disappeared. By morning, no trace of the night's events was left on the Netanya beach.

At the National Immigrants House, Maxim and Dima joined in on the various jobs there were to do. They began learning Hebrew, and after a few months there were already able to chitchat in their new tongue. But between themselves, they still spoke Russian. In their free time, they enjoyed walking along the Tel Aviv promenade, sitting at one of the cafés that looked out onto the Mediterranean, drinking a cold beer, and watching the multitudes pass by. Most of the immigrants were like them. The many different shades of skin and ways of dress showed that they all came from different places. They were alone, but they never complained, despite the fact that during this time, their lives were anything but easy. Their sole focus was to find a steady job and make a living. And then, one day in the spring of 1940, they were given the chance to work. There was a restaurant that specialized in Eastern European food. It was located in their favorite place: The Tel Aviv promenade. Maxim began working as a dishwasher, while Dima shadowed a waiter. The pay was terrible, but the restaurant provided them meals that tasted like home. They were still staying at the National Immigrants House, but their goal was to become independent –

meaning they hoped to find a small apartment to rent where they could do whatever they wanted.

One day toward the end of the year, two young men sat down at a table. Dima waited on them. The two customers asked Dima for advice regarding the menu, and he recommended a particular hearty dish. They took is suggestion and did not regret it – the food was delicious. At the end of the meal, when they got their coffees, one of the young men began talking with Dima. In response to his questions, Dima told him that he'd been in Eretz Yisrael for a year and a half and that he'd come from the Ukraine. The youngster told him that they lived on a kibbutz.

"Have you heard of a kibbutz?" he asked. "It's like a commune in your country." Dima said that he had heard of kibbutzim, but he had yet to visit one.

"We're from Kibbutz Sdot Yam. Just this year we moved to our new location on the coast south of Caesarea. Our main industry is fishing. The kibbutz was founded in 1936 in the Krayot region on Haifa bay. Have you heard of Hannah Senesh? She's also a member of the kibbutz. Anyway, we're looking for young people who are dynamic and motivated and are ready to join and work together. Maybe on one of your breaks, you could come and get acquainted? If you decide to join the kibbutz, you would be accepted for a trial period. Just know that you will have to meet the criteria and a council will vote to accept or deny your application. If you decide to visit one day, ask for me. My name is Eli Eshel."

Dima told Maxim about the kibbutz members and about the way of life there. He didn't reject the idea.

"It's worth a visit. We don't have anything to lose," Maxim replied. "Washing dishes and waiting tables for a few meager coins isn't how we pictured our lives to turn out. We have to try something else."

On one of their following days off in December, they took a bus to Kibbutz Sdot Yam. They were each almost 24 years old, young enough to begin a new chapter in their lives. Eli Eshel was happy to see them. He took them to see the kibbutz secretary and there they put down their things and signed up for a trial period. Eli explained the acceptance procedure to them.

"I'll guide you on your first steps. If any problem arises, you can come to me and I'll try to help solve it. We have a joint dining hall for all the members and a set meal schedule. You will live in a two-story residential building. There are four entrances and for each entrance there are four one-room apartments. For each entrance there is also a shared bathroom. The showers are shared by everyone and are located near the dining hall. Clothing is also shared. There's a clothing warehouse where you can get clothes for work and for afterward. Next to the clothing warehouse is the laundry; every Friday you bring in your dirty laundry to get washed. On Friday evenings, movies are shown in the dining hall. Meetings also take place there, and sometimes a visiting artist or band comes to play there, usually from surrounding kibbutzim. The foreman will assign you a job. Your building houses others of your same age group, and I'm sure that soon they'll all make your acquaintance, so that you will not be bored for long."

Maxim was assigned to work on the kibbutz's fishing boat, while Dima was given work at the fishponds. Both of them, of course, were designated as beginners with no experience. Maxim swabbed the decks, did paint repairs, and sorted fishing crates. Over time, he joined in more and more with the other fishing duties: Lowering and raising the trawlers, repairing the fishing nets, lookout for fish concentrations, and he even began learning to steer the boat. Once he gained some experience, he felt that his coworkers were satisfied with his work and recognized that he was serious. They started to get close to each other and a strong friendship began to form.

One evening, as Maxim and Dima sat on the grass next to their building with a few other friends, Maxim glanced over discreetly at a girl sitting nearby. He felt that she was also stealing glances at him. He was tall, slim, considered to be quite handsome, and over his short life, he understood that he was attractive toward those of the 'weaker sex'. But the relationship between him and the girl advanced at a snail's pace. Here and there they'd have inconsequential small talk, and over time a connection developed. They began finding themselves in each other's company more often. Her name was Rena and she enjoyed hearing stories about his past. His journey to Eretz Yisrael especially interested her. Eventually, they became a couple and spent most of their free time together. Rena was a born in Eretz Yisrael – a 'sabarit'. Like Maxim, her parents had also immigrated from Ukraine. Her father worked in road construction while her mother was a librarian in the Haifa Public Library. She was born at the Rothschild Hospital in Haifa. Her parents were among the founders of the kibbutz, which was first founded in the Haifa Bay. She had two older brothers and a younger sister.

On the evening of July 30, 1941, a kibbutz member meeting was held in the dining hall. Among the issues discussed were Maxim and Dima's applications. The fishing boat crew and the team in charge of the fishponds spoke favorably about the two of them. A vote was held and they both were accepted as full members, with all the corresponding rights and obligations. Three months later, Maxim and Rena were married. They moved to a modest apartment in the young couples building, and it seemed that there was no one as happy as they were.

They received a day's vacation for their honeymoon, and they chose to spend it on the shores of the Kinneret, in the town of Tiberias. They dipped their feet in the waters of the Kinneret and dined at a fish restaurant on the beach. They walked along the streets and alleyways of the city, visited the souvenir market, and even bought a decorative plate painted with a picture of Tiberias with the Kinneret in the background. Toward the evening, they boarded a bus for Haifa, and there they transferred to another bus that stopped at the kibbutz entrance bus stop. They reached their apartment tired but happy. The following day they were back in their routine – Maxim on the fishing boat, and Rena at the children's house where she worked as the assistant kindergarten teacher. Dima and his girlfriend – a young woman named Hannah – would visit them often. Rena would serve hot water over tea leaves and lemon peels with cookies. Hannah and Rena were childhood friends and they liked to sit and reminisce about their past.

One night, Maxim told Rena that he'd decided to change his last name to a more Hebrew one. Instead of Shaulov, it would be Shauli. He asked her what she thought. She didn't object.

"What's good for you is good for me," she said.

The next day, before going to work, Maxim stopped by the kibbutz secretary and informed her of his decision. The change was made with support and understanding.

One evening in January 1942, as Maxim returned home from working on the boat, Rena was waiting for him at the door. Bright and happy with eyes sparkling, she told him that she was pregnant. He burst with joy. He hugged her, caressed her belly, kissed her lips, and whispered in her ear:

"You're going to be a mother, and I a father. We're going to be parents. This is so wonderful. You've made my day so happy."

That evening, when Dima and Hannah were visiting, Maxim told them the good news.

As the days, weeks, and months passed, Rena's belly grew. She would occasionally have checkups with the kibbutz doctor and nurse. Everything was healthy, but she suffered terribly from morning sickness. Her favorite foods were suddenly unappealing and left untouched. But all in all, she continued as usual, working in the children's house with no special requests or requirements. Maxim tried to do anything to make her more comfortable. He loved her with all his being. She liked to take Maxim's hand and place it on her belly so that he could feel the baby move. She was a part of him and they were like one.

In the last month of September, Rena went into labor. It was already evening when she turned to Maxim and said:

"Contractions have started." She was calm and resolute. "Send for the nurse, my darling." Maxim, full of excitement, ran straight for the nurse and brought her to Rena. The nurse checked her and said to Maxim:

"The time has come. We need to take her to the hospital in Hadera."

He prepared a bag with toiletries, a change of underwear, slippers, and other things that he thought would be useful for her. Rena got registered at the maternity ward's reception desk and was sent to a delivery room, where she was checked again and then waited for the oncoming birth. Her contractions intensified and beads of sweat trickled down her face, but she did not complain. Maxim didn't leave her side for a second. He wiped her face, caressed her, and tried to encourage her as much as possible.

At 7:42 in the morning, on September 30, 1942, their little boy was born. They named him Shaul, after the king of Israel.

Five years had passed since the day he had left Nastasia, the woman who raised him lovingly as her own son, in the province of Zaporojye. Maxim felt a strong need to sit and write a long letter telling her everything that had happened to him over those years, starting from his time with Dima in Constanta, the journey to Eretz Yisrael, their first days in Tel Aviv, and finally becoming a member of Kibbutz Sdot Yam and his work on the fishing boat. He wrote happily about his marriage to Rena and the birth of his son Shaul. Maxim closed his letter saying that he loved and missed her. He also asked her to send his love and gratitude to Irina, Gregory, and their children, for all that they did for him. He wrote his return address in Sdot Yam on the back of the envelope. The next morning, on his way to the boat, he dropped the letter off at the secretary.

Maxim had always had a dream that he cherished and hoped to achieve one day: To visit Jerusalem, the eternal capital of Israel. He shared his thoughts with Dima, and they decided that at the soonest opportunity they would travel to Jerusalem and spend nearly an entire day there. One evening, as they sat together, they told Rena and Hannah about their plan. Both women encouraged them to go and gave them their blessings. Now all that remained was to go to the secretary's office and request a day's vacation in order to visit Jerusalem. The trip was coordinated with the secretary's office and their places of work – Maxim's fishing boat and Dima's fish ponds – and now they just needed to make the travel arrangements. Eli Eshel agreed to take them to the bus station in Hadera.

"I'll pick you up tomorrow at 7:00 at the square in front of the dining hall." And so it was agreed. At dawn the next morning, Rena packed a bag with sandwiches, fruit, a bottle of water, and paper towels. Dima and Hannah arrived at 6:45. Dima was carrying a similar bag. They said goodbye to Hannah and Rena and walked to the dining hall. Eli was already waiting for them, leaning on his car and smoking a cigarette. After a short drive, he dropped them off at the Hadera bus station. They took their bags and said goodbye. He wished them luck on their trip and started back to the kibbutz. Maxim and Dima looked for the sign for the Tel Aviv buses. It was the first in the line of buses. It was a beautiful morning – the sky was blue and the air was clear. On the bus, their eyes watched the passing views and they enjoyed every minute. At the Tel Aviv Central Bus Station, they transferred to the Jerusalem bus. At 10:00, they were already making their way to the Western Wall. Once in a while they'd stop a passerby to ask for directions. The neighborhoods, pathways, and streets that they passed through left a deep impression on them both. They could feel the holiness enveloping them; the special scents, the sounds, as if nothing had changed in ages.

After a long way on foot, the Western Wall appeared before them all at once. They took out their yarmulkes from their backpacks and placed them on their heads. A great crowd of men, all wearing prayer shawls and *tefellin*, was praying in the square, each body swaying back and forth. Maxim and Dima approached the stones of the wall and touched them lovingly. Between the cracks were hundreds of little pieces of paper, put there by people who had written notes of prayers, requests, and wishes for the Almighty in hopes that they come true. The two continued their tour and ascended the Temple Mount, also known as Mount Moriah and earlier as Mount Zion. On it had stood the First and Second Temple. In its center is a large stone – the Foundation Stone. Caliph Abd al-Malik built upon it the Dome of the Rock in 690. Next to it stands the Al-Aqsa Mosque, which was last rebuilt in 1035. In the Muslim tradition, this was the spot from which the Prophet Muhammad ascended to heaven. And so, it was a holy place for both peoples.

It was getting late, and the two sat down on the side of the road and took out their food from their bags. Afterward, they began walking back toward the bus station. On the way back, they passed by the same places on their way to Tel Aviv, such as Latrun, Ramle, and Mikve Israel. In Hadera, they hitched a ride to the junction near the kibbutz. Tired but satisfied, they returned home.

Gertie Van der Giessen

Gertie thought about Henrik's proposal for a few days. Finally, she came to the decision to go for it. She discussed it with her father, emphasizing her wish to become independent. Hans did not object. He knew that there was tension between Gertie and Tineke. Perhaps this would be better for everyone. Gertie called Henrik and told him that she would arrive in Rotterdam by train at 4:00 p.m. the following day. Henrik said he was happy about her decision and that he would of course meet her at the train station. The train pulled up to its destination at exactly the scheduled time. Henrik helped Gertie with her luggage and they walked together to his car that was parked in the train station parking lot. The two then drove straight to the apartment that Henrik had arranged for her. It was a beautiful apartment. It had a living room, a bedroom, a bathroom, and a kitchen.

"Take your time to settle in," Henrik said. "I'll be back in two hours to get you. We'll go to the club – it's near here. You can get to know your knew workplace, as well as meet your coworkers. We'll talk about the rest of the details later." He gave her a quick hug and left.

After Henrik had left, Gertie began to unpack her luggage and arrange her things in drawers. She then filled the bath with warm water and let herself sink into it. There were six stacked towels in the bathroom and a cupboard full of cosmetic products. Gertie dried herself off, massaged herself with scented lotion, applied deodorant, and put on clean clothes. She then went to the kitchen and opened the refrigerator. It was full to the brim. *Henrik has gone above and beyond for me*, she thought to herself. In the living room she found the liquor cabinet. There were several unopened bottles of liquor and half-a-dozen packages of snacks. Gertie poured herself a third of a glass of gin, added ice cubes, and tonic water. She sat down on the couch and thought about her future and about how fortune had sent Henrik to her.

He returned after two hours, just as he'd promised. Gertie thanked him for all the trouble he'd gone through and added that she really appreciated that he was looking out for her. He put her arm in his and together they went to the club. On the sign above the entrance a single word was written in gold lettering on a blue background: "Eldorado" – the name of the mythical golden kingdom in South America. Two bouncers gave Henrik a slight bow and he nodded his head back. Henrik and Gertie entered the club. The place was packed and reminded her a little of his friend's Rudy's club in Amsterdam. Henrik led her to his office. The office was elegantly decorated in the latest fashion. He went to the liquor cabinet and asked:

"Alcoholic or soft drink?" As per her request, he made her a gin and tonic. For himself he poured a fine French cognac. They then each took a seat at his desk.

"As I told you in Amsterdam," he began. "You'll start out as a waitress, just to get yourself acquainted with everything. I'll speak to the head waitress tonight and make sure that she does all that she can to help you learn the ropes. I'll always be there to back you up, for any problem or question that may arise. You can always come to me, at any time, and I'll try to solve it for you. Today you're free. Tomorrow is a new day and a new beginning. I wish you the best of luck."

After everything was agreed upon, he invited her to dinner at the club.

Five months passed since Gertie first arrived in Rotterdam. She was a force at work. Her particular beauty turned every head, but her own feelings were reserved for Henrik, and he encouraged this growing attraction between them. They were increasingly seen in each other's company. Sometimes they would go out to other places; the theater, the movies, or a fine restaurant. One day, Henrik told her that he was in love with her and that he wanted her to move in with him. Gertie beamed with happiness.

"I would love to live with you," she said.

He helped her pack her things and move. His place was a one-story house that covered a large area, surrounded by green with a fountain in the middle of a manicured garden. There was another residence on the grounds where the housekeeper, the cook, the steward, and the gardener lived. The house itself had six rooms, including a giant living room. Gertie couldn't believe her eyes. Wealth flowed from every corner. She hadn't known how rich Henrik actually was – he'd always been modest about his money. He never showed off or spoke about his luxurious house. That night Gertie lost her virginity. She was in love with him, and her life had been given meaning. Two weeks later, Gertie began managing the club, under his loving guidance. She was happy. The whole world belonged to her and everything – the moon, the stars, the sun – smiled down on her.

This idyllic life – the tranquility and harmony – continued for five years, at least in Gertie's mind. Though during this long period unanswerable questions did come up, though she dared not confront Henrik with them. For example, why he never mentioned the word marriage. Or what would happen if she became pregnant. Several times, without his knowledge, she skipped using contraception – with a clear motive – but nothing happened. She even secretly went to the gynecologist a few times to get checked out, but after some tests it was determined that she was completely healthy and fertile and that she had no reason to worry. These and other questions disrupted her general mood somewhat, but she pushed them out of her mind and did not allow them to control her happiness.

One day Gertie's worries were realized. It came down on her from out of the blue. She tried to deny the inevitable change this knowledge would have on her stable and happy life. She now understood how naïve and ignorant she had been not to have seen the plain truth. Everything began to become clear when a young waitress – whom she liked – came to her asking to speak in private about a very important subject pertaining to Gertie. They sat together in a corner table, out of anyone's earshot.

"Listen, Gertie," the waitress began. "You hired me, you helped me out during the early stages, you encouraged me and gave self confidence, which I had been missing. I am grateful for your patience and for everything that you've done for me. We all like you here. But I must tell you: There are a lot of whispers among the girls about Henrik. One of the girls – a good friend of mine – says she saw him a few times hugging another woman and going into a café in front of her apartment, and she's not the only one. It really hurts me to tell you this, but I'm begging you, for your own good: Don't be stupid. Open your eyes and pay attention to what's going on around you."

She refused to believe what she was hearing. It seemed like the whole world was crashing down on her. An inner storm began sending shock waves outward and upward. Her racing heartbeat felt as if it could be heard by all. Despondent, she sat down at one of the tables and began analyzing what the waitress had told her. Perhaps it was just gossip? And if there were truth to it – what must be done? What was next? Gertie came to the decision that she needed proof, and until then she wouldn't reveal to Henrik any glimpse of the storm that was raging inside her.

Proof came quickly – only two days after Gertie's conversation with the waitress. Henrik told her that he would be home late that night because he had a very important business meeting. Before he left, he gave her a hug and a kiss. She thought about the five years she had spent with him and wondered how she could have been so blind. The next morning, when Henrik left early for work, she decided to look through the laundry basket. She found his shirt from the night before and smelled it. It had a faint odor of women's perfume. She began to look for more evidence in his study. There, she found a photograph of a beautiful woman tucked away in a folder. On the back of the photo was written: "To Henrik, with love and kisses. Yours always, Dorothea." It was dated August 17, 1967. At the bottom of the drawer was another folder labeled "Medical Records". In it she found a stunning discovery: Henrik was infertile. That was enough for her. Gertie packed her things without thinking twice, called a cab, and wished Henrik to go to hell.

She had enough savings to rent a small apartment in town. She locked herself up for days, lamenting her misfortune. Her love for him had not disappeared, but she knew that she would never go back to him. She had to get over it and begin anew. Days and weeks had passed without any change. She needed to get out of bed, go out into the world, and find a job that fit her skills. Her decision to go outside encouraged her, but it was not easy to find a suitable job. Week after week passed by, and she'd found nothing. One day, after a long and futile search, she decided to take a break and order a soft drink at a café. She sat down and pulled a cigarette out. A man sitting at a nearby table got up and gave her a light. She thanked him.

"I'm Willem," he introduced himself. "What's your name?"

Priel Porat

After finishing the prep work for unloading the bananas and arranging the port shifts, I got Shauli and together we went to Bondi Beach to watch the surfers. We sat at a café and ordered a cold beer. It was a sunny spring afternoon; warm and pleasant. Gorgeous girls in tiny bikinis lined the beach, exposing their skin to the sun's caresses. Once evening turned into night, we made our way to King's Cross, where the bars and clubs are located in Sydney. We passed the night from pub to pub, enjoying the atmosphere and the pretty girls. Around 3:00 a.m., we got back to the Jalopy, happy and satisfied, but tired. We crawled up the gangway, and it's a good thing no one saw us in that state. When I got to my cabin, waiting for me on the doorstep were six letters, all from Gertie.

The bays and beaches of Sydney are truly beautiful. Originally, it was actually founded in 1788 as a penal colony for prisoners exiled from Britain. Captain James Cook, who explored and even mapped Australia, first claimed it for Britain in 1770. But the whites who settled in Australia were not the first inhabitants – settlement on the continent began almost 50,000 years before. Now, descendants of Aborigines account for less than 1% of the population.

We enjoyed nine days in that beautiful city, but as all good things do, so too our vacation came to an end. We found ourselves passing under the Sydney Harbour Bridge on our way to Melbourne, Australia's second largest city after Sydney. The directions that came from the ship agent included: Loading of apples, lamb meat, and lobster destined for New York. The refrigeration officer needed to set the temperatures of the different cargo holds according to the cooling temperature of each product stored in them. Two crewmen had to help check and record the temperatures.

After several days of sailing through calm waters, we arrived at Bass Strait between Tasmania and southern Australia, and then into Port Phillip Bay outside of Melbourne. At the entrance of the port a pilot boarded and immediately went up to the bridge and directed the ship to the waiting dock for the company inspectors to embark. The ship passed the inspection. Loading permits were issued to the captain, who requested the pilot again, this time to direct the ship to the loading dock.

Like Sydney, the city of Melbourne – the capital of the state of Victoria – is a bustling place. It's located near the mouth of the Yarra River, next to Port Phillip Bay. The first settlers arrived in 1804. Once again Shauli joined me in going ashore, but this time Yoav Artzi, the replacement carpenter, also came along. He stayed in the cabin next door to mine. The bulkhead separating the cabins was made of simple wood with an oak finish. Sometimes you could hear muffled, nameless voices from the neighboring cabin.

We first asked the cab driver to take us to the city center. We walked through the streets, among the crowds, we watched the Yarra River that split the city in two, but we didn't find it all too interesting. Here and there we would stumble upon an Aboriginal didgeridoo player making strange noises while inhaling and exhaling without stopping the music – a cyclical melody. We continued on, looking for different kinds of entertainment. There had to be a place in that city to use up the adrenaline that was pumping through us. We called another cab. Luckily, the driver was a young guy who liked to talk. He straightaway started a conversation, asking us where we were from and where he could drive us. We asked him where we could find an area where there were bars, clubs, and good restaurants. He said he'd take us to the perfect part of the city called St. Kilda.

"It's near the beach and not far from the port, and I'm sure you'll like it there. I myself spend most of my free time there," he said. He dropped us off on Acland Street and said: "This is the place you're looking for – it has everything you want." We thanked him, paid the fare with a generous tip, and got out of the taxi into the lively street and started scanning the area. The driver was right. Clubs, pubs, restaurants, and food stands filled the entire length of the street. A didgeridoo player used his vibrating lips on the end of the long wooden tube to make rhythmic, tribal Aboriginal sounds, pleasing the ears passersby and hoping for a generous hand to reach out to his overturned wide brimmed hat. Suddenly, we ran into a very Israeli name – Eilat – a bar-restaurant advertising oriental cuisine. Without hesitation, we went in. The restaurant was long and narrow, like a train car. The tables were arranged in a line, one after the other, along the right-hand wall. Opposite them was a buffet and a bar. The place wasn't full, there were only a few couples sitting there. The stereo played Israeli songs – old ones – out of two speakers. We sat down at an open table. A nice-looking, smiling waitress brought us menus.

"Would you like to order some drinks in the meantime?" she asked. We ordered some beers and looked over the menu. It listed foods that we hadn't seen for a long time. When the waitress came back with our beers, we ordered hummus, a Mediterranean salad, eggplants in tahini, kebabs, and lamp chops. While we sat sipping our beers and waiting for our food, Yoav caught my attention:

"Listen, Perry, that waitress keeps checking you out," he said. "Try something, she's worth it."

I looked over at her – she really did look good, you could even give her a high score. Nice, ample breasts, looking like they could pop the buttons off her shirt at any moment. A body that was curvy and in the proper proportions. Straight black hair cascading to her shoulders, green eyes, a short nose, and a sensual mouth. When she returned to our table with our order, she turned straight to me and asked if we were Israelis.

"Yes," I replied. "We're Israeli sailors. We got here today from Sydney, and our ship's anchored at port." She said that the owner of the restaurant was also Israeli and that he would come over at any minute. The meal was excellent. We ordered another round of beers. This time the waitress came back with a good-looking man who had a full head of curly black hair. He held out his hand in greeting and introduced himself in Hebrew:

"My name is Erez. I moved to Australia 20 years ago. I'm

originally from Netanya and am happy to meet friends from my homeland."

We gave him our names and added that we were happy to meet a Hebrew-speaking Israeli.

"This is Nicole," he said, gesturing at the waitress. "If you please, the next round of drinks are on the house."

Nicole smiled broadly and told us it was a pleasure to meet Israelis. She was looking at me, her eyes sparkling.

"What's the name of your ship?" she asked me.

"The *Cormoran*," I replied. She asked a few more probing questions before Erez called her over to him. She came back and asked what we would like to drink. Erez was buying. Shauli and Yoav preferred to stick to beers. I switched to whiskey. Erez joined us at the table, with a shot in his hand. He took in thirstily all the news about Israel that we could think of. We told him that we'd bring him some Hebrew newspapers the following day. One round led to another. Nicole would sometimes sit with us, devouring me with her eyes. Finally, we decided to leave the restaurant and find a bar somewhere. Erez recommended one nearby. We thanked him and said goodbye, promising that we'd come back the next day, possibly with other people. Nicole was reluctant to let us leave – it seemed that if she could, she would lock the door and keep us there.

The place we went to was a typical Australian pub, where the beer flowed like water. Some billiard tables were set up toward the back, where a few cheerful groups tried their luck at knocking the balls. We sat at the bar and ordered a pint each from the tap. I always have the good fortune to sit next to hot women, maybe I look for them subconsciously or consciously. Sitting on the stool next to me was a sexy redhead. I drooled at the sight of her.

"How does a beautiful girl like you sitting alone at the bar like this not get snatched up right away?" I said to her, smiling.

"I know how to fight and I've got pepper spray in my purse for harassers like you."

"I just wanted to pay you a compliment. I had no intention of harassing you. I'm here with two friends of mine. Anyway, my name's Perry," I said, turning my back to her.

Shauli then asked me, in Hebrew: "So, how's it going?"

"Terrible," I answered. "A waste of time, no chance." While we were still talking, I felt a hand touch my shoulder.

"Excuse me for asking, but what language are you speaking?" she said.

"Hebrew," I replied. "We're Israelis. Israeli sailors. Nice to meet you, I'm Perry."

"My name's Julie. I'm sorry about how I reacted before."

"No problem. Apology accepted. Perhaps you'll allow me to buy you a drink?"

"Gladly," she answered. She ordered a half-pint of beer and I went back again to the damn whiskey. Because she asked, I told her a little about myself. She also began to reveal a bit about her own life. She'd been divorced for five months. She had a two-year-old daughter. They lived with her mother, who was helping her take care of her daughter. At present, she wasn't working, but she was looking for a job as a legal secretary, which was her line of work. As the night went on, the conversation between us flowed more easily until I worked up the courage to ask her to come back to the ship with us and join us for a drink and some Israeli atmosphere. I was sure she'd turn down the offer, but to my delight, she said yes. Yoav and Shauli exchanged looks. They couldn't believe what was happening before their eyes. A taxi took us to the ship. I helped Julie up the gangway and led her to my cabin.

"One drink and then you guys disappear," I told Yoav and Shauli.

We were in high spirits. Yoav ran off to get a tray full of snacks and dips while Shauli, as usual, turned over a trash can and showed off his drumming and singing skills, to Julie's – and all of our – delight. The vibe of the room and the drink started having their effects on Julie, and if she had still had any reservations, they began to dissolve. She scooted closer to me, and I didn't stand on the sidelines. I spurred her on, and signaled to Yoav and

Shauli that they should raise anchor and set sail anywhere but with us. That redhead was a fireball. Instead of me taking her on, she tore me apart into little pieces. She burned so hot and passionate that it seemed like she hadn't had a man in ages. I saw that it was true that redheads had special powers. Their nature is more alert, energetic, and fiery. Their inexhaustible energy is a wonder to behold.

Dawn broke slowly. I went into the shower and washed myself up. Julie was curled up under the blanket in a deep sleep, looking as though a gong would not wake her. I went to the crew preparation room, poured a cup of hot water from the boiler and made myself a strong cup of coffee. It was still early. There was still an hour until breakfast, and afterward: the crew's work arrangements for the day. There was still time for a quickie, I thought. I went back to my cabin and started touching her body, but she growled in her sleep and turned away from me. Grudgingly, I gave up. *What had happened to her redheaded heat?* I muttered to myself. I went below to Itzik Shahak's office. He was already there, bent over piles of papers on his desk.

"Morning, Chief," I said.

"Good morning," he replied. "What did you do yesterday?"

"It wasn't bad. I went out with Yoav and Shauli. We found a great Israeli restaurant. Then we went to a pretty good bar where I met a nice redhead, who came back with me to the ship." He smiled up from his paperwork.

"I see you never stop. At every port you land on you cast your rod and catch a fish. Maybe we'll go out together sometime and you can throw me a bone?"

"No problem," I said. "Whenever you want, I'm at your service."

We agreed on a work schedule: Paint touchups on the portside hull, swabbing of the decks, and scrubbing of the bulkheads. Yoav the carpenter would measure the ship's bilges, the ballast tanks, and the fresh water. He would then submit the list of measurements to the officer on duty in the afternoon. He would also need to be prepared to get fresh water from the onshore pipes. A fresh supply of food would be delivered by the afternoon. The crew would have to be ready to receive and load it onto the ship. Following the coffee break at 10:20, there would be a lifeboat drill, which would include lowering the boat into the water.

When I finished breakfast, Yaacov the messman prepared – at my request – a tray for Julie. She was already dressed once I got back to my cabin. I placed the tray on the table.

"Perry, I have to go and see how my daughter is," she said. "I promise I'll come back toward the evening. Don't be mad." I hugged and kissed her.

"It's fine," I said. "I'll be waiting on the ship."

The crew began working according to the schedule agreed upon with Itzik. At 10:30, we lowered the lifeboat into the water. The drill went smoothly. In the afternoon, the supply truck arrived. The crew unloaded the crate from the truck and began loading the supplies onto the ship. The chief steward checked the amounts and the freshness of the produce, also cross checking to make sure it matched the list that he had. The crew then brought the supplies to the galley and the cook and the rest of the steward's department sorted and arranged them in the food refrigeration holds located one deck below the galley. The long workday came to an end. All that was left was to eat dinner, take a good shower, pour a glass of whiskey, and wait for Julie. Would she come? She did indeed show up – and how. While I was sipping my drink and listening to the radio, I heard a light knock on the door. I thought it was Shauli or Yoav coming to visit, so I answered in Hebrew:

"Yes, come in."

The door opened and the fiery redhead stood at the threshold. I got up and went to her. I took her into my arms and kissed her on her expectant lips. We sat at the table, I poured her a glass of whiskey, and we drank to our meeting. She then took out a colorful package from her purse.

"Perry, here's a small gift for you."

I opened the package. Inside was a lighter with a picture of a penguin against the backdrop of Melbourne. I appreciated the attention she gave to me. I kissed her again, while thanking her for the present. A short time later, we found ourselves in bed making passionate love. At the height of the lovemaking, there was a knock at the door. Julie put a finger to lips, hinting clearly not to answer, not to open the door. An hour later I heard a bottle crash against the bulkhead separating my cabin from Yoav's. Five minutes after that there was another knock on my door. Yoav's voice was heard from the other side:

"Perry, open up. I have to talk to you about something important."

Without a choice, I got out of bed and wrapped a towel around my waist. I opened the door. Yoav stood there looking agitated.

"Perry," he said. "Don't ask what happened."

"I will ask. Spill."

"Nicole, the waitress from that restaurant, is going crazy in my cabin. She destroyed a half bottle of whiskey and she knows that you're here. She heard voices coming from your cabin and didn't understand why you didn't answer the door when she knocked. I tried to calm her down, but it didn't work. She's insisting that she sees you, you have to fix this problem. I can't hold her back."

It really was a problem, like Yoav had described it. *Now what?* I hesitated. Suddenly, lightning flashed. They say cats have nine lives, but in that instant I found the tenth.

"Listen, Yoav, I've got an idea," I said. "In ten minutes, come back here and say with all the seriousness that you can muster that we have to move the ship forward 20 meters. Leave the rest to me." When he left, Julie called from the bed:

"What did he want?"

"He reported that he'd heard the ship was to move forward along the dock. I sent him to check with the first mate."

Yoav returned ten minutes later.

"Perry, the first mate asked that you go to his office. We're moving the ship soon."

"OK," I answered. "I'll get ready. Make sure Nicole stays in your cabin until you get my signal." He left and closed the door.

"Julie," I turned to her. "Soon we have to move the ship. According to protocol, all visitors must disembark immediately due to insurance reasons in case an accident occurs." Reluctantly, she got out of bed and began getting dressed.

"Will I see you tonight?" she asked.

"Of course," I replied. "We'll meet at the pub again." I walked her to the gangway. I waited until she disappeared behind the shipping containers on deck. She kept looking back to see if I was still standing next to the gangway. I waved at her goodbye.

In the cabin, I straightened the sheets and hid away any traces that a woman had been there. When everything was in order to my satisfaction, I went and knocked on Yoav's door. He opened it. Nicole was sitting at the table, a half-empty glass of whiskey next to her, her eyes a bit foggy.

"Hello Nicole. What are you doing here?" She turned to me and, slurring, said:

"I wanted to visit you and see how an Israeli ship looked like. Why didn't you open the door when I knocked? And what were those voices I heard?"

I didn't owe her any explanation, but something told me that I should answer politely and carefully. She was quite good looking and her plentiful bosom was enticing.

"Firstly, I didn't know you were behind the door," I began. "Secondly, I was in the middle of an argument having to deal with work and we didn't want to be disturbed until the problem was solved." The answer seemed to satisfy her, as her mood began to lift.

"Perhaps we should move to your place?" she offered.

"Sure, Nicole," I answered. She got up, wobbling. I supported her so that she wouldn't trip and we went to my cabin. I set her down gently on a seat next to the table. She looked terrible. I turned to the door.

"I'll be right back," I told her, out of the corner of my mouth. I lay below to the crew preparation room and made a strong coffee with no sugar.

"Drink this. It'll help you recover. It doesn't look like you're used to heavy drinking."

"Yes, you're right," she said. "I don't know what came over me. I'm sorry for the way I acted and barging onboard. I couldn't stop myself from coming to the ship to see you, even though I only just met you yesterday. To be honest, I liked you from the first moment I laid eyes on you. I'm embarrassed to say it to your face."

I poured myself a glass of whiskey and asked her to tell me a little about herself. She began to speak openly and with remarkable honesty.

"I'm 29, married, but in the process of getting divorced. I have two children, a boy and a girl,"

"OK," I said.

"I'm also Jewish," she continued. "My parents immigrated to Australia from Austria when the Nazis took power. My husband isn't Jewish, he's Australian from an Irish family. I met Erez at a party of mutual friends, and from that day we became good friends."

"How close are you two?" I asked.

"We've never had sex. Our friendship is more important to both of us. I help him out at the restaurant sometimes, without asking for compensation – I have more than enough money already. That's it for now. Now, tell me about yourself." I did.

The sex was wild, but not my taste. She went crazy when she climaxed, roaring like an animal and scratching in deep red lines into my back with her fingernails. I didn't tell her what I thought, but I made a note to myself that that would be the first and last time with her.

"Nicole," I offered. "Let's maybe go to Erez's restaurant for a nice dinner? I promised him that I'd bring him some Israeli newspapers. I won't be able to stay long, though. I've amassed fatigue over this week and I still have to get up early tomorrow morning."

We both went to take a shower. The water stung on the scratches that she'd left on my back. She noticed.

"I'm sorry Perry," she said. "I wasn't really aware of what I was doing. You were so good and I just lost control."

"It's OK, it's nothing. Scratches heal. But in the future, you should try to control yourself better. Not everyone finish lovemaking with scrapes and bruises."

Erez was very happy to get the newspapers.

"I'll have some decent reading material for the next few days," he said.

Dinner was more or less the same as the previous time. Afterward, Erez joined the gang again for some drinks on the house. Nicole asked to use the telephone to call her kids. When we were alone, Erez began to talk about her.

"She's a woman with a heart of gold, always wanting to give and help. It's just too bad about the marriage crisis that she's going through. They're very wealthy, and aren't in need of any money, but they just don't have anything to keep them together. Her husband goes out in public with some young thing and doesn't care what she or anyone else thinks. It kills her. We have a deep friendship and I'm like the priest she confesses to. She tells me everything that happens to her. I try to give her helpful advice and to calm her troubled mind. Just so you know, she fell in love with you at first sight. I know this because she told me."

Nicole came back. The kids were alright, but they wanted to see her. It was my chance to yawn and show that I was getting tired. I called a cab that stopped outside the restaurant. I said goodbye to Erez, but Nicole walked me to the cab.

"Will I see you tomorrow?" she asked.

"Yes, I'll come by the restaurant at the end of the day." Her eyes, full of adoration, were locked onto me until my taxi pulled away. I told the driver to take me to the other side of Acland Street, and when he stopped, I got out and made my way to the pub to meet Julie.

The clock read 9:30 p.m. when I entered the pub. The fiery redhead was already waiting for me, her face looking a bit angry about the delay. I apologized and blamed my heavy workload. *You can't compare Nicole and her animalistic aggression to the delicate softness of Julie*, I thought to myself.

"Perry," she said, breaking my reverie. "I know of a good restaurant on the beach, a five-minute walk from here. Wanna go?"

"I'm not really hungry," I admitted. "I had dinner onboard the ship. I'll just have a drink and you can order whatever you want." My little white lie was satisfactory – though it's actually against my nature. Usually, I'm as straight as an arrow.

The restaurant did look very unique and romantic, against the twinkling lights on the water. Inside was a long, crowded bar. We chose a table on the terrace overlooking the ocean. Julie ordered a plate of shrimp, fried calamari rings, a green salad, and a glass of white wine. I ordered a double whiskey and some fries. Julie enjoyed the meal and the pleasant atmosphere of the place. Later, we decided to go back to the ship together. We didn't waste any time, throwing off our clothes and jumping straight into bed for a night of intense lovemaking powered by thunder and lightning. She left early in the morning, but not before we agreed to meet again that night.

The loading of the cargo dragged on. It looked to me that we would stay in Melbourne for at least another week. The day was warm and pleasant; springtime in the Southern Hemisphere, compared to the Northern Hemisphere's autumn. At 08:00, I handed out the day's work assignments to the deck crew: Jeremy the deck boy – to the control bridge to swab and clean the accumulated dust; Carlos Antonio, Ben-Tzur, Shauli, Ehud, and Jackie – to the funnel to prep the scaffolding, scrub and carry out paint repairs on the funnel; Yoav – to take measurements of the tanks and grease the winches at the bow and stern; Doron and Yonatan – free, because they worked loading the cargo. I felt a deep thirst in my throat and decided to quench it with a cold beer. I went to my cabin, opened a bottle, and sat down to write a list of the crew's overtime hours, for which they get extra pay according to their contracts, in addition to their monthly wages. At around 11:00, I lay topside to the funnel deck to make sure everything was going as planned. The work was progressing to my satisfaction. They'd completed preparing the scaffolding and scrubbing the funnel by the coffee break. Now they were halfway through the paint repairs and it looked like they'd be finished by lunchtime. I went to Itzik Shahak's office and updated him about the work and recommended releasing the crew in charge of repairing the paint on the funnel once they'd completed their task. He authorized it. In the afternoon I sat with a beer on the wood deck below the lifeboat deck on the side facing the ocean, enjoying the sun and the quiet. Shauli found me.

"I've been looking for you all over the ship," he said. "I didn't know where you'd disappear to." I told him to join me and enjoy the view, but first to go to the fridge and bring back two cold beers. We sat together in silence, sipping our beers and looking out onto the harbor and the ocean beyond.

The sun's rays were so powerful that it felt like the middle of summer. A ship entering the harbor passed in front of us. Two tugboats were attached to it, sounding their horns every once in a while to the directions of the pilot, maneuvering the ship to the landing dock.

"You've got your finger in a lot of a pies," Shauli said to me, breaking the silence. "How's that going for you?"

"It's not easy," I said. "But the waitress was just a mistep. I hope I don't see her again. With the redhead, it's something else. We've got chemistry. I was attracted to her when we first got to the bar." He changed the subject:

"I got two letters from Nellie. She misses me and is waiting on bated breath until the day that we'll meet again. She sent you warm regards."

I remembered that I had also received a letter from Gertie,

which I'd placed in a drawer and hadn't opened yet. Apparently, because of all of the stress with work, I'd forgotten about its existence. Shauli had to get up a few more times to get more cold beers from the fridge. Our conversation slowed; we just sat, sipping our beers and watching the water in front of us. Sometimes he would go back to the subject of his Nellie, his deep longing showing clearly on his face. I nodded as if I understood what he was saying.

At around 15:30, Carlos Antonio approached us. It had taken him awhile, too, to find me.

"Boss, there's a woman near the gangway. She's looking for you. You weren't in your cabin or anywhere else. She's been waiting for twenty minutes already. It doesn't look like patience is one of her virtues."

"Thanks, Carlos. Get a beer for yourself from the fridge and bring her here, please," I said, then turned to Shauli. "I hope it's not the waitress."

Carlos came back with Nicole at his side. She was wearing a beautiful floor-length gown, a sparkling necklace around her neck, and holding a pair of white gloves.

"Perry," she said. "There's a gala show at the theater. It starts at 4:30 p.m., so there's not much time left, and I'd like you to come with me as my date, you'd really enjoy it."

I glanced at Shauli. He raised an eyebrow that said, 'Do what you like.' I was wearing a white T-shirt and faded blue jeans. They were clean, but they were my work clothes, not an outfit for going out. Shauli was dressed similarly. I didn't feel like changing, and that's what I told Nicole, but she straightaway answered:

"It doesn't matter, come as you are, I don't think it's a problem, but we have to hurry."

I tried out another excuse: "If I go, then Shauli has to come with us." Once again she replied without hesitation:

"I'd like that. It would be a pleasure if Shauli joined us."

Out of options, we reluctantly got up and walked to the gangway.

On the dock near the gangway there was a bright, shiny blue car parked and waiting.

"Make yourselves comfortable," Nicole said as she started the engine. Twenty minutes later, we arrived at the center of town. She steered the car through Flinders Street and pulled up at the front of a magnificent theater.

"We're here," she said. The engine was still running when two men dressed in valet uniforms approached the car. They opened the doors and after Nicole got out, one them sat in the driver's seat and went to park the car. The other man led us to the entrance, while mumbling compliments. A third man, dressed very well, greeted us at the door and brought us into the hall. As soon as we entered, the whole crowd stood up and began applauding. The men, without exception, were all dressed in suits, while the women were all wearing gowns. I felt ashamed for wearing my shabby clothes. Shauli felt the same. I wanted to turn and go, but Nicole squeezed my hand, hinting, 'Don't even think about it.' The applause did not die down until we sat down in our seats in the front row.

The curtain rose. A silver-haired man in a black-and-white striped suit went to the microphone onstage. He opened by welcoming the audience and then gave some information about the program, and finally, he thanked Mrs. Nicole Archer who was gracious enough to sanction the play and the art program that was to follow.

"Thank you, and many thanks again to Mrs. Archer for donating and allowing us to put on this show." The crowd rose again to its feet and applauded in honor of Nicole.

It was difficult to follow the play. My eyes kept closing involuntarily. The fatigue and the beers had their effects on me, but Nicole made sure to shake me awake whenever she saw me nodding off. When it was all finished, we were once again accompanied to the exit, to the applause of the crowd. Once outside the theater, Nicole turned to me and said:

"You see this building? It's mine. And wait, come see

something else." She gave us a tour of the city, showing us more buildings that she owned.

"Perry," she said. "This can all be yours, if you only say yes." Gently as possible, I declined her generous offer. Disappointment showed on her face. It looked like Nicole wasn't going to accept my offer. *She's still married, and we barely know each other*, I thought to myself. *And who's promising her that she'll keep all this property she's pointing out after her divorce?* Fatigue overwhelmed me. I knew that I would cancel meeting Julie that night. All I wanted then was to get back to the Jalopy, to be alone, and to lay my head on my pillow. I asked Nicole to drive us back to the ship.

Shauli decided to go out with Yoav. I was left alone in my cabin. I poured a glass, took out the Gertie's letter from the drawer, and began to read it. Among the pages, there was a photograph of her standing in front of the Oasis. On the back of the picture she'd written: "My love, I miss you so much. My heart aches with longing. Take care of yourself out there, far away. Love always, Gertie." The lines written there truly moved me. Suddenly I felt how much she meant to me. I placed the photograph in a prominent place on the table and sat down to write her back.

The *Cormoran* was loaded. The cranes were lowered and returned to their spots and the ship was ready for its long trip to the New York Port. While we were waiting for the pilot to arrive, I thought again about Gertie. *Would we sail from New York to northern Europe? Or maybe to another port?* Anyway, I knew that by the end of December my contract would be up and I would leave the ship – that is, after the next port following New York – and the thought gave me some comfort.

I awoke the next morning as a storm was raging at sea. Waves surged over the deck, gusts of wind and sprays of salt water engulfed the hull of the *Cormoran*. I knew that it would be impossible to complete outdoor work, so I had to arrange indoor duties that are kept for times of bad weather. At 07:15, I went to the bridge. As usual, when he heard the door of the chartroom open, Itzik jumped out of the captain's chair and stood beside it, looking out toward the storm.

"Morning, Chief. How's the shift going?"

"Good morning, Perry. The shift's passing just like the previous one."

I suggested that the living quarters' bulkheads be scrubbed, paint repairs be done in the galley, and the supplies in the stern holds be cleaned and organized. The first mate authorized the work schedule, and so it was agreed. He then offered me a cup of coffee from the boiler in the corner of the chartroom. I leaned on the bridge window railing, sipping my coffee and watching the terrible weather and following the rolling waves crashing on the foredeck, between the cargo holds and the deckhouses. I thought I saw something white go back and forth with each wave that washed over it. I decided to go check out what that white object was. I used a pair of binoculars and focused onto the spot, and it dawned on me that it was a wing of a sea bird, possibly a seagull. I told the first mate that I was going out to see what it was exactly.

"Are you crazy? Don't you dare go out there! That's a direct order!" I nonetheless insisted that I go out.

"Chief," I said. "You know that I'm careful. I'll position myself between the cargo holds and deckhouses. I'm requesting permission to go out and check. Keep me in sight."

Reluctantly, he allowed me to go and check. I went below to my cabin and put on my storm clothes. I decided to go out on the starboard side of the deck, because there was better cover there, even though the white object was on the port side. I approached carefully, taking cover ever so often when I heard waves crashing. I was amazed to discover that the white object was in fact a helpless albatross. It looked like his left wing was broken. He was near death, his head hanging, unresponsive to the water tumbling over him, but he was still alive. I knew that Itzik was watching me, impatiently. Carefully but quickly, I picked up the albatross and began making my way to the protection of the stern. It was almost

08:00 and I had to return to give out the crew work assignments for the day. At 08:30, when Itzik finished his breakfast, he came with me to the stern. On our way there, he said to me:

"Good for you, Perry. No one else would have dared to do what you did."

I told him that I had once raised birds in a cage that I had built myself for a whole year, and that I still had powerful feelings for the creatures. Itzik studied the bird, who looked terrible.

"He has to be fed," he said. "Go get a can of sardines and a bowl of water from the galley." The albatross didn't have enough strength to open his beak.

"Grab his beak on both sides and try to open it," Itzik said. "I'll feed him the sardines, and if necessary, force them in with a stick." His beak was large and strong. It was about 15 cm long and curved at the end. I worked hard to pry the beak open and allow the sardines and water to be pushed in. In the end, we successfully force-fed the bird. Itzik asked me to get from the carpentry shop a wooden plank that measured a meter-and-a-half long, about half the albatross's wingspan. He would go get a first aid kit from the sick bay.

"We need to set his wing, and the he just might survive," Itzik said.

After the albatross received medical treatment, we let him alone to rest. About every half-hour I went back to the stern to check on him. Every morning for the following few days I would go inspect the deck for flying fish that had lost their way in the middle of the night and, with the help of some waves, had found themselves stuck in the corners of the ship. If our albatross was lucky, he could enjoy a meal of two-to-three fresh fish a day. The albatross has unique strength for survival. It is of the order *Procellariiformes*, which comes from the Latin *procella*, meaning storm, because they are not afraid of stormy weather. It is capable of flying several days straight without stopping. To rest, it sits on the waves of the ocean. It returns to land only to nest, and there it lays a single, large, white egg. The bird feeds on fish, squid, shellfish, and scraps from ships. The average lifespan is about 30-40 years.

Over the following days, the albatross began to recover and show signs of life. He was able to stand on his legs and to eat and drink without help. I made sure to tie a long rope to his leg, allowing him to walk around the stern, but not further than that. On the tenth day, we removed the wooden splint. It looked like the wing had begun to heal, but was still loose. It was obvious that he had yet to regain the ability to fly.

The bitter end of the albatross

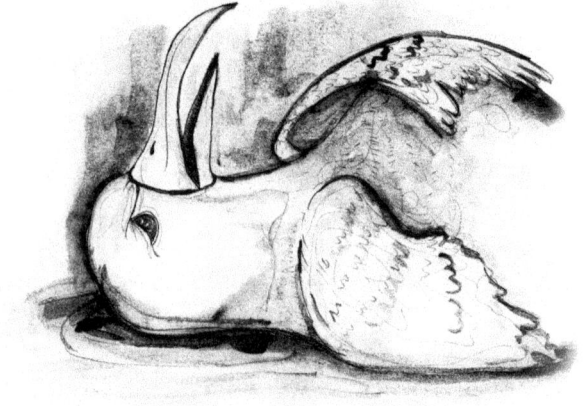

On Friday afternoon, preparations began for a barbecue on the stern deck. It was the albatross's thirteenth day with us. The weather was wonderful and besides a scattering of high cirrus clouds, the sky was blue and clear. The ocean, too, was blue, quiet, and calm. Albert, the donkeyman, split lengthways a 200-liter barrel, which usually contained lubricating oils. He welded four legs onto it, drilled a few holes in the bottom, attached a hand-cranked spit, and a grill below. Earlier in the morning, I sent two crewmen to the cargo hold to bring a nice looking lamb to Arieh the cook so that he could prepare it before the barbecue. This was explicitly forbidden, but everyone, including the officers, turned a blind eye to it. After all, who's willing to resist a beautiful lamb roasting over a spit, with the cook basting it in intoxicating sauce and the fat dripping onto the grill?

Barbecue day happened once a month, if the weather and sailing conditions permitted. The deck crew would swab the stern deck in advance and would set up the barbecue tables and benches, stored in the hold containing equipment particularly for these types of events. The ship's electrician would string colored lights around the after cabin. The cook and the galley crew would prepare salads and all of the tasty side dishes. The chief steward would take out cases of beer, Coca Cola, and bottles of wine, included in the budget set aside for these purposes. There would be an overall holiday feeling for everyone. While dinner is usually served at 17:00, on barbecue day dinner is at 18:30. Someone from the crew would bring out a stereo and cassettes and the electrician would connect two powerful speakers to it. The officers' messman and the crew's messman would set the table for the decadent meal that awaited.

But it was going to be a sad day for me this time. While I was showering and getting ready for the dinner, Shauli burst into my cabin.
"Perry, come quick. A disaster has happened to the albatross."
I sprinted to the stern deck. I arrived to see the albatross

receding with a trail of foam, trying desperately to use his wings to fly above the water, unsuccessfully. Cruel fate ambushed the unfortunate albatross in the innocent waters of the ocean.

Shaul Shauli

Shaul brought a lot of pride to Rena and Maxim. They raised him with love and devotion, especially Rena, who gave him the nickname Shuli. She nursed him until he was a year and two months old. In the late afternoon on weekends, they would take out the stroller and walk with him along the pathways of the kibbutz. During the rest of the week, Shaul would be at the nursery with other babies his age, under the supervision of dedicated teachers and carers. Rena worked as a nursery school teacher for three-year-olds while Maxim still worked on the fishing boat. He had become a skilled fisherman. On his free time, he began learning how to steer and stabilize the boat. In addition, he learned about the boat's systems and the engine room. He also studied meteorology, seafaring, and maneuvering. His hope was to one day pass the sailing license exam and have command of the fishing boat.

When Shaul was three years old, a baby sister was born, and she was given an extraordinary name. She was called Bossem, meaning perfume. The name was Rena's idea, and Maxim had no objections to it. Now it was up to them to solve the matter of Bossem's living arrangements. Their apartment had a master bedroom, a children's bedroom, a living room, and a balcony. They debated between putting her bed in Shaul's room or closing off the balcony to turn it into another room. In the end, they preferred the balcony.

Hannah, Dima, Rena, and Maxim would spend time together regularly. Sometimes on their free time on weekends, they liked to walk along the beach of Sdot Yam or through the spectacular ancient ruins of Caesarea, breathing in the scents of history and the sea breeze of the Mediterranean. Toward the evening, with the sunset, Maxim and Dima would lay a blanket on the sand, while Rena and Hannah would unpack the cooler: A variety of sandwiches, drinks, and fruit would be spread out on the blanket. Hannah and Dima had been married for a year and Hannah was in the early months of pregnancy.

Shaul and Bossem grew up beautifully. There was no question that the good food, open spaces, cool sea breeze, kibbutz environment, rural tranquility, and the abundance of love showered upon them influenced them for the better. They gave their parents much happiness and pride. One Saturday when Shaul was six, Maxim brought him on the boat for the first time. They walked along the boat between the fishing nets and equipment and next to the large crane. Afterward, Maxim showed him the bridge with all of the devices there and even let him turn the wheel left and right. Shaul was enthusiastic and interested in everything he saw on the boat. He asked his father about all of the different devices on the bridge, and Maxim happily and patiently explained what they did in simple language, in order to satisfy his son's curiosity.

Shaul was tired when they'd gotten home. Rena made a light dinner and then gave the kids a bath. Maxim put Shaul to bed and read to him until he was sure he was asleep. He shut the book, placed in on the shelf, covered Shaul, kissed his forehead lightly, turned off the light, and silently tiptoed out of the room, making sure to close the door behind him. Rena did the same with little Bossem. They met in the living room. Rena made two cups of tea with mint, took out some honey cookies from the pantry, and sat down next to Maxim in front of the radio. The news on the airwaves were difficult. Fierce fighting was breaking out across the country, which had only recently been born. Names of the fallen filled the public notice columns in the newspapers. Photographs of noble youths peered out from the pages of the papers day after day. The pain was shared by everyone, and the situation was all anyone ever talked about in the dining hall, between friends, on the pathways of the kibbutz, and in their own homes. Instructions were distributed to all kibbutz members regarding behavior during wartime. Everyone gathered in the dining hall, where they were explained the struggles that the country was facing.

Instructions were also pinned to the bulletin board, as a reminder, which included: *After sunset, total darkness must be maintained. At the sound of a long siren, everyone must go as quickly as possible to the bomb shelter, which has been prepared in advance.* All kibbutz members received strips of tape for the windows. A fire and damage control squad was formed and the clinic was staffed on a 24-hour basis. Despite the labor shortage due to members joining the war effort, the kibbutz economy continued more or less as normal. The war broke out on November 30, 1947, the day after the UN announcement of the Partition Plan (Resolution 181). The Declaration of the Establishment of the State of Israel was proclaimed on May 14, 1948, at the Dizengoff House at 16 Rothschild Boulevard in Tel Aviv. It was also the last day of the British Mandate in Eretz Yisrael. The armies of five Arab countries invaded Israel and irregular Arab forces rebelled against the UN Partition Plan. Thus began the second stage of the Israeli War of Independence. On June 1, 1948, the Israeli Defense Forces were established, replacing the Hagana paramilitary organization. The war was brutal, threatening the very existence of the young state. It resulted in more than 6,000 Israeli deaths, about 1% of the Jewish population.

On June 27, 1948, the kibbutz secretary received six draft letters by special messenger from the army. The names of both Maxim and Dima were among them. Maxim could have requested an exemption due to his slight limp from the injury he'd received as a child, but he preferred to fight alongside everyone else. The army messenger asked that they not delay – they were to join him in his vehicle that same day. He stressed that every hand capable of wielding a weapon was greatly needed and that he would return within a few hours to pick them up from the dining hall square.

Rena shed a tear when they said goodbye. She helped Maxim pack his bag – the same bag that he had taken on his trip to Jerusalem. Maxim hugged and kissed his children, Shaul and little

Bossem. As he began walking toward the square, Rena called out:

"Take care of yourself and don't be reckless. You have a wife and children who love you, who need you and are waiting for you at home."

The six new recruits were driven by the messenger to get enlisted and divided into forces at the Sarafand base, located in the country's Center near Lod and Rishon LeZion in the area of Be'er Ya'akov. About two weeks before, on June 11, the base was attacked and soldiers and commanders were lost. The six recruits began intense training in preparation for the front lines. Two weeks later, after their brief military training, all the new soldiers were sent to various units. Dima was sent to the Southern Front, to the 12th Brigade ("HaNegev") under the command of Gen. Yigal Allon, while Maxim was sent to the Northern Front, to the 2nd Brigade ("Carmeli") under the command of Moshe Carmel. Dima fell in the battle to take Beer Sheva on October 20, 1948, during Operation Yoav, whose goal was to break the Egyptian line that had cut off the Negev. Nine days after him, Maxim was also killed. He fell on October 29 during Operation Hiram in the battle to take Malkiya. He was only 31.

It was Rena who gave Hannah the bad news about Dima. She stayed with her as much as possible, to comfort her and ease her suffering. Hannah was now eight months pregnant.

"It's so sad that Dima won't be able to see the fruit of our love," she would say, over and over.

Dima was buried in the military section of the kibbutz cemetery. His coffin, wrapped in the Israeli flag, was lowered into the grave by his comrades-in-arms. A three-volley salute was fired and an army rabbi delivered the eulogy. Hannah collapsed on the dirt the covered her husband's fresh grave.

Eli Eshel was the one who gave Rena the news that Maxim, too, had fallen. She looked into his eyes, refusing to believe him, shaking her head and raising her hand as if she could drive away the terrible news. Maxim was buried next to Dima. The two friends would rest, together, in peace forevermore. Hannah and Rena did not leave each other's side during those hard times. They encouraged each other and each woman was there to ease the other's pain of her own tragedy. They had to pitch in together, for the sake of Shaul, Bossem, and the little one who was about to come into the world, a world that now looked cruel and brutal. The war ended on July 20, 1949, after the last ceasefire agreement was signed with Syria.

Shaul and Bossem continued to grow and mature. Rena spared them nothing. She did everything she could to ensure that their father's absence was not felt. However, sometimes questions about Daddy would come up. Rena would explain that Daddy was like an angel in heaven and was watching over them from above. His body may have been in the earth, but his soul was floating somewhere between the stars and infinity. At night, after she would put the children to bed, and she would be alone with herself, she would think again about Maxim. She would lament over her fate and would always return to the same question: *Why did this happen to us? We could have been such a happy family together. It's a terrible loss that he could not see his children develop or be a part of their growth.* She very much missed his strength and mental fortitude, as well as his seriousness and sense of responsibility.

One day, when he reached the age of twelve, Shaul asked his mother to take him on the fishing boat. He still remembered the outing he had with his father, and the large steering wheel, the navigation devices, the fishing nets, and the big crane. He felt a strong need to visit again. Rena bent over, scooped him up into her arms, and embraced him. She said that at the first chance she'd get, she'd take him and Bossem to the boat. Bossem was now nine years old, a smiling, boisterous girl with boundless energy. She was curious about everything and would often ask her mother questions about anything that popped into her fertile mind. Bossem adored and admired her brother. They got along wonderfully and it was impossible to separate the two of them.

Between them, it was perfect, and Rena was thankful for it.

Two weeks later, on a Saturday morning, Rena took her kids Shaul and Bossem to the boat. It was the beginning of a blisteringly hot August. The sun beat down, and there was no breeze, but the air was clear and clean, and the bright colors of nature that shone on the three of them seemed to be a sign that their outing would be perfect, and indeed it was. Shaul teemed with excitement from the moment they stepped on deck. The crew was busy repairing the fishing nets, swabbing and scrubbing the main deck, and making paint corrections. Everyone waved hello, but continued working. Rami, the captain of the boat, came to greet them. He was impressive. He was tall, sturdy, and quite handsome. His hands were large and weathered, and his face was wrinkled – a result of constant weather changes and being bombarded by salt water during storms. His blue eyes were kind and gentle. On his head he wore a green baseball cap and around his neck a silver chain with a pendant of a large anchor pressed against his chest. He remembered Maxim. They had spent a long time together on the boat, but Rami preferred not to talk about him, unless he was asked. They walked together around all the parts of the ship. Rami explained to them how to spot a school of fish and described the process of casting the nets and raising them and bringing them back in with the cranes. Shaul once again played with the steering wheel, under Rami's guidance, and no one was happier than he was. *One day, I'm going to be a proud fisherman, just like Dad and Rami*, he thought to himself. Rami invited them for a cool drink in the boat's mess. At the end, before they disembarked, he gave the kids two seashells and said:

"If you press the seashell against your ear, you'll be able to hear the sea winds, sounding melodious as a symphony."

Rena, Shaul, and Bossem thanked Rami for his wonderful hospitality and for the all of the fun that they had on their amazing visit.

Rena and Hannah stayed close over the years. They often spent time at each other's house. Alex, Hannah's son named after his father, was now six years old, and his resemblance to Dima amazed everyone who saw him. Neither Rena nor Hannah were in relationships, though they had no shortage of suitors. They were just not yet ready to begin a new chapter in their lives at that point.

At the beginning of the autumn of 1960, Shaul received a draft notice. After completing basic training, he was assigned to serve in the Navy, and was sent to the deck of the INS *Eilat*. His fellow sailors called him by his last name Shauli, and the nickname stuck, following him for the rest of his life. Their base port was in Haifa, separate from the civilian port. Sometimes, Shauli would watch the merchant ships going in and out of the port, to the sounds of the tugboat horns. He was particularly moved to see the Israeli merchant ships, proudly flying the Israeli flag on the stern staff. He'd already come to the decision that after he finished his service, he'd join the merchant marines.

Shauli's service on the destroyer passed uneventfully. The destroyer and its crew would go out to sea often, to engage in training with other vessels and to patrol the coast. They would also be involved in combined training exercises, including with Shayetet 13 (elite Israeli naval commandos) and different Air Force squadrons. The INS *Eilat* had previously been the British destroyer HMS *Zealous*. She was built in 1942 and first launched in 1944. Her job as part of the Royal Navy during WWII was escorting supply convoys in the Arctic Ocean. Israel purchased the ship along with her sister ship, the INS *Yaffo*, in 1955. After undergoing the necessary refurbishment, she was given to the Israeli Navy. Her end was tragic: In 1967, the destroyer was sunk off the coast of Port Said in the Sinai, in a planned ambush by Egyptian missile boats. Forty-seven sailors were killed and drowned, and 100 more were wounded.

On days that he had leave, Shauli would always return to the kibbutz. He had a routine: He would buy some sort of present for

Bossem and a bouquet of flowers for his mom. Bossem was now 16, in the prime of her youth, lively, energetic, and active. She looked good, and most of her free time was spent with friends, either walking along the kibbutz pathways or at the beach. Shauli usually preferred to rest in his room, reading a good book, or to sit on the grass near the house.

At the end of his military service, Shauli received an offer from the kibbutz organizer to join the fishing boat crew. It had been his childhood dream, but now all he wanted – what he was passionate about – was to join the merchant marine ships and sail to faraway places, far beyond the horizon. He requested some time to think about the offer, even though he already knew his answer would be negative. He decided not to say a word to his mom or to Bossem, until he was certain everything was arranged the way he wanted. Until then, he thought, there was no reason to talk about it. On the morning following the conversation with the organizer, Shauli put his navy discharge papers in his wallet and got on a bus to Haifa. Once at the central bus station, he got on another bus downtown, and there he found himself climbing the stairs to the Seamen Bureau. The bureau was on the second floor of a building on Independence Street, the main street downtown. He went to the secretary and she took down his name and told him to wait in the hall to be called for an interview. He waited about an hour until they finally called his name. In the room, a man was standing next to a boiler, making himself a cup of tea. He gestured toward a chair and told Shauli that he'd be right with him. He then sat down at the desk and introduced himself.

"My name's Chaim. I'm the director of the bureau. How can I help you?"

"My name is Shaul Shauli," he began. "I've recently completed my military service on a Navy ship. I'm from Kibbutz Sdot Yam. My greatest wish is to sail on a merchant marine ship. My father was also a seaman – he worked on the kibbutz fishing boat."

Chaim stared at him. For a few excruciatingly long moments, he didn't open his mouth and just played with a ballpoint pen.

Finally, he looked straight at Shauli and said:

"If you have on you your ID card and your navy discharge papers, I'd like to see them." He took them, and wrote down Shauli's information on a white piece of paper. "I understand from what's written here that you completed a full military service as a sergeant on the deck crew and that your behavior was commendable. That's a very good start. All that I can say to you at this point is that you have to pass the admissions committee, which convenes in the next few days. I will give you a warm recommendation for the deck department. Within two weeks from today, you'll receive the committee's decision in the mail. Good luck."

After ten days, the committee's letter arrived. Shauli opened the letter, his hands shaking. He skimmed over the formalities and got straight to the main message:

The committee has accepted your application for the deck department as ordinary seaman (OS). You are to report to the Seaman Bureau within a week of the above date for registration and to receive instructions regarding embarkation on merchant marine ships.

Sincerely,

The National Labor Federation in Eretz-Israel, The Seaman Bureau,

The Deck Department Acceptance Committee.

Shauli underwent thorough medical examinations at the mariners clinic and received various vaccinations. He registered at the Ministry of Labor, Shipping and Ports Division, where a file was opened for him and he was finally issued a seaman's book. He was also asked to visit the Border Patrol at the Haifa Port in order to do a background check and get a certificate of good conduct to show that he didn't have a criminal record. Without it, he was told, he wouldn't be allowed to go to sea. No one was happier than he was. As he walked into to his house on the kibbutz, with the seaman's book in his pocket, Rena asked him about his frequent outings. He told her, and added that when he'd return from his first voyage, he thought he should leave the kibbutz and rent an apartment in Haifa.

Over the following days, Shauli began a regular habit: He'd take a comfortable chair, and pack a bag with a bottle of water, a sandwich, and some sort of fruit, and then go to the beach. He'd stretch out on the sand or in the chair, looking out onto the blue water of the Mediterranean, all the way to the horizon. When a ship would pass, he'd follow it with his eyes until it disappeared. *Soon, I'll be on one of those*, he'd think to himself. One morning, he decided to board the fishing boat and visit the crew from the kibbutz, and in particular Rami, the captain. Rami was happy to see him. They walked around the bridge and the rest of the ship. Shauli was impressed by the all the equipment. The nets ready to be lowered, the marker buoys, and the complex pulley system used to lower and raise the nets. Even the crane impressed him, as it looked bulky but powerful. It probably wasn't easily operated – it needed a skilled crane operator who was good at his job.

At noon, Rami invited Shauli to lunch. He readily agreed. The meal was made up of fresh fish that had just been caught and they tasted like a delicacy fit for a king. On the side of the fish were fries and a vegetable salad. As they enjoyed their meal, Rami began a more serious conversation:

"So, now that you've finished your service, are you joining us on the boat? Why do I ask? Because I'd like to see you as part of our crew. I overheard in the dining hall that you were offered a job on the boat, and that it was in your favor that you had experience at sea. And I'll let you in on a little secret – I spoke with the kibbutz organizer to assign you to work with us."

Disappointment washed over his face when Shauli told him about the merchant marines, about being accepted to the deck department, about having already passed all the checkups and completed all the requirements. In the next few days, he explained, he'd be getting a call to embark. He was happy about his decision, and it was final.

"You need to know," Rami said, "that a move like this could disqualify your membership on the kibbutz, unless you get official permission from the kibbutz general assembly. And if it is approved, you'll receive a small portion of your salary for your own use and the rest will go to the kibbutz."

"Rami," Shauli said. "I thought about that, too. My plan is to rent an apartment in Haifa."

Two days after his visit to the fishing boat, while he was sitting on the comfortable chair watching the beginning of the sunset with the waves lapping at his feet, Bossem sat down next to him.

"It's too bad that you're leaving us," she said. "Mom's taking it hard. Seeing you leave will be difficult for me, too. To see my brother only once every few months, after always being together, is really sad. Even though you were gone a lot during your service in the navy, and mom and I really missed you, you were never gone for such a long period of time as it looks like you're going to be now. I know that for Mom, you're always going to be her little boy, who needs her protection, warmth, and love."

"But I've grown up, Bossem," Shauli replied. "I've got a dream, and I'm on my way to realizing it. The day will come that you, too, will feel the same way. Get a little older, and you'll have your own dreams, or in the end you might get married and follow your husband. Mom has to understand that when her chicks grow up, they spread their wings and leave the nest. But you and I will always come back to visit, to help her and support her."

Bossem agreed with her brother. *He's right, really*, she thought. Her brother had changed before her eyes into a handsome man, radiating with confidence and strength, and his wishes were honorable. *His path should guide me and be an example to me.*

A week later, the long-awaited call came: "You are to report to the company's offices in Haifa, ready to sail. You will board the cargo ship *Teverya*."

Gertie Van der Giessen

It was hard for her to be in a relationship again. Everything was still fresh, the wounds in her heart had yet to heal, but Willem had made an impression on her. Especially after she'd told him about her experience at Henrik's nightclub, and about the two of them, and that it was over. He told her that she might suit him, since he was a co-owner of a bar downtown. She was welcome to join the crew, in the same position she'd had before, because just recently – *what a coincidence* – the position had become open. Gertie didn't know how much he liked her, or that he planned to immediately fire the girl currently in the position. Willem was attracted to her and was interested in more. He was ready to give her above and beyond what she expected, just so that she would be near him. If Gertie had been able to decipher a person's soul, to read his hidden thoughts and personality, it would've been clear to her to run away as quickly as possible from the man standing in front of her. But – what is it that they say? – when emotions are at play, the eyes go blind.

The bar that belonged to Willem and his partner was right in the center of town. In the area were several clothing stores and in the square in front of it were some cafés. It was crowded and there was lots of traffic. The bar itself had a modern, yet simple, design. There was a fan and light shone in from the windows; nothing like the dim bars she was used to. It could take up to 150 customers. The bar was quite impressive and spacious. After Willem introduced Gertie to his partner Rod and to the rest of the crew, he explained to her the basics of the job. The work was familiar, and besides the few requirements that were specific and unique to the place, she had no problem integrating into the role. At the beginning, Willem was very patient with her and their relationship was relaxed. After a relatively short time, she moved in with him. Then she quickly learned his true nature. He was so jealous, that it was frightening.

He became physically and verbally abusive toward her and their shared life became unbearable. *He's a wolf in sheep's clothing*, she thought. *I have to leave him right away*. And so she did, at her first opportunity.

The second-floor apartment that she found and began to rent was located on the neighboring street to William Street, in the Katendrecht district, which was the city's center of entertainment to which everyone flocked. The apartment looked out onto the port and to the movement of ships entering and exiting. Gertie felt a great relief to be on her own and to do what she wanted, without the disturbing presence of Willem. That same week she got the job at the Oasis. Her striking beauty, her patience, and knowledge of the job all contributed to her fast rise up the ranks, so that within a few months she became the head hostess. She felt content and happy. Additionally, she was paid a generous salary and often received tips from satisfied customers. She bonded with one hostess in particular, whose name was Nellie. They became best friends and would often stay at each other's place. The club was flooded every night. Couples and single people alike enjoyed spending their time on its floors. The level was high and the atmosphere – electric.

One evening, she caught of a glimpse of two nice-looking guys who were led by a waiter directly to the center table near the dance floor – a table that was usually reserved for club VIPs. Almost immediately, one of them got up and approached Nellie, the blonde. He looked like he said something to her, and she nodded her head and they went out onto the dance floor. The man who stayed behind at the table intrigued her. She felt a need to check him out. In contrast to her status at the club, and despite the fact that her job didn't include serving customers, she decided to do something different, just this one time.

"How 'bout a drink?" she said, almost whispering, when she'd gotten near him. His studying glance went over her body up to her eyes. He had a challenge in his look, and his playful response made her interested. He was also handsome – tan and brawny – which was a nice bonus. For the first time, Gertie felt shy, and the unbelievable happened: She blushed uncontrollably. When she came back with his order, at his special request, she sat down next to him at the table.

"My name's Gertie," she said. "And you?"

"Priel, Priel Porat. You can call me Perry," he replied.

Priel Porat

When the albatross disappeared among the waves of the ocean, I felt a terrible regret, since he could not survive, though he'd been so close. I looked at the rope that had been tied to his foot and abandoned food and water bowls. Suddenly I didn't feel like a barbecue and all of the racket that went along with it. I preferred to be alone in my cabin with a bottle of Vat 69. Shauli came into my cabin about an hour later, in his hands a plate piled with various grilled meats. He set the plate down on the table and sat next to me. I slid over the bottle of whiskey and gestured toward the cabinet for him to get out a clean glass. We sat silently like that for several minutes, until Carlos Anotonio also showed up bearing gifts: Under his arm he was holding a bottle of Vat 69. He set it on the table, a warm smile appearing from beneath his groomed moustache. *It's nice of them*, I thought. *They care about me, even though they're under my command. I guess they like and respect me and the way I behave while giving orders.*

As usual for a Friday night, more crewmen began showing up. As the time passed, so too did my sorrow for losing the albatross, with the help of the drink and the presence of the guys. The mood was its normal cheerful self. It was Yoav Artzi who made the request for another song from my notebook. Shauli agreed. I couldn't refuse. I went to the drawer and got out the notebook.

At port

Under the sky of a foreign port
I think of the land that I love
I think of the love that I lost

The silvery fish dance
In the passing beam of the lighthouse

All is silent and calm
Under the sky of a foreign port

The looks on everyone's faces were of fond remembrance. Shauli asked for the words to the song so that he could set it to music and Carlos Antonio took his place at the trashcan drum. We all soon found ourselves singing along to the song of the evening. After we finished the sing-along, and the drinks really began to take their effect, it was time for storytelling. This time it was Yoav Artzi who wanted to share a past experience at sea. Here is how he told it:

"One August day, when we had finished loading a bulk shipment of corn kernels at the Port of Baltimore, and when the ship was preparing to go out to sea, a small truck stopped near the gangway. The driver asked about the first mate. In his hand, he held documents for him. Shortly after, the ship's boatswain came to me and asked to prepare a loading crane as well as additional crewmen to load special cargo from the truck onto the ship. As we lowered the loading hook toward the truck, the driver removed the canvas that had covered the cargo and attached the ropes to the hook. The cargo was made up of two sealed metal containers – most likely aluminum – upon which was written a description of the contents. That same evening, when we went out to sea, the mystery was revealed: These were the bodies of a Jewish American couple whose wills expressed their wish to be buried in the Holy Land. Their family had made all of the necessary arrangements – both with the local government and with the Israeli embassy to receive the certificates of authorization – in order to fulfill their last request. Since transferring the containers by plane was expensive, the family finally turned to the Israeli shipping company Zim, and their passage by sea was approved. So these are the background facts. Now began the strange series of events.

"One night, in the middle of the ocean, a few of us sat together in the boatswain's cabin. We drank, listened to music from a

stereo, and told stories, just like we're doing now. We had with us
one able seaman, whom I won't name, and soon you'll understand
why. He was a bit arrogant and not particularly liked by any of
the crew. He always talked about himself: 'I was there, I did this,'
All the time 'I, I, I...' and 'you guys should know that I'm not
afraid of anything.' And here's where the boatswain got an idea.
He turned to the showoff and said:

"'If you're such a big shot, I'm willing to make a bet with you.
If you lose, you'll owe me a bottle of whiskey. If I lose, I'll give
you two. What do you say?'

"Our Tarzan agreed to the terms without hesitation, and held
out his hand to shake on it. The boatswain went to his desk and
pulled out his work knife, which was sheathed.

"'Your mission is simple,' he said. 'All you have to do is
take this knife, and exactly at midnight go to the forward deck
equipment storeroom, without any lights, and place the knife on
top of one of the containers and come back. We'll be waiting for
you here.' Our hero smiled widely and said:

"'Are you joking? Isn't it a waste to lose two perfectly fine
bottles of whiskey?

"The boatswain just answered: 'We'll see about that once
you've returned.' So, we continued sitting there, drinking and
telling stories, only now we purposefully steered towards more
gruesome, scary stories. Finally, the clock showed five minutes to
midnight. The time had come. The boatswain asked me to escort
our hero to the stairs that went out to the main deck. We had in fact
agreed ahead of time – when our hero had taken leave to hit the
head – that I'd take him to the portside exit. As is typical with bulk
carriers, the deck was long. He would need a good few minutes to
reach the bow, and the night was dark with no moonlight. As soon
as we left, the boatswain took out a white sheet from his cupboard
and his flashlight and went out the starboard side exit. He knew
that I'd try to stall our hero. The boatswain quietly snuck to the
bow, ducked into a corner, cut three holes into the sheet for eyes
and a mouth, pulled the sheet over his head, and put the flashlight
in his mouth, while it was still off. His eyes began to get used to

the dark and he waited for our hero. He soon arrived, opening the bow door and hesitating. It was pitch black. He then began to take careful, unsure steps toward where he thought the two containers were located. Suddenly, he thought he heard a noise coming from deep in the hold, some kind of metallic sound. He instinctively turned his head toward the noise. That's when he saw something that nearly gave him a heart attack. From out of the darkness came a shapeless form, shrouded in white, a yellow-orange glow coming from where a mouth should be. Its arms – or perhaps not its arms – were outstretched, a crowbar hanging out in front of it, strange unrecognizable noises were coming from inside, and it was heading straight for him. He was paralyzed by fear. His hair stood up and beads of sweat came trickling down his face. The shapeless figure continued to approach him, and then, at the last instant, he shouted 'Mommy!' He turned and ran as fast as he could out of the hold and across the deck. He bumped into obstacles, fumbled and tripped, but got up and kept running, muttering and not daring to look back until he got back inside. While fleeing, he'd dropped the knife somewhere on deck or in the hold. He knew that we were waiting for him, but he had to first wash his face in his cabin and catch his breath. Once he finally returned to the boatswain's cabin, he saw that everyone was still sitting around the table. They stared at him. The boatswain asked if he'd completed his mission.

A mysterious ghost at the bow of the ship

"'Of course!' he replied gruffly.

"'Great,' the boatswain said. 'before we all go check that you did indeed succeed, I want to show you something.' He went to his shower and a few seconds later called out, 'Yoav, turn off the lights.' A shrouded white figure, with glowing yellow-orange mouth, came out from the shower.

"Our hero shouted: 'Oh, god! It's the ghost I saw in the bow! Help!' and he ran out, with our laughter trailing behind him."

"Nice! Good one, Yoav," I said. "That's an incredible story."

The albatross flew into my mind again. I hadn't processed its disappearance. For some reason I had the feeling that someone had released its leg from the rope without understanding the consequences. We continued sitting together, sipping from our drinks, listening to music. It was still early, relative to when we would normally disperse for the night.

"Perry," I heard Yoav say. "Besides songs, do you have any good stories to share with us?"

"Yeah," I said after some thought. "I'll tell you about something that happened to me a few years ago, that sounds unbelievable and untrue, but it really happened."

"One day," I began. "Our ship was anchored in the Haifa Bay, waiting for its turn to enter the port. The wait already lasted more than a week. In actuality, it was good for the crew, since being docked at the home port felt good for everyone. At the end of the work day, whoever wasn't on duty could take the service boat, which would arrive every two hours from 06:00 until midnight, to land. At that time I was still working as an able seaman and port shifts were part of my job. As you all know, you can't get out of them. And so, Friday came and I was on duty for the weekend. The remaining crew was very small, just the bare minimum to keep the ship functioning and secure. On that Friday evening, I decided to make myself a sandwich from whatever I could find in the crew refrigerator, since dinner had been terrible and I was still hungry. In the serving room there was a motorman who I didn't recognize. He'd joined the crew as a regular substitute crewman as a shore gang while the ship was docked in Haifa. We sat to eat and introduced ourselves to each other. I won't say his name. We talked while eating and then afterward, while having tea. Suddenly he said:

"'I have something interesting to tell you. Four months ago, I sailed onboard the ship *Yarden*, to eastern Africa ports and to the Asia. One day we arrived at the Cochin Port in southern India. After we tied up at the dock, several merchants approached us to hawk their wares, which included souvenirs like carved wooden elephants, Indian clothing, bedding, cushions, spices, and more. Among them was one with a very strange look. Is head was wrapped in a turban with a diamond-looking stone pin in the middle – like the Sikhs wear, or maybe not. I heard him say to one of the crewmen: 'If you want, I can read your past and your future to you. The Sikh's eyes were dark, piercing, and hypnotic. The guy was curious, so he invited him to his cabin. After a half hour, I saw them coming back. The sailor look dumbfounded. He told me that the Sikh knew everything about his childhood, his parents' names, his brothers and his sisters. Regarding the future, he'd asked for more money, but my friend had refused. Just out of fear of learning what was to come. The Sikh then turned to me and offered to read my past, present, and future. Just so you know, Perry, I'm a free thinker, not superstitious, I don't believe in coffee ground readings or tarot cards, only in what my eyes can see and what's in my pockets. But there was something so entrancing about this man, that I decided to listen to what he had to say, and not just for the fun of it.

"'I led him to my cabin and we sat at the table. I offered him a drink, but he declined politely. The Sikh took out from his bag a small, weathered notebook and began to flip through it. After a little while, I heard him say:

""You have a brother and a sister, both of them are younger than you. Your sister's name is Rachel and your brother's is Menachem," he didn't wait for a confirmation, but continued,

"Your parents live in northern Israel in a small town near the bay, to the other side of it is the large city of the region. When you were nine years old, you chased a cat, but tripped and cut your left knee. As a result of the fall, you still have a scar there." He continued this way, mentioning facts that I had long ago forgotten about. But to my amazement, it was all correct. I didn't know and couldn't understand where he had gotten all of that information about me. At that point, I was already curious and wanted to know about my future. The Sikh said that it was possible, but that I had to pay more money. With no choice, I handed over several rupee notes.

""When you return to your country, you will have to leave the ship, even though you'd planned to go on another voyage."

""Why?" I asked.

""I cannot tell you, even though I know the reason. You will find out on your own."

""And what about the coming years? My health, for example, my finances, a wife, children?" He flipped through his notebook. He was silent for a while and then said:

""I do not see a good future for you. Perhaps it's better if you do not know. But if you insist anyway, you will have to add another 20 rupees." I felt like he was playing me. He probably had some sort of trick. He looked at me with his hypnotic black eyes and waited for me to speak.

""Fine, let's continue," I said and gave him the money. He put the bills in his pocket and said:

""In six months from today, you will sail on another ship, you will be in an accident, and you will die." Perry, all I wanted to do in that moment was to shake him off of me.

"'What happened when you got back to Israel?' I asked him.

"'The Sikh was right. On the day the ship was to sail on the next voyage, I felt excruciating pains in the pit of my stomach. The second mate, and then the captain, determined after a checkup that I had appendicitis and that I had to disembark immediately and be taken to the nearest hospital.'

"'How much time has passed since your conversation with the Sikh?' I asked.

"'Five months.'

"'And that's why you prefer to work as a substitute crewman at port until the day the 'ultimatum' passes.'

"'That's not actually the reason. Truthfully, I'm sure that the Sikh had some kind of trick to figure out my past. Regarding my disembarkation, it's just a coincidence.'

"That Sunday, we entered port, and three days later we went out to sea. I didn't see the motorman again. Two months later, when we were anchored at Portland, Maine, the ship agent brought us letters, newspapers, and magazines from Israel. When we were at sea, the boatswain gave me one of the newspapers. In one of the inner pages, I saw a photo of the motorman, with his name in the caption. The headline read that an Israeli seaman had been killed at sea. In the article, the name of the ship and all of the details of the event were given. I looked at the date of the newspaper. The Sikh had been right once again. The man had died exactly six months after his prophecy."

The strange Sikh from Cochin, southern India

"That really is an unbelievable story," I heard Shauli say. "If it hadn't come from your lips, I would never buy it. How did that strange Sikh know? Where did he get his abilities? That story is too amazing and inexplicable. I'm sure any reasonable person would agree with me. But who knows? Maybe there are people with supernatural powers beyond the comprehension of common men?"

"I agree with you," I said. "But these are the facts. You can even check the incidences at the company's office, both the day he disembarked from the *Yarden* and the day that he died at sea."

It was already past midnight. Fatigue began to overcome me, so I hinted to the guys that it was time for me to clock out. Each one said goodbye one after the other, thanking me for the nice evening. Before I fell asleep, the figure of the albatross floated toward the back of my mind. That's how I drifted off, apparently, my thoughts accompanying him to the depths of the ocean.

By 08:00 the next morning, I'd already showered, shaved, and eaten breakfast. I went to check up on the two crewmen on duty cleaning and swabbing the living quarters passageway, the laundry room, and the garbage room, before the captain's usual 10:00 inspection. This cleaning inspection takes place every Saturday at sea and is considered routine. Captain Bar-Noy, the first mate, the first mechanic, and the chief steward, wearing their ranks, would meet in the bridge and from there make the rounds throughout the ship. Special attention was given to the mess and serving room, the galley, the food storage, and the living quarters.

On Saturdays, lunch was always *cholent* (slow-cooked stew) and an oven-roasted chicken quarter with salad. There are some who prefer the chicken breast while others prefer the leg and thigh. To prevent arguments, the chicken was distributed on rotation, where one week a department would be served the breast and the next week they'd be served the leg and thigh. Once I finished eating lunch, I went out for a walk around the main deck. It was a beautiful day. The surface of the water was as smooth as a baby's bottom. The sky was clear, besides a few high cirrus clouds, and a light westerly wind caressed my face. I lit a cigarette and slowly and calmly strolled toward the bow. I climbed the stairs to the deck and continued until I got to the edge. I leaned forward, watching where the bow cut through the water, splitting the ocean in two and creating two frothy waves on its sides. A pod of dolphins jumped at the side of the bow, playing along with the waves. The dolphins were making shrieking noises with their blowholes. It is so relaxing to watch them play. Seeing them gives you a feeling that you're not alone in this vast expanse. The dolphins continued playing along the bow for a little while longer, until they were no longer interested and went on their way, leaping and jumping into the distance until they disappeared into the ocean.

Upon returning to my cabin, I poured myself a glass of Vat 69. All of a sudden, I thought of Gertie. I missed her, I really did. I didn't want to be alone with my thoughts, so I went to visit Shauli in his cabin. He was resting in his bed, but as soon as he saw me, he jumped out of bed, went to wash his face, took out two beers, and sat with me. I glanced at my watch – it showed 14:00. We sat in silence for a few minutes, sipping our beers. Suddenly Shauli said:

"Perry, your story yesterday about the unlucky motorman really affected me. Do you have any other interesting experiences up your sleeve that you can share?"

"Yes," I said after a little thought. "I've got loads of experiences, just like everyone else." And so I began:

"I'm going to tell you about the best fuck of my life. It's an incredible story, and it would be a shame to keep it to myself. One day we arrived at Port Elizabeth in Newark Bay, where the Passaic and Hackensack Rivers meet in New Jersey, connecting to New York Bay. Since New York City was nearby, I decided one evening to take the train in to the city. After walking around 42nd Street and its surroundings for a while, I stopped a cab and asked the driver to take me to the Village in Manhattan, which is considered to be a bohemian area. I knew that there was an Israeli club there called Finjan. With a little help from a passerby who gave me directions, I found the club. The place was packed. An Israeli singer was on stage accompanied by musicians. The bar was crowded and it took me a while to get the double whiskey that I ordered. I stood in a corner, listening to the singer and looking around the club. There was a couple there, and I noticed that every time I caught a glimpse of the man, he was looking at me with a smile on his face. At first I thought he was looking at someone behind me, but his eyes were focused on me alone. His gaze made me a little uncomfortable. Finally, the guy got up from his seat and started to come toward me, with the smile still on his face.

"'You don't remember me,' he said in Hebrew. I didn't recognize him, but I politely answered that he looked familiar and maybe we'd met a long time before. 'That's right, try to remember,' he said. I couldn't.

"'We studied together at the agricultural school in Mikve Israel and we'd walk to Tel Aviv together on foot and go to my house, which was by the Carmel market. Your name's Perry, right?' he continued to smile. Now I remembered.

"'You're Yitzhak, right?' He nodded. During the time we'd studied together, we shared a lot of youthful experiences. After we finished studying, our paths separated and never crossed again, until now.

"'Come, join us at our table and meet my friend.' His friend was a very nice looking girl who looked me over as she introduced herself.

"'My name's Maureen, and yours?'

"'Perry,' I answered. Yitzhak asked what I had done since those days at the agricultural school. 'Military service – the navy – and afterward I joined the merchant marines, rented a bachelor pad in Haifa, which means I'm still unmarried. Now, tell me about yourself.'

"'So,' he began. 'My parents couldn't find their way in Israel and decided to move to New York. After we got settled in, my dad opened up a small clothing store in Brooklyn. About a year later, the opportunity of a lifetime fell into his lap. He rented a warehouse in the harbor, after realizing he had the potential of working with the many merchant marine ships there. He filled the warehouse with clothing and other goods and sold them wholesale to the ship crews. He would go meet the ships as soon as they docked, passing around his business cards, on which the details of his wares were described. He was very successful and has done well. As time went on, my parents bought an apartment on Park Avenue. They bought me a bridal salon that is doing quite well. I've got a great team, very professional. Now I'm renting an apartment near the salon. By the way, here everyone calls me Isaac. Americanization, you understand.'

"'Nice, I'm glad to hear you've been successful.' We sat, recalling memories from the past. Suddenly, Maureen turned to me and asked if I danced. I looked over to Isaac and he nodded his head. The band was playing a slow jam. She pressed up against me and I felt her the curves of her perfect body. Her perfume tickled my senses.

"'Are you Isaac's girlfriend?' I asked.

"'No, we're just good friends, and sometimes he takes me out with him, if I'm free.'

"'And what do you do?' I continued to investigate.

"'I'm a senior journalist at one of the country's major press agencies, UPI. I get to travel the world and interview big shots.' I then told her a little about myself, after she'd inquired. When we got back to the table, Isaac invited me to join them at an exclusive club for members on Fifth Avenue. All the VIPs went there.

"'You won't regret it,' he said. Of course I accepted.

Maureen, the New York journalist

"The club was on the second floor of a building. Three bouncers stood at the door checking people coming in. One of them asked Isaac to see his membership card, to which he obliged. Our hands were stamped with stamps that could only be seen under the club's ultra-violet lights. The club was packed to the brim. Some of the revelers were in various states of undress. Isaac pointed out some celebrities, while explaining to me who they were. When Maureen went to the ladies room, I took the opportunity to ask Isaac about their relationship. He answered that besides friendship they'd never been intimate. He then added that I should make a move, because she'd told him that she was interested in me. We danced together again. This time she rested her head on my shoulder and let me feel the warmth of her body.

"'Maureen,' I whispered into her ear. 'Would you like to come back with me to my ship? I'm sure that you'd enjoy the Israeli atmosphere.' Her reply surprised me:

"'No, Perry. That's not part of my plan. But I'd like to see you again tomorrow. Let's get a hotel room.'

"She was waiting for me in the cafeteria where we'd set to meet. It was exactly 14:00 when I arrived. Maureen was sipping a glass of juice that she'd ordered before I'd arrived. I ordered an espresso.

"'Listen, Perry,' she said. 'I'd invite you to my place, but I have to confess that technically I'm a married woman. My husband is much older than me. He's a wealthy man with a good heart. I have everything that I want, but we don't have sex. You could call it a marriage of convenience. I like and admire him very much, but nothing more.'

"The hotel that Maureen took me to was five minutes away from the cafeteria. We stayed there until evening. We made amazing love. She was completely free, with no inhibitions, and I loved it. But this wasn't the fuck that my story is about, Shauli, that's still to come. Anyway, we continued to meet everyday. We would meet at the same hotel, and afterward would go out to a new place every time. She showed me interesting sites in the city and she even took me to her office and introduced some of her fellow journalists. It was great to be together, but like every good thing, it had to end. After ten perfect days, it was time for me to set sail. The ship had finished unloading and loading and was ready to sail for Montreal, Canada. It was difficult to say goodbye. Especially since I knew I would probably never see her again. Maureen embraced me warmly and I finally took a cab for the ship.

"According to the plans, the ship was to stay two days in Montreal and from there sail to Yokohama, Japan, via the Panama Canal. We arrived in Montreal on the morning of the third day since we left New York. As we docked, I saw Maureen standing there, waiting for the gangway to be lowered. I was completely surprised. When the gangway was lowered and secured, I went to meet her. She saw the look of shock on my face and immediately explained that she had contacted the shipping company and had gotten all of the information – the date and time of our arrival and where we were to dock. She had been decisive: She had to come see me. She had finished all of her tasks at work, gotten on a plane, and here she was. We closed ourselves up in my cabin. We made boundary-breaking love, but that still wasn't the fuck that I'm going to tell you about. That's later. Anyway, in the evening, we called a cab and drove to Saint Catherine Street, a place I'd remembered from a previous visit two years before. There was a particular tavern that I'd gone to a few times during that trip, so I decided to take Maureen there. We sat down at a side table. A charming waitress came and took our order – a bottle of Riesling, shrimp, and a salad. As we were talking and waiting for our food, I felt two hands cover my eyes from behind. I touched them – they were a woman's hands. I pulled them off gently and turned around. In front of me stood a gorgeous bombshell, smiling from ear to ear. I thought she must have mistaken me for someone else, since I didn't recognize her at all.

    "'You don't remember me, Perry? I used to work here. I'm Sharon,' she said. I then remembered that I had known a waitress named Sharon, but that she had been extremely overweight. She noticed that I was confused.

"'I lost a lot of weight. That's probably why you don't recognize me,' she said. My doubt over her true identity was kept hidden. I nevertheless introduced Maureen as my friend from New York. Sharon held out her hand in greeting, but Maureen refused to acknowledge it. I exchanged a few more words with Sharon, and then Maureen turned her back to us, mumbled unintelligently, and looked frustrated. There wasn't much time left. Maureen was anxious to get back to the ship. Showing my disappointment, I paid reluctantly and we left."

Shauli poured another round and asked me to continue the story.

"So, we got back to the ship and Maureen asked to discuss something with me, something of utmost importance, even more important than the bed that was beckoning us. I poured the two of us a drink and we sat down at the table.

"'Listen, Perry,' she began. 'I am very serious about what I'm about to discuss with you. My plan is like this: Tomorrow, you take some documentation to the doctor, and I'll go with you, but let me talk to him in private. You'll then leave the ship, and fly to Israel. Three days later, I'll meet you in Israel, with divorce papers in my hand. What do you say to that?' Shauli, I was stunned. To disrupt the voyage like that, to suddenly quit and go back to Israel, it all seemed weird and unrealistic. But, don't forget, she was something special, and the adventure that she had put in front of me actually seemed worth it. The next morning, the ship agent brought us to the clinic. As we'd discussed, Maureen went in to see the doctor and after a short while, she came out and in her hand was a signed paper from the doctor recommending that I disembark from the ship and seek medical treatment for an illness. The captain authorized it and wished me a speedy recovery. The chief steward gave me my salary and issued my disembarkation papers. In the afternoon, the ship agent came to get me. He brought me – with Maureen at my side – to a hotel and arranged my stay there until the following day.

"'A driver will come get you in the morning with your plane ticket and will bring you to the airport,' he told me before going on his way. An hour later, while Maureen and I were having a drink at the hotel bar, she ordered a taxi.

"'Perry, I've got an evening flight to New York. This is only a short goodbye. I'll see you in three days,' she said. 'I'll give you the flight number and my arrival time. I'd like it if you could meet me at the airport.'

"You're going to think badly of me, Shauli, but that same evening I went back to the tavern with the intent of seeing Sharon. And that's what I did. I wanted to feel her body, to forget for a moment my sudden betrayal to my ship and to not think about what was waiting for me on my return to Israel.

"I had a cute little bachelor pad in Haifa, next to the beach of the Bat Galim neighborhood. I organized things ahead of Maureen's arrival. I stocked up the fridge and freezer with goodies and, of course, I made sure we weren't missing any drinks. That day a telegram arrived with all of the flight information, including the date and time of her arrival. The next day, in the late morning, I went to the airport, still in disbelief over what I was doing. It was the beginning of August and it was hot, there were no clouds in the sky, and no breeze was blowing. Inside the arrivals gate of the airport the air conditioning was working at full blast, slightly cooling the hot day. I looked at the arrivals board. Maureen's plane was scheduled to land at 14:35, final. I glanced at my watch. It was 13:30. I still had plenty of time, so I went to one of the airport restaurants and ordered a bottle of beer, with no glass.

"Maureen spotted me right away in the crowd of people waiting in the arrivals terminal. She came over to me and for a moment we stood together wrapped in an embrace. Her eyes sparkled at seeing me again. Outside, I flagged down a cab, which sped us to my bachelor apartment in Haifa. On the way, Maureen explained to me how her husband didn't put up a fight when she'd brought up her wish to divorce. He was many years her senior, and hadn't had sex together in some time, but he also just did not want to stand in her way. He wished her luck, but requested that she keep in touch with him from time to time. The next day, they flew to Reno and soon after got the divorce certificate. Her manager at the news agency heard of her plans to move to Israel and offered that she work as a correspondent in their Tel Aviv bureau. He assured her that they'd find her a suitable apartment and rent her a car. She'd only be able to stay at my place for a week – until her apartment situation was worked out – and then she'd have to go to Tel Aviv and focus on work.

"We had a stormy week, like the ocean during a hurricane. We spent most of the days in bed, steeped in sex and our inexhaustible love. In the evening, we would go out to one of the local bars and then go to a nice restaurant to eat a satisfying meal and replenish our energy. The days passed quickly, and soon I found myself walking her to her cab, which was taking her away from me and to the bustling city of Tel Aviv. Two days after she left, I was asked by the company to substitute as a shore gang on a ship that was docking soon that evening, to allow the crew to take a short shore leave. A week later I returned to my bachelor pad. On the answering machine were several messages, all from Maureen. I listened to all of them, each one sounding nearly identical: 'Perry, my love, I've got a nice little apartment in north Tel Aviv and even a car. I started work. Call me, and come see me as soon as you can. Love, Maureen.'

"Here, Shauli, is where I get to the real deal that I promised you.

"I took a train at the Haifa Central Station, which departed to the sounds of the train whistle announcing its exit. When I got to her apartment, it was already late afternoon. She opened the door, and her eyes shone with joy at seeing me. It seemed like we held each other at the door for almost an eternity, until we finally let go. Maureen went to her liquor cabinet and took out a bottle of whiskey and two glasses, and from the refrigerator she took out ice and some mini appetizers. Once we settled into the couch, Maureen started to tell me about her time in the city – finding the fantastic apartment, the car she was using, the office where she was working, her boss, the rest of the employees, and of course the other reporters, some of whom she'd known from New York.

"Evening began to fall, replacing the daylight. While I was still sipping my glass of whiskey in the living room, she got up abruptly and went to the bedroom. The door was left open. I followed her steps with my eyes. She began to shed her clothes, first, her shoes, followed by her dress, then her floral bra, and finally, maddeningly delicately, her silk panties.

"I put down my whiskey and followed her into the bedroom. Maureen was lying out on the bed, her arms behind her head, her legs slightly apart, and her eyes fixed on me. A light breeze came up from the sea, playing with the window curtains. Her perfect body once again intoxicated me and my senses. Quickly, I let my clothes fall to the floor. Whiskey numbs the senses, but not those related to sex. It releases the inhibitions in the recesses of the brain's grey matter and you become free and loose, like the ripples that kiss a ship's body in port.

"My tongue brazenly headed straight for her valley of Venus, lingering carefully at its
    crest. My fingers searched and stroked her wisps of hair and then climbed up her body to her nipples. She began to moan and her pelvis rose and fell at an uneven rhythm. I held back from finishing, but she must have had a number of orgasms, from how wet she became. *She's going to need a couple of bottles of water*, I laughed to myself.

"Shauli, that was an explosion, but listen to the rest."

"First, refill the glasses," Shauli said. I did, and then continued:

"Well, we rested a bit, caressing each other, and then Maureen went behind me, stuck her tongue into my anus, then moved to my testicles and inserted them both in her mouth, while she fingered my member. I was a volcano on the edge of eruption, and I could feel the flaming lava about to gush forth. We were moving wildly and in waves and once I couldn't resist, I flipped her over and mounted her. My climax was immediate and with a force previously unknown to me."

Shauli sat dumbfounded. "Listen, Perry, I'm going to have to go take care of myself soon," he said with a toothy grin. "How did the saga with Maureen end? Or is it still happening?" he asked with interest.

"No, it ended like all good things do," I said.

"So, don't leave me in the dark, finish the story."

"Well," I said. "It fell apart just a few days after that stormy night. Maureen came to my bachelor pad and begged me to go to Tel Aviv.

"'Leave the sea life and I'll pay for you to go to university and do something. My work is in Tel Aviv and I have a beautiful apartment, as you've seen. Even if I could stay in your apartment, I wouldn't survive without air conditioning and other essentials that you don't have, and I need them for my work as a reporter.' I didn't hesitate much when I answered:

"'I love being with you. You've given me wonderful days that I'll never forget, as I'll never forget you, of course. But you're in second place and the sea is in first. I wouldn't leave it for any offer, no matter how tempting. For me, the ship is my true wife.' And that's how it ended. Maureen ran off furious, and I never saw her again. Sometimes I think about what she might be doing now and where she might be, but not more than that. My life continues to flow along the ocean and the waves. They and only they are what make up my life in a world where all of us live in a bubble that will pop one day."

"Perry, let's go get dinner," Shauli said. "It's time."

A glance at my watch agreed with him. Saturday dinners were

always more festive than the rest of the week. The first course was an assortment of salads and steaming vegetable soup, main course was meatballs and sides, and for dessert, pineapple compote in sweet syrup.

I leaned against the wooden railing on the starboard side lifeboat deck, drinking a beer and looking out over the ocean expanse. The horizon was clear and bright, and evening began to fall on that part of the world, painting the few clouds in brilliant colors, indicating the setting of the red sun behind the skyline. I lit a cigarette, enjoying it, but knowing that one day I'd have to quit the harmful habit. I flicked the cigarette butt overboard and downwind, and decided to go back to my cabin. I took out a bottle of whiskey and a glass from the liquor cabinet, sat down at the table, filled the glass three fingers tall, and once again my thoughts flew to Gertie. I opened the desk drawer, took out the bundle of her letters, and read them over for the umpteenth time wistfully and longingly. They dripped with love and yearning against a background of hope that the next meeting would be soon. In a cabin, without the magic of a woman, the loneliness is oppressive, especially after a long workday at sea. Not everyone on land can understand this. They finish a day of work, go back home to their family and kids, dinner is ready, the easy chair and newspaper too, and finally, they get into bed next to their loving wife and her body. But on the other hand, they don't have the peace and tranquility of a sailor. I've always told myself: As long as I sailed on ships, there'd be no chance that I'd settle down and tie myself to a woman, no matter how much I loved her. It was clear to me that the sea and love 'didn't go together,' and that one day I would have to choose between the love of a woman with whom I'd want to share the rest of my life, and my love of the sea. Many thoughts go through the mind of a seaman when he's alone in his cabin. Married men think of their wives and children; the bachelors about all of the ones they left behind somewhere, about plans for the future, and of course, about the last fling that they had. Shore leave is relatively short, and if one of the crewmen happen to catch the occasional love, he feels like the peacock spreading his tail feathers, or the rooster straightening his crest. I gathered up Gertie's letters and returned them to the drawer. I poured myself another whiskey. As I sat down, there came a knock at the door and Shauli walked in.

"Listen, Perry, your story really hit me. I'm still thinking about it," he said.

"It happened in the past, and it's over," I said. "Now, go get yourself something and join me." Shauli took out a beer from the fridge.

"Do you remember sailing together on the *Deganya*?" he asked as he sat down.

"Of course," I said. "But I really remember sailing together on the tanker *Samson*, when you worked for the El-Yam company and when the Six-Day war broke out in June 1967. I still think we done a great injustice, but I need proof. But let's not talk about it; just the thought of what we all went through makes me sick." Shauli agreed with me. He added that two and a half years had already passed since that voyage, but he would never forget it. It would follow him for the rest of his days.

The night went into overdrive and I wanted some time to myself. So I asked Shauli to close the door behind him when he left, because I needed to be alone when I got into bed. Even though it was still relatively early, Shauli understood what I meant. He bid me a goodnight and even thanked me for the day we'd spent together. When he left, I poured myself another drink and lit a cigarette. I really liked Shauli, both as a friend and as an extraordinary sailor, the likes of whom there weren't many. This was the third ship on which we sailed together. My thoughts returned to the tanker *Samson*, but I quickly banished the memories. I was still angry about lack of attention and consideration toward everything that we'd done, gone though, and contributed to that voyage.

Loneliness exists at sea, but isn't felt. There's always something to do, whether it's during the workday or afterward. You can watch a movie being screened in the day room after dinner, or you can play board games with someone, or read newspapers – even though they were a bit old, or you can listen to the stereo playing Israeli music. Listening to those songs gives you a feeling of closeness to your homeland. Sometimes you don't want to listen, because it can cause you to miss home, or a deep sadness could emerge inside of you, about all those you left behind, who are thinking about you, and you them. The thoughts kept running through my mind, bouncing and changing identities. My difficult childhood, my wish to seek refuge at sea. To escape my wicked stepmother and my weak father who barely functioned and didn't even know the soul of his only son.

Shaul Shauli

Shauli packed his luggage according to the list he had prepared ahead of time. In his side bag he packed a few small, important items, including his seaman's book and his embarkation papers. One of the documents, labeled with the date of his embarkation and his wage information, was in duplicate, one for the chief steward and a copy for himself. Another document, this time in triplicate and in different colors, was for the arrangements upon boarding; the green paper would go to the border police, the red to the ship's captain, and the yellow was his own copy. After everything was sorted and packed to his satisfaction, all that was left was to say goodbye to his mom. Rena took him into her arms, wished him a good voyage and success in his endeavors. Her eyes were moist. Shauli knew that his mother hadn't fully accepted his decision, but he felt mature enough to decide his own fate, and she knew that. Bossem insisted on accompanying him to the bus stop, and he accepted her request happily.

When he reached the gate at the Haifa Port, the guards stopped him and asked for his entry permit. Shauli opened his side bag and showed them his embarkation papers. They waved him in and even pointed out where the border police building was located. When he got to the building, a nice policewoman in a brown suit asked to see his embarkation papers and seaman's book, which he gave her. After a computer check showed he had no criminal record, he was not wanted by authorities, and the certificate of good conduct was still valid, she swiftly and skillfully pounded her stamp into the inkpad and stamped the documents. She took his seaman's book and placed it in a small compartment labeled *Teverya*. At the same time as she was doing everything, she asked Shauli for a passport photo. She then stapled the photo to his port pass, upon which she wrote in English his name, the ship's name, his rank, and his boarding date. The policewoman wished him a good voyage and handed him his pass. He thanked her, feeling a great relief and an indescribable sense of happiness. Once he left the building, he started in the direction of the ship. He asked where it was located at one of the piers. He couldn't resist; he took out his pass and read it over and over: "Seaman's name: Shaul Shauli; Ship's name: *Teverya*; Rank: Ordinary Seaman; Embarkation date: June 27, 1962."

Shauli began to march along the docks, from one ship to another, reading their names until finally he spotted the *Teverya*. Her hull was black, the superstructure was painted white, and her name on the bow was also painted white, in English and in Hebrew. The funnel was also painted white, with seven gold stars between two blue stripes painted on top. She was beautiful. He fell in love at first sight. Shauli noticed that the ship's derricks were working a full strength, loading and unloading cargo. He ascended the gangway aboard the ship. When he reached the door to the superstructure, he was stopped by a sailor in a blue cap, asking what he wanted.

"I have embarkation papers as a ordinary seaman," he said.

"What's your name?" the sailor asked.

"Shaul Shauli," he replied.

"Nice to meet you. I'm an able seaman, my name's Shimon, but everyone calls me Shimi. Welcome aboard. I'll take you to the first mate's office, you need to see him." Shimi left him at the opening to the door and went off to his work. The first mate was sitting at his desk, busy with complex paperwork. Shauli lightly knocked on the door, and the first mate lifted his eyes. When he didn't recognize him as someone he knew, he asked how he could help. Shauli introduced himself and showed his papers. He looked over the papers, checked the stamps from the company, the transportation authority, and the border police, and finding them acceptable, went to a glass cupboard that was filled with rows of keys, took one bunch, and told Shauli to follow him. They lay below through the passageway for the living quarters.

"From what I read, you're Shaul Shauli. Your name is already on the transportation ministry's list for this voyage. My name's

Avichai, but to you, it's 'Chief' – that's the practice." He opened the door to cabin number 114.

"So, settle into your new home. Afterward, go see the chief steward. He'll get you clean sheets. After him, go find the boatswain – he'll probably be on the main deck – and introduce yourself." And with that, he turned toward the steps. Shauli looked around the cabin, opened and shut doors and drawers, pushed aside the curtain and looked to the foredeck, watching the derricks unloading and loading cargo into the belly of the holds. Shauli turned away from the porthole and began to unpack his luggage. He hung clothes on hangers and organized others in the varnished mahogany closet. He put his toiletries in the shower room and his important documents in a drawer. When he finished, he headed to the chief steward's office.

Shauli introduced himself to the chief steward and gave him the form the company had given him. The chief steward's appearance wasn't very appeling – stout, fat, and balding – but he had a kind face.

"Well, Shauli, you've come to the right ship. Welcome," he said, taking out the contract crew list and signing his name. "Nice to meet you. Now, go find Eli the cabin steward. He'll take you to the clean linen supply closet and there he'll give you clean sheets and soap."

Shauli thanked him and left to locate Eli. When he found him near the galley, he told him that he had just boarded the ship and that the chief steward had told him to get clean sheets. Eli gestured with his head to follow him to the linen supply closet. There he was given a pair of bottom sheets, two top sheets, two towels, a blanket, soap, and a pack of matchboxes, asking – or rather, stating – that "you probably smoke."

Shauli made his bed, hung up the towels in the shower room, and when he finished, went below to find the boatswain. He found him in the ship's forward deck equipment storeroom, busy closing up paint cans and cleaning brushes. As he'd already learned to do, he

called him "bos'n". Shauli told him that he'd boarded the ship as
an ordinary seaman and that the first mate had sent him to see him.
The boatswain was a hulk. He was 190 cm tall, with a thick neck,
giant hands, and his whole body rippled with strength.

"What's your name?" he asked.

"Shaul Shauli," he said. "But you can call me Shauli." The
boatswain thrust out his hand.

"My name's Carmel. We're getting close to dinner, they
serve it at 17:00. At 18:00, I'm putting you on deck duty until
midnight with able seaman Shimi. He'll help you learn the shift
procedures. Tomorrow evening, we're set to sail to a few ports
in the Mediterranean, and afterward to the length of the United
States' eastern coast, starting in New York and ending in Mexico.
The voyage will last about three months."

Dinner wasn't particularly appetizing, but from what he
understood from the rest of the guys at the table, "that's how it
is at port – once we're at sea, everything changes for the better."
After dinner, Shauli went to his cabin to change into work clothes.
Fifteen minutes before 18:00, he was already standing at the main
deck door near the gangway, ready and raring for any task that
would be asked of him. Toward the start of the shift, Shimi arrived
on deck and together they went to check out the various loading
areas on the main deck. Shimi began to give him the basics.

"You have to watch the cargo, to make sure no damage is
incurred. While this is the specific task of the officer on duty,
we're his eyes. Most importantly, we have to check the rigging
to make sure that nothing's too loose or too tight, and sometimes
we have to tighten or release the ropes as the need comes, with
the help of the electric winch. Another important thing is to check
the status of the gangway, since during loading and unloading
the ship sometimes leans port or starboard, because of uneven
distribution of cargo on either side of the ship. The officer on duty
will make sure to stabilize the ship, by distributing water between
the ballast tanks, but sometimes the pace is so crazy that we have
to pay attention to any situation. Another factor – and maybe the

main one – is the strong winds and wild waves that push the ship away from the dock. Of course, there's lots more to learn, but I'm sure that while working, you'll get the hang of everything." Shauli absorbed everything that Shimi said. No one was as happy as he was – to walk on the deck of an Israeli merchant marine ship!

The *Teverya* was a freighter that transported general cargo primarily to the Gulf ports of the US. She was built a year before in the Bremer shipyard in Germany, with a deadweight capacity of 10000 tons and had a speed of about 15 knots.

Shauli listened to all of Shimi's explanations. He wanted to learn everything as quickly as possible for two main reasons: Firstly, so he wouldn't be a burden on the rest of the crew, and secondly, to improve his personal knowledge. Though he did already have some prior knowledge, from visiting the kibbutz fishing boat and learning from its skipper, Rami. And his service on the destroyer *Eilat* also contributed to his general knowledge. But on that big ship, everything looked different to him. At around 22:00, Shimi suggested that he take a short break.

"Go to the crew preparation room. In the fridge, you'll find vegetables, sausages, cheese, fruit, milk, butter, olives, and other things. Make yourself something. You'll also find a boiler, so you can make yourself a cup of coffee or tea. When you get back on deck, I'll also go get something to eat."

The deck shift passed by without incident. Shauli learned a lot and was very happy. At midnight, a deck crewman came to switch him out. Shimi briefed him and afterward, when everything was clear, they returned to the structure. Shimi liked Shauli. He felt that he had a strong will. He also seemed serious and sincere.

"You want to have a cold beer with me in my cabin before you go to bed?" he asked, or more accurately, stated a fact.

Shimi's cabin was incredibly clean and organized. He took out two beers from his fridge and a Hungarian salami that he bought on his last voyage. He cut some slices of salami and put them on a plate and brought everything to the table. Shimi asked Shauli if it was his first voyage, and in general, what brought him to sea? Shauli's answer came quickly: He was a kibbutznik from Sdot Yam, bordering the Mediterranean, and he spent his childhood swimming for hours, tanning, and watching the sunset behind the horizon. He would often watch the faraway ships make their way to the coast, and from this came his love of the sea. Also, his military service began and ended on the destroyer *Eilat*. Shimi also told him a little about himself, and when they finished their beers, they bid each other goodnight. Shauli headed to his cabin to have his first night's sleep on the ship. Before falling asleep, he thought of his sister Bossem and his mother Rena. They would be so proud to see the happiness that engulfed him.

The next day, after finishing breakfast, Shauli and other crewmen made their way to the paint storeroom in the bow. The boatswain distributed paint and tools, then he divided them into different jobs around the ship. He put Shauli together with a sailor named Raanan.

"Go down to the dock and walk along the hull as much as is possible, and scrape and polish wherever there's damage. At least two coats of base paint and then a top coat." Raanan nodded his head. They collected the paints and tools and went ashore. Raanan explained to Shauli the basics of their task. First, they had to scrape off any peeling paint or rust, then polish the edges of the peeled paint and brush with a steel brush.

"You begin at the stern and I'll begin at the bow, until we meet in the middle. But first, I'll help you out to get things started."

At around 10:00, Raanan came by his side and checked out the work.

"Good, you picked it up quickly. Now lets go aboard, coffee break is 20 minutes long and afterward, we'll continue working until 12:00." When they boarded again for lunch, Shauli's stomach already growled with hunger. The meal tasted delicious, even though it was a little bland.

After the 15:00 coffee break, the boatswain asked that they finish the maintenance work, return the paints and tools to the storeroom, and begin the various jobs related to preparing to set sail. Shauli was put with Shimi again.

"Let's check the lifeboats," Shimi said. They checked that the drainage plug was open and that the lifeboat was tied correctly and securely in place. They also made sure that the tarp on the winch was secure and tied in a knot for immediate opening in order to prevent sea water from entering. They did another round inside the boats and outside, to make sure that everything was correct.

"Now we'll go to the storerooms in the bow and tie everything down to prevent movement in the rocky sea. The crew is divided into teams like us, and everyone has different tasks," he explained.

They used ropes to tie down the numerous paint cans and the water barrels that held the used paintbrushes and rollers. They set the long bamboo rods that were used to paint high places in the corner of the storeroom in a way that they wouldn't move. Once everything was tied and secured, they lay topside to the bow deck.

"Now we have to seal all of the vents with their covers, and we'll do the same on all of the decks on both sides of the ship."

When they were finally finished, it was dinnertime. As he entered the structure, Shauli noticed that on the notice board was written: "Shore leave ends at 22:00." They both had free time and neither was on deck duty. Shimi again invited Shauli to his cabin after dinner.

"Let's go have a cold beer."

"Gladly," Shauli answered. He was happy for the invitation. He had heard so many stories of new sailors being bullied, and here, he was in luck. He felt that they were already good friends and that he could trust him to not let someone else pull one over on him.

Sailors love telling stories about their voyages, and Shimi was no exception. As they sat sipping their beers and talking about the coming voyage and the first port where they'd be docking, Shimi said:

"Hey Shauli, let me tell you a story about a voyage I had about a year ago. It happened at the Port of Piraeus, which, by the way, is going to be our first and last port on this voyage. We arrived at port on the morning of a beautiful summer's day. It was the last port before reaching our home port of Haifa. After we docked, the boatswain came up to me and said:

"'Shimi, you're released today. Go to town, go shopping, or go out, whatever you feel like doing.' After lunch, once I was clean and put-together, I went ashore with the intention of taking public transportation into Athens and see the Acropolis, and really, it was worth it. The site that left the biggest impression on me was the Parthenon, a temple dedicated to the goddess Athena, the protector of the Athens. Most of the beautiful buildings in the Acropolis, including the Parthenon, were built during the rule of Pericles, 495-429 BCE. Pericles was a statesman, an orator, and a military commander. He also promoted art and literature, leading Athens to become the cultural center of Ancient Greece and prompting what is now known as the Golden Age of Athens. And now, I'd thought to myself, I was standing on its ruins, in awe and admiration of all the sights before me.

"Once I had had my fill of antiquity, I began to make my way to the main street in the modern city of Athens. There I found a quaint tavern, so I went in. A band of musicians all dressed in traditional white outfits played and sang, filling the place with pleasant sounds of bouzouki – Greek folk music. I found a corner table set for two and sat down. A waitress arrived and asked what she could get me. She set down a menu on the table and said she'd return shortly. I went over the menu and knew what I'd order. When she returned, I asked for a Greek salad, roast lamb, baked potato, and a beer. Shauli, I was licking my fingers it was so good. The lamb was at the level of a three-star Michelin restaurant. If we have the time, I'll take you there," Shimi promised, then continued his story:

"Toward the evening, I returned to Piraeus. I decided to have a beer or two at a bar I knew before returning aboard. I checked how much money I had left in my pocket, and it turned out there wasn't much. I had to take into account the cab ride back to the ship. I finally found the bar that I was looking for and went inside. I sat at the corner of the bar and ordered a beer. *I'll have this one beer and get back*, I told myself. I drank, and thought about the Acropolis, the tavern, and going back to the ship after the successful day. I reached into my pocket and took out my pack of cigarettes and lighter, and enjoyed the smoke. I noticed that a pretty broad sat down in the seat next to me. For the next ten minutes, she didn't say a word. She looked over at me every once in a while, but nothing more. But then, when I took out another cigarette from the pack, she picked up my lighter and lit my cigarette for me.

"'What's your name?' she asked.

"'No name,' I said.

"'Great, so why don't you buy me a drink?' she said. I knew she must be the bar's hostess, it was written all over her face, and her fake drink wasn't cheap at all. I reached into my pocket and pulled out a few coins.

"'Darling, this is all I have left – just enough to finish this beer and return to my ship.'

"'OK, I understand,' she said. 'Would you mind if I got you a beer?'

"'If you want to, I'll gladly accept a beer.' She gave a nod to the bartender and he gave me another beer.

"'Thanks,' I told her. 'I appreciate your kindness. Cheers!'

"As the time passed, the place started to fill up with people. At some point the hostess, whose name I still didn't know, stood up.

"'I have to earn my keep. You can stay, the bartender already knows – he'll serve you as many beers as you want, no charge. You should wait for me, you won't be sorry.' And with that, she turned to one of the crowded tables. I had already started my fourth beer when she came back and asked me if everything was alright.

"'Yes,' I said. 'I'm enjoying the place, especially the music.'

"'Listen, No Name,' she said. 'You should wait for me. I finish my shift at 4:00. We'll go straight to my apartment.' She didn't wait for an answer, but just went back to the customers. I waited, most definitely. A girl that doesn't even know me buys me drinks and offers to have a fling. Who am I to say no? But the more I sat alone with my beer, the more I got the gut feeling that something wasn't right. *She's up to something*, I thought. *Maybe I should go back to the ship. I'll finish the beer and leave.* I looked at the clock, it was 3:30. *There's not much more time to wait, I may as well wait out the last bit*, I decided."

Shimi went to the fridge and took out another two beers and the salami.

"So, what do you think of the story?" he asked Shauli.

"Continue," Shauli said. "I want to know how it ends."

"OK, so a little before 4:00, the hostess came back, smiled, and said that she's going to go the dressing room and freshen up. She said that she'd be right back.

"'Don't go anywhere,' she told me and asked for a cigarette, and then 'borrowed' my lighter. 'I'll light the cigarette in the dressing room.' She smiled and turned to leave. This, Shauli, is where I get to the interesting part. Now, just so you get the whole picture, this was a Ronson V lighter. It was special because it was blue, not the standard metallic. Of course, it also needed flints, cotton wool, and lighter fluid. I bought it three years before at a port and after a few months it had become part of my personality. I loved it and it was very precious to me. Sometimes I would feel it in between my fingers like nuns play with rosary beads. Most of the other patrons had already left the tavern. It was already 4:30 and there was still no trace of the tramp. *You've been duped, Shimi*, I smiled to myself. *There's no lighter and no screw*. I decided not to give up. I asked the bartender where I could find the owner of the tavern. He told me that his office was on the second floor. I lightly knocked on the door and then opened it. The owner said something in Greek, which I of course didn't understand. I spoke in English. I described the hostess and told him that my lighter had been robbed.

"'Ah,' he blurted. 'You must be talking about Melina. She left.'

"'She couldn't have,' I said. 'I sat next to the door and she didn't pass by me.'

"'Right, she left out the employee exit, so you didn't see her.'

"'Just so you know, I'm not going to leave this quietly. I'm going straight to the police.' This time his face looked serious.

"'You shouldn't report to them for some stupid lighter. Forget about this and save yourself some more trouble, especially since you're a foreign sailor.'

Melina and the Ronson V lighter

"The police station was really close to the tavern, on the next corner. I told the dispatcher what happened with Melina and the response I got from her boss, the tavern owner. The officer didn't show any interest in helping me.

"'Listen to me, you should take the bar owner's advice. You look drunk. You should call a taxi and return to your ship.'

"'That's exactly what I'll do,' I said. 'I'll go back to the ship, I'll see the captain and I'll submit a complaint to our embassy in Athens, and I'll make sure to emphasize that the local police did not handle the matter properly.' This seemed to sway the dispatcher. Finally, he picked up the telephone, and then two policemen arrived.

"'Come with us in our patrol car and show us the place.' When we got to the tavern, they said:

"'For your own safety, stay in the vehicle. We'll go inside.'

"Five minutes later, they returned, with my blue Ronson V in their hands. I thanked them and they brought me to a cab that took me back to the ship."

"Wow, way to go," Shauli said. "Because of your tenacity and determination, you succeeded. Where's the lighter now? I don't see it."

"Stolen…" Shimi said.

At 23:00, a pilot boarded the ship. The crew waited in the small mess room, used for coffee breaks, when they heard the announcement on the intercom:

"Deck crew report to the communication stations, coxswain – to the bridge." Carmel sent Shauli to the aft communication station, which was under the command of the second mate. Shimi was also part of the crew that was sent to the stern. He asked that Shauli be next to him when they unhitched the ship from the dock, and explained to him that when there were only two mooring ropes left connected after the rest were released, a lot of pressure gets placed on them as the ship begins to drift. This creates a dangerous situation for inexperienced sailors.

"So, watch how I release them, the moment that the second

mate gives the command." And indeed, the command was quick to come. The tugboat that was connected to the stern sounded its horn, and began to pull the stern away from the dock. The captain's call from the control bridge echoed through the intercom:

"Release the stern." The second mate immediately repeated the command and the crew simultaneously released the pressure from the cables. The mooring crew ashore unhitched the two cables and they were raised on deck quickly by the winch in order to ensure the safe operation of the propeller. When the mooring ropes were past the water's surface, even before they touched the deck, the second mate immediately reported that they were above the water's surface and that the stern was free.

"Thank you," the captain's reply sounded on the intercom. "Keep two men with you to release the tugboat and the rest send to fold and secure the gangway."

In the serving room Shauli made himself a sandwich and went on deck. The ship plowed through the water, leaving behind a long trail of white foam. The night was clear and the sky was full of stars. A cool wind came up from the sea that June night. He watched the blinking lights of Haifa grow distant and knew that the next time he'd see that view, three months would have passed. Fatigue fell upon him. *That's it*, he thought. *Time to go to sleep.*

Morning began when he heard several knocks on his door the voice of the on duty crewman:

"Good morning! It's 07:00."

Shauli got out of bed, went to the porthole, and pulled back the curtain. His eyes saw the fore of the ship cutting through the water. He took in a good deep breath, turned from the window, and went to the head.

The food at breakfast was more abundant than he'd ever seen. On the table were bowls of salad, dishes of olives, butter, cereal boxes, a pitcher of milk and a pitcher of coffee, white and yellow cheeses, crisp hot rolls, a jar of honey, and a jar of jam.

A messman asked him how he'd like his eggs and he ordered a two-egg omelet.

At 08:00, he was already standing near the paint supply room with the rest of the crew, waiting for the work assignments from Carmel the boatswain. Shauli was sent with three other crewmen to scrub the superstructure and swab the deck, from the control bridge to the main deck. They took with them a can of liquid soap, a plastic container that held a gallon of rust remover, two buckets, and several scrubbing brushes, both long and short. Raanan was in charge of the team. He gripped the water hose while the others scrubbed the bulkheads and swabbed the deck, dipping their brushes in the buckets full of a mix of soap and rust remover. Another team rinsed the main deck with seawater from bow to stern. The work continued through the entire workday, ending at 17:00, but by then the *Teverya* was clean and shiny.

The next day, the Aegean Islands came into view. The ship made its way through the water between the many islands. The view intoxicated Shauli's senses. He looked at the islands' white houses, their bays of turquoise water, the scattered lighthouses – each lighthouse different from the next, the fishing boats, sailboats, and yachts, sailing between the white-gold beaches. He thought that he'd like to lie on one of those fine beaches, sipping Ouzo and eating seafood, and maybe trying a nice tourist girl for dessert.

On the following afternoon, the Port of Piraeus was picked up on the ship's radar. The crew began the preparations for arrival at port. The Israeli Merchant Marines flag was hoisted on the stern mast. The Greek flag, the pilot flag, and the quarantine flag were flown from the upper bridge deck (monkey island). The Israeli flag was hoisted on the foremast of the ship's bow. The boatswain sent the coxswain to the bridge. Excitement permeated through Shauli ahead of arriving at his first foreign port. The ship stopped its gears when the pilot boat approached. Soon after the pilot boarded began the slow approach of the ship toward the port entrance, where two tugboats were waiting. One was tied to the bow and one to the stern. Their task was to help maneuver the ship to its intended dock. Shauli helped lower the gangway to the dock, then watched the people climb aboard to the deck. First – the port authorities, afterward – the ship agent and other shore personnel.

Gertie Van der Giessen

Seeing Perry leave at the dock was very difficult for her. She felt a great love for him. As soon as the ship disappeared beyond the horizon, she felt a deep emptiness and sadness inside. Gertie remained on the dock for several long minutes, staring into the water. While she was lost in her thoughts, she heard a voice from behind her:

"Gertie, where's the ship?" It was Nellie, who had come to say goodbye to Shauli.

"Sailed away. It left five minutes ago," Gertie answered.

"How did I miss him? I really wanted to surprise him. Even though we said our goodbyes yesterday night and we had a wonderful time together, but still, when I woke up this morning, I knew I had to see him before he set sail."

They walked out of the port together.

Club Oasis was packed with partygoers when Gertie got back to work. She glanced over at that table where she first met Perry. Sitting there now where two cheerful couples, laughing, drinking, and enjoying themselves. She again felt a longing for him begin to drip inside of her, making her feel helpless. Now she understood that love had its own kind of pain. Gertie decided to focus on work. She made the rounds between the tables and the other sections of the club to make sure everything was going smoothly. Sometimes she gave an instruction of one kind or another to a hostess or a waiter, if only to keep distracted. She noticed Nellie sitting at one of the tables with two customers, hosting them as a friend, in order to justify her presence. *She must feel like me*, Gertie thought. The hours passed slowly. All she wanted was to go home and crawl into bed, but she knew that there was no chance of that happening before 4:00 a.m. At midnight, Nellie came to her and requested to end her shift early.

"I know how you feel – I'm going through it, too. Of course, you're free to go," Gertie said. Nellie thanked her and turned to leave.

It felt like an eternity before her own shift ended. Now she could finally be by herself.

The days and the weeks – and after them, the months – passed one by one. She had a routine of every week visiting the office of the *Cormoran* ship agent and getting updated on where it was in the world. She purchased a world map and colorful pins. She taped the map up onto the wall of her kitchen and tracked the ship's route. She was the happiest person on earth when she'd receive a postcard or letter from Perry. She read what he wrote countless times, each word having great meaning. On those days, she would feel the blossoming of spring, the smell of tulips, the pristine lake of swans.

Nellie and Gertie shared with each other their feelings for Shauli and Perry, bringing them together, joined in fate. Indeed, their loves were themselves close friends, and somewhere out there, they were together in that tub on the water. Gertie told Nellie about the map in her kitchen and about the letters and postcards from Perry and Nellie told Gertie about the love that emanated from Shauli's letters.

Gertie's beauty was astounding, and there were many visitors at the club that tried their luck with her, but she knew how to turn them down gently and sweetly. One day in November, she checked her mailbox and found a letter from Perry. Not much was written there, but it made her float on air. She read it over and over again:

Gertie my love, tonight we're leaving the port of Melbourne in faraway Australia for New York. And apparently, the following port on the schedule is Rotterdam. So we should be meeting again this coming December. In any case, even if there is a change in our schedule, my contract is up at the end of that month, so I will come to you even if it is by plane.

Love, kisses, hugs, yours always,
Perry

His letter moved her immensely. Love and happiness engulfed her completely. Her love for him was powerful and uncontrollable. She knew that he was the man with whom she wanted to spend the rest of her life.

Priel Porat

At the end of dinner that Saturday, I felt the need to relax a bit in my cabin. Sitting together with Shauli all afternoon and the meal itself really weighed on me, not to mention the constant drinking. I barely began to rest before I heard a knock at my door. At the sound of my voice, the door opened. Shauli, Carlos Antonio, Ben-Tzur, and Yoav Artzi stood at the entrance.

"Can we come in?" they asked, and before I could answer, they were already inside, sitting down on the couch near the table. Without a choice, I pulled myself out of bed, hit the head, relieved my bladder, and washed my hands and face. Now I felt clean and refreshed and I could host them. Carlos Antonio had brought a bottle of whiskey, while Yoav had a plate piled high with cheeses, olives, sausage, pickles, vegetables, and rolls from the crew preparation room. What can seamen talk about among themselves? About their past experiences ashore, about their triumphs over the 'weaker sex', about a good meal, or a good buy at a port. You won't hear them speak about going to the theater or a gallery, or about a trip to a famous site. Though maybe a few do. Shauli felt that it was his turn to tell a story, and in the meantime, he also had written a song about his childhood on a kibbutz.

"So first I'll read the poem," he said.

Wildflowers

Tell me, my girl,
why have you gone, to never return?
Thinking upon your wild laughter,
my heart aches with longing.

As the spring breaks, and fields turn green,
I remember how we used to walk together,

amid the stalks of wheat,
along the furrows of the plows.

In fields of wildflowers,
I will whisper loving words,
I will gift you bouquets of wildflowers,
on the beautiful days of spring.

Come back to me, come back.
show me your glorious face.
How have you gone forever,
cut at the stem like a wildflower.

We all applauded Shauli. Ben-Tzur made the comment that the song reminded everyone of long lost loves that had never been fully realized. Carlos Antonio poured another round, while I asked Shauli to begin his story.

"OK, friends, this is a short story about Alejandra at the Port of Veracruz, Mexico. One morning we arrived at Veracruz and the weather was wonderful. When we docked, three Mexican mariachi players approached us, wearing sombreros on their heads and Hawaii-style leis around their necks. They plucked their guitars and sang in honor of our arrival. None of the crew understood the meaning of this surprise reception at the dock, but the mystery was soon solved. We had arrived in the middle of the annual Carnival celebrations. After finishing work and eating breakfast, the boatswain released three of us, me included, for a short shore leave, since the ship was to set sail in the early evening. Well, I was happy with what leave I was given, so I took a shower, changed clothes, and waited for my two friends to disembark. We caught a cab that had just left off other sailors at the adjacent ship and it sped off to town.

"The streets were crowded with people. Girls playfully threw confetti on us. People gathered on both sides of the main street waiting for the colorful parade that was to pass by at any moment.

We settled into a long one-story building that looked out onto the main street. It had many archways, which led to various cafés, restaurants, and souvenir shops. We sat down at one of the cafés and watched the people coming and going. A charming waiter arrived and since we wanted to try a typical Mexican drink, we ordered tequila. The drink went down so nicely that soon additional rounds started coming. The parade started passing our part of the street and we could hear the music of the accompanying band. Hundreds of men and women dancers dressed in fantastic costumes danced along the whole length of the parade. It kind of reminded us of Purim parades in Israel, but this was much, much grander. Every once in a while, young girls passed through the tables giving out celebratory kisses. We were in seventh heaven. We thoroughly enjoyed ourselves, and each passing moment the good feelings doubled, and tripled, and quadrupled, especially as the tequila began to work its magic. When the buzz in the street began to die down, we decided to check out a nightclub. When we asked, the waiter recommended a popular place. When I tried to stand up, something strange happened. I just couldn't stand up straight. It felt as if my butt was stuck to the chair. Only after a few tries did I succeed in getting up. I'm telling you, that tequila is like still waters running deep. It goes down easily, and without warning, it explodes.

"A taxi took us to the entrance of the club. We didn't have much time left. We had to return to the ship in two hours. As we walked in, we were immediately pounced on by three pretty Mexican maidens. The place was full of dozens like them. Alejandra, the one who 'picked' me, was very sweet and cute. She laughed and joked a lot, and I enjoyed her company. I didn't want to touch tequila again, and neither did my two friends, so we ordered beers for ourselves and some local drink for the girls. Sometimes I would go with Alejandra to the dance floor, but my head was still hammered by the tequila. At some point, I asked Alejandra if she'd agree to be alone with me. She said yes, so we went to one of the rooms upstairs intended for privacy. The room itself was modest and minimalist, but at the end there was a door to a bathing room. I didn't pay attention to the time. When we got out of bed, we went into the shower to wash up, enjoying ourselves, singing, and laughing together, not having a care in the world. Suddenly, the shower door opened and the chief steward burst in, ignoring our nude state, yelling at me:

"'Get your clothes on now. The ship is delayed because of you. The captain sent me to find you.'

"'How did you find me?' I stammered.

"'The guys that you were with told us where you were and one of the girls in the club pointed out the door to this room.'"

That's how his story with Alejandra ended. When the ship went out to sea, the boatswain came to Shauli and said that the captain had ordered that he go to the bridge. He demanded to know why he was late. In the end, he was given a fine and a note was made in the official log, a copy of which was submitted to the commissioner at the shipping division in Haifa.

The next morning, on Sunday, I went to the command bridge to sort out all the planned work assignments for the day together with Itzik Shahak the first mate. As usual, after our initial 'Good mornings,' he offered that I make myself a cup of coffee from the boiler in the chartroom.

"OK, Perry, today I want you to send a team to cargo hold one's tween deck. It doesn't have any cargo. It's empty, and that gives us the opportunity to swab and scrub it and to repair the wooden pallets. Also, today we're going to conduct fire and damage control drills. They're planned for 16:00. We'll stage a fire in the galley and afterward a water breech in the stern's cable storeroom."

When I was dividing up the jobs, I decided to send the carpenter Yoav Artzi to the storeroom, together with Ben-Tzur, Carlos Antonio, Ehud, and Jeremy the deck boy. I knew that the wooden pallets that were used to transport refrigerated cargo were heavy and would need four pairs of hands to move. Yoav took a toolbox with him, containing a hammer, pliers, a saw, nails, and a crowbar to repair the pallets. Yonatan, who had been on the midnight shift, would join them after lunch. According to the plan that was outlined to him, he was to work on paint repairs at the stern. Last but not least, my friend and companion Shauli was to take care of the gangway. That is, to grease and oil and the moving parts, check the status of the cables wound on the winch, and of course, to grease them and make sure everything was up to code. The day passed uneventfully. The two drills – the fire drill and damage control drill – were successful and to the satisfaction of those in charge, and then came dinner and afterward – free time.

I showered and changed into clean clothes. I barely managed to sit down before Yoav knocked on my door and invited me to his cabin to drink and chat. Here and there, another crewman would arrive, and the cabin began to get crowded. Well, the stories continued to flow, and this time it was Yoav's turn:

"This is the story of a very unique nautical clock," he began. "About eight years ago I sailed on a very old ship. She was in such bad shape, that sometimes we had to plug holes where seawater had begun to seep through. But she still stood up to waves and we never worried about a disaster. On this same voyage when my story occurred, my wife and two kids had joined me on ship. One evening we were sitting in the mess with a few other crewmen, when suddenly the first officer entered, holding two clocks in his hands.

"'Guys,' he said. 'Does anyone want a clock, or do I throw them overboard?' I immediately jumped at the chance and asked for one of the clocks. It was a Smiths Empire clock, made in Great Britain. It was an antique, maybe over half a century old. It was round and made of copper, which had to be polished with Brasso every once in a while. It had a glass hinged cover and it was engraved with Latin letters. The clock also had a key that needed to be wound every three days. The reason why it was being replaced was because electric clocks had been purchased for the ship. When we returned to Israel, I respectfully hung it up in my living room. When I looked at it, I would be reminded of the open sea, my short leaves, and the voyages, even though to others – landlubbers – it sounded strange.

"Days passed and then years, and one day, my marriage ended. I left the house, leaving everything behind, including, of course, my dear clock. Years later, about five, I was invited over to have lunch with a sailor friend of mine. On the wall of the living room hung a clock that looked very familiar. It was a little different, however, because it had an added lacquered wood frame. When my friend noticed that I was eying the clock, he smiled.

"'What's that smile?' I asked. He kept smiling and then answered:

"'This is your clock. Your ex-wife gave it as a gift to my wife. But take it, it's yours. I know how important this unique clock is to you.' Since that day, that clock hangs on the wall above my bed in my apartment, and I wind it every three days. That's the story of the antique nautical clock."

Ben-Tzur and Shauli simultaneously asked me to open up my notebook of songs. I didn't really feel like it, but everyone piled up on me.

"OK," I said, and went to my cabin to get the notebook

Novice

The sea thrashed and foamed
The ship rocked and rolled
And Moishe the novice
Threw up his whole soul

Chorus:
The white albatross
He knows he's in luck
He dives and he catches
All Moishe's muck

Yankele comes
To wipe Moishe's face
But poor Moishe's had
Enough of this place
Chorus

To go back ashore
Moishe pleads and he begs
But Yankel just laughs
From his head to his legs

Chorus

Months and years pass
And Moishe the new
Has become a skilled sailor,
A tough sonofabitch too

Chorus

And when he looks back
At those first days on deck
He laughs and he chortles
At all of that dreck

Time flew by, and it was late, so I decided to go back to my cabin. I couldn't sleep. I kept thinking about Gertie. I got out of bed and sat at the table. I poured myself a drink and lit a cigarette. I was consoled by the fact that I would see her again soon. The ship was sailing the Pacific Ocean for a few days already, en route to the Panama Canal, and from there to the Port of New York. The last port before crossing the Atlantic to Rotterdam, where Gertie was expecting me and waiting for me, I hoped. Melbourne, Julie, and Nicole, had already been behind me for ten days. The Jalopy had already crossed Phillip Bay, the Bass Strait, the Tasman Sea, Cook Strait between the North and South islands of New Zealand, and now it was sailing the ocean in a large circle. That is, the further south you go toward the pole, the Earth's latitudinal lines become smaller. Therefore, this type of sailing shortens the distance. But you always must take into account the weather and the state of the water. It isn't safe for the ship to sail during the harsh winter months or the storms that come with them.

The next morning when I went up to the bridge, Itzik told me that we were changing our route. The wireless operator gave Captain Bar-Noy a weather forecast, warning of an approaching storm with winds hitting 9 on the Beaufort Scale.

"At the end of breakfast, get two teams together. One will go with you to check the bow and make sure everything is tied and secure, and the other one will do the same at the stern, including the decks of the structure."

"OK, chief," I said, repeating his instructions.

I sent Shaul Shauli with a few crewmen to begin checking the stern while the rest of the crew came with me to check the bow. During the deck work, I noticed that the sea was rising. At first, it became covered in a thin film of foam, but toward noon, deep waves were forming. Winds began to blow and only grew in intensity. Even the white foam became thicker and flakes rose up from it. Our checks were completed right before the cruel sea attacked us. We secured all of the doors to the superstructure and sealed all the portholes and skylights to insulate them from the sea's wrath. It really is unbelievable how quickly the weather changes out on the ocean. The Jalopy began to be tossed around, up and down, left and right, but we were shielded within the structure. In the galley, they secured the pots to the stove in order to prevent them from moving, and in the two messes, officers and crew poured water from a kettle onto the tablecloths to keep the dishes in place. A rough sea is unpleasant. The rocking is not easy on any of us. Who doesn't love a calm sea, with a red sun setting over the horizon, dolphins jumping out of the water and playing with the bow, seagulls hovering in hopes to pick off food thrown overboard? But sometimes – and it happens often – the sea does not care about our feelings, and it rages and raves, because it is his kingdom, and we – whether we like it or not – are subject to his will, until his anger passes.

The storm raged for three days before the sea calmed down. Finally, the sky changed and began to smile down on us. The blue sky with streaks of high cirrus clouds along with the calm waters created in us a holiday atmosphere. We were now in the heart of the Pacific Ocean, counting the days before we finished crossing and entered the Panama Canal.

Work at sea is really quite routine. Three crewmen divide the sailing shifts, while they help out with the deck duties during the daytime hours. The rest of the crew are usually busy with paint repairs, swabbing the decks, fixing damaged cables, greasing moving parts, etc. Once a week a lifeboat drill or fire drill is conducted. Even the meals are set according to schedule. On Wednesdays and Saturdays lunch is chicken with rice. And that's where the problem arises regarding the distribution of chicken pieces, as most of the crew prefers dark meat over white meat. So – besides the "privileged" crew, such as the boatswain, carpenter, and donkeyman – the crew is divided so that half get the leg and thigh and the other half has to be satisfied with the chicken breast, until the next meal's rotation.

The crew also spends time in the day room, where there are newspapers, games, a stereo system, and television. They can watch fairly new releases, since the ship agent brings movies to the ship when it's docked at port. There's also a pretty well-stocked library available to the crew. And of course, once a month there's the BBQ, which is the star of the voyage.

The days passed one after another, and there we were on another Friday night. This time we sat in Ben-Tzur's cabin, drinking, chatting, smoking, and tasting the delicacies that he'd prepared for us. At some point, I began to tell them a story about something that happened to me years before, when I was still an able seaman, and this is how it went:

"One day, I was sailing on a ship that was transporting wooden logs from West Africa. The ship's captain, in addition to his official position, was also a professional hunter. During the voyage, he would carve handles out of fine African wood for his hunting rifles. He also fashioned a target on the far bow deck for target practice, testing out the handles he'd made every once in a while.

"Work onboard was very physically demanding. We had to weave an endless amount of steel hoisting cables for raising logs; change worn derricks cables; inspect and repair pulley wheels on which the hoisting cables lifted and lowered the wooden logs; and of course the regular work of day-to-day ship maintenance. Since I was still serving as an able seaman at the time, I couldn't really 'spoil myself' much. The ship would usually stop at the Port of Las Palmas in the Canary Islands in order to get equipment and fresh supplies before continuing to the African ports. Our first stop was in Freetown, Sierra Leone, where we began to unload various cargo we'd taken on in Haifa. We continued unloading the cargo at the different ports, as the ship sailed southward. At the final unloading port, a special crew of African men boarded the ship. They would remain with us on the voyage as we loaded the new cargo at the various ports. Their job was to load the wooden logs into the ship's holds, and when they were full, to continue loading into the tween deck and on deck. We arranged for them living quarters in the bow stowage, which was large enough to accommodate them. They had their own cook and in all practicality, they were separate from the ship's crew. Our relationship with them was shaky. Eventually, we reached the mouth of the Nyanga River in Gabon, where we laid anchor A guide arrived for the ship's captain to accompany him on a hunting trip. Once he was dressed in his khaki hunting outfit – including a hat, binoculars, sunglasses, and a pistol at his hip – he disembarked. His guide carried three of his hunting rifles, of different types. The ship remained in the charge of the first mate for the next three days.

"Gabon is located right on the equator, and most of its land is covered in rainforest, hence the flourishing logging industry. Bunches of wooden logs would travel along the river to the estuary. They were bound – five at a time – by iron chains hooked to rings fastened to the wood. The logs were marked with different colors, whose meanings I never understood. The next morning, the first mate decided to conduct a lifeboat training drill. The portside lifeboat was lowered to the embarkation deck and was immediately raised back into place and secured properly. The second mate, who was in charge of executing the drill, gave us a secretive smile.

"'Now let's lower the boat into the water and take a spin.' When we were in the boat, strapped in our life vests, we released the lines and sealed the drainage plug. We lowered the boat to the embarkation deck and got in. The carpenter and third mate remained on the embarkation deck, and at the second mate's orders, they lowered it into the water, while the engine was running on idle.

"We sailed up the river for about a half hour, amazed by the wild landscape that we saw; the monkeys jumping through the trees, the parrots and other colorful birds, the crocodiles sleeping along the river bank, and the sounds of hidden, unknown animals. At one point, we saw a hut, and beside it a man gesturing for us to come over. He was surrounded by six women, but the second mate declined his offer. Reluctantly, we returned to the ship and raised the boat back into place.

"The African crew's work was grueling. They had to separate the logs from the bunches and secure each one of them individually to the derricks cables that were lowered to them. Each log weighed a few tons. And it was in shark-infested water. Sometimes, one of the men would slip on a log and fall into the water. If he wasn't quick enough to jump back onto the log, he could be lucky and only lose a leg or two, but if he wasn't, he wouldn't be heard from again, and only a bloodstain could be seen rising to the water's surface, hinting at the tragedy that struck the pour soul below.

"On the ship were a few officers' wives who traveled with us. After a backbreaking day of work, the black men would strip out of their clothes and wash themselves with the water hose on deck. They were packed with tools that any white man would be jealous of – something hard to imagine – and sometimes during their regular shower time, we could see the wives peeking out of their portholes to enjoy the view.

"On the third day, the captain returned to the ship with the carcass of a crocodile that he successfully shot along with a few fowl. His plan was to skin the crocodile and dry it out, along with its head and jaws. When he was finished, he gave the remaining meat to the black crewmen, and of course, they were happy with the unexpected gift.

"The ship was set to sail the next morning to the next loading port. That day, after lunch, I went aft to smoke a cigarette and watch the Africans work. Suddenly, I saw a large shark approaching the ship. I ran to Arieh, the ship's cook and a friend of mine, and asked him for a large piece of meat and the hook that he usually used to hang a quarter beef. When he gave it to me, I went back to the stern, connected a steel cable to the end of the hook and wound it around the winch drum, while I stuck the sharp end of the hook through the meat. I used the winch to lower the hook with the meat into the water and waited for something to happen. I leaned on the stern's railing, watching the water, and then the unbelievable happened. Suddenly, the cable went tight with a loud crack and a giant shark, ravenous and greedy, got caught on the hook.

"'Shark!' I shouted, and several crewmen ran toward me. I asked one of them to help reel in the hook using the winch and the shark slowly began to rise out of the water, until he was close to the railing. At this point, I asked someone to raise the stern derrick so that I could wrap hoisting cables around the shark and at the same time release him from the winch. The shark was so close to me. He could have swallowed three people at once with his mouth. Soon, everyone began to hear about the shark's capture, including Arieh the cook. While the derrick was being prepared, a single shot was heard. I saw the shark jerk and then the cable straighten. The shark slipped into the water and disappeared. I glared at the captain, standing calmly on the deck of the bridge's starboard side wing, dressed in his hunting outfit and holding his rifle. I was furious about what he did, but I couldn't do anything. The shot had endangered many of the crewmen who had crowded the stern. It was such a shame, I felt so bad for losing the shark. I'd wanted to dry out the jaws for myself and give the meat to the Africans, who had suffered so much from the animal."

Everyone shared in my sadness over losing the shark and also added that the arrogant captain had made a mistake in killing it, since he hadn't been part of the capture itself. As we all know, the captain is the 'god' of the ship, even if he isn't always right. We continued to sit, drinking and telling stories from the current voyage and previous ones. We loved those evenings where wet gathered together and enjoyed ourselves. People on land cannot understand life at sea. To them, it looks crazy. It doesn't 'sit right' with them. But to us, this is life at its essence, and we wouldn't trade it for anything – even if they wanted to dress us up in a fancy suit and give us a swanky office and a fat paycheck. The main problem is that it's much harder for the married ones among us than for those of us who are still single. They always speak about their families and their children who they've left behind, and of course, it isn't easy for them at all. When one of them receives a letter from back home at one of the ports, he usually shuts himself in his cabin and thirstily reads its contents. For him, these are the moments of happiness and longing for family, for the rooms of his house filled with familiar objects – souvenirs he brought back from his travels, and for the space where he spends time with his children.
The night began to turn into the wee hours of the morning and yawns began to emerge from some of us, including myself, a sign of the end of a great evening. We separated with 'good nights,'

but not before we thanked Ben-Tzur for the wonderful hospitality. I went back to my cabin, and the first thing I did was empty my bladder. All that was left was to undress, get into bed, and dream about all that is sweet and nice in the world, including, of course, loving Gertie.

The harsh winter began to return as the ship went northward toward the Panama Canal. The ocean waves rose higher and higher and the wind conditions only worsened, due to the weather and the sea. Spray covered the ship, halting deck work. The fierce wind whistled through closed doors and the portholes were washed with every wave that battered the deck. The meteorological forecast that we received showed no change for the coming days. In addition, a dense fog made hindered visibility, which forced Captain Bar-Noy and his pipe out of his cabin to the bridge, to turn on the fog lights, put steering into manual, add another sailor as lookout, and focus his eyes on the radar. That's normal procedure when visibility is down. There were instances when the captain had to stay on the bridge for two days or more; the messman had to bring meals to the bridge, and he would sometimes need to catch a few winks on the couch. Those days, we worked on indoor jobs – we swabbed the passageways and made paint repairs where needed. Crewmen waddled like ducks along the passageways because of the constant rocking of the ship. In the mess, the messman poured water over the tablecloths in order to keep the dishes in place and also to prevent falls and breaks. Some members of the crew lost their appetite, while others became especially hungry. How can that be explained? Perhaps it's psychological – to spite the storm and show how much it doesn't affect them, how it's just like another day. But if we're completely honest, who doesn't love to see the bright blue sky, the round disk of the sun, the still, marble sea, and the clear horizon?

There were a few days left in November before December would arrive. That was the month when I contract would finish. I could feel Gertie waiting for me, counting the days until we'd see each other again, just like me. Sometimes in the evening, I would go through her letters again, reading them passionately. I had a few surprises for her – gifts and souvenirs from the various ports wrapped in colorful boxes. They were sure to make her happy. I thought about trying to convince her to leave the Oasis and come with me to Israel. It could be a good idea. I'll leave the sea and try to do something else. Maybe we could use the money from my pension to open a small business or store and make an honest living together. I continued toying with my dreams about the future, even though I knew somehow that it wasn't realistic. There wasn't anything for her in Israel, and me – I could never leave the sea.

The ocean kept raging and surging, accompanied by ferocious, cold winds, until we reached the bay at Balboa, the entrance to the Panama Canal. The portside anchor was dropped and gripped the bottom in order to prevent the ship from drifting into the many other ships waiting to enter the convoy into canal. The bay was calm, in comparison to the ocean, but a tropical rain poured down on us nonstop. Toward 04:00 the next morning, the crew was woken up in order to prepare for entrance into the canal. A pilot boat approached the starboard side and two pilots climbed aboard. Immediately after, another boat arrived and a Panamanian hitching crew also came on deck. Half of the crew turned toward the bow and half to the stern. Four tugboats also approached – two at the bow and two at the stern. The Panamanian crew began to hitch them on. Two crewmen helped them using the winch.

Even though we'd crossed the Panama Canal a number of times before, it was always exciting to sail on it; to watch the movement of the engines connected to the sides of the ship with steel cables, guiding it through the locks that are secured by gates. To watch how in minutes, the locks are filled with water, raising or lowering the ship according to the heights of the lakes the ship was to enter. The surrounding green rainforests tangled around the waterfalls through which the canal's water flows are, too, a sight to behold. Monkeys can be seen jumping between the trees' thick branches, along with colorful tropical birds flying and singing above, and perhaps even an alligator lazing on the bank.

Toward the evening, we'd arrived at the other end of the canal, in the waters of the Caribbean and the Atlantic Ocean. Two crewmen folded up the tents that had been set up on both wings of the bridge for the pilots to protect them from the tropical rain. This kind of rain usually falls in those regions nonstop. Another crew was busy securing the connection cables, and the carpenter Yoav Artzi secured the heavy anchors in place. Steering was set to automatic, and helmsman Carlos Antonio could lay below to the crew preparation room and make himself a hot cup of coffee. Traversing from one ocean to another gives you the feeling of shifting between worlds, even if they are no different in color or foam. Despite this, you enter a world that is more familiar than the one you've left. Even the passing ships are more familiar than those you encounter in the Pacific, even though they, too, are the same. It's just a feeling that you get. New York was ever closer, and with it, mood had improved toward the end of the long voyage that had started all the way in Melbourne.

Shaul Shauli

In the evening, Shimi invited Shauli out.

"Let me take you to the 'Ronson lighter' club," he said. They hailed a cab and drove to the Piraeus city center. The two walked with the rest of the crowd, who had taken advantage of the summer evening to walk along the promenade bordering the Aegean Sea. Mothers pushed babies in strollers with their husbands at their sides, smiling at each other and occasionally leaning over to look at their babies, happiness beaming on both of their faces. There were also couples in love, young and old, along with children. Everyone enjoyed the pleasant evening, including Shimi and Shauli. When darkness fell, they went to a fashionable tavern and ordered a typical Greek meal to the sounds of bouzouki music. At the end of the delicious meal, they went to the club, sat down at the bar, and ordered a drink. Shimi looked around for Melina, but she was nowhere to be seen. Finally, he gathered the courage to ask the bartender about her.

"She doesn't work here anymore," he answered.

They didn't really like the place – it was boring and lifeless – so they ended up returning to the ship.

As time passed, Shauli began to gain experience. He was a curious and disciplined sailor and was always ready for any task or mission that was put to him. He worked swiftly and spared no effort to please his superiors. The crew liked him a lot and enjoyed his company. At port, girls would always chase him. Shauli was charismatic, charming, and knew how talk to women. He was also very handsome, which attracted the nymphs like bees to a flower. Shimi was his best friend onboard and if they weren't on loading duty at port, they would always go out together. Shauli continued working on the ship with Shimi for more than two years. Its set route allowed them to return to Haifa every two-and-a-half months. The stay in Israel would last about two weeks. Over the stay, Shauli always made sure to invite a substitute crewman from the shore gang to his cabin. He'd leave him a bottle of liquor, beers, and a few packs of cigarettes. On these breaks, Shauli would fill his apartment with good things to eat, most of which he'd purchased at the various ports and the rest he'd get at the local supermarket. Of course, he'd always dedicate a day or two to visit Kibbutz Sdot Yam. Bossem was now 19 years old, beautiful, tall, and curvy. He would open his bag, tell her stories from the voyage, but not get into details. Rena asked worryingly if he was settled in the apartment and wondered if perhaps he should return home, where his room had remained the same since he'd left it. But Shauli explained that he needed his privacy and that she needed to accept his decisions and the life that he'd chosen. At his age, he needed to be independent and live they way he wanted. When it was time to leave and go back to Haifa, sadness would wash over Rena's face. Shauli's features reminded her of her late husband Maxim and she felt as if the world had left her alone in her sorrow. Bossem, on the other hand, would hug and kiss him warmly and would wish him luck on his next voyage.

The first day out at sea would leave a feeling of emptiness. There was a feeling of disconnecting from the solid land and from the loved ones left behind. But within a day or two that feeling changes and you get into a new routine at sea and a new journey. Who knew what adventures lay ahead or how the voyage would end?

Shauli gained enough sailing days to apply for a specialization to get the rank of able seaman, a level that designated a skilled sailor and resulted in a higher paying job. The first mate gave him a very good recommendation. After two years aboard the *Teverya*, when it once again returned to the Haifa Port, and after his replacement boarded the gangway, all that was left was to say goodbye to Shimi and the rest of his fellow crewmen. He gathered his things, which were already packed and ready, and disembarked. Every few steps he'd turn his head and look back in sorrow and longing. Shauli registered for able seaman studies at the Ministry of

Transport, Administration of Shipping and Ports, following a letter from the shipping company in addition to the first mate's recommendation. The classes were held on a small ship that was moored permanently at the Kishon Port and had been converted especially for studies and training courses for all the ranks. The specialization including knowledge and expertise regarding all the various types of ropes, the different knots that are used on ships for different purposes, braiding and splicing ropes and cables, and general knowledge regarding anchors and the parts of the ship, putting out fires, damage control, life boat lowering and understanding all of the crewmen's tasks in lowering the life boat. He also learned about survival and inflatable rescue raft. At the end, the trainees had to pass both a practical and theoretical exam. The course was ten days long, and at the end, he received a temporary certificate for the Ministry of Transport stating that he successfully passed all of the necessary exams. A month later, he received in the mail his official able seaman's certification, which included his name, the official certificate, and a red wax seal. Another week passed and he received a letter from the shipping company Zim, announcing that he was accepted for a contract in the company. Now he would no longer have to stand in the long line at the Seaman Bureau. Two days later, he received a phone call. He was told that he was to report to the company's office, at the crew division, to arrange his embarkation.

Late in the summer of 1964, Shauli found himself climbing the gangway of the ship *Deganya*. She was the sister ship to the *Teverya*, and he was of course happy about that. After reporting to the first mate, and then to the chief steward, Shauli went to look for the boatswain. He knocked lightly on his cabin door. A muffled 'yes' came from the other side. When he opened the door, he saw the boatswain sitting at his table, a bottle of whiskey at his side and the whole cabin cloudy with cigarette smoke. Shauli introduced himself as an able seaman who just then boarded the ship and told him that he'd already reported to the first mate and the chief steward.

"Nice to meet you," he replied. "My name's Priel, or Perry, as everyone calls me." When the boatswain asked Shauli how long he'd been sailing he answered:

"More than two years," and added that he knew the ship as he'd sailed on her sister ship, *Teverya*.

"Great," Perry said. "Now I'll show you your cabin. After dinner, you're on deck duty from 18:00 until midnight."

The next evening, the *Deganya* went to sea. Shauli was assigned to the stern crew. After the lines were raised and the tugboat released, the crew were busy with securing the ropes, by first placing the eye around the bitts and then wrapping them in three figure eights, so that once at sea, the rope wouldn't be swept up during a storm. The winches were also covered with canvas tarps to protect them from the salty seawater. The sparkling lights of Haifa on the coast and the Carmel ridge began to fade away against the background of the yellow moon, its reflection dancing in the water along with the silver wake of the propeller. When the work was finished and the gangway was in place and the doors to the superstructure were hermetically secured, the crewmen went to the small mess adjacent to the preparation room for a special night meal, which Perry the ship's boatswain had prepared ahead of time. Finally, tired but happy, Shauli went to bed.

The *Deganya* sailed to the same ports as the *Teverya*, so that Shauli was already familiar with the route, the places, the ship agents, and the suppliers. Perry noticed that Shauli was an exceptional, skilled sailor. There was no need to repeat things, he would immediately understand his duties and perform them without any mistakes. His dedication and attitude toward any task that was asked of him was above that of the average sailor. Shauli was a great help to Perry. Every boatswain wished for a sailor like him. When they left the Port of Piraeus for the Port of Livorno in Italy, and after they'd completed their work, Perry invited Shauli to his cabin for a toast after dinner. Shauli accepted the invitation with gratitude.

Perry's cabin was spacious, clean, and very orderly. The whiskey was already set on the table, with two glasses next to it, along with a plate filled with cheeses, sausage, sardines, vegetables, and two rolls. When Perry asked where he lived, he answered that he was already living in the Carmel, but that he came from Kibbutz Sdot Yam, and his mother and sister were still there.

"And what about your father?" Perry asked.

"My father fell in the War of Independence," he said.

So they sat, having an exploratory conversation, with the liquor bringing them closer to one another. At one point, Shauli asked Perry what had brought him to the sea.

"My love for the sea began when I was still just a boy. It's a long story, and I've never talked about it, but if you want to hear it, I'll gladly tell you."

Perry refilled the glasses, tasted something from the plate, and began his story.

"I was born in the winter of 1942 in the Hadar neighborhood of Haifa. My mother went into labor and my father went to call the ambulance to take her to the hospital. But by the time he returned, I'd already emerged into the world. During the events leading up to the founding of the state, he was seriously wounded by Arab rioters and had to spend long months in various hospitals. He suffered from terrible pains, for which there was no cure. His everyday activities were impaired. He also was on painkillers. When I was four, my mom got sick with cancer and was hospitalized. Left with no choice, I was moved to a facility. My sister, who was also still a child, couldn't take care of me. When I turned five, my mom passed away and escaped her agony. A year later, my father remarried. She had a nice apartment in the Bat Galim neighborhood, on the Mediterranean Sea, and we all moved there. Until this day, I don't know why my stepmother hated me. She would punish me for no reason. I suffered greatly from her. It was hard for me to be near her, so I would find refuge in my little room. One day, I went down to the beach, which was only a few meters from our yard. I walked along the soft sand, looking for seashells and picking up the most beautiful ones. To this day I love seashells. I have quite a collection and I even bought a catalog of different shells from around the world. As I grew older, I would spend more and more time on the beach; I learned to swim and to dive. I studied the seabed, the rocks, and the sandy clearing between the rocks. I even managed to catch fish with my bare hands and there wasn't anyone happier then me when that would happen. Most of all, I loved to dive into the depths, sometimes until it got dark. I always wondered what lay beyond the horizon. The sea was so huge and vast and my curiosity swelled. I discovered sea adventure books, like *Robinson Crusoe*, *Martin Eden*, and *Moby Dick*, and many more like them, and I read them hungrily and passionately. My stepmother didn't allow my classmates to visit me and didn't allow me to go see them. One day my teacher came to our house and really gave it to the wicked stepmother. She even warned her that if she continued her appalling behavior, she'd call social services and the police. But nothing helped to improve her attitude toward me.

"I was nine when I first discovered the Haifa Port. It was about a kilometer-and-a-half walk from the house. The smells of the port, the many ships, the boats, all of these left an indescribable impression on me. At the southern end of the breakwater, I saw a group of kids about my age practicing with a rowboat. Once I got closer, I saw that they were part of the 'Sea Scouts' sporting league. I went to the office that was next to the equipment storeroom and requested to sign up for the league. I was told that I needed to go to the Haifa branch for registration and issuing of a membership card, and that's what I did. I went the whole way on foot. I had to get to the port twice a week for rowboat training. It was on Tuesday afternoons and Saturday mornings. For an entire year, I rowed with the other children in the group. It was a very integral experience for me and it helped me forget my stepmother. Sailing the length of the port and between the ships increased my curiosity even more. Already at that age I had come to the decision that one day, I'd sail on one of those ships."

Perry paused his sad, absorbing story to refill the glasses. He lit a cigarette and said:

"Now you're starting to understand what brought me to the sea – at the beginning it was a way to escape the awful reality of my childhood, but it quickly turned into a love that can't be defined."

Shauli sipped his whiskey, sitting quietly in hopes to hear the rest of the story of Perry's life, with whom he already felt a close friendship.

Perry continued: "After a whole year of rowing training, we began learning how to sail. We learned how to raise the sail, how to sail upwind and downwind, how to steer, how to reinforce the rigging, and the correct knots. During this period, my situation at home had become unbearable. The wicked stepmother bothered me nonstop. My father could not function and never intervened against her deeds. One day she sat in front of me, hiked up the hem of her dress, and exposed her vagina in front of my eyes. I was not yet eleven. My sister – who had begun to work and was basically funding the whole family with her paycheck – pushed hard to take me out of that hellhole and finally succeeded. I was sent to a kibbutz. My years on the kibbutz did good for me. I was happy; it was a time of peace and calm. I loved the fields of clover, the hills surrounding the kibbutz, the children in my age group with whom I grew up, the fish ponds, and of course the swimming pool.

"The period during which I was sent to the kibbutz was only a few months after the beginning of the gradual end to the regime of austerity in 1952. Austerity measures were placed on the citizens of Israel, which had been established after the declaration of independence and the following War of Independence. Many immigrants had flooded Israel and the population had doubled. Construction, transportation, and agriculture had to be financed. The country's revenues could not cover its expenses. This created a difficult situation for the new country. There was a food shortage, and in order to survive it, Prime Minister David Ben-Gurion instituted a period of austerity, during which food and goods would be rationed in equal portions to the citizens. A special department was created called the Ministry of Rationing and Supply, headed by Dov Yosef. There was a severe cut in food allotments, as well as clothing, shoes, and furniture. Each citizen was given coupons to buy goods. People would stand in long lines at the ice and fuel wagons. A bell would ring when they arrived. At the butcher shop and the grocery store, people would clutch their coupons distributed by Dov Yosef and his ministry, knowing that when it would get to their turn, they'd be able to buy, for example, a dozen eggs a month, 750 grams of meat, 200 grams of cheese, and luckily, 3500 grams of potatoes. Of course, the rest of the foodstuffs were assigned similar amounts. Fortunately for me, at the kibbutz there was an abundance of everything and we did not lack anything.

"Kibbutz life was great. I hiked around Israel, getting to know the country intimately. We participated in many night activities, like night field training in the open hills and fields. There we learned to listen, recognize, and identify the calls of the various wild animals, birds, and reptiles. There were also many sports, which led to competition between the kids. Later, I was earned the right to take the mare out to the pasture and the cows to the fields of clover. My happiness soared, and yet the call of the sea and its mysteries had not left me, even during this wonderful time. I was always thinking about it and about what lay beyond the horizon.

"When I was approaching my 15th birthday, an event happened that changed my life. On her latest visit, my sister told me that my father was getting divorced and that his evil wife had left the house. She was to thank for this, as her father had finally come to understand that he had made a mistake. I immediately told her that I would come home."

At this point, Perry asked to take a break in his story, as the memories of his childhood were difficult for him.

"Don't push yourself," Shauli told him. "What you went

through was harrowing and fascinating. Let's have another drink, and when you feel the need, I'd love to hear the rest."

There was a heavy silence. Perry looked deep in thought. They sipped their drinks quietly, and eventually, they changed subjects and began to talk about the upcoming work that was expected of them. Perry felt a growing affection for the sailor that sat in front of him. His face revealed curiosity and anticipation. So he decided to continue his story.

"I said goodbye to the kibbutz and to my friends. My sister came to help me and we returned together to the house in Bat Galim. Swimming in the sea, diving, and trying to catch fish with my hands returned to me all of those things that I'd longed for during my time on the kibbutz. Despite that, I would only look back in fondness on my time there. I heard later about the naval school and I immediately applied. For two months I studied diligently for the entrance exam, but unfortunately, I failed. The kibbutz's school curriculum – with its focus on agriculture and water – was very far from what they taught in the city. So, I tried to get into the Mevo'ot Yam naval school in Moshav Michmoret, which focused less on entrance examinations, but my father strongly objected.

"'You lived on a kibbutz! Go learn at an agricultural school.' And so, without choice, I studied an entire year, successfully, at that same school an hour and a half away from home. After the first year, I was sixteen and old enough to know what I really wanted to do. I had no doubt at all that my heart's desire was the sea. I returned to Bat Galim and the next day I took myself off to the port. I went to the fishing boats and asked for a job, but they turned me away. While I wandered the port, I arrived at the service boats pier, which transported sailors to the ships moored at the breakwater and the ships anchored in the bay outside of port. The office wasn't far away and after I was told where it was exactly, I went there. A tall, thin man wearing a black cap sat at the desk speaking into a walkie-talkie, probably with one of the boats. He gestured for me to sit and when he had finished, asked what I wanted. I told him about my great love for the sea and that

I wished to work on the service boats. He then asked for my age.

"'Sixteen,' I replied. He stared at me and after a little while said:

"'At the moment, we don't have any space for a student on the service boats. In the meantime, you could work in our small shipyard. You would help building the boats, which is interesting work. You would also become familiar with the structure of the boat and how to construct it.' I was happy and grateful for the opportunity. He got up from his chair, came over to me, and shook my hand.

"'I wish you good luck. Go to the shipyard – it's located at the southern end of the port, near the breakwater. I'll already let them know by phone that you're coming. By the way, what's your name, kid?'

"'Perry,' I answered."

Perry paused his enthralling story again. He poured another round, got up, and hit the head. When he came back, Shauli noticed that his hair and face were slightly wet.

"OK, Shauli, let's continue," he said.

"I worked at the shipyard for two months, and I really got an education. And then one day, a lanky man from the service boats office came to tell me that I was to report to him the next morning, as I was being appointed as an apprentice on one of the boats. Shauli, you have no idea how overcome I was by happiness. I was walking on air and felt as if the whole world was smiling at me. They put with a veteran skipper, and from him I learned how to operate a boat. At the beginning, my job hitch or unhitch the ropes, to check the rubbing strake and make sure there was no damage to the boat, to swab and scrub, and to make paint repairs. But with time, I began to learn the steering and to sail the boat under the skipper's supervision. The sailors would arrive to the bay on ships, and after we helped them release their belongings that they'd tied to the ropes, they'd give us cigarettes – that's one of the reasons I began smoking. I admired them. They were dressed in the types of clothes that you didn't see in Israel then. I ached for the day that I'd become one of them.

"I worked for an entire year on the boats. I was already more than 17-years-old, trained and experienced, but the urge to sail had not left me for even a moment. At the same time, I made friends with someone my age; smiling, happy, and cheerful. We would hang out together and even tried our luck with one of the prostitutes who worked the streets around the port. It turned out that his uncle was a partner in a small shipping company. They had one small ship with a capacity of 850 tons gross, and their office was near the port. He suggested that we go by the office and talk to his uncle and maybe we'd sail together. His uncle strongly opposed letting his nephew go to sea, but he did take me on as deck boy. At the Shipping and Ports department, they told me that without a signed written consent from my father, I could not be issued a seaman's book, as I was still a minor. At first, my father refused outright, but after a heated argument, and some help from my sister, he finally relented and signed.

"We went out to sea on a winter's evening. The small ship rocked in the water and I felt my stomach rise. Even though I'd already experienced that type of situation on a boat, this time it felt different. Perhaps because the living quarters were in the bow next to the paint storage and the fumes would drift back to us. Anyway, that was my first and last time that I threw my guts up during a storm at sea.

"The voyages were short, to the ports of Turkey and Cyprus. We'd return to Israel every two weeks and stay there for over a week. The boatswain really abused me, but I accepted his behavior with understanding. He was a Cypriot Greek and didn't understand Hebrew, so he would speak to me in English, which I hadn't yet gotten the hang of. When he would ask me to bring something from the storeroom, I knew that he'd get angry if I didn't bring what he wanted, so I would always bring back a few different things, hoping that one of them was what he'd asked for. After a while, I began to pick up the language and understand more and more names of tools and parts of the ship. Nautical language is very different than what they speak on land, so much so that people on land wouldn't even be able to decipher it.

"Six months had passed since I started working on the ship, I was raised to the rank of ordinary seaman, and one day the captain let me take the place of the regular veteran sailor at the helm while the pilot boarded the control bridge to direct the ship into port. The fact that a novice sailor took his place enraged him.

"I worked on the deck of that small ship for ten months, a period that will follow me for the rest of my life, and of course, only for good, but I had to leave once I got my military draft notice. At the end of that same year, I found myself on a bus with other new recruits on our way to base. At the end of basic training, I asked to be accepted to the navy, but I was told that our class was not intended for the navy, but rather to other corps. My world fell into darkness; I didn't know how to accept the bad news. But serendipitously, two days after I'd completed field training and just before I was to be assigned to a particular troop, a few officers dressed in naval uniforms came to visit. All of the recruits gathered outside of our tents. They sat us down in front of the officers, who gave us a serious presentation praising Shayetet 13 (Israeli Navy special forces). At the end, they said that anyone who felt suited for it and had the necessary motivation, should report to the designated tent to sign up. I felt like a drowning man being passed a lifeline, an actual ray of light in the dark.

"About thirty soldiers reported to the tent. We were asked questions and our medical record was checked. The instructors were also asked to give their opinions regarding the candidates. A truck arrived the next morning. Seven candidates were called by name and told to climb aboard, myself among them. Shauli, this was in the middle of a cold and rainy January and my balls froze. At the end of the trip, we'd arrived at the Shayetet base. I won't go into the details of the exercises, tests, and medical exams that we went through that day. Don't forget that when I was a kid, I'd swum and dove like a fish in his natural habitat, and this of course helped me. After a personal interview with the fleet commander and the field officers, I was told that I'd get answer at the training base. The truck brought us back and we still didn't know whether or not we'd get in. On the following day in the afternoon, I was called into the platoon commander's office. He handed over a draft notice for the naval special forces. He looked at me with admiration and said:

"'You're the only one who got in. I wish you good luck.' I thanked him, saluted, and left the room.

"We were a small group that was put into the long training course, but before we began, we had to sign on for a year and half of extended service. The girls on base would steal glances at us and the food was basically gourmet compared to the terrible stuff we got in basic training. I felt as if I were on the top of the world, but not for long. During training, I'd see merchant ships peacefully sailing by. During my free moments – which were few and far between – I'd sit on the cliff and look out onto the horizon, watching for merchant ships. All I wanted to do was to serve on a destroyer and then return to the merchant marines. It had never occurred to me to do extended service. I knew that they'd tempt me to sign on more at the end of the first period. One day I went to see one of my commanders and simply requested to be moved to a destroyer. He looked me over and then began a Zionist sermon:

"'I've been following you during training and you've made no errors. Quite the opposite. You've been selected out of hundreds of applicants and we're investing everything in you. Don't disappoint me. Forget this stupid idea and go back to your room.'

"'No,' I said. 'I'm serious. I have a seaman's book and I'm returning to the sea once my service is over. I can contribute much more with the knowledge that I have aboard a destroyer.' Silence fell, and then suddenly, with a stern look on his face, he said:

"'Think very carefully before you answer me. You can leave the special forces, but forget about the navy.' I couldn't believe what he was saying, I mean, I was in the navy, and he was apparently just trying to scare me.

"'I stand by my decision,' I said.

"'Fine. Now leave.'

"The next day I received a notice to report to the naval base on the Carmel. The girls on base and my fellow trainees gave me resentful looks as I headed for the gate. *There*, I said to myself. *The commander just wanted to scare me. I'm on my way to a naval base and from there I'll be sent to a destroyer*. But that's not what happened. For two weeks I worked my ass off in awful jobs like cleaning toilets, peeling potatoes, guard duty, and the like. After the two weeks ended, I was given an order to report to a transfer base in the center of the country. My face fell and my mood went with it. I could not believe what I read. But that was the reality and I couldn't do anything but make my way to the transfer base. On the base, we took psychological tests and, really, didn't do much else. Every day we hung out in front of our tents or went to the canteen to buy candy and such. In the evening, we were free to go out into the big city, Tel Aviv. Once a day, usually in the afternoon, we reported to the office. A few names would be called and those soldiers would be sent to various bases. My name, too, was called a few times, but I always refused, insisting on military jail or the navy. There were discussions. I was explained that there'd never been an instance where a soldier was thrown out of a corps and then returned to it. I was told to choose any other force, but I remained stubborn. Soldiers came and went but I stayed stuck on base. One day, I was called for another meeting. I was firmly told that the situation could not continue and that in the coming days I would be sent to some troop or another. An idea formed in my head and I wanted to see it through.

"'Give me a 24-hour order to see the navy's personnel commander. I'll try to meet with him. If I don't succeed, do with me what you will.' They agreed and signed the order.

"I went back to the Carmel base where I'd been kicked in the ass.

In the afternoon, I was called to the commander's office. I saluted and remained standing. He pointed at the chair and in a baritone voice said:

"'Sit.'

"The commander was tall and had a broad belly. He leafed through the pile of papers in his hand and finally asked why I was insisting on returning to the force. I told him my life story, about the Bat Galim beach, my work on the service boats, my voyages, and how I could contribute to the navy.

"'My love for the sea would hinder my integration in any other force,' I said. The commander listened until I finished and didn't ask questions.

"'OK, soldier. I'll think about your request. I won't promise anything. Return to your base. You'll get an answer within two days.'

"And yes, the unimaginable happened. I was issued an order to report to the naval base in Bat Galim, my own neighborhood. The large rock that had been sitting on top of my chest disappeared, as if it had never existed."

Shauli felt a kinship with Perry. The story of his life amazed him and he waited for him to continue. They refilled their glasses and lit cigarettes. A sailor knocked on the closed door of the cabin and asked to come in, but Perry told him nicely that he was having an important discussion and wouldn't be able to host him that evening. Shauli urged him to continue, he wanted to know if in the end he'd served on a destroyer.

"Patience," Perry said. "Let's go back to the training base."

"They put me with the person in charge of landscaping. It turned out that he knew my sister, who had also done her military service in the navy. This eased relations, which were fine to begin with. It was pretty boring taking care of the gardens, but I was allowed to leave base every evening and return in the morning. There weren't any duty rotations or any guarding to do. I'm sure any soldier would welcome those conditions, but I didn't. I still dreamed of joining a destroyer. One day, the drill sergeant came to me and said:

"'I have a proposition for you. I'm going to be finishing my service soon and I'd like to recommend that you take my place.'

"'I really appreciate your offer and am grateful for everything you've done for me, but I just want to board a destroyer,' I said. 'I've gone through a lot to try to make that happen. It's true that right now I'm living in a utopia, going home every day, but that's not want I expected.'

"A month passed since I arrived at the base, when I received an order to report to the INS *Haifa*. I was swept up in joy. I took on the task readily and willingly.

"Service on the destroyer was not easy. Most of the time we were out at sea, training. But I had no complaints. I was just happy. Two months after I finished my military service, I already found myself sailing on a merchant marine ship. Now you understand what brought me to sea. It wasn't easy for me to share my story, especially those difficult parts about my childhood. Actually, you're the first person who's heard the whole story. I feel kind of like a weight has been lifted, because this whole time I've had this hidden part of me locked away – locked and bolted."

Shauli felt close to the boatswain sitting in front of him, and knew that they'd be good friends. At port, Perry would always invite him to go out when they were free from deck duty. They'd usually spend their times at nightclubs or bars. As they were both quite good-looking, they had no trouble catching a couple of pretty ladies and bringing them back to the ship with them. They sailed together on the *Deganya* for about a year and a half, up until Perry had a long shore leave. Another boatswain replaced him, but unlike Perry, he kept to himself.

Shauli continued for another two voyages, until he too went on shore leave. In his apartment in the center of the Carmel, he began to unpack his bags, taking out his clothes, including several new items. He arranged his clothes neatly into his drawers and began to fill his fridge with the various delicacies he'd picked up at the different ports where the ship had docked. He also placed a few bottles of liquor in his cabinet in the living room. After he finished organizing everything, he decided to go out to one of the local restaurants that served Mediterranean cuisine. One was located not far from his apartment, so he went there. A waitress gave him a menu and asked if he wanted to order a drink.

"I'd love to get a bottle of Carlsberg," he said.

"Right away," she said. When she came back with the beer, he ordered a plate of hummus with *ful*, a chopped Israeli salad, four kebabs, and fries. He also ordered a bowl of pickled vegetables and hot sauce. It had already gotten dark outside once he'd finished the tasty meal. The price was reasonable and Shauli left a tip for the nice waitress. When he left the restaurant, he started making his way to the popular Club 120 on Yefe Nof street. The street was covered in greenery – grass and trees, with beautiful houses hidden among them. All of Haifa, the bay, and the port were spread out before his eyes. House lights sparkled like stars in the night sky. An astounding view, by all accounts. Shauli went in, sat down at the bar, and ordered a whiskey. The place was pretty full, but not crowded. *The night's still young*, he thought. But fatigue began to set in, caused by the long day he'd had with the ship docking at port and him arriving home, so he decided to go back to his place and get some sleep. The next morning, after he'd showered and had a satisfying late breakfast, he decided to go have a short visit at Kibbutz Sdot Yam. He packed his bag with the gifts he'd bought for his mother and sister. At the central bus station, Shauli went to a pay phone and dialed Perry's number, but there was no answer.

The bus stopped at the kibbutz and Shauli was the only one to get off. When he rang the doorbell, his mother opened the door. As soon as she laid eyes on him, she opened her arms and took him into a motherly embrace, tears of joy flowing down her face. When she asked, he told her about the voyage, about his apartment in the Carmel, and about how happy he was with everything. Shauli then opened his bag and took out the gifts.

"Where's Bossem?" he asked.

"In the army," his mother replied. "She was recruited to the paratroopers and she's intended for officer's training." Rena took out of the fridge a pitcher of orange juice and a cheesecake, set them on the kitchen table, and they both sat down. Shauli noticed that his mom's hair had begun to grey and wrinkles had begun to form on her forehead and at the corners of her eyes. He felt sorry for her loneliness – without her husband and her two children – but didn't know how to cheer her up. Toward the evening, Shauli said goodbye, but promised that he'd come visit before his next voyage. Rena took him into her arms once again and kissed his forehead.

"Take care of yourself," she said.

At the Haifa central bus station, Shauli caught a cab that brought him directly to his apartment. He turned on the electric water heater and took out a bottle of whiskey from the liquor cabinet. He then took out some cola from the fridge and ice cubes from the freezer. He also took out some cubes of salty cheese, some tomatoes and cucumber, which he chopped up, drizzled on some olive oil, and sprinkled with a little salt and ground black pepper. He stirred the cola into the whiskey, turned on the new stereo that he'd just bought on the voyage, and lay out on the couch, sipping his drink and listening the music. The image of his mother then floated in front of his eyes and he became sad. Shauli felt uneasy about not having seen Bossem, but he hoped that everything was going well for her and that she was enjoying her service.

At 11 p.m. he decided to go out again to Club 120. He sat at the bar and ordered a black label Scotch whiskey. This time, the club was full of partygoers, but surprisingly, there were still free seats at the bar. Someone was singing and pounding out loud rock songs on the grand piano, with a crowd of people surrounding him and clapping whenever a song was over, waiting for him to start another. On the dance floor, couples danced to the rhythms of the piano keys and his vocals. Shauli locked eyes with a striking and sexy redhead, who seemed to know everyone and everyone knew her. She was accompanied by one of the 'pretty boys' from the city, who had a reputation of being a heartbreaker. Shauli remembered seeing her the last time he'd been at the club. She had a haughty look on her face and she radiated confidence. At one point, she approached the bar, stood right next to him, and ordered two drinks. As she turned away with the drinks, their eyes met, but it was as if he were transparent. The clocked showed 1 a.m. It was time to go home. Shauli walked back on foot, taking in the smoke from his cigarette.

Another day would begin soon. Shauli ate something light to soak up the alcohol in his stomach and before falling asleep, he thought of the redhead from the club.

The next day in the afternoon, Shauli went to the company's office. There, he found out that Perry was sailing on the ship *Netanya*. Shauli remembered that there was a restaurant on Plumer Gate Street, not far from the entrance to the port, which sailors often frequented. He hoped to see some of his colleagues there. And indeed, he met there the one and only Shimi, his friend from the *Teverya*. They were both happy to see each other again and Shauli joined him at his table. There were a few empty bottles of beer in front him and he ordered another round. They exchanged stories about the time they spent together and afterward. Shimi was happy to hear of his friend's success with the able seaman exams.

"I always knew you were a better-than-average sailor," he said.

The restaurant specialized in Eastern European cuisine and they couldn't resist the temptation to order the chef's specials. Neither of them were disappointed; the meal was excellent.

Daylight gave way to nightfall and they went out to the street. Shauli asked Shimi if he'd ever been to Club 120.

"I've heard of it, but I've never been," he said.

"Well, the time has come for you to see the place. Let's get a taxi."

"Alright, sounds good," Shimi said.

When they got to the club, they sat at the bar and ordered a glass of fine whiskey. The pianist played rapturously and a crowd of people circled him just like before. Shauli glanced around. His eyes fell on the gorgeous redhead who made everyone crazy. This time she wasn't with her pretty boy. She went to the bar to order a drink, once again standing right next to him. "Mr. Transparent" asked the redhead if he could buy her a drink – no strings attached. She politely turned him down. Shauli told Shimi that this was at least some progress, compared to last time. Patience was needed. She'd eventually get caught in the net. Shimi and Shauli continued to talk together, every once in a while ordering another round of fine whiskey and listening to the piano player's music, whether they wanted to or not. The redhead came back to the bar and again stood next to him. Shauli focused his eyes on her and said:

"This is the third time that you're coming to stand next to me. That means you either get some charm, or a drink. Again, no strings attached."

This time she looked at him more closely. A smile came across her face, revealing two rows of pearly whites.

"Thanks for the offer, but not this time," she said. "Try a little harder and maybe I'll think about accepting."

The bartender handed her the drink and she turned and disappeared into the crowd.

"She's like a slippery eel, but I've been blessed with patience," Shauli said.

"Yes," said Shimi. "You were always calm, cool, and collected."

The two friends met often over the following days. They would sit at the same downtown bar-restaurant where they'd first met, which was known as a place sailors would go to during shore leave. Shimi – who was a veteran compared to Shauli – would bump into lots of friends, some of whom would join them at their table. In those instances, the drinking would gain momentum and their mood would soar. They would all tell stories of their times at sea, gossip about officers and other sailors, and of course, they couldn't go without talking about their various sexual conquests at the different ports of the world. To accompany their drinks, they usually would also order something to snack on, such as sardine dip, liver pâté, salty cheese cubes, anchovy toasts, hard-boiled eggs, assorted vegetables, and fresh rolls. The restaurant's owner had actually been a chef on cruise ships and he had a reputation among all the sailors for creating delicious delicacies that were also pleasing to the eyes and nose. Often when a plate would be licked clean of its contents – and that happened regularly – he would come and offer another one as a replacement. He opened his establishment early every day except Saturday. All of his thoughts were devoted to the sailors. He knew that there were many who wanted to catch the 8:00 service boat to arrive on time at their ships anchored in the bay, or others who were in a rush to begin their workday on a ship docked at port. From him, they could always get a hot cup of coffee, whose aroma would give a good start to the day. At 6:00 a.m., he would make his rounds in the nearby outdoor market to pick his produce for the day. As soon as he'd open the doors to the restaurant, he'd begin cooking and assembling sandwiches, which were his specialty. It was no surprise that the majority of his clientele were seaman, as they felt almost as if their were at sea when they came to his place. Shimi and Shauli would usually sit there until the evening, and even though they were a bit unsteady on their feet when they left, they'd want to continue into the night.

A cab drove them to a popular nightclub on Mount Carmel, where there were shows, but also hostesses whose entire jobs were to take drunk customers for all they've got – suckers, basically. And indeed, two girls just like that sat down next to Shimi and Shauli. One was quite pretty, but the other – oh boy – she was fat, old, and looked like a foggy night. Even if she would parachute down onto a ship in the middle of the ocean, no one would fuck her, apart from the rare exception. Their cheap drink cost a fortune and the girls' mundane questions, such as 'What's your name?' and

'What do you do?' brought them the same conclusion – that they had to be sent to another table. Even though the drinks that they'd consumed all day were sitting heavily on them, they still clung to some minimal amount of sanity.

The show at the club – and the announcer's voice who introduced the act to a loud round of applause from the audience – didn't much impress the two friends. At this point in their drinking, it was difficult for them to follow the act. Dawn began to break once they finally hit the street, barely able to walk, yet happy and satisfied. They even broke out in traditional Israeli songs, about their beloved and holy land. On their way, they stumbled across a crate of milk on the doorstep of a house and the temptation was so strong that they swiped a bottle to quench their terrible thirst – a result of their heavy drinking. But they decided to be generous and rummaged in their pockets until they found enough money to cover double the cost of the bottle and placed it in the crate as compensation. Then they stopped a passing cab and, since Shauli wasn't far from his apartment, the cab drove there first. Shimi immediately fell asleep in the cab and Shauli shook him to wake him up. Before he left the taxi, he gave the driver Shimi's address and paid for the fare, to prevent any trouble.

A week after, Shimi went out to sea. Shauli felt all alone. *Now's the time to visit Club 120*, he thought. That whole week, he hadn't set foot in the club. He wanted the redhead, but he knew that this next time, he'd have to switch up the bait.

He sat on the same seat at the bar and before he could even order, the bartender asked if he wanted the usual.

"Yes," he answered. *Nice of him to remember me*, he thought.

Not much time passed before he felt a light tap on his shoulder. The redhead, smiling and prettier than ever, stood in front of him.

"Hello," she said. He looked at her, nodded, and went back to playing with his glass of whiskey. Her surprise at his behavior was perfect.

"Where's your friend?" she asked.

"Out at sea," he answered tersely, without looking. The bartender handed her her drink. Shauli noticed that she turned toward the club reluctantly, perhaps even in disappointment. Shimi should have seen this. He knew that she'd come back. The fish had taken the bait. And she did return.

"I'm ready to take you up on that offer," she said.

"What are you drinking?" he asked.

"Rum and coke."

"Why don't you sit instead of standing? This seat is free," he said. He turned to the waiter and asked for her drink and ordered another whiskey for himself. She held out her hand.

"My name is Alma. What's yours?"

"Shauli."

While they sipped their drinks, Alma asked what he did.

"I'm a sailor on shore leave. And you?"

"I run a boutique in the center of the Carmel."

"So your store is near my apartment," he said. Shauli spoke sparingly, but was generous and polite. He answered all her questions and made sure their glasses were always full. Suddenly she said:

"I don't understand one thing. The first two times we met, you seemed interested. But now your face – which is quite handsome, I must admit – is as blank as the stone Sphinx."

Priel Porat

When we left the breakwater of the Panama Canal, near the city of Colón, deep waves began rocking the *Cormoran*, but not wildly. The ship worked its way through the Caribbean Sea on its way to the Atlantic Ocean. Two-and-a-half days passed and we arrived at the Jamaica Channel, the passage between the two islands of Jamaica and Haiti. The Jalopy entered the dark waters of the Atlantic in the middle of the depressing winter. At least I was comforted by the fact that there wasn't much time left before we would reach New York. There was a month until we'd reach the English Channel and then on to Rotterdam, and the end of my long contract, where Gertie was waiting for me.

One thing I really enjoyed was to watch the lighthouses as we passed. Every lighthouse has its own fascinating story – when it was built, how it was built, the colors of its tower and its flashing lights – which set it apart from the rest.

In the evening, as usual, Shauli, Ben-Tzur, Carlos Antonio, and Yoav invaded my cabin. They really felt close to me. To them, I wasn't just the boatswain, but also a friend. Especially Shauli, who, as soon as he learned I was boarding the *Cormoran*, asked to join the crew. I was pleased, of course. I thought of him as a good friend. He was a good and skilled sailor and any boatswain would have been glad to have him on his crew. Yoav left the cabin and returned a little while later. He held a plate of "tastings" in one hand and a bottle of whiskey in the other. Because everyone liked my last story, and since they asked, I decided to tell them about Lena:

"One day I arrived at the Port of Houston, Texas, which is located on the Buffalo Bayou. The river meandered through the heart of the city. In the evening, four of us decided to go out on the town to see what kind of nightlife it had to offer. We found a bar in the south side of the city that looked nice, so we went in. It wasn't particularly big; a few tables, a corner for pool – the American version of billiards, as you know – and the drinks bar with ten stools. The heavy wooden furniture looked to be from the colonial era of the 17th and 18th centuries, during the British rule. Since there were enough places at the bar – probably because of the early hour – we sat there. I was still busy with taking out a pack of cigarettes and my lighter from my pocket when I noticed all three of my friends staring at a point behind the bar. I, too, lifted my eyes and was stunned. In front of me stood a bartendress who was out of this world. Beautiful and sensual, with the body of a supermodel, a challenging smile across her face, and her whole body exclaiming freedom and openness.

"'What can I get you?' she asked. The friendly way she spoke was as if we'd known each other for years. Her attitude, her looks, and the way her body moved thrilled all of us. Each of us ordered our drink and she poured them with a professional zest.

"'Your English ain't perfect. Where are you guys from?'

"'We're Israeli sailors. We came into port today,' I said.

"'Interesting,' she said, adding: 'I actually have a close girlfriend who's volunteering on a kibbutz in the Galilee and she writes me all the time about your beautiful country.'

"As the time passed, more and more people crowded the place. Another bartenderess joined to help out with the orders. At one point, we went to play pool in teams of two. Our drink rotation went into high gear, since we decided that the losing team would buy the next round. The Americans have a method: If someone wants to play, they place a quarter next to one of the pockets and when the game finishes, he plays the winner, and uses the quarter to release the balls and start a new game. Since I was the best pool player out of the four of us, it was decided that I'd play the next guy. During the game, another few quarters began to stack up at the pockets. I beat at least three other players and then our bartendress came over to challenge me. All eyes were on her, as she skillfully sunk the balls into the pockets. The way she dressed, the way she stood, her movements, and the happy grunts that came from her throat, all this came together to make a perfect woman who any man would desire to have. She barely let me have a chance and beat me in the end.

"'Well done,' I said. 'Now I have to buy you a drink.' She laughed.

"'You're not the first one to lose to me. Some days there isn't much work, so I spend hours at the table. I love the game.' On her way back to the bar, she asked for my name.

"'Perry, and you?'

"'Lana.'

"Lana kept busy making drinks, but when there was some down time, she came over and talked with us. The night was ending and it was time to go back to the ship. Lana didn't accept the invitation to come have a drink on the ship and get a feel for the Israeli atmosphere. Her answer was evasive but polite:

"'Thanks, but not tonight. Maybe another time.' So, the four of us went back to the ship and crawled into bed. The next day, I waited for the deck work to finish and for the cargo shifts to be arranged so that I could go back to the bar, this time on my own.

The astonishing Lana, at the Port of Houston

"Except for a few people, the place was empty during the early hours that evening. Lana looked even more beautiful than the night before. She smiled warmly at me and asked how I was feeling.

"'I'll feel better if you agree to another game of pool. Yesterday you kicked my ass, even though I'm considered to be a good player. And hey, my alcohol levels are still low.' She gave a full belly laugh.

"'Come on, cowboy, show me what ya got.'

"We went over to the table with our drinks and I racked the balls. Lana went first, but this time I was clear-headed. We played two games and I beat her both times. At that point, customers had begun to file in, so Lana had to go back to the bar. The evening flowed into night. I stayed until the last customers left. Lana began to close up the bar. I suggested that we go to a nice restaurant that she knew of. She agreed, which made me happy. We took her car to a steak restaurant at the mouth of the river, about a half hour away. We ordered two rib eyes in a mushroom sauce, with a side of baked potato and salad. We also ordered a bottle of semi-dry Merlot. I repeated my previous night's offer, and this time Lana accepted, driving us back in her car to the ship.

"'I won't stay long, just a short visit,' she said.

"'Better than nothing,' I replied.

"Lana looked around my neat and orderly cabin and paid special attention to my souvenirs that sat on the corner table and hung on the bulkhead, as if she was trying to analyze my personality.

"'Let's sit at the table,' I suggested. She set her purse down on the bed, pulled up a chair, and sat down.

"'I've got whiskey, beer, soft drinks, coffee, or tea. Which do you prefer?'

"'I'd love a cup of tea,' she said.

"'I'll be right back,' I said. I went out to the crew preparation room and made her some tea in a glass cup, set it on a saucer, and on it placed some lemon slices. On another saucer I put some sugar and a spoon. I also made up a plate of cheese, tomato, cucumber, and green olives.

"As Lana began sipping her tea, I poured myself a glass of whiskey.

"'How long are you staying at port?'

"'Probably about another four or five days,' I said. When she asked, I told her a little about myself. She listened to what I was saying without interruption.

"'Now how about you?' I asked.

"'Well, my sister and I came to Houston about a year ago, from Salt Lake City, Utah. We rented an apartment together not far from the bar where I work. My sister also found a job as a waitress at a nightclub down the road from the bar. Our salaries are good and we're able to support ourselves nicely, and even put some away in savings. We don't have steady boyfriends, because we're just not interested at this point, even though we have flirtations here and there.'

"Lana finished her tea, got up, and took her purse.

"'I've got to get going. It was very nice to spend some time with you on this ship. Tomorrow I'll take the day off and I'll come visit you, I promise.' I accompanied her to her car and we said goodnight, with a light kiss on the cheek.

"The next morning, before arranging the crew's work schedule, I felt a need to be alone for awhile, and unlike my usual behavior, quench my thirst with a drink. At around 11:00, Meir, the first engineer, came into my cabin. I poured him a glass and while the two of us were drinking, he began to tell me how he was feeling better ever since he went over a letter he had received. The conclusion that he'd reached was that he should finish up the business with his wife as soon as possible.

"'She's not worth all the trouble it would be to get her back. I'm still young, not bad-looking, I'm high-ranking with a good salary, so I don't see any problem in just continuing my life without her.'

"I then told him about Lana and her sister, how she came aboard the ship, and that I was expecting her to visit again today, in hopes that I won't be disappointed.

"After lunch and work, and in preparation for the upcoming drinking, I felt the need to rest my head a bit. I had only shut my eyes before the door opened all at once and Lana's silhouette appeared before my sleepy, and somewhat hazy eyes. Something in her body language seemed off. Her eyes were glazed over. She understood, from the quizzical look on my face, what I was thinking.

"'The bottle of wine's to blame,' she said, laughing hysterically. 'This morning my sister and I sat and polished it off together. We were having an early birthday celebration for her. But I'm here, because I promised to be. Remember?'

"'If you'd like to continue the celebration with me, I can bring some wine. Or would you prefer a different drink?' I said.

"'This time I'd like some whiskey,' she giggled.

"While we were still sitting and drinking, Lana suddenly got up and started unbuttoning her blouse.

"'Do you have anything that plays music?' she asked. I turned on the radio and searched for a song that fit the mood. Lana swayed to the music, taking off items of clothing one after the other. Her body was unbelievable, and I'm sorry, but I won't go into detail. We're in the middle of the ocean and I want to save you from using up your soap reserves. But I will say this: She had a marijuana leaf tattooed on her right breast. Anyway, we spent the afternoon in orgasms, until the smoke in the funnel started up. After dinner, which I served her in bed, Lana suggested that we visit her sister at work. Of course I agreed, but I asked if a friend could join. My friend Meir was glad for the offer, if only to forget his deep depression.

"The night club where Lana's sister worked was packed. We were barely able to find a place to sit our asses down. Her sister came over to us right away.

"'This is Scarlett,' Lana said.

"'Nice to meet you,' I said. 'This is Meir and I'm Perry.' Scarlett took our order and went to the bar. We continued sitting there until her shift was over, enjoying the atmosphere of the place and the shows. We were some of the last people there when we all left in Lana's car. We decided to go to a diner that the sisters recommended, and while we ate and drank, I noticed that something was happening between Meir and Scarlett. They were deep into a discussion, their eyes shining. I was happy for Meir, because he needed to recover from the crisis that he was going through and this was the best way for it. The pleasant evening ended in a disappointed for both of us, as Lana offered to give us a ride back to the ship and said that we should meet up again the next day. Next to the gangway, I kissed Lana goodnight, while Meir gave Scarlett a peck on the cheek. It was obvious that he liked her, and maybe only sought some comfort, but who knows what goes on in someone's mind?

"The next day in the afternoon, Scarlett and Lana surprised us by coming aboard the ship. Both seemed cheerful and free.

"'We took a day off,' Lana said, and her unique laugh filled the air of the cabin. 'Go find Meir, we're going to go have a good time. And bring a bottle of whiskey along to lighten the mood.'

"'Sounds great,' I said. 'But we have make arrangements with our supervisors to get off of work. In the meantime, sit, make yourselves at home. The fridge is right there, and there's the radio. I'm going to settle things.'

"The first mate had no problems and authorized my leave, as long as I'd organize everything before leaving, including finding a replacement. I found Meir in his cabin, busy with complicated paperwork and drinking a glass of whiskey. I told him the plan, and that the sisters were at that moment in my cabin, waiting. Meir put away the paperwork, downed his whiskey, and said:

"'I'll arrange it with the chief engineer. Give me a half an hour to take a shower and change clothes. I'll meet you at your cabin when I'm ready.'

"As Lana started the car and began driving away from the ship, Scarlett mentioned that we would stop at a friend's house and pick him and his girlfriend up, too. We went to a house in the outskirts of the city and Scarlett hopped out to get the couple that would be joining us. Five minutes later, all three were in the car.

"'Meet Bill and Linda,' Scarlett said.

"'Nice to meet you,' we said. 'Perry and Meir,'

"'We're going to a beach near Galveston,' Linda updated us. 'It's right on the Gulf of Mexico.'

"On the way, we stopped at a supermarket and picked up a case of beer, cheeses, meats, rolls, and vegetables. The whole way to the beach, we drank and sang, imitating the pop songs emanating from the radio. The beach came into view when it was already late afternoon. We unpacked the beer, the whiskey, and the food from the trunk. The sand was soft and pleasant. Lana had taken a blanket from the car and began laying it out on the sand. We all sat down and began passing the time drinking and singing, chatting and dipping our feet in blue gulf water. If we had had any reservations, the drinks took care of those. As the evening began to set, hands and lips went into action. Bill with Linda, Meir with Scarlett, and I with Lana. You won't believe it, but our clothing began to come off one by one. We made mad love on the beach, shamelessly, in public. At one point, we decided to try something different. We went back to the car and Linda took the wheel, with Bill in the passenger seat. Meir and Scarlett climbed into the trunk, while Lana and I put the blanket on the roof of the car and climbed on. Linda started driving slowly down the beach, with the radio turned up. Every once in a while, I'd reach my hand down to Bill for the whiskey bottle, and Lana and I would take a few swigs. In the end, we ended up making love on the roof of the moving car, to the applause of the few couples still on the beach. That was an extraordinary experience for all of us. A day later, the ship went out to sea, but not before I gave Lana the contact information of the ship agent and the phone number at the office. I promised to return, but I didn't know whether or not it was an empty promise."

All the guys said at once: "So, did you see her again?"

"Yes," I said. "It actually happened pretty soon after. On the next voyage we sailed to Houston again, but this time we were set at economic speed, so the voyage there only took thirty long days. We docked in the morning and prepared the ship for the longshoremen. During the coffee break, I went to chief steward's office, who granted my request for a $1000 advance. From there, I lay below to my cabin to begin celebrating our arrival at port. I took out a bottle of whiskey, a glass, and ice. I sat there drinking and thinking of Lana, who I hoped I'd see that evening at the bar where she worked. I felt like resting a bit after lunch, but it didn't last long, since Lana burst through the door, her laugh reverberating through everything in the cabin. She came straight to the bed and kissed me, as wisps of sleep still clung to my eyes.

"'Alright, cowboy of mine, get up and get dressed. We're going out to have some fun.'

After I received permission from the first mate, we went down to the dock. A bright blue sports car, sparkling in the rays of the sun, was parked next to the ship. Lana reached into her jeans pocket and pulled out a set of keys, her unique laugh indicating this was her car.

"'Where did you get the money for this kind of car?' I asked.

"'My grandma passed away. She left Scarlett and me $50,000 each.'

"As she drove, I noticed that she'd gotten a new tattoo on her arm. Lana stopped in front of a bank and said she'd be right back. When she returned, she handed me a thousand dollars.

"'Put this in your pocket,' she said.

"'What's this for? I have my own money,' I said. She laughed.

"'Don't worry, it won't last long,' she said, and continued driving to a bar she knew of. 'We're going to a lesbian bar. The bartender is a friend of mine. But just a friend. I haven't experimented yet. Who knows? Maybe I should try it once.'

"We sat at the bar. I was, of course, the only guy there, and I didn't feel very comfortable. Lana ordered a Tom Collins and I got a beer. I took out a hundred dollar bill to pay and Lana said:

"'Don't ask for the change. Leave the rest as tip.' That's how it continued for every new round of drinks. Lana was deep in conversation with her friend, as if I didn't exist. The truth is, the place got on my nerves. I wanted to go somewhere normal and a half hour later, we left. When we were in the car, Lana took out of her wallet a small golden box. She opened the lid and sniffed some white powder.

"'What's that? Cocaine?' I asked.

"'Yeah,' she said.

"'When did you start with this garbage?' I pressed.

"'Not long ago. All that money kinda blinded me and I started doing stupid stuff.'

"I felt bad for her. Such a beautiful woman on her way down to rock bottom. It'll be hard for her to climb out of that.

"That night we went to the bar where Lana worked and continued our drinking. We tried to play pool, but Lana couldn't tell her left from her right. She hardly could stand and started to speak nonsense. There was no reason to stay, and besides, from the thousand dollars that had been put into my pocket, there was barely $150 left. I offered to take Lana to her apartment and from there, I thought, I'd take a cab back to the ship. I helped her climb into the back seat, while I went behind the wheel and drove straight to her place. I helped her get into bed and she fell asleep right away. I gave her a kiss on the forehead and left quietly. That's it, guys, I never saw her again. I went on shore leave, and after that I sailed on a ship that traveled to the Far East. The end of the story is that one day, months after I had seen Lana last, I met a friend who'd sailed on the same ship that would dock in Houston. This friend told me that one time in Houston a real babe showed up to the ship asking for Priel Porat, the boatswain. She apparently looked very sad when she was told that I was on shore leave."

"What happened with Meir?" Shauli asked.

"He also never saw Scarlett again, but she had helped him overcome the crisis he'd been going through. When he returned to Israel, he divorced his wife. Today, he's remarried and has a beautiful daughter."

When we reached the Bermuda Triangle, the sea was especially stormy. Waves furiously swept over the whole length of the main deck. Violent, freezing winds blew, bending the high antennae into half circles. Showers, accompanied by snowflakes, fell down upon us from dark, gloomy cumulonimbus clouds. Once again, the order was given to secure the doors and hatches and to not stick our noses outside. The Jalopy's groans and moans went on endlessly. Without another option, I gave indoor work assignments to the crew, the ones that we always pushed off for bad weather.

In the evening, the guys came to my cabin. One brought a bottle of liquor while another brought a plate of snacks from the crew refrigerator. But this time, Carlos Antonio brought with him a box of Cuban cigars. Shauli asked to hear another song, so I took out my notebook.

Proud Israeli Seamen

Once, we were Hebrew sailors,
today we're proud Israeli seamen.
The flags of Israel and the Merchant Marines
fly defiantly on the ship's masts.

The rope's unhitched, the anchor's aweigh,
the ship's slowly leaving, out to sea.
Our beloved country disappears in the distance,
but our deck flows with milk and honey.

At some foreign port somewhere,
cranes unload our cargo,
blue and white exports filling their docks,
Israeli-made products for the world market.
Once, we were Hebrew sailors,
now we're proud Israeli seamen,
representing our land with love and honor,
through the wide ocean and the seven seas.

There was a quick round of applause, but it was time to go to sleep, so my guests filed out one after the other. The *Cormoran* rocked from side to side. I had to spread out my legs in bed in order to maintain stability, and that's how I spent my fitful night.

The ocean continued to rage in the following days. The sun didn't peek out from behind the clouds for even a second. It seemed like the weather would follow us to New York. If I had wings, I fantasized with a grin, I'd fly away to some tropical island, lie out in the white sand under a coconut tree, and watch the turquoise water while sipping a cold cocktail. But what can you do when reality is not what you dream of?

The crew was satisfied with the indoor work, especially Shauli and Ben-Tzur, who were assigned to do paint repairs in the ship's galley. Arieh the cook treated them with delicious beef and chicken steaks – outside of the normal menu. He also set a platter of fruit on a side table for them. He only had one request:

"Don't gloat. If someone comes into the galley, it would be wise to not let them see you in the middle of eating."

"Of course, Arieh, there won't be a problem," they said in unison.

This time it was Ben-Tzur's turn to invite us to his cabin.

"Don't forget to bring your song notebook," he said to me.

The rocking of the ship didn't cease for even a moment, but it's a part of our normal lives at sea, and sailors fully understand accept these situations. We sat for about an hour, drinking and chatting, until Ben-Tzur asked that I read them a song.

"Alright," I said. "And since we'll be arriving at the mouth of the Hudson River soon, I'll read a poem that is fitting for the end of a voyage."

Arrival at Port

The helmsman is called to steer,
The pilot comes aboard,
The deck crew at their stations,
Ropes are ready, tugs are hitched.

The captain is at the bridge, giving orders
The floating buoys remind the sailors
Of the voyage that was,
And voyages before.

The pilot navigates the piers
The tugs sound their horns
The ship's bow cuts through the water
Along the docks, to be hitched.

Ropes are lowered,
Tugs help straighten
The engine stops, the gangway's lowered
While the shore waits patiently for the sailor.

"That's nice, Perry," Ben-Tzur said. "You really captured the feeling of going ashore. I mean, we're all practical men, needing some release, a good restaurant and some fun, and we also want to relax and forget days like we're having now."

In the early hours of the morning, at the beginning of the month of December, 1969, we reached the rendezvous point in the Port of New York. It was a beautiful morning at the end of the long voyage that had begun in Australia. Even the sun showed its face and smiled between the clouds. The ship agent brought letters, two of which were for me. By the Dutch stamps, I knew they were from Gertie. I waited until I had a free moment, so that I could read them alone in my cabin without any interruptions.

After breakfast, I gave out the work assignments in coordination with First Mate Itzik Shahak. We agreed to release three crewmen on shore leave until 17:00, after which two of them would be assigned to deck duty – one from until midnight and the other from midnight until the next morning. The three that received the shore leave were Ben-Tzur, Doron, and Jeremy the deck boy. The rest of the crew knew that their turn would come the next day. After everything was in order, I hurried to my cabin so that I could focus on Gertie's letters. I was overwhelmed with excitement, and even though it was still early, I could resist and poured myself a double before opening the first envelope. I lit a cigarette and picked one of the letters to read first. Love and longing poured forth from them. She spoke of her work at the Oasis club and about her apartment, where she felt my absence. The most important message that came through was that she agreed to come with me to Israel. She also asked that I send Shauli love from Nellie, who also wanted to follow him, if that was what he wished for. Happiness washed over me. I felt that I could actually renounce my love for iron – which had been my life's essence – in favor of the love of flesh and blood, and that perhaps it would symbolize a new beginning for me, and who knew what could happen?

At the end of the workday, after I had showered and changed, I went back to read the letters over again. The whiskey bottle was already on the table, and of course, I had to quench my thirst. My old radio played music from a local station, creating an air of arrival ashore, back to civilization, after the prolonged loneliness of being out at sea. While I was lost in my thoughts, Shauli came into my cabin.

"Perry, are we going down?"

"Yeah, sure. I'm already dressed and ready to go. By the way, I got a couple of letters from Gertie and Nellie sends you her love. She's ready to follow you to the ends of the earth."

"Yes, I know," Shauli said. "I received four letters from Nellie, and she sends you her love, too."

We raised a toast to arriving safely ashore. Now there was only one thing left to do – to go out and enjoy a night in the big city after so long on the water.

At our request, the taxi drove us to Greenwich Village, the bohemian neighborhood in the west side of Lower Manhattan. We walked the streets of the neighborhood, looking for a good place to spend the night. My eyes fell on a place that had a weird sign: "Your Father's Mustache."

"I think we should check this place out," I said to Shauli.

"Alright, let's go," he replied.

We weren't disappointed. The place was packed and full of people dancing in rows between the tables to the sounds of a banjo. The men wore straw hats with sashes and the women held colorful kerchiefs in their hands. Everyone was singing and having a good time, and the atmosphere was electric. Shauli stood next to a real fox, and they stayed together the whole night, until one point when he winked at me and left the club with her. I was left alone, but I thought to myself: *Good for him, he found a nice screw.* My bladder ached, but every time I went to the bathroom, it was occupied. Finally, I couldn't take it anymore. I paid the bill and ran outside to look for somewhere to piss, but I couldn't find a place. There were lots of people walking past and I couldn't just pull out "what's his name." I felt the world ending, I couldn't hold it in anymore. I opened the first door that I found and urinated on a red rug. From a distance I heard:

"Motherfucker! What are you doing?"

I looked over at a man behind a counter and saw him lift a telephone receiver. I put my finger to my mouth, meaning *Shh!*, gave a shake, and left. It was a five-star hotel. I immediately flagged down a cab and went back to the Jalopy, good and tired.

Shaul Shauli

Alma waited for Shauli to respond.

"Sweetie," Shauli said. "I was trying to be nice to you. I just wanted to buy you a drink and made sure to tell you that I didn't expect anything in return. But you just gave me the cold shoulder. I don't chase after women – even Miss Universe – if they don't seem interested, and you weren't."

"Well, anyway, I'm sitting next to you now, having a drink," she said. "I'm just curious about you, and maybe a little more. And I am interested in you, but maybe you didn't realize it. Let's see how it goes, what do you think?"

"Sure," he told her.

As the hours passed, the distance between them grew shorter and then disappeared altogether. Alma felt that a great guy was sitting across from her and that it would be easy to fall in love with him. Shauli, too, in addition to the lustful thoughts that raged inside him, saw Alma as not only a beautiful woman, but one that was interesting and easy to talk to. He noticed that every once in a while, a guy at the club would approach her, try to hold her hand and say something stupid or inappropriate. They would also check out the "creature" sitting next to her. Alma did her best to answer each of them politely. Eventually, Shauli was fed up and wanted to leave the club. He suggested that Alma join him, but she apologized and said that while she would love to go with him, she couldn't that night. He paid the bill, said goodbye to Alma, and left the club without setting up another date, but he felt that they would meet again soon.

Shauli was asked to report to the company's office. He was told that he was to board a tanker that would sail to Persain Gulf within a week. He knew that the pay onboard a tanker was higher than that of a regular voyage, so he didn't hesitate to accept the embarkation papers. He'd also never traveled that route. As was his routine before leaving – and after arriving to – Israel, he decided to visit his mother and sister in Sdot Yam the following day. He went to a candy store and bought beautifully wrapped box of chocolates and at a well-known perfumery, he bought a two French perfumes. He arrived at the kibbutz in the evening. Bossem opened the door, looking wonderful with cadet insignia on her shoulders. They embraced warmly, her face revealing how happy she was to see him. When he entered the house, he saw his mom sitting on the couch in the living room, watching the news. When she saw him, Shauli noticed that it was difficult for her to get up from the couch. He went to her and said:

"You don't have to get up, I'll sit next to you." He kissed her cheek and she squeezed his hand. Shauli took out the gifts he had gotten them, while Bossem went to the kitchen to bring some drinks, cake, and fruit. They sat and talked together for about two hours. Shauli told them about what he'd been up to and about the apartment, and also about his upcoming voyage. Bossem was proud to tell him about her work in the officers training course and told him that she had a boyfriend who was a captain in the Armored Corps Special Forces Unit. His mother didn't say much, and her face expressed weariness and sadness. Even her eyes were dull. Finally, Shauli felt that it had gotten late and that he should return to Haifa. He said goodbye to his mother and Bossem walked him to the door. Outside the house, Shauli turned to Bossem.

"What's going on with mom?" he asked.

"She's been deeply depressed lately," Bossem said. "She's even started a new habit of visiting dad's grave once a week."

They said goodbye on the main road to the bus stop.

Shauli didn't visit Club 120 that whole week. He finished all of the preparations before the departure. The company office issued him a plane ticket from Haifa to Eilat. On the day before the voyage, he packed his bags and made sure he hadn't forgotten anything. In the late evening, he decided to go to Club 120. As usual, he sat at the bar and the bartender poured him is regular glass of whiskey. A pair of delicate hands covered his eyes from behind and he gently pulled them off and turned around to see Alma's smiling face.

"Where did you disappear to these last few days?" she asked. "I've been here every night hoping to see you and spend some time with you," she added. "Besides, tonight I feel like having a drink, letting loose, and getting a bit crazy."

"No problem," Shauli said. "I think you should drink as much as you want and do whatever you want."

The piano player started rocking away on the ivories to the amazement of the people who encircled him. Alma put her hand in Shauli's and began to caress it gently. He noticed that this time, uncharacteristically, she drank a bit much. She looked at him hazily and softly. Shauli decided not to tell her about the following day's voyage yet.

At around midnight, they left the club. Alma was unsteady on her feet and he supported her as they walked along the road. Suddenly, she said:

"Shauli, take me home with you. I feel like being in your company tonight, if you don't mind."

"Of course," he said. "I'd be happy to spend more time with you. My place isn't far, we'll be there soon."

He put his arm around her shoulder and continued ambling along. Her body heat rose from her breast and brought his adrenaline up to astronomical levels. He knew that he'd get her tonight – the fish had been hooked.

When they got to his apartment, Shauli offered to make Alma a cup of coffee. She declined, almost aggressively, and asked for whiskey instead. He poured two glasses of whiskey, brought out some snacks from the fridge, and put it all on the table. He went over to his new stereo system and turned it on, filling the room with mellow sounds. He felt electricity in the air, but waited to make a move, because he saw how drunk she was. *Before I touch her, she needs to sleep it off some*, he thought.

"Alma, you need some sleep," he said to her. "I'll also get some rest on the couch."

"No, Shauli, I'm here so that you'll sleep with me. I want to do that with you."

He dimmed the lights and threw off his clothes, his member fully erect. Shauli went to Alma, kissed her softly, and helped her take off her clothes, too. Her divine body was revealed. In the soft light, he saw that she was a true redhead. He began to touch her, giving her everything he knew about the game of love. Finally, after she asked for it explicitly, he entered her, but something stopped him. Alma screamed. He tried again, but she screamed again. Shauli couldn't believe what was happening. He had a slight suspicion, which Alma confirmed.

"I'm a virgin," she said. "You're the only person I want to have my first time with. But it hurts." He tried to calm her down.

"Alma, at first it isn't pleasant, it even hurts a bit. Relax and let me help you. I assure you that your future experiences will be wonderful."

The mission was difficult, her hymen seemed to be made of tough canvas. Alma was almost dazed by the time he was inside her. He went to the sink, wet a towel, and wiped her face. She fell asleep right away.

Shauli went to take a shower. While he was washing himself up, he thought about the game she'd played with all of the guys at Club 120. By the way she was with the pretty boy and with all her other admirers that huddled around her, she seemed like the kind of girl who knew a thing or two. *She played everyone, even me*, he thought, rinsing himself.

It was almost 10:00 in the morning when they woke up. While Alma was still rubbing the sleep out of her eyes, Shauli went to the kitchen. Alma got up and went to take a shower and he could hear her washing her body while he made breakfast. He would have to leave in less than two hours. The hard part would be telling her about it. Alma came out of the shower and sat down to eat the late breakfast with him. Only then did she notice that there was a suitcase and tote bag sitting next to the door.

"What's that, Shauli?" she asked. Shauli cleared his throat.

"Alma, yesterday you weren't in a state where I could really tell you, but in about an hour, I'm going out to sea. That is, right after we finish breakfast." She looked at him in disbelief.

"For how long?"

"My contract is for four months. The route leaves from Eilat for the Persian Gulf, but every two-and-a-half weeks we'll stop at the Port of Eilat for two days. It's on an oil tanker."

"Shauli, you made me fall in love with you and now you're leaving me?"

"No, it's not like that. This is a short separation because of work. I'll see you when I'm on shore leave. I promise."

Shauli caught a passing taxi.

"Alma, I'm going to the Haifa airport. I'll tell the cab driver to stop at your apartment first."

"No, Shauli. I want to go with you to the airport and from there, I'll get a taxi home," she said.

They waited together for a half an hour before boarding. Shauli got two cups of coffee from a drinks stand and brought one to Alma.

"I had a very significant night with you and I'll never forget it," she said. "Now this unexpected separation is going to be really hard on me. I'm going to miss you, especially after what we had."

"Alma, you're a woman now. I don't think you'll regret it."

The call for boarding was heard over the loudspeakers. Shauli embraced her and said goodbye. She remained standing in that spot until he disappeared from her view.

The flight to Eilat was less than an hour long. Shauli stared out the window, watching the changing scenery – at first green, but then morphing into a dry brownish-yellow. But it was something extraordinary, primeval, like some untouched landscape. Eilat, Aqaba, and the Red Sea emerged before his eyes, as the plane began its descent. The exit from the plane was accompanied by a dry desert heat. There was no wind, which made the heat even heavier. Outside of the airport stood a line of taxis; he went into the first one and asked to be driven to the oil pier. The pier was a few hundred meters long and he needed to walk the whole way on foot. At the other end, he spotted the tanker. It was enormous, a real monster. The gangway was lowered onto the narrow edge of the pier, while the rigging at the bow and stern were tied to buoys. All around, there was sign after sign prohibiting smoking in all areas of the dock. Petrol fumes wafted through the air and he sensed that one tiny spark could blow the tanker to smithereens.

The deck crew was busy with loading supplies from a barge hitched to the hull. The work took several long hours, since the tanker was only restocked with these kinds of supplies once every three months. Once they'd loaded the supplies, they then loaded the barge with all kinds of machinery and parts that were broken and needed to be repaired at the shipyard, since the repairs couldn't be made onboard the ship. Empty oxygen tanks were also loaded onto the barge, in order for them to be refilled and returned, as well as empty oil barrels and other materials. The boatswain showed Shauli his cabin, which was located at the stern with the rest of the living quarters besides the captain's and other senior officers, whose cabins were in the central bridge structure. The only crewman who Shauli knew was Shimi, from his time on the *Teverya*. They were both happy to see each other. After both of their long days – Shimi with the supply load and Shauli with his flight – they moved to the cabins and helped with the other jobs that were left to do; work only finished at eight in the evening. Afterward, they decided to go out and have a good time in the southern tourist city. They found a nice pub in the new city center with long wooden tables and benches set up outside. The place was full of young tourists their age, mostly from England, Scandinavia, Germany, etc. It looked like most of them were backpackers traveling the world, stopping here and there to take on a waitressing or other job to make a little money before continuing on to their next stop. While they were sitting and drinking their beers, Shimi asked how things ended up with the girl from Club 120.

"Did the fish catch the bait?" he asked.

"Completely," Shauli said. "But you won't believe it – she was a virgin and I was her first. Now she's waiting for me to return on shore leave."

At the next table sat two nice-looking English girls. They exchanged a few glances until Shimi finally went over to them. Soon, the three of them came to join Shauli. After they introduced themselves and exchanged a few pleasantries, the guys ordered a round of drinks. The English girls each ordered a pint from the tap. As the drinks continued to flow, so too did their conversation, and their intimacy. They were eventually sitting in pairs, with roving hands exploring their possibilities. They then decided to go walking along the promenade, from which they continued on to the beach, walking arm in arm, until they found a somewhat secluded spot. Each couple went off in a different direction, and they made passionate love in the moonlight, with the waves splashing against their skin.

Shauli and Shimi returned to the tanker happy and exhausted, but not before they promised the girls to meet them the following evening at the same place. Shimi invited Shauli for a last drink at his cabin before turning in. They talked about the English girls – whose names they couldn't remember – and about their great luck right before setting off to sea. They also talked about the upcoming voyage to an oil port on the coast of Iran in the Persian Gulf, about the fishing that they could do from the tanker's stern, and everything that awaited them in one of the hottest points of the globe.

Shauli was assigned to the loading shift, so he couldn't go meet the English girl that evening. Shimi, however, was free, so he went out and took the boatswain along with him. The shore leave was set to end at 06:00 the following morning. At 07:30, the tanker was unhitched from the dock and began making its way through the waters of the Red Sea toward its destination in the Persian Gulf. It took nine days to arrive in the Gulf. On their way, they had passed through the Straits of Tiran in the southern Sinai Peninsula and from there had continued through the Red Sea to the Port of Djibouti, where they stopped for a few hours to receive a supply of drinking water. From there, they sailed through the Gulf of Aden, circling Saudia Arabia into the Gulf of Oman and through the Strait of Hormuz. A few hours later, the tanker was docked at the oil port in Bandar Abbas in Iran.

The crew wasn't allowed to leave the area of the port, but a shuttle was organized to bring them to a large hangar where there was a cafeteria and some shops that sold foods, like pistachios and caviar. They could also buy souvenirs like Persian rugs and copper plates. Onboard the tanker, anyone who had some free time would let out nylon lines with hooks all the way down to the seabed. The cook had defrosted meat for bait ahead of time. You could hear the glee of the "fishermen" whenever a fish was hooked and hauled up onto the deck. Some of the fish were frozen for future use and the rest were brought to the cook, who prepared a glorious feast.

Once the four-month contract period was coming to an end, Shauli was busy getting ready to disembark from the tanker. Finally, all that was left was to wait for his replacement. Shimi had disembarked a month before, when his contract had ended, and he hoped to see him once he returned to Haifa. Shauli arrived home at around four in the afternoon. After he'd unpacked his bags, he went to the local supermarket to stock up on food and other essentials. Evening fell and he was satisfied with what he'd accomplished. His thoughts then went to Alma. He decided to go check out Club 120 a little later with the clear goal of seeing her.

The bartender remembered him and, without even asking, his regular drink was set in front of him. The virtuoso piano player wasn't there that night and in his stead was a young songstress accompanied by a few musicians who played nostalgic songs from the Fifties and Sixties. Shauli looked around the club. The place wasn't crowded. *It looks like the magic is gone*, he thought to himself. He suddenly caught sight of Alma. She wasn't alone. Her arm was around the waist of that same pretty boy he saw on his first night at the club. Alma went pale when she saw him, but Shauli turned his back to her, paid the bill, and left the club without looking back at her. That was the last time he visited the club. He wasn't angry with her, but felt disappointed.

The next day, he went to visit his mother on the kibbutz. When he arrived, she was sitting on a swing next to the flowerbed in front of her house. A book lay next to her. She looked like she was sleeping. When he called out, she lifted her head. Her face lit up when she saw her son.

"You look good!" she said. "The sea is good for you. Come inside, I'll get you something to eat and drink."

Shauli helped her inside. While he nibbled at the food his mother had prepared, he asked about her day-to-day life.

"Not much is new with me," she said. "Sometimes I meet up with Hannah and once a week we go visit the graves – we water the plants, drink tea, and talk."

"How's Bossem?" he asked.

"She hasn't finished officers training yet. She's still going out with her boyfriend the tank captain. He was here a few times. His name is Amir and they look happy together."

Shauli had almost forgotten the gifts he'd brought his mother. He opened his bag and took out two copper plates – works of art – one for his mom and one for Bossem. She thanked him for the present. At the end, he stood up, went to his mom, and gave her goodbye hug and kiss. Rena walked with him to the door. There, she stopped, watching him until he disappeared at the bend in the road.

Shauli waited nearly an hour for the bus to come. Darkness had nearly overtaken the dim light of evening when he arrived at his apartment. He poured himself a glass of whiskey and turned on the stereo. *Tomorrow I'll go downtown to the sailor's restaurant near the port. Maybe I'll see Shimi or Perry*, he thought. He felt exhausted; it was time for bed. He washed the whiskey glass in the sink, took off his clothes, and got into bed.

Shauli didn't see anyone he knew at the restaurant. He sat down at a table that faced the street and ordered a bottle of beer, a steak, a baked potato, and an Israeli salad. From the sailor's restaurant, he called a cab and was driven to a beach in the southern outskirts of Haifa. There, he sat down at one of the many cafés located along the promenade. A light breeze rose up from the sea, easing somewhat the heat of the day. Girls in bikinis lined the beach, sending his vivid imagination to wild places. Other girls ran along the beach, with their feet in the water. Of course, there were also men, but he didn't really notice them. All he wanted to do was to catch one of the fish and release some tension, but it didn't work out and he had to go back to his apartment alone.

The days and weeks passed peacefully. One morning, the telephone woke him from a deep sleep. It was the manager of the crew department.

"Good morning Shauli," he said. "I know it's early, but you have to come down to the office immediately."

"OK, I'll come right away," Shauli answered.

Shauli arrived at the office and reported to the crew assignment department.

"We need you on a ship ASAP," the manager said.

"But I haven't finished shore leave," Shauli said.

"We know, but there's been an emergency. You need to fly this afternoon to Vancouver, Canada. You'll be replacing a sailor that's been injured and is in the hospital. It's a bulk carrier and it'll be back in Israel in about a month and a half. We'll let you continue your leave after you return."

Shauli didn't end up taking advantage of finishing his shore leave when he returned to Haifa. He stayed on the ship for many long months until May 1967. Then, at the sailor's restaurant, he met up with Perry and from then on they were inseparable. They would usually go to the sailor's restaurant for lunch and then in the afternoon they'd go to the beach promenade, and by evening they'd be at one of the dozens of nightclubs that could be found in Haifa.

On May 15, during the Independence Day celebrations, Egyptian troops crossed the Suez Canal and invaded the Sinai Peninsula, breaking the ceasefire agreement. Two days later, the UN Emergency Force was expelled from the Sinai. On May 23, Egypt closed the Straits of Tiran to Israeli ships and cargo ships containing Israeli-made goods. The deliberate closure was a pretext for war. Egypt had blatantly broken the ceasefire agreement that had been in effect since 1957. These actions, in addition to increased tensions with Israel's neighbors to the north, led Israel to recruit reserve forces. The IDF entered a period of waiting, as long as there were negotiations being led by the United States president, who had proposed a plan to break the blockade with a convoy of international ships. Israel agreed to hold off and give the proposal a chance.

The reserves unit of the Merchant Marines, under the Ministry of Transport, Administration of Shipping and Ports, recruited two crews of officers and seamen. After completing all of the necessary arrangements, they were flown to two different locations – one in Kenya and one in Ethiopia. In the afternoon of May 28th, Shauli and Perry met at the sailor's restaurant. They ordered two cold beers. As they drank, Perry told Shauli that he'd volunteered to sail on an El-Yam company ship, which was still looking for volunteers.

"What's the name of the ship and where is it sailing to?" Shauli asked.

"The company hasn't released the destination yet, but the name is *Har Gilad*, though I think that's fake."

Shauli asked Perry to go with him to the company's office. As he registered and was accepted as a volunteer, he was warned not to speak about it to anyone. It was top secret. All of the volunteers who were accepted were bachelors – that was probably the decision of the overseers. The following day, all of the volunteers received a notice of cancellation, without any explanation.

"This is still classified and you cannot speak to anyone about the little that you know," they were told.

On June 1, they were given an urgent call to report to the company's office.

"We've been given the green light. Tomorrow morning at eight, come ready to set sail. You need to wait at the entrance area."

Shauli told himself that it may be a dangerous voyage, especially in light of knowing that two teams were recruited, perhaps for the same task. He learned from the newspapers that the IDF was waiting and that the convoy was prepared to break the blockade. He got the feeling that he might never return. They were possibly 'guinea pigs', intended as the official reason for a war to break out. In the evening, he packed his bag. When he finished, he poured himself a glass of whiskey on ice. He wasn't afraid of the forthcoming unknown voyage, but as he sat drinking his whiskey, he thought of his mother and sister. He came to the decision to organize his apartment and to write a farewell letter, just in case something did happen. He put the letter in an envelope marked "For Bossem Shauli".

At 07:30, Shauli was already waiting at the entrance to the El-Yam company's offices. Perry smiled at him when he arrived. One after the other, the rest of the officers and seaman began to arrive. They were a total of 24 in number. At exactly 10:00, a bus stopped in front of them and they were asked to board, still not knowing where they were going. Shauli looked out of the window as they passed the familiar streets of Haifa, on their way to the international airport named after David Ben-Gurion, the first prime minister of Israel. The crew gathered in the departures terminal and waited for instructions. During that time, there were those who fled Israel fearing what may come. The incumbent prime minister called them 'wimps'. Since so many had decided to leave, the running joke was that "the last one out would turn off the lights." Seeing this group of young people, the ground crews and terminal workers said angrily that they should be ashamed of themselves for not helping the country in its hour of need. A few even spat at them in disgust. None of the crewmen could answer, because of the top-secret nature of the mission, and so they suffered the insults in silence. After two hours, they were called to the VIP terminal. A long table was filled with delicacies. The president of the company and other people whom they didn't recognize shook their hands and gave each crew member a silver coin from the Port of Eilat that read, "Go in Peace and Return in Peace." Only aboard the plane were they told of their destination. The captain told them that they were flying to Teheran and the following day they'd arrive at the Persian Gulf, where they'd board the oil tanker *Samson*, which had already begun loading the black liquid into its tanks.

"That evening, we'll leave for the Port of Eilat. On the way a small merchant ship will join us."

There was still daylight when the plane landed at the airport in Teheran. They were then brought to a hotel in the city center. Curiously, the sign on the front read "Sinai Hotel". It made them think about the meaning of the name and its connection to God. In the evening, Shauli, Perry, and a few others went out to a club. It was strange for them to watch the waitress bring drinks to the table with a veil covering her face. On the morning of June 3, they continued their journey to the oil port in the Persian Gulf. The tanker was loaded and ready. They replaced an Italian crew, most of whom were already waiting with their bags on the dock. Toward the evening, the tanker set sail, its bow facing in the direction of Eilat. According to the plan, they were to arrive at the Port of Eilat on June 10. After it was apparent that diplomatic measures had not been successful, Israel's newly formed National Unity Government gave the IDF the authorization to launch an offensive, in order to remove the existential threat. The first military steps were taken against the Egyptian forces, who constituted the main threat against Israel. On June 5, while the tanker was still on its way, the Six-Day War broke out.

All the crewmembers who were free sat around the radio – which had been changed to shortwave – listening carefully to the announcer describe the battles in the Sinai Peninsula. When the tanker had passed through the Gulf of Aden, one of the ship's two boilers malfunctioned and as a result, the tanker was forced to slow down. By June 9, when it was clear that they wouldn't arrive on time to the rendezvous with the *Dolphin*, the small merchant ship was told to make the short voyage through the Straits of Tiran and on to Eilat. A crew of navy reservists who had been waiting the whole time at a hotel in the city of Massawa on the African coast of the Red Sea, boarded the ship on the way to Eilat. Three frightened sailors were removed from the ship and joined a second crew, which waited for the tanker to arrive. Once the *Samson* reached Massawa, the second crew of reservists boarded the ship, along with the three deserters from the *Dolphin*.

The Six-Day War ended on June 10, after Israel achieved huge victories, stunning the entire world. At the same time, the *Dolphin* crossed the Straits of Tiran and arrived at the Port of Eilat, making international headlines. The *Dolphin* was immortalized in the history books and a model of the ship was even erected at the port. Twenty-four hours later, the *Samson* also arrived at the Port of Eilat, fully loaded with crude oil. A single line was written about it in the newspaper. The first oil tanker docked at the oil station in Eilat after crossing the Straits of Tiran. A few company representatives boarded the ship and thanked the crew for volunteering for the special mission. Some refreshments were brought and set out on one of the tables in the day room, and with that, the ceremony was over.

The campaign ribbon for the Six-Day War was awarded to the crew of the *Dolphin* and to the crew that joined the tanker at Massawa, as well as the three deserters. The 24 officers and seaman of the *Samson* were not recognized or given the campaign ribbon. To this day, those men harbor the feeling that they were wronged. No one could understand the thoughts that went through their minds that last night before setting off on a voyage from which they were not sure they'd return.

Perry disembarked from the tanker, as did most of the other volunteers. Shauli continued for another voyage and then he too went on shore leave. A few days later, when he was visiting his mother on the kibbutz, he noticed that her hair had become even more grey, that more wrinkles had appeared on her face, and that she had difficulty walking. She even needed the aid of a walking stick. He was sorry to see his mother in that condition, and so lonely. In order to distract himself from those thoughts, he asked Rena about Bossem. Her eyes flickered with life.

"Bossem is very successful – she's now an officer, a lieutenant. Her boyfriend Amir comes to visit often and they're planning to get married. I so want to live to see my grandchildren."

"There's no reason you wouldn't," Shauli said. "Where are these crazy ideas coming from?" He then asked about Hannah.

"We see each other almost every day," Rena answered. "She's my only real friend. She's well, and she looks fantastic."

Shauli took out some gifts he'd brought for her and Bossem. Before making his way to the bus stop, he decided to go visit his father's grave.

At the end of his shore leave, Shauli signed on to board a merchant marine ship once again. The voyages were to be two-and-a-half months long, starting at the Dagon silo dock in Haifa, to one of the Gulf ports in the US, and back. When the ship would return to Haifa, it would anchor in the bay for several days, waiting to be cleared to dock and unload the grain. One day, while they were anchored, a service boat arrived with Bossem on board. Shauli was busy painting on the embarkation deck when the boatswain came and said:

"Go to the entrance passageway. There's a female officer with a rank of captain there asking to see you."

Shauli had a bad feeling. He knew that it was his sister who was waiting for him. She'd never visited one of his ships before. As soon as she saw him, she said:

"I have bad news and I needed to tell you in person so that you wouldn't hear it from someone else. Mom died this morning from a heart attack. The only thing that comforts me is that she didn't suffer – it happened all of a once."

His eyes swelled with tears when he heard of his mother's death. Bossem told him that the funeral was at 4:00 in the afternoon that day and that they had to go to the kibbutz as soon as possible. When they left the port, Shauli ordered a private cab that took them all the way to the kibbutz.

The kibbutz members accompanied the coffin to the small cemetery. Hannah, weeping and clutching a handkerchief, walked quietly behind her friend's coffin. Amir held on to Bossem, who laid her head on his shoulder, tears streaming down her face. Rena was laid to rest near Maxim. A rabbi gave a eulogy. Dirt covered the fresh grave and some flowers were placed upon it. Shauli said *kaddish*. The undertakers took the stretcher back to their car, painted black with prominent Stars of David on the sides. The funeral goers began to disperse, not without first offering their condolences to Bossem and Shauli.

A year and a half after their shared time on the *Samson*, Perry and Shauli met again at the sailor's restaurant. Perry told Shauli about the ship the *Cormoran*, which was setting out on a long voyage. Shauli did not hesitate – they went together to the office of the company's crew department, where he signed a 15-month contract with the *Cormoran*. From the offices, they then went out to celebrate their upcoming voyage to sail the seven seas.

Priel Porat

The ship agent's good news raised my spirits, and of course, Shauli's, too. After unloading and loading the cargo, the ship would sail to Rotterdam. We would depart within a week. After assigning the daily tasks to the crew, I went back to my cabin to be alone with Gertie's letters. They were so full of love. Waiting for me to arrive was difficult for her and she was counting the days until we'd see each other again. She also wrote about how she was preparing for my arrival and about the Oasis. My fingers trembled a bit, so I went to the liquor cabinet and poured myself a nice-sized glass of whiskey. I then took out some paper and an envelope from my desk drawer. My letter to Gertie was short: I wrote that I loved her and missed her, that the ship would arrive in Rotterdam at the end of the month, that is, about two-and-a-half weeks from the writing of that letter. I also sent greetings to Nellie.

In the evening, Shauli and I went out to one of the clubs on 42nd Street in Manhattan. He told me about Nellie's letters. We planned our upcoming shore leave in Rotterdam. The company had authorized a two-week shore leave before our return to Israel. We'd also been told that our replacements would already be waiting for us on the dock and would board the ship as soon as we'd arrive.

When we returned to the ship, Shauli suggested that we have another drink before bed. We went to my cabin and as Shauli stretched out on the couch, I poured two glasses of whiskey. Gertie and Nellie were the focus of our conversation, but not for long, as Shauli asked to hear one of my stories.

"OK," I said. "This time I've got an emotional story about my good friend Roni, who's also a veteran seaman. Actually, he was my boatswain aboard one of the ships I sailed on. During one of our voyages, as we sat together in his cabin, just like we're doing now, he began telling this story, which I'll now tell you in the first person.

"One day, we arrived at the Port of Rosario, which is on La Plata River in Argentina. We were aboard the first Israeli ship that had ever docked at the port and the news reached everyone in the Jewish community there. Many of them came to visit the ship, met the crewmen, and were excited to see the Israeli Merchant Marines flag flying in the breeze. They invited us to a special evening, which included an elaborate dinner. The cargo unloading went slowly and our stay at the port ended up lasting a month and a half. There was a nightclub in town that the crew would go to nearly every night that we had free, and of course we had plenty of flings. One night while out at the club, I felt a sudden pain in my stomach. I soon found myself bent over the toilet, puking my guts out. One of the waitresses gave me an antacid, which did help. In the following weeks, I kept going back to the club and drinking the usual amounts, and the pain didn't return. I wrote it off as a one-time incident and pretty much forgot about it altogether. The days and weeks passed, and then it came time to raise the ropes and set sail for our next destination – Buenos Aires.

"The short trip from Rosario to Buenos Aires couldn't relieve the fatigue that had built up from the month and a half of working all day and going out all night. But as soon as we docked, we forgot all about being tired: The big city, vibrant and full of life, opened up her inviting arms to us. As soon as you exit the port, you arrive at Alem Avenue, with all the great meat restaurants. Sometimes there's a long line just to get in. Of course, we would choose one of the restaurants where various beef cuts were roasting on spits out in front. We usually ordered some fine cuts served on coals at the table, along with some excellent salad in delicious dressing and warm fresh bread. For the second course, we'd order a tenderloin steak, in their language it was called *lomo* – a tender, juicy cut of meat. It tastes like heaven and melts in your mouth like butter. We'd wash down the whole meal with a fine bottle of semi-dry Argentinian red wine.

"Right near Alem Avenue is 25 de Mayo Avenue, a known center of entertainment, where we spent many of our nights. Corrientes Avenue is a bustling main street known for its famously impressive Obelisk. We enjoyed many wonderful days on that street. In short, we had a great month in Buenos Aires, but we finally reached the time to return to Israel.

"The crew began preparations for the long voyage ahead. In the afternoon, I once again felt the pain starting in my stomach and enveloping my whole body. I ran to the head and my whole lunch was flushed down the toilet drain. I felt an ongoing nausea and my face had gone pale. There was no choice but to go to see the second mate. He checked my pulse and blood pressure and after consulting with the captain, they called a doctor through the ship agent. The doctor boarded the ship and after an initial checkup, he recommended that I go ashore to get an X-ray done on my stomach. I was nervous, since we were supposed to set sail that evening. At the Sanatorium Metropolitano Hospital's clinic, I was given a white liquid to drink before the X-ray. When the doctor returned with the results of the X-ray, he gave me the bad news: I had to disembark from the ship.

"'You have a duodenal ulcer, which requires surgical intervention,' he told me.

"The pilot boarded the ship the moment I disembarked.

"The hospital was privately run, but was large and spacious. I shared a room with two other sick seamen. I became friendly with one of them, who was from Trinidad. Eventually, because of our friendship, he came to Israel and sailed with the Israeli shipping company Ofer Brothers for several years. One day, he disappeared and I never heard from him again. Anyway, Dr. Domopolos, who was Greek, was the one who took me off the ship and was also my surgeon. When I opened my eyes for the first time after the surgery, a cute redheaded nurse smiled widely at me. She looked at me with kindness and sympathy.

"'My name is Lishka,' she said. 'I'm a surgical nurse and I was in the operating room during your surgery. I'm Jewish and when I heard that an Israeli sailor was hospitalized here, I requested to be present during your operation in place of the scheduled nurse, and the doctor agreed.

"'Nice to meet you and thanks for helping me, I'm Roni.'

"During the rest of the time I spent at the hospital, whenever she finished her shift, Lishka would come my bed, pull up a chair, and sit next to me. She told me about her family, her time in nursing school, and even her boyfriend, or to be exact, her fiancé. She was interested in hearing about Israel and also about me. I was hospitalized for two weeks before I was discharged. The ship agent brought me and Lishka to a small hotel on Alem Avenue, where I stayed for another three weeks to recover from the operation. Sometimes, I would go with Lishka to visit her parents. She even introduced me to her fiancé, who made a good impression on me. We would also visit some of the sites in the city and enjoy the beauty that shone from every corner. She revealed to me that the surgery had not been simple. There'd been a complication, and because of her discerning eyes, she had alerted the attending physician and serious damage was prevented. He immediately treated the complication, which had been nearly unnoticeable.

"On the day of my flight back to Israel, Lishka accompanied me to the airport. It was difficult for her to say goodbye and she began to cry. There was still some time, so we ordered some coffee at the airport cafeteria. She asked that I write to her once I arrived to Israel and I of course promised I would.

"'I really appreciate everything that you've done for me,' I said. 'I won't forget you.' We hugged each other and I turned to board. Lishka stayed standing in her place, perhaps even until the plane took off.

"The day after I landed in Israel, I went to the seaman's clinic. The doctor who looked at me was one of the best diagnosticians in the country and told me that it had been a mistake to operate on me. I could have been treated with medication. This didn't make me feel any better. I had been a healthy and strong young man and now a part of me was missing. *They deceived me, and the company*, I thought. The doctor authorized sick days for me and so I stayed ashore for a relatively long period. At that time, I had a daughter, but I was divorced. When I arrived to Israel, my sister cleared out a room for me in her apartment.

"Three months passed since the day I'd returned the country. One evening, the doorbell rang and Lishka was standing in the hallway, beaming. I was very surprised. After we calmed down a bit, I poured some soft drinks for us and we sat on the balcony facing the street, Lishka updating me about everything that had happened since I left. She'd left her boyfriend and quit her job at the hospital and immediately began making preparations to immigrate to Israel. Despite her family's dismay, they supported her decision and even wished her good luck on her new life in a new country. She'd been sent from the airport to Kibbutz Dovrat in the Galil and shared a room with two other new immigrants while studying Hebrew at the kibbutz *ulpan*. She asked for some special time off in order to come visit me.

"'And here I am,' she said.

"We sat on the balcony until the wee hours of the night, talking about everything we'd done together and about her future plans. We continued meeting this way for about two months. Sometimes I would visit her in Dovrat and sometimes she'd come to me in Haifa. She was serious about our relationship, but I wasn't. I wasn't yet ready for a new relationship since the separation from my wife, especially since I enjoyed tasting the nectar of many wild flowers, of which there was no shortage.

"During one of our encounters, I told Lishka my true feelings about our relationship.

"'Listen Lishka,' I said. 'I don't think anything serious can really develop between us. At least, I'm just not serious. I'm still going to sail for many more years and that just isn't healthy for a relationship. We can of course continue being friends and I'll always be around if you need help or advice while I'm in the country. However, I would like you to meet a good friend of mine. He's single and a really good guy, and he even fluent in Spanish. If you'd like, I can introduce you to him and we can see how it goes? What do you think?"

"Her face dropped. We sat in silence for a few minutes, but in the end, she agreed.

"My Spanish-speaking friend Eran was a big-hearted guy. He was always smiling and joking and everyone liked to be around him. He was even financially 'well off.' I told him about Lishka and he agreed to meet her. After a few days, we drove together in his car to Kibbutz Dovrat. Lishka was happy to see us. I noticed that they 'clicked,' and I knew that they'd be good together. A week later, I left on a three-month voyage. When I returned to Israel, Lishka and Eran came to meet me at the dock and they were holding hands, looking happy. When the gangway was lowered, the royal couple came aboard. In my cabin, I served them some drinks and then Lishka took an envelope out from her purse and handed it to me. I opened it and saw that it was a wedding invitation, for a week from then.

"'We waited for you,' she said. 'Your presence is important to us.'

"The wedding was set for seven in the evening. That same day, I sat with a female friend at a bar not far from the wedding hall. I drank quite a bit and at one point I told my friend that I had to go, because I had somewhere to be. I didn't want her to join me. The hall was full of guests when I arrived, a bit late. As soon as I entered, I heard a scream:

"'Roni! Come over here! The ceremony has been delayed – we're all just waiting for you!'

"I didn't feel very comfortable, as her gaze was fixed on me instead of Eran.

"I didn't see them for years after their wedding day, until just before the current voyage. But before I tell you about that emotional meeting, I'll say that I did hear about them over those years, and how. They had a beautiful boy, who I still haven't met. A few years after they were married, Eran became ill with cancer and passed away. Before that, however, Lishka joined the police force and had climbed the ranks pretty quickly. One day on duty, she had a terrible fall and had to undergo several surgeries, though there wasn't much that could be done. Her doctor delivered the bad news that she'd never stand or walk again. During her rehabilitation treatments, Eran passed away, and she hadn't even been able to visit him during his darkest hours. Despite all of her hardships, her spirit had not broken. She began training at a shooting range and won several trophies and medals for marksmanship. Her greatest honor was winning the national marksman competition in the disabled category. I even remembered reading about her in the newspaper.

"Soon before our voyage, the phone rang. An unfamiliar woman's voice asked for Roni.

"'Do you remember me?' the voice said. 'It's Lishka.'

"'How did you find me?' I asked.

"'I know an old friend of your sister's. I asked for her information. He told me that he wasn't in contact with her, but that he had her brother's details. I told him that that's who I was really looking for, for years, and I didn't know how to contact him. He gave me your number, and here we are talking after such a long time apart.'

"She asked about what I'd been doing for all those years and told me about her current life. I promised that I'd stop by her house a few days later and she gave me her phone number and address.

"Her house was in a great location, overlooking the glorious bay, radiating peace and relaxation in a place called the Valley of the Sun. On the way to her place, I stopped by a candy store and bought a nicely wrapped box of chocolates. I didn't feel it was enough, so I stopped at a flower shop and bought a nice bouquet as well. The salesman wrapped it and added a card, on which I wrote a few simple words. I rang the doorbell and a large dark man answered. He already knew that Lishka was expecting me. Apparently, he was from Ghana and worked as Lishka's helper for the past several years. The house was shiny and polished. It was tastefully decorated, but the doors to the rooms were all closed. There was also an uncomfortable silence that hung over the place. The helper brought me to her bedroom, where I found her in bed. A blanket covered her up to her face, which came to life when she saw me. I set the flowers and chocolates down on the side table and bent down and kissed her cheek. She hugged me with her right hand – her strong side. The helper brought me one of the beers from out of the six-pack that I brought. According to her explicit request, I told her all about the life that I'd had in the many years that we hadn't seen each other. Lishka told me that she hadn't left the house for three years. She was recently hospitalized again, because of some complication in her stomach. She's paralyzed in most of her body and had a catheter. It was difficult for me to see her like that, but I tried not to show how I felt. Her left hand didn't function well, but her whole life was performed through her computer, which was her window to the world. Her mind was clear as a young woman's, and her face was beautiful, despite her misfortunes. That's it Perry. And Roni finished his story."

Lishka's story moved Shauli, but I'd become tired and told him that it was time to sleep.

"Tomorrow is a new day," I said.

The tired, good-old Jalopy, with her cargo holds loaded to their full capacity, sounded her horns and left the Port of New York on the morning of December 18, 1969, on her way to Rotterdam. The two tugs that had accompanied her out also sounded their horns, wishing her a safe voyage and calm seas. But the voyage was not calm at all. The forecast that was received warned of a raging sea with winds reaching 10 on the Beaufort scale, the highest rating before hurricane. And indeed, as soon as we moved away from the safety of the shore, the water turned ferocious. During the following days, the *Cormoran* rocked violently in the storms. Powerful, shrieking winds battered and shook the ship's antenna mounts on the bridge deck. The rain – mixed with ice crystals – fell interminably. The dark, grey-black clouds completely blocked out any sunlight, and visibility was close to zero. The crew had never experienced this kind of storm. Some worried that their trembling ship would not survive and would sink into the depths of the sea. On the morning of the fourth day of that frightful storm, I was called urgently to the control bridge. I saw Captain Bar-Noy, worn pipe in his mouth, standing wide-legged and gripping the railing, watching the wrath of hell surrounding him. Next to him stood First Mate Itzik Shahak and Second Mate Moti Lev. Carlos Antonio stood at the helm, attempting to somehow steady the ship. Bar-Noy turned to me:

"Listen Perry, a huge wave crashed onto the portside gangway and destroyed it. I want you to get two of your best crewmen and gather up some of its pieces, before the sea takes them. I recommend Shauli and Ben-Tzur. Leave one at the portside door, to maintain visuals. Bring the other with you to gather the gangway parts. Bring them to the protected aft storeroom and don't leave before I give you an explicit order. I'll turn the ship so that you'll have safe access."

That's all I need, I thought. *Only a few days left in my contract, with Gertie waiting for me, and I've got to go out into the middle of the ocean's fury*. Shauli and Ben-Tzur, like the rest of the crew, were still in the middle of breakfast when I went to tell them about our urgent mission.

"Go put on boots and storm uniforms and wait for me at the portside exit to the main deck."

A glass of whiskey warmed me up while I put on my own storm clothes. Then the three of us waited at the portside door for the order. After five minutes, Moti the second mate came and gave us the captain's go ahead to exit to the deck. I left Ben-Tzur at the door.

"Keep us in view while we're out," I told him.

The gangway was completely shattered and its pieces were

strewn over dozens of meters. We began picking them up and bringing them to the storeroom in the stern. Some parts were nearly washed overboard, and we went to get them first. Skillful Shauli hurried to complete the task as quickly as possible. Suddenly, I heard a sinister sound. I lifted my head and saw a rogue wave moving swiftly toward us. I managed to scream "Shauli!" before it crashed into us. My world went black.

Gertie Van der Giessen

Gertie began preparing for Perry's arrival. She'd gotten an approval from the managers at Oasis for some days off. She went to the market and bought all of the necessary ingredients to make Perry a typical Dutch meal. *I'll do all of the cooking, cleaning, and flower arrangements on the day before he arrives*, she thought. She even helped Nellie get days off. Both women were blissful. Those final days before Perry and Shauli were to return felt like an eternity. Gertie checked with the office of the ship agent to be sure of the date of the ship's arrival at port. She was told that the *Cormoran* was scheduled to arrive within a week, but may be delayed by a day or two, due to being caught in a rough storm. The next day, she received the letter Perry had sent her from New York. It was short, but very meaningful.

Both Gertie and Nellie had become impatient at work ahead of their vacation. It was difficult for them to focus and it did not go unnoticed by the managers, however they preferred to turn a blind eye and not reprimand them. Both women were a great asset to the club, and management knew that, despite the fact that at that time, they both looked lost in their jobs.

In the afternoon on the following day, while Gertie was cleaning her apartment, her doorbell rang. When she opened the door, she saw Nellie standing before her, crestfallen and tearful.

"Nellie, what happened?" she asked, startled.

"I came here straight from the ship agent's office. A tragedy happened on the deck of the ship. Two sailors were washed overboard while securing some equipment during a violent storm. The agent said that these were only the initial reports and that he's in contact with the captain. As soon as he has more information, he'll be in touch."

Everything turned dark. They hadn't received the sailors'

names, but they were already tormented. Dread penetrated their hearts. Gertie went to change her clothes.

"We have to go to the agent's office right away," she said. "We'll sit there until the information comes in."

The agent had no news.

"I haven't received any new messages. Neither has the office in Haifa. I suggest that you two go calm down in the waiting room and as soon as I get anything, I'll come tell you."

One of the secretaries came and offered them something to drink – coffee, tea, or a soft drink. They accepted some coffee. They thanked the secretary for her consideration. After two nerve-wracking hours, the agent called them into his office.

"More information has come in," he said. "They've confirmed the first message. The two sailors are Boatswain Priel Porat and Able Seaman Shaul Shauli. As per the captain's orders, after he'd turned the ship to enable them access, they went out on deck to collect important equipment. Instructions were given to an additional seaman to maintain eye contact with them. The disaster occurred when a rogue wave crashed toward them without warning and washed them into the stormy water. One of the seamen was lucky in that a second rogue wave carried him up and crashed him back on deck. The name of the survivor has not yet been released, but I'm sure that we'll receive the message soon."

The two friends went back to the waiting room crying, each one taking comfort in the other's arms. They still didn't know which one of them had lost her love. The tension was unbearable, but they could do nothing about it. Time stood still as they waited to hear who had lived and who had died. Who would be joyful and who would grieve.

An hour and a half passed until the office door opened once again and they were asked back inside.

"Please come in," the agent said. "I've just received a message from the ship summarizing the events. The survivor is Able Seaman Shaul Shauli. The boatswain is considered missing.

The ship and other additional ships are scanning the area, but the chances of finding him are slim. Visibility is poor and the sea is unusually stormy."

The next day, Gertie received the bitter news. There was no chance of finding the boatswain. He was declared lost at sea. The incident was recorded in the ship's official log. The search ships, including the *Cormoran*, returned to their original course toward their destinations.

Shaul Shauli

Shauli had heard Perry's scream, but he could do nothing. All he could manage was to lift his head and see the rogue wave crash on both of them. In an instant, the water washed them away – as if they were lifeless rags – into the dark ocean. Ben-Tzur, who had had them in his view, was stunned to see what had happened. One moment, he was watching his two friends, full of life, rushing to collect the gangway pieces, and the next, they'd disappeared as if they were never there. He stood frozen in place, not believing what he'd seen. Suddenly he saw another giant wave coming up from the sea and covering the entire main deck. When the water rolled back out, Ben-Tzur noticed a body lying motionless between the portside railing and the storeroom nearest to him. Without hesitation, and without thinking about the danger it posed to him, he sprinted toward the slightly distorted body.

Captain Bar-Noy had also seen the gigantic wave crash onto the deck and sweep away everything in its path.

"Steer thirty degrees left!" he told Carlos Antonio. He immediately called Moti the second mate.

"Get four crewmen and bring a stretcher and first aid equipment! You may need them. Go on deck from the portside door. Ben-Tzur is there. Do it as quickly as possible!"

He asked Zevik the third mate, who'd also been called to the bridge, to throw overboard two lifesavers and orange flares from both sides of the bridge.

Ben-Tzur reached the body within less than a minute. He ignored the threatening sea, the roar of the waves, the pelting rain, and the bitter cold. He immediately identified Shauli. He was alive, his entire body bruised, and breathing unsteadily. But he was conscious, though disorientated.

"Shauli, it's me, Ben-Tzur. Do you hear me? Do you see me?"

Shauli nodded. The second mate and the crew arrived with the stretcher. Moti began examining the injured man, making sure nothing was broken and that there were no open wounds. When he found none, he put in an IV line. They carefully lifted Shauli onto the stretcher.

"We'll take him to sickbay."

The captain began the search and rescue procedures after the missing boatswain. He sent out a distress signal and requested the help of the other ships in the vicinity to search for a man overboard and gave the location where the disaster occurred. A telegram was sent to the company's offices to report the incident. The ship was in the middle of the ocean, far from any shore, which made it even more difficult to receive assistance in the search and rescue.

Shauli lay in bed in sickbay. Moti checked his blood pressure, pulse, and pupils thoroughly and attended to his wounds, bruises, and abrasions. After finishing his treatment, he concluded that the patient was extremely lucky. He'd come out of this within a few days, and return even stronger. He wrote down everything that he'd done in his medical log.

As evening came, the captain knew that the chances to find Perry had disappeared. It was nearly impossible to see anything in the terrible weather conditions. He thanked all of the surrounding ships for their assistance. The state of emergency was lifted and the men on lookout returned to the warmth of the superstructure. The order to return to the ship's original course came swiftly. The captain recorded the incident in the ship's official log and the second mate submitted to him a copy of the medical report. Bar-Noy wrote up a detailed report, including the ship's delayed arrival at the Port of Rotterdam, and gave it to the wireless operator to send to the offices in Haifa. Bar-Noy also requested that he send it to the Ministry of Transport, Administration of Shipping and Ports and to the agent in Rotterdam.

On the following day in Israel, all of the newspapers published articles detailing the catastrophe. It was covered on the radio and TV as well. Everyone was talking about the miracle of the sailor being returned to the deck from the depths of hell. Shauli recovered quickly: He spent two days in sickbay and then returned to his own cabin. He only thought of Perry, his friend and companion, whom he'd never again see alive. Eight days after the tragedy, the tired and wounded *Cormoran* arrived at the Port of Rotterdam, with two tugs hitched at the stern and bow easing her to the dock.

Nellie and Gertie were waiting on the dock as the ship arrived. The boatswain and able seaman replacing Perry and Shauli onboard were also waiting there. Standing next to them were also the marine inspector from Transportation Ministry and a representative from the company there to investigate the events surrounding the loss of the boatswain. Perry's belongings were packed and brought to the offices of the company. They would be given to the agent who would arrange for them to be sent back to Israel. When the gangway was lowered, Shauli disembarked to meet Nellie and Gertie. He was still bandaged up, but in general, he looked okay. He took Nellie and Gertie in his arms. All three of them looked mournful and in pain. Shauli invited them to his cabin onboard, where he'd tell them everything that happened once they were alone.

Gertie listened closely to everything Shauli had to say. Sometimes she'd stop him to ask for some clarification or another. It was very hard for her to hear about Perry's last moments. Tears flowed down her face, which she kept wiping with a handkerchief. Shauli poured some drinks and said that his replacement was already onboard, so he'd soon receive his disembarkation papers and would be free to leave. Nellie asked him to go stay with her in her apartment and he said yes.

The marine inspector and company representative went to the captain's office onboard. They asked for the sequence of events that led to the disappearance of the boatswain. Without concealing anything, Captain Bar-Noy explained how he'd come to his decision and what steps he'd taken in order to protect his two most experienced sailors, who were sent to retrieve the pieces of the broken gangway. The inspector asked to look at the official log and the captain handed it to him. He read it over carefully, asking questions about each section. Finally, he asked the obvious question:

"It is still unclear to me why you risked the lives of three men during stormy seas for unnecessary gangway parts. You could have of course used the second gangway when docking and could have even ordered by telegram that shipyard workers meet you on the dock to repair the damaged one. Know that I am returning to Haifa with an unfavorable report about you. A commission of inquiry and you will be asked to appear before it."

The company representative wrote something down in his notebook, his face also looking stern and unhappy.

Gertie said that she canceled her days off from work, since it was supposed to have been a special vacation dedicated to her and Perry. But now it was meaningless since he was gone.

"At least I'm happy for you and Nellie, that you survived. From what you've described, it was a real miracle."

As they sat in the cabin, the chief steward came and asked Shauli to go with him to his office. There, Shauli signed his disembarkation papers and received his paycheck.

"Be ready in an hour at the gangway. A taxi will come to get you. I wish you a pleasant leave, you deserve it after everything you went through."

Besides the boatswain, all of Shauli's friends onboard bid him farewell. He also said goodbye to the officers and crew and wished them a comfortable voyage in calm waters. When he returned to his cabin, he told Gertie and Nellie that he'd signed the papers and that a cab would be waiting for him within the hour.

"We have time to drink another glass before we disembark."

Ben-Tzur came to help him with his bags and to walk with him to the gangway. On their way, Ben-Tzur told him that the new boatswain seemed strict and unfriendly.

"Luckily, I don't have too much time left on my contract," he said.

Carlos Antonio was waiting by the gangway when they arrived. He asked to shake Shauli's hand one more time. He also spat out a few words about the new boatswain. Shauli knew that Perry had been liked and admired by all the crewmen as a professional boatswain and a big-hearted friend. It would be hard to fill his shoes.

The cab pulled up to the ship. Nellie, Shauli, and Gertie went to meet it. From window of the car, Shauli looked back one last time to the Jalopy. His eyes wandered over the whole length of the ship; the decks, the life boats, the bridge and living quarters structure, the black hull, and also the gangway from which he just now had descended. The ship would be inscribed permanently onto his heart, not only because of the fifteen months he spent aboard, but more because of his dear friend Perry. He was supposed to be with him in that cab, sitting next to his Gertie. The cab sped through the port gates, toward the bustling city and a new horizon. He knew that his time at sea had ended.

Epilogue

Nellie and Shauli were married in a civil ceremony and once she had converted properly, they wed once more, this time under the *chuppah*. They made their home in the northern part of Tel Aviv and opened up a souvenir shop with both of their savings. They had two sons; the first-born was named Priel "Perry". Nellie studied Hebrew at an *ulpan*. Today, she speaks fluently, though with a Dutch accent. They are happy to this day.

Gertie Van der Giessen continued working at the Oasis for two more years, until the day she met a Greek captain named Nikos Pastrikos. Gertie quit her job and joined him on a voyage. At the end of the voyage, they disembarked at Piraeus and then took a ferry to the island of Kos, where he lived. They had a Catholic wedding ceremony and later Gertie gave birth to a beautiful daughter. Nikos's villa looked out over the Aegean Sea, from the hilltop of a quaint village.

Captain Bar-Noy stood before a commission of inquiry conducted by the Ministry of Transport, Administration of Shipping and Ports. The commission came to a unanimous conclusion that he had erred in his decisions and they had cost a seaman his life. Therefore, he would be on suspension for three years. The sentence had sealed his fate. Two days later, he was found at his desk at his apartment, with a bullet in his head. Blood and brain fragments were splattered on the wall behind him. A signed letter lay on the desk.

Bossem completed her military service with the rank of major. She married her sweetheart Amir, who had also finished his service with the rank of lieutenant colonel. She went to live with him in Moshav Megadim in the north of Israel. They had a son named Maxim. Every Rosh Hashana and Passover, they host Shauli and his family at their home.

Hannah, Dima's widow, passed away three years after her friend Rena, beside whom she was buried.

Eli Ben-Tzur became an officer. He's still unmarried, but is in a committed relationship. Marriage is not on his radar at this point in life. Today, he serves as second mate on a Zim ship.

The *Cormoran* went out of service two years after Perry drowned. Her final voyage was to southern India. There, she was scrapped and deleted from the Israeli registry.

The ocean continues to sweep away sailors and vessels. It happens every day in different parts of the globe. Despite all of our technological advances, meteorological services, and satellite imagery, the ocean will not quiet. It will continue to sweep into its depths everything given to him and will not stop until it is satisfied. A passing ship is an intruder that interferes with his time of rest, and must pay with his blood. It is a daily struggle. At times the ocean is calm and then suddenly it can turn frothy and violent. Tranquil days are a pleasure for sailors, who fall in love with the calm breeze, the clear horizon, the sunrise and sunset, the moonlit sky and twinkling stars – but it is all a farce.

Cast of Characters,
in order of appearance

The Cormoran - The name of the ship upon which much of the story takes place. Also lovingly called "The Jalopy".

Priel "Perry" Porat - A boatswain, the story's hero.

Shaul Shauli - Able Seaman, a central figure in the story.

Mordechai "Moti" Lev - Second Mate.

Carlos Antonio - Able Seaman, the ship's helmsman.

Bar Noy - The ship's captain.

Yitzhak "Itzik" Shahak - First Mate.

Eli Ben-Tzur - Able Seaman.

Yerimiyahu "Jeremy" - Deck boy.

Gertie Van der Giessen - Hostess at the "Oasis" nightclub, Perry's girlfriend.

Nellie - Hostess at the "Oasis" nightclub, Shauli's girlfriend.

Maxim Shaulov - Shauli's father.

Igor - Shauli's grandfather.

Katia - Shauli's grandmother.

Svetlana - Katia's midwife.

Nastasia - Maxim's nanny.

Irina - Nastasia's sister.

Gregory - Irina's husband.

Brigitte - Hostess at the "Oasis" nightclub.

Zeev "Zevik" Tichon - Third Mate.

Doron - Ordinary Seaman.

Yossi - Ordinary Seaman.

Gershon - Ship's carpenter.

Ehud - Ordinary Seaman.

Yonatan - Ordinary Seaman.

Avraham - Second Engineer.

Hans - Gertie's father.

Joanna - Gertie's mother.

Wilhelmina - Gertie's grandmother.

Margareta - Gertie's childhood friend.

Sonia - Irina's eldest daughter.

Maria - Irina's younger daughter.

Nikolai - Irina's son.

Alex Dimitry "Dima" - Maxim's best friend.

Yaacov - The ship's messman.

Willem - Gertie's ex-boyfriend.

Yoav Artzi - Ship's carpenter.

Mikhailovich - Shoe factory owner.

Marina - Girl Maxim meets at a bar.

Natasha - Marina's friend.
Tineke - Hans's second wife.
Henrik - Owner of a Rotterdam nightclub, Gertie's first boyfriend.
Rudy - Owner of an Amsterdam nightclub.
Gabi - Perry's good friend during his time on a bulk freighter, the ship's cook.
Marie - A prostitute from Jamaica.
Arieh - The *Cormoran*'s cook.
Yaacov "Jackie" - Ordinary Seaman.
Mr. Schwartzman - A leader in the Jewish community of Constanta.
The Berkoviches - A Jewish couple who take in Maxim and Dima.
Moshe - An *aliyah* representative in Europe.
Eli Eshel - Member of Kibbutz Sdot Yam.
Rena - Maxim's wife.
Hannah - Dima's wife.
Erez - Owner of an Israeli restaurant in Melbourne.
Nicole - Waitress at Erez's restaurant.
Julie - Redhead from a Melbourne bar.
Bossem - Shauli's sister.
Rami - Skipper of a kibbutz fishing boat.
Alex - Dima's son.

Chaim - Director of the Seamen Bureau.
Yitzhak "Isaac" - Perry's childhood friend.
Maureen - Journalist from New York.
Sharon - Waitress from Montreal.
Shimon "Shimi" - Able Seaman aboard the *Teverya*.
Avichai - First Mate aboard the *Teverya*.
Eli - Cabin steward aboard the *Teverya*.
Carmel - Boatswain aboard the *Teverya*.
Raanan - Able Seaman aboard the *Teverya*.
Melina - Girl at a bar in Piraeus.
Alejandra - Girl at a club in Veracruz.
Alma - Redhead from Club 120.
Lana - Sexy bartender from Houston.
Meir - First Engineer who sailed to Houston with Perry.
Scarlett - Lana's sister.
Bill - Lana's friend.
Linda - Bill's girlfriend.
Amir - Bossem's boyfriend, a tank commander.
Roni - Shauli's friend, who sailed to Buenos Aires.
Lishka - Nurse at a Buenos Aires hospital.
Eran - Roni's friend.

www.ingramcontent.com/pod-product-compliance
Lightning Source LLC
Chambersburg PA
CBHW071118170626
46809CB00002B/418